Mansart Builds
a School

The Black Flame: A Trilogy

Book Two

Mansart Builds a School

W.E.B. DU BOIS

KRAUS-THOMSON ORGANIZATION LIMITED, MILLWOOD, N.Y.

First printing 1976

Library of Congress Cataloging in Publication Data

Du Bois, William Edward Burghardt, 1868-1963.
   Mansart builds a school.

   (His The black flame, a trilogy ; book 2)
   Reprint of the ed. published by Mainstream Publishers,
New York.
   I. Title.
[PZ3.D8525Man7] [PS3507.U143]   813'.5'2   75-42390
ISBN 0-527-25271-9

Printed in the United States of America

EDITOR'S NOTE

The introduction to *The Black Flame* appears in the first volume. Below are listed, in tabular form, the errors which appear in volume two. They are particularly numerous; Dr. Du Bois, in a letter to me, dated March 14, 1960, referred quite correctly to "the terrible errors" in this volume. What accounted for this in particular I do not know; at any rate they are indicated below:

Page	*Line*	*Error*	*Correction*
14	4	defferences	differences
27	5	quesiton	question
43	11	Grogman	Crogman
49	34	anomoly	anomaly
55	32	estra	etra
55	37	oby	obey
67	29	Howell	Howells
70	4	cary	carry
70	8-9	distubed	disturbed
79	16	who's	who've
86	36	many	man
89	5	progaganda	propaganda
99	3	grouhd	ground
118	6	stubborness	stubbornness
121	3	tonerres	tonnerres
121	16	add "of" at line's end	
132	29	trouble	troubles
134	10	woudl	would
134	34	stone	store
141	16	despite	despise
166	23	forget	forgot
169	8	businsses	businesses
179	30	intrigues	intrigued
181	35	aboslute	absolute

Page	Line	Error	Correction
182	14, 21	Cerokks	Scroggs
185	26	Douglas	Douglass
199	17	Captail	Captain
200	39	concsious	conscious
202	28	mandhood	manhood
202	30	ot	to
204	10	sympathteic	sympathetic
207	24	indigation	indignation
208	22	effection	affection
214	31	delibertaely	deliberately
216	last line	platform	plantation
218	37	nad	and
227	24	nohting	nothing
239	32	an	on
252	22	inio	into
253	5	traetment	treatment
259	14	traetment	treatment
261	27	five	fine
265	3	cototn	cotton
265	5	Memphas	Memphis
266	12	Mooe	Moore
269	10	figting	fighting
269	32	husabnd's	husband's
270	9	a-bighty	a-mighty
271	2	omit "This movement"; add: The owners	
276	2	pirtuses	parties
286	11	Heman	Herman
287	29	Cagnes	Cannes
297	27	though	thought
300	27	began	begun
303	28	milliowners	millowners
303	34	bgan	began
304	2	cnditions	conditions
307	38	yleld	yield
308	12	Phohibition	Prohibition
309	39	sumit	submit
310	27	1914	1915
311	20	Unlses	Unless
318	9	confidence	conference
324	3	omit "she"	
325	22	him	his
332	25	Grinnel	Grinnell

Page	Line	Error	Correction
333	last	stubborness	stubbornness
335	4	juzzled	puzzled
337	27	cotnrol	control
340	2	stubborness	stubbornness

MANSART BUILDS A SCHOOL

The Suppression of the African Slave Trade to the United States of America *(Harvard Historical Studies, No. 1, 1896)*

The Philadelphia Negro *(Publication of the University of Pennsylvania Series on Political Economy and Public Law, No. 14, 1899)*

The Souls of Black Folk *(1903)*

John Brown *(1909)*

Quest of the Silver Fleece *(a novel, 1911)*

The Negro *(Home University Library, 1915)*

Darkwater: Voices From Within the Vail *(1920)*

The Gift of Black Folk: The Negro in the Making of America *(1924)*

Dark Princess *(a novel, 1928)*

Black Reconstruction in America, 1860-1880 *(1935)*

Black Folk: Then and Now *(1939)*

Dusk and Dawn: An Autobiography *(1940)*

Color and Democracy: Colonies and Peace *(1945)*

The World and Africa *(1947)*

In Battle for Peace *(1952)*

The Ordeal of Mansart *(1957). First Volume of trilogy,* The Black Flame.

The Black Flame

A Trilogy

BOOK TWO

MANSART BUILDS A SCHOOL

By W. E. B. DU BOIS

MAINSTREAM PUBLISHERS: *New York*

1959

First Printing, November, 1959

MAINSTREAM PUBLISHERS

832 Broadway   New York 3, N. Y.

PRINTED IN THE U.S.A.

CONTENTS

To Shirley Graham

CHAPTER 1

THE COYPELS

It was in 1912. Mrs. Coypel was visiting in Atlanta. She and her husband had often planned a visit there; but while Arnold had come several times on hurried business trips, they had never managed to come together for a good social time, which Mrs. Coypel was convinced might lead to something.

She was thrilled when she learned that John Baldwin, the social leader, rich banker and mayor of Atlanta, was actually the son of old Dr. Baldwin.

"Well, I never!" trilled Mrs. Coypel. "Just to think! And my husband speaks of him so often. Arnold was one of Dr. Baldwin's favorite students. Of course he must have known John, Your John Baldwin. Yes, I'm sure I've heard him mention him—often, yes!"

She was sitting at tea in young Mrs. Baldwin's beautiful living room. And such a home as this was, and how intimately the conversation with the elegant but often silent hostess was progressing! Mrs. Coypel was talking rapidly, almost without pause. Her thoughts and senses were darting here and there.

"What beautiful flowers! Arnold loves flowers and is quite an authority. I know he would be thrilled by your garden. His garden is quite a show place in Lanark: zinnias, cannas, roses, sage—well, I really wouldn't know. I am sure one of those persons who loves flowers and birds and all that but I never can remember the name of a single one. It must be expensive to raise such a profusion of lovely things in the midst of this great city!

"Your husband and mine must renew acquaintanceship. Since your husband is mayor—so perfectly splendid for so young a man, yes, of course—"

Mrs. Baldwin had murmured something conventional, but Mrs. Coypel swept on. "That makes our husbands interested in the same work, education. And education is such a great occupation. Arnold has done wonders in Lanark. He's superintendent of schools there, I think I told you, and has really brought them up from nothing.

9

But you know how these stodgy little country towns are—not that Lanark is so little, after all, but they cannot appreciate talent like —O yes, I am so glad to meet Mrs.—what did you say the name was?"

Then, as a second guest forced her way into the conversation, Mrs. Coypel's mind ran silently on with a slowly maturing plan— piling up and expanding and making beautiful and astonishing vistas on the far horizon. Arnold must get out of Lanark; that pokey little town was driving her crazy, so small and personal and torn up and excited over the silliest trifles. Mrs. Coypel had lived there all her life but it seemed that with this visit to Atlanta she had suddenly become aware of how tawdry and sordid this little North Carolina town in the foothills really was. Yes, Arnold and John Baldwin must meet.

John Baldwin was a coming man. He was a leader in Atlanta. He was already well-to-do; he was sure to be rich; he was mayor, possibly would be governor, then certainly senator and then, well, who knows? Now, if Arnold could attach his wagon to this rising star, think of the possibilities! They would be dragged out of that backwater of small town gossip and provincial interest and set in the midst of a great, swirling, pushing, powerful city. Atlanta, she gathered from the people she had met, from the talk about dinner tables and in social gatherings, was bound to be a great city, easily the greatest in the South, one of the greatest in the country. Seated in such a center men of ability in any line could go far. Of course, Arnold was not showy and he seemed to have very little ambition, but he really had ability and learning. He read an astonishing number of books. How he managed it, Mrs. Coypel could never understand, but he did, and really seemed to enjoy it. Now just suppose for a moment—then she jerked her mind back.

"It's nice to have you back," said Mrs. Baldwin, languidly, to a newcomer. "Did you see Jim? Naturally; well, things are about as usual here; of course you heard of Callie and John; what a stink! Yes, I'm thinking of a new fur, but the styles are so short for me. No, not a thing; I simply don't believe it. More tea? And you, Mrs. Coypel?"

"Yes, yes, of course," she found herself saying just a little vaguely, as she was not really following the conversation. She quickly adjusted herself. "But you must really run up to Lanark, Mrs. Baldwin, you really must—and you, too, Mrs.—er—, just a little outing, you know, from the noise and rush of the great city. You and Mr. Baldwin. I'm sure you both need a change—oh, you are? How splendid! You'll be going right through Lanark. Of course, the best trains do not usually stop but I am sure we can arrange it, and remember now, we are going to expect you."

And then Mrs. Coypel's mind went off again, as other guests wandered in and out. John Baldwin would come to Lanark; he would see that Arnold was offered a place in the city schools of Atlanta. Already the Lanark schools under Arnold's superintendency had an excellent reputation. The General Education Board had commended them, and Arnold had been asked to read a paper before the National Education Association. Of course, he hadn't; he was so slow and uninspiring about such chances.

"Yes," she said aloud, as Mrs. Baldwin arose. "Arnold is really a remarkable school man. You just ought to have seen our system before he took it over. Old dilapidated buildings, poor teachers, no system. He got the city system established with special school taxes and fine new buildings, and has been attracting some of the best teachers of the state. He even persuaded the Rosenwald Fund to put up a school for the 'niggers' in the county. Rather too elaborate, to my way of thinking, but Arnold was very pleased. Well, I must be going. I shall see you tonight, of course, at the Johnsons'. It has been so very lovely of you to let me see your home and to give me such entertainment. I am thrilled. Good day and good-by."

Arnold Coypel was a North Carolinian by birth but had taken his college course at the University of Georgia when its educational program was under the good old Dr. Baldwin. Then he had returned to his home state and gone to teaching. He was a tall, thin, light-haired man with blue eyes and a characteristic stoop. He had, however, a good deal of firmness under his mild manner, and was distinctly an idealist. He was glad to become, in 1902, the city superintendent of the schools of Lanark. Lanark was a small North Carolina town, the center of a fairly prosperous farming district, and had a few small industries. It was in the western part of the state, and the population was mainly of middle class whites with a few Negroes as servants and as farm tenants and laborers in the outskirts.

Mrs. Coypel returned from Atlanta in such a whirl of plans, all so logical and compelling, that she could not understand her husband's lack of enthusiasm as she unfolded them. Arnold must plan to leave Lanark immediately and establish himself in Atlanta under the patronage of John Baldwin, the son of his old Dr. Baldwin.

"John Baldwin? I don't remember any John Baldwin."

"Why he's old Dr. Baldwin's son; you must remember him."

"Oh yes; there was a young wife and a son; but he was educated at Princeton. I was graduated before he came home. We used to wonder why a son of Baldwin should go north for education. I supposed it was on account of the flighty wife he married."

"Arnold! She was a Breckinridge and is now a most respected leader of Atlanta society. And as for John, he's a coming man of Atlanta. He's wealthy—"

"Sure, from his mother's family."

"Well, he's in banking,—and listen: He is mayor, and under thirty. See?"

"See what?"

"You must cultivate him, visit him, get him to visit here and see your schools. He remembers you, and his wife was very cordial."

"But my dear, I don't know him and don't want to. I doubt if he knows me. I don't want to go to Atlanta. I'm satisfied here."

"That's just it. Satisfied! My God! Satisfied, content, in this little one-horse town."

Arnold smiled tolerantly. But he demurred at writing Baldwin and inviting him to visit.

"I don't know him. I don't know how he has turned out—successful? Oh yes, young Baldwin would be very successful, but after all what is success, and moreover, what of it? Why should I leave Lanark? I am doing a good job here and I am happy. What more do I want? I'm not at all intrigued by the idea of living in Atlanta. I've been to Atlanta once or twice and found it noisy and dirty and no place for either thought or flower. Doubtless the rich John Baldwin can afford a flower garden in Atlanta, but the poor Arnold Coypel has, I am convinced, a much finer garden at less cost right here in Lanark; so that if it is a matter of flower gardens—"

"But it is not a matter of flower gardens and you are silly to talk that way and you know it. It is a matter of getting on in the world and meeting people and being in the midst of things and not vegetating in this hole."

Arnold smiled. "You didn't call it a hole when I first came

here and we were courting. I was given to understand that it was one of the finest towns in the South, very aristocratic and with a noble history."

"Nonsense. You are just making fun. Lanark is all right as small stodgy towns go; but for people who want to live in the twentieth century it is simply impossible. It is off the track. It leads nowhere. You have got to make a change."

Now it was probably a mistake, and Mrs. Coypel ought to have realized it, to use imperatives with Arnold. He was apt to get silent and stubborn, which was exactly what he did now. She tried tears and had hysterics in mind, but according to his usual method he walked out and left her alone. It was then that she remembered Zoe. This was their first and only child born a year after their marriage in 1903. Zoe was now eight years of age and mostly in the care of her black nurse. Mrs. Coypel, finding Arnold fond of children, had hinted soon after Zoe's birth that her physician advised against further pregnancy for a number of obscure reasons. Of course Arnold was too kind to object or inquire further. They settled down to one child until this crisis arose and Mrs. Coypel saw Zoe as the path to Atlanta. She was convinced that the education and future of the child could make Coypel see the need of more money and wider opportunitny.

She therefore rather suddenly discovered that Zoe's education was being woefully neglected and that a Negro nurse was the last person to be entrusted with any part of it. She dismissed the nurse and took increased and personal care of Zoe; read books and learned of Atlanta's new and efficient kindergartens and grades for white children. Arnold was much pleased with his wife's new interest in the child, although the child itself was not and violently bemoaned her black nurse. The family was a bit upset. Arnold naturally hearkened to the increased and reiterated argument for going to Atlanta. He, of course, was aware in a way of some cogency in what his wife was saying. He had drifted into this town almost accidentally after graduation and some experiments at teaching. Because of a local emergency he had been made superintendent of schools and he had taken hold of the job. He had been rather successful, because here was a job that he could grasp and forces that he could influence and largely control. He had made this community of some five thousand white people education conscious. The town consisted of well-to-do farmers and merchants in the commission business, and a few industries. There was no depressed white working class, most of the whites being pretty well-paid clerks and artisans. On the basis of income there was some, but not great nor impassable social defferences. Service and menial work and common labor were performed by Negroes, mostly from colored families long resident in town or the surrounding county.

The white people had become rather proudly aware of their schools. They paid their extra taxes quite willingly and the simple but beautiful high school on the main street was a source of great civic pride. He had had some difficulty with teachers, of getting rid of old driftwood and securing salaries large enough to attract young and well-trained people, but even here he had considerable success.

Living expense was low in Lanark, and the social contacts not uninteresting, although, to be sure, not exactly inspiring. Most of his teachers were satisfied. The town did not have, or at least was not conscious of any considerable racial problem. The number of colored people in town was rather small and somewhat larger in the country. No provision was made for them in the city school system, but in the country they used an old church. He had arranged for a new Rosenwald school and the county had helped. There were fairly good school facilities for the Negroes throughout the county except, of course, some of them had to come long distances and he had not been able to get the county to undertake the transportation for Negroes like that provided for whites. But this was not in the line of his particular work, and he could do little about it.

Personally, Coypel had been rather happy. His work kept him busy. He had married without any particular forethought one of the pretty girls of the town, well-connected and widely acquainted. He had built himself a six-room cottage in a pleasant neighborhood, with a large yard, and he had to confess to himself that of the compelling objects in his life his flower garden loomed first, and he would not have dared to admit to Mrs. Coypel that nothing held him to Lanark so strongly as this yard.

On the other hand, Arnold Coypel was naturally a little troubled by the fact that he was out of the main currents of the world; that he did not have contact with people who were doing things and thinking new worlds into being. The interests which he served in this little town were, after all, rather narrow and of themselves unimportant. What, for instance, was he educating these young people for? They would become businessmen; they would go into the employ of the large corporations; they would get into the tobacco industry either for planting or for manufacture. Some would teach in the country, in small towns, preferably in large cities. But there were in their minds no large thoughts of development, social uplift, new forms of living.

It would have been difficult to make students, teachers or the town itself aware of any demand for social thinking. Practically none of them knew any race problem. In Lanark a few Negroes voted, and of course none held any office. There was little real poverty among them and no serious crime. Personally, he would have liked to get in closer touch with a certain kind of world. He would like to be part of some movement or movements toward wider realization of what human life might mean. But how? He could not see any conspicuously open door in Atlanta. From what little he knew, and he did know little, the doors opening in Atlanta were not doors leading to what he had in mind. They were leading to great and conspicuous wealth, to despotic power over human beings and their lives, to expansion in dubious directions and for ends that he could not quite see.

If he had been more conscious of himself as a source of power and direction he might have thought of helping to make this tre-mendous dynamo and ganglion of Atlanta into a world-changing force; but see how difficult it had been in the comparatively little spot like Lanark to make something reasonable decent and com-monplace out of indifference. He somehow shrunk at trying to do anything or the dreaming of the possibility of his doing anything in Atlanta. Then again (and this was more personal), he hated patronage; he hated to ask things from people in power; he thought he had a right to expect voluntary initiative on the part of the powerful if they saw in him any indications of usefulness or suc-cess. He was not going to toady and beg of John Baldwin.

Beyond this, he realized that what his lovable but rather silly little wife wanted in Atlanta was nothing like what he would want. She was overwhelmed at the society and luxury, the chance to show off and to meet conspicuous people. He knew he would hate that kind of thing and be very uncomfortable and therefore he shut his lips rather grimly and the subject was not opened again until after the miraculously increased importance of his little daughter's education. That did change things—just why, Coypel did not realize, except that his wife seemed of a sudden to take on the responsibilities of motherhood. She was now tireless in making over the home for Zoe's enjoyment, and was all the more convincing because she really felt a difference and enjoyed the new work with her hitherto unknown child. She continued talking of the future.

"What on earth can one do with $1,200 a year? Barely live decently; but when it comes to bringing up children (she used the plural advisedly) why we can't save a cent. Whatever will we do when it comes time for Zoe to go to college? It'll cost at least a thousand a year. Even in High School and at home, what with the sororities and goings-on, why we just must make more money now that Zoe is growing up." Zoe herself soon began to pray for a heaven in Atlanta.

The invitation to read a paper at the Regional Teachers' Meeting which convened in Atlanta, which soon came to Arnold, was, as Arnold half suspected, arranged by his wife through Arnold's loyal teaching staff. They felt it would be a great honor. Arnold went, not with any clear idea of procedure, but with some thought of trying out the possibilities of getting a better paying position and one nearer "things," as his wife put it. Of course, this would take time, but it would not hurt to make acquaintances and get the lay of the land. Moreover—and this seemed more likely and personally more pleasing—perhaps if he seemed in possible demand elsewhere, Lanark might voluntarily offer him the raise in salary which he had never asked.

He came to Atlanta at a critical time in the public school situation. New blood had been injected into the school board, led by young John Baldwin. He represented "Business," and Business thought it high time to take a hand in education. There had been a good deal of parlor radicalism afloat and a pronounced labor upsurge. Under the present superintendent, an opinionated old fogy, the schools were a hotbed of personal favoritism, old-fashioned methods and new ideas hopelessly jumbled.

John Baldwin attended the afternoon session of the teachers, when Coypel read his paper. He was scouting for new material in teachers and less definitely for a superintendent. On the Board he had the votes to overturn the present setup, but he was going slow. He was on hand today, because the superintendent of schools of Trenton, New Jersey, would speak, and he had applied for the

Atlanta position. Baldwin listened to him coldly. He seemed trying to be more Southern than the South. He expressed all but contempt for "demands of the masses," having doubtless in his own mind the colored people; while, of course, his hearers thought only of the white workers whom they more or less directly represented. The colored folk did not come into their minds at all. Baldwin sensed this.

"He won't do," he muttered, and half arose to go. Then he paused as the next speaker arose. He instinctively liked him. He reminded him a little of his father, that half-legendary impractical old man. The speaker had the same introspective air—with just a touch of the ascetic. Baldwin sat down and listened. It was a very clear, sensible speech, combining frank honesty with long and sympathetic knowledge of human beings.

Baldwin did some rapid thinking. Referring to his program, he saw that this Arnold Coypel was from a small North Carolina town. He could be had cheap—far cheaper than a northern man. Of course he would not have the advertising value, but on the other hand he was Southern; he neither forgot nor exaggerated the race problem. He would excite little jealousy; most Atlanta folk would feel superior to him and try to use him or eventually supplant him. But if Baldwin was any judge of character, this man could handle men. He decided quickly and met Coypel at the foot of the platform stairs. He assumed his most disarming manner—bluff, hearty, full of frank good nature.

"Thank you, Mr. Coypel—thank you. That was an excellent statement."

Coypel was surprised. People often listened to what he said, but they seldom praised it.

"Why—I'm glad if—"

"Baldwin is the name—John Baldwin; perhaps—"

"Yes, of course, you are old Dr. Baldwin's son."

"Yes, yes—did you—?" Then some memory clicked in Baldwin's mind and he changed. "You knew him—?"

"Yes, I knew him very well. In fact I have never known another human being quite so well—or in the same way."

They began to walk and talk. They passed through the groups of people, greeting them mechanically. Coypel talked of old Dr. Baldwin. He asked about his health, saying apologetically that he had lost track of him since his retirement.

"He was a queer man, unusual in his mental manners and methods. He had a fund, a vast fund of knowledge—of what was transpiring at the moment here, in Europe and Asia; of what had happened a decade, a century, a thousand years ago. And it was all known, all at his finger's end; he did not have to search for it and put it together. He applied it right here to the problems in this country, in this student. Of course, for this very reason people did not understand him. He seemed always to be talking of something of which they hadn't the foggiest idea, and coming to the most extraordinary conclusions about them and their business."

Baldwin mused. He must have been a man worth knowing, the kind of friend a boy would need. And he was his own father—why hadn't he really met him? Coypel continued:

"Yet everybody liked him. His honesty and selflessness were so apparent, so ingrained. He went right to the Right and Wrong of things, and yet with such knowledge of the human soul that he always understood, and people knew he did. Vicariously he was always suffering for the sins of others."

Baldwin was startled. This was the funny old man whom he recalled as slow, shabby and always in the way. How he and his gay young mother had secretly mocked and made fun of him. He even remembered with a strange pang, the hurt look he had often surprised in the old man's eyes at some unusual bit of impudence. He could almost see him now, climbing up to his study, that eyrie of dirt and books, where he himself was never allowed to go lest he dirty his pretty clothes.

He began to be a bit uneasy; he wondered if Coypel knew that Old Dr. Baldwin still lived; imprisoned, incredibly old, watching the world and mumbling from his mountain home. He was afraid Coypel might ask some unpleasant questions and hastened to turn back. But as he parted he said: "Mr. Coypel, I want to see more of you. I have something in mind which might interest us both."

Young Baldwin the next summer went north and sat in close conference with members of influential people on various subjects. Incidentally, he inquired further about Arnold Coypel. So that when he came south with Mrs. Baldwin he took pains to arrange to have the through express stop and let him off at Lanark and then to visit the Coypels, to Mrs. Coypel's hysterical surprise and delight.

Baldwin was the jovial, well-dressed, clearcut young business man with his foot on the first round of political preferment. His mind was made up and he had no questions as to procedure. He liked Arnold Coypel. There was about this man something of spiritual sonship to his half-known father. This was the kind of man he wanted to put at the head of the schools of Atlanta. They needed a hell of a lot of refurbishing and revolutionizing, and this metropolis of the southeast must have a school system that would make the United States sit up and take abundant notice. They had just had trouble in Atlanta in the unfortunate lynching of that Jew. They must brace up and become civilized. Education would do it. He believed that Coypel was the man to start it. He could found a good system. Whether he had the hardness and drive to complete it was a question, but he could start it.

So almost without preliminaries young John Baldwin offered Arnold the position of superintendent of the city schools of Atlanta, at a salary four times that which he was receiving. He hardly waited for an answer. He dandled the pretty little daughter, and his wife was suitably and elegantly silent under the rush of words and almost tearful exuberance of Mrs. Coypel. When, like a subdued tempest, the Baldwins moved out of the little home and took the train to Atlanta, Arnold Coypel, walking among his flowers, realized that he had made an important life decision and that this decision involved saying goodbye to his flowers. He was not sure just whether he ought to feel elated or to give way to a rising lump of emotion closely akin to tears.

So the Coypel family moved to Atlanta and Arnold started his new work. He gave much attention natutrally to the white schools and literally forgot about the colored schools until Baldwin brought them to his attention. He was ashamed of his neglect, but colored schools, like colored people, had never engaged his attention. Of course they must work and eat and be educated; but there had been so few in Lanark and they were mostly outside the town —well, he had not realized that one-third the population of Atlanta was black and that their schools must engage much of his attention and plans.

Baldwin broached the matter. It seemed that old John James was dead. "Good old 'nigger,' of the old faithful sort. Sorry to lose him."

"Who was he?"

"Superintendent in charge of the colored schools."

"Oh, you have a colored superintendent?"

"Oh, just a name—no power; just a figurehead to save the Superintendent from annoyance. We have now an application from the ranking principal of the colored schools to succeed and that poses a problem."

"Is he a good man?"

"Yes and no. He's pretty well trained—graduated at Atlanta University and has done some graduate study there—"

"Atlanta University? I did not know—"

"Oh no, it's not what you think. It's a colored school supported by Northern missionaries. Its name is a thorn in our flesh. But it's a good school. This colored principal is named Manuel Mansart. I met him once when he came to Princeton with his colored singers. Later I helped him to his first job. He's done pretty good work here, but I don't know. He's got brains and ideas. He can't be treated like old James. But how can we treat him and not run into trouble? We can't have a firebrand on our hands. If he gets the appointment he's got to be a 'good nigger' or go. So that's your problem, Coypel. Go to it."

Manuel Mansart was thirty-seven, a stocky man of dark brown skin and close-curled hair. He had been born in Charleston, S. C., in 1876, on the night his father was lynched. He had secured an education in Atlanta and taught a country school. He had married a school-mate and had four children. For eight years now he had been teaching in Atlanta. He had lived through the riot and wanted to get out of the South. But just as an offer came for him to teach in Indiana, John James, the Superintendent of the Atlanta colored schools, died. James had been nothing more than a frightened figurehead, but his successor might be a real power. To the disgust of his family, Manuel applied for the job. This morning the new white superintendent had asked him for an interview.

Today, as a result of the interview, Coypel was embarrassed. He sat in his office on the fourth floor of the City Hall and looked rather helplessly out of the window across the forest of roofs with chimneys in the background, all wavering in the summer heat an obbligato of curiously divergent and ugly sounds. He had just had an interview with Manuel Mansart and they had been talking about the colored schools of Atlanta. Of course, it was possible that Mansart had exaggerated the situation and naturally he must check that carefully. Yet, there was no doubt but what Mansart believed in the truth of all he had said.

It seemed to Coypel almost unbelievable that a great, rich, pushing city like Atlanta should so neglect and ignore one-third of its population. Of course it must be largely forgetfulness, or was it in part deliberate? It could hardly all be deliberate, and yet here were 40,000 children crowded into five schools; all the buildings old, the newest built twenty years ago for white pupils and then turned over to the Negro when a shift had taken place in the residential areas of the Negroes and new and better sections were opened for the whites. All of these Negro schools had double sessions, that is, the children did not go to school all day. One part went half a day and then in the afternoon an entirely different set crowded in. Indeed, in some of the primary grades three sets tried to get tuition. The same teachers bore a load of sixty to eighty and more pupils, and they were paid from $800 to $1000 a year. They were not simply overworked; in fact, those among them who were at all conscientious were almost driven to distraction.

Coypel stirred uneasily. There could easily be some exaggeration here. What was the corresponding condition in the white schools? He must look into this thoroughly. In the first few months of his incumbency he had devoted almost all his time to getting the family settled physically, trying to satisfy Mrs. Coypel with a place to live.

His mind drifted out in that direction. He had left a salary of $1,200 for a salary of $5,000. It seemed to him first that this was riches. He envisaged travel to the North, to the West, to Europe. His financial troubles were over. But wait! Mrs. Coypel had chosen a house whose rental would be $200 a month! It was fantastic when he heard of it. It would call for two or three regular servants. He would need a salary of at least twice as large for the upkeep, yet only this morning she had gone into tears over the prospect of anything less.

With a sigh Coypel pulled his mind away from that and came back to Mansart. He felt ashamed of himself. Here was a man with a large family living, or trying to live on $1,200 a year. Of course, he did not have to pay much rent. He could not rent a pretentious house in Atlanta even if he had wanted to. He didn't have to buy a new automobile. He was driving a second-hand Ford. His clothes and the clothes of his family didn't cost much, or did they? Coypel found himself rather at sea. How did colored people of Mansart's class dress? He remembered that Mansart looked very neat. Probably his suit cost about as much as Coypel's own suit, and his linen was clean and whole. But the main thing after all was the man himself.

Fundamentally he was undoubtedly honest. He was terribly in earnest and really excited and yet reasonable. They soon learned that they were of the same age and that both had families. They talked about flowers and about human beings. They were frank and confidential in many ways, and yet there were certain reticences and omissions. Some matters they deliberately skirted briefly. Others they omitted. He remembered that when he had mentioned John Baldwin, Mansart said nothing. Yet, on the whole it had been a real communion of souls and both men were impressed and to a degree changed by the meeting.

Mansart had arrived in a belligerent mood. He tried not to forget what his family would think. His oldest boys would expect his father to knuckle under to the whites. His younger boys would stare at him coldly. His wife would weep at the prospect of living longer in Atlanta. He was not soothed by a ride to the fifth floor in a freight elevator. There were white people with him but they took this elevator because it was the first one going up. He took it because he was ordered to after the two passenger elevators had gone on and left him. The secretary who received him was deliberately insolent. She took down his name, looked it over, and said: "Sit down, Manuel; I will see when Mr. Coypel can see you," and then went back to her work. Coypel came out accidentally, discovered him, shook hands cordially and ushered him in. He sensed the office disapproval when he called him "Mr. Mansart."

Mansart was mollified but immediately gripped himself. He must let neither small courtesies nor small insults influence him. He had a job to do and he started in immediately, perhaps a little abruptly, with his "demands." Coypel dexterously intervened with an offer of a cigar. It indicated rather more thoughtfulness than he was ordinarily credited with, but he felt the discomfort of the situation. He wanted to get down to frank exchange of feelings and attitudes. Then he asked for the facts of the situation. His secretary interrupted him somewhat unceremoniously and was rather insistent. It would seem that an important personage without wanted to talk with Coypel, but Coypel was quiet and firm, and after he had given the secretary a level glance, she withdrew.

Coypel was quite different from the type of white school official with whom Mansart had hitherto come in contact. He felt in sympathy with him, and Coypel liked the forthright young black man. They talked frankly. Mansart showed that the colored schools were not getting more than a tenth of the school expenditures despite the fact that Negroes formed a third of the population. He brought along pictures and plans of the dilapidated schools. He showed how they were overcrowded and understaffed, with double sessions and wretched equipment and low salaries. He mentioned his own miserable salary.

Coypel was both astonished and sympathetic. He had never been face to face with the problem of Negro schools before. His small experience in Lanark was of little help here. In fact he was indignant to think that a big rich city like this was acting in so selfish and thoughtless a way. He knew, however, that he must be careful, that Georgia was not North Carolina and that the state of white schools was going to call for money, time and hard work.

He listened to the story of the colored schools and the story of Mansart's own life. He arranged for a trip to inspect the schools day after next. Then they came down to personalities and frank comparison. Finally Coypel arose.

"Of course you know I can't actually promise you anything now. I am new; newer than you are. I don't know my real power or my sources of support; but I wish you would believe this, Mr. Mansart; I am going to do everything that I can to see that the colored schools of Atlanta have a fair deal. I am going to try. Please believe that."

He spoke almost pleadingly with a certain absent-mindedness, because way back in his head he began to realize just the sort of thing he was up against. In theory, to some extent in practice, he knew about the race problem in the South. He had grown up in its shadow and yet it seemed that never before had he actually come in contact with it as a matter of flesh and blood. Or at least, not in just this guise. He had seen poor Negroes, Negroes neglected, ignorant and even criminal; but this phase of opportunity and group treatment, this was new to him, at least as a real experience.

"You will believe me, won't you?"

And Mansart said yes, shook his hand and was gone.

But his real belief was expressed when he got home. He wrote to Gary and said, "I am deeply obliged but I am not going to accept your kind offer." His wife was resentful. She had built on the idea of getting out of the South, of getting away from this discrimination, of having a modern house and decent income and here was Manuel, like all Negroes, putting his trust in a Southern white man's word. She sat in silence and looked at him and the tears began to fall down her cheeks.

Coypel came home a few days later thoroughly depressed. He had for two days been visiting the colored schools, just as a week earlier he had gone through the white schools. He had expected discrimination not only against Negroes but against all poor whites and all ignorant people; and in some respects the discrimination was not really so great as the figures or even the sight would indicate. And yet, as he sat back and closed his eyes, he felt that there was a certain blatant, ostentatious and deliberate discrimination against Negroes that was beyond his comprehension, that stirred only wrath and protest.

For instance, the newest white school with its beautiful grounds on a new street, off Peachtree, was almost like an opera house, flamboyant and screaming with opulence and ostentation. It was a show place rather than a center of thought and learning. He doubted if many of the white mill hands' children were going to feel comfortable there or be able to pay the fees for fraternities, sororities, games and excursions.

On the other hand, one had to delve down in unpaved alleys or decadent streets to find the colored schools. Most of them were firetraps and unsanitary, and the confusion of overcrowding made functioning impossible. The teachers were harassed or indifferent. The discipline was a matter of threats and yells and helplessness; and yet out of it and through it there was a certain push, spirit and inventiveness and uncurbed efficiency and a jolly spirit of comradeship. If all this was harnessed and housed, disciplined and directed—but pshaw! So what? He turned to his telephone and called up Mayor Baldwin.

"Yes, come right over. I was just about to call. I have the first draft of the budget before me which the finance committee passed last night. I want to talk with you about it."

Coypel went over and was conducted immediately into the mayor's office. Mayor Baldwin was a young man, handsome and well-proportioned, exceedingly well-dressed, and punch and ambition radiated from his personality. He was a shrewd man, one who had never had to worry about money to spend and who now was spending it on a scale that called for considerable wealth. He had a quiet, alert, thoroughly capable secretary. He looked at Coypel with keen, frank eyes. He saw a man of thirty-five, ascetic looking and thin, with certain indications of impracticable idealism about him, something of hesitation in thought and action, and a tendency in the midst of accuracy and decision to wander off into day dreaming and theories.

He sensed immediately that Coypel was upset and hastened to forestall him with the offer of a dry Martini which Coypel refused. There was a rapid exposition of the school budget. He showed he had gotten out of the Board of Education a large appropriation for the public schools, larger than ever before, and that he was going to put the Atlanta public system on the map so that the whole nation would see it.

Coypel got in his query quietly and rather before Baldwin had planned. He said, "Yes, yes, but what about the colored schools?" Baldwin frowned a little. He wanted to get the main picture outlined before he came to the difficulties; but he was too frank and enthusiastic to dodge an issue, especially when he saw what Coypel had at heart. Coypel went ahead and outlined rapidly what he had seen in the last two days. Baldwin pushed back his cocktail and laid down his cigar and looked at Coypel steadily. He said:

"Coypel, I know just how you feel, and I sympathize with you. I am no 'nigger hater.' On the whole I like colored people, at least most of those I really know, and I am frank to say that I don't know many and I don't seek to know more. But they are here and they are going to stay here. They are not going to die out nor be deported. They are going to become, if we have sense enough to guide them, a good reliable class of laborers and servants as intelligent as we can make them.

"The chief source of danger is a certain number of educated or perhaps I should say half-educated leaders. Their existence cannot be avoided, but they are a source of danger. They want to go too fast and too far and we have got to curb them. Their number is small and I don't think we need to fear them much just now. What we want to do is to outstrip them, keep the white race so far ahead that they will be breathless from trying to pursue us.

"Now there is another thing. In all this we have got to be fair to them. I may be wrong about their ability but so far as the facts go I am right at this moment. I propose to do something for Negro schools. They have been wretchedly neglected but—" he bent forward and jabbed the desk with his forefinger. "This is a poor white town, and a poor white section. The white aristocracy of the South was disinherited by the war and the abolition of slavery, and has been superseded by a pushing, determined set of newcomers. They are beginning to rule the South and especially they founded and are ruling Atlanta. They form on the whole a ruthless, ambitious group of people who are lurching forward at a tremendous rate. They can't be stopped and I don't want to stop them. They can be made to want better things when they understand what better things are.

"Now, see what I mean. The most difficult man on the Board of Education is a fellow named Scroggs. He represents the lurching rear guard of this pushing poor white army. He broke into the white primary and got himself on the Board of Education. He has no education himself but he is ruthless, profane, and is going places. His God is Tom Watson. Now he wants schools but he doesn't want schools for Negroes. If I tried to push through the proposition of giving the colored people of Atlanta their proportional share of school expenditures according to population, he would kill the thing in a minute, and in the end the Negroes would get less than they are getting now.

"What, therefore, we have got to do, Coypel, is to improve the white schools tremendously and improve the colored schools a little. What we do for the colored schools must be substantial but not conspicuous. Later, in ten or twenty years we can go forward with the colored schools, but that will only be when the whites have advanced in still greater degree. Now this is my problem and I tell you it's the only way we can do anything. I hope you are going to play ball with me and I hope this Negro Mansart will have sense enough to play along with you. If he hasn't, kick him out. I know him. He means well. I once got him a job. But he must bow. He must bend. It will be easy enough to get someone who will go along with us, if he won't."

"No," said Coypel energetically. He knew when he said it he was really dodging the issue. "No," said he, "I will not let Mansart go. He wants his salary increased and if he will work with me

I will do what can be done under your plan. Otherwise I am through."

He knew when he said this that instead of joining issue with Baldwin's main thesis he had grabbed rather desperately at a side issue and made that his fight rather than the main quesiton; but he did not know just where to take his stand on the main question.

"All right," said Baldwin jovially, "keep Mansart if you can! Give him $1500 and promise him two new schools and perhaps a little extra salary for the teachers. But keep him in line. Don't let him become a firebrand and blow us all up."

CHAPTER II

ATLANTA BURNS

There began in 1914 not simply a war, nor simply a World War; but rather a war of many worlds against each other; of nations against nations, of races against races. Many white Georgia preachers sensed Armageddon and sonorously rolled out the text of those terrible Last Days, "When nation shall rise against nation, and Kingdom against Kingdom!"

But their words, while eloquent in the pulpit of Dr. Barnswell, and vivid in the words of Dr. Swain, and even bloodcurdling as yelled among the hard-shelled Baptists, somehow lacked conviction from long overuse, until in the Fall of 1914, word began to circulate concerning a new prophet down from the mountains into Atlanta, at dusk, on Sunday evenings.

Crowds began to await him and he was impressive: incredibly old, with long, snow-white hair, clothed from neck to instep in a long and not too clean black gown. But his words held the hearers. He was not a conventional preacher but more of a teacher; he used low conversational tones and one had to press close to catch all he said. But what he said was frightening and the crowds grew. It took on the form of one sermon, broken into parts arbitrary, by pauses and absences sometimes of weeks and even months. His message seemed like this:

"All this is written. It is an accumulation of hates and animosities; a clash of counter-strivings covering centuries. Paradoxes have at last met. Europe, Asia, Africa and all the Americas have been preparing for this for centuries. It has announced itself in Trilogies: African slavery, Asiatic wealth and White Supremacy; Slums and Poverty, Ignorance and Crime, Disease and Death; Aristocracy and Power, Comfort and Luxury, Society and Gambling; Philosophy, Science and Technique. We have talked of Absolute, Final, Longest, Biggest, Highest. We have pretended to distinguish Truth, Lies, Good, Evil."

Then he wandered away; he awaited no questions, he furnished no answer. Months later he appeared again, talking at first to a few, who swelled finally to hundreds. He seemed more disturbed and eager:

"Greed nailed the world together into one snarling, scratching, fighting ball of human hatreds. We are One, cried the priests with black hypocrisy; we are One, cried Science with pale contradiction. We are not One and never will be, cried the Crowd as they chased bawling scoundrels and bitches into the dens of Gain. They made armies, well-regulated whorehouses and rationed gin mills. They built beautiful battleships to spew out at frequent ports great bunches of wild young stallions to rape the frightened women of lowly races and cheaper classes.

"They lied with prayer and cheated on the altars of sacrifice. Yesterday men like angels of the Resurrection flew up into the sun-kissed skies and burned the homes and flattened the shops and ripped the guts out of women and children to the Glory of God and Love of Man. Valiant knights sneaked beneath the blackness of deep waters to rip the bellies out of unsuspecting argosies filled with clothes and food and steel for the starving and freezing, whose cries swept the Seven Seas.

"Such was the brave and heroic battle of the bastards and skunks who were decorated with medals and stars. They did to others just what others did to them and more and worse if anyway possible. They kicked the Prince of Peace in the teeth and crowned him with bayonets. Great nations, too poor to build schools, libraries and hospitals, were rich enough to build magnificent warships at ten million dollars apiece, to prowl the seas for prey or scare the weak into slavery. They could not cure Cancer, but they could spread Syphilis. They tore the towers of cathedrals neck from jowl to erect offices for profit.

"Now come the statesmen in serried ranks, brave in apparel and venerable in mien: the Sons of Beliel from London; the snakes from Paris; the jackals from Vienna; and rats of the First Families of Germany. Stupid old generals and half-baked colonels; ignorant Admirals and Captains who will now blunder and waste, kill and cripple, strut and whore and swagger, and come home to be made rulers of men, to talk wisely of matters of which they knew nothing, while hysterical women gape, dribble and applaud.

"It will be One War, from 1914 on and on for a century, a war with only interludes of Starvation and Insanity. The preachers and priests—the bishops and metropolitans begin to run, begin to climb their towers to escape the rising, licking filth of blood and spittle, begin to explain, begin to remind and prophesy: Hear ye, hear ye! Make straight the way of the Lord, God of Greed! The rapt Buddha of the East, reincarnate in Christian machines, seize arms and beat Nirvana into the brains of Moslems, while Moslems mad with hate preach Holy War.

"The lowly white Jesus of the West will turn the other cheek and kick his black brother in the jaw so hard that all his bloody broken teeth will seed the earth and popup as well-oiled machine guns, spraying death on vermin called Men.

"The Son of God went forth to War, a kingly crown to gain; only he was twins, he was quintuplets; he fought himself. Protestant fought Protestant; Catholic killed Catholic; Moslem murdered Moslem; Jew electrocuted Jew; and Buddhist butchered Buddhist, and all killed each other. Even Baptists baptized Baptists in pools of hot and filthy blood. It was a Last Supper of the Lords of earth, sky and Hell.

"We produced to destroy and destroyed to produce and paradox birthed maniac, made men murderers and women prostitutes and children foundlings and turned the world insane.

"The kingly crown was a wreath of colonies, studded with gold and diamonds and festering with tubercles, cancers and syphilis; packed with care and suspicion in ships and trains plastered with mud and oiled with human blood.

"In 1906 the San Francisco earthquake roared the warning of outraged Nature; in the same fatal year Atlanta spilled the first blood; in 1911 Italy ran amok in the Balkans and then came August, 1914. It was all one piece. It all moved one way."

He started away but walked so slow that night overtook his followers, and becoming superstitious and afraid, none learned where he lived or what he was. But word got around. It appeared to many church folk that here was irreligion and even blasphemy. The police were notified and kept watch for a month, until after that Battle of Flanders where black Africans fighting for France walked by tens of thousands straight into the mouths of German artillery, raising their ancient war cries in a dozen tongues until no black man lived and silence reigned.

Suddenly at early sunset he broke silence. He talked rapidly and more loudly than before. He stood on a pedestal instead of squalling on the turf. Some colored folk listened on the edge of the crowd.

"War is Murder and murderers murder, until all is done and there is Peace and Nothing. After the Phantasmagoria, learned jackasses, spawning like flies, in lovely old universities will explain it all in thick books and cadent lectures: Everybody was right; nobody was wrong; all was Logic and Rhythm and Evolution; all was Good for the greater Good. And all readers and hearers will be silent for none will believe a word of what is said.

"Ends fighting Ends; War ending War; Good to stop Evil; Evil to birth God. Virtue, Bravery, Honor and Disease.

"Then the silent, hidden God of gods—how he will flay the liars and the scoundrels; how he will loose more Hell on earth to show the sacred world what Sons of Bitches we are—"

"For I have been wrong. I have blamed Generalities and Others. But it's me, it's me, O Lord, standing in the need of prayer. It's me and you who are guilty of this war. We right here sought Liberty and established Slavery. We preached Brotherhood and built the Color bar. We taught our children that Negro Slavery was right and Negroes stupid, inferior and nasty. We declared that we never fought to defend slavery or made every effort to restore it. We set the world the example of a democracy founded on inequality and the world answered with the world wide serfdom of colored peoples. We helped turn the abolition of the African slave trade into the Factory system and the private ownership of tools and materials and captivity of labor by low wages for whites and none for blacks. That white world today is fighting itself for a new division of the no wage area. And we of all men are seeking to share in this new division of the spoils. Shame on the world which seeks thus to rule the world and shame on Atlanta and the white South which tries to buy the domination of white folk over yellow, brown and black. Come, black brothers. . . ."

Here the crowd began to murmur menacingly, and drown out his words. "Who is this old man?"

"This is nigger equality! Hustle him away! Drive him home! Stop his mouth! Call the police!"

The police came and accosted him: "See here, old man, we can't have no such language about here. Who are you? Where do you live? Have you got a license?"

The old man turned wearily and smiled on the crowd which

had now swelled to a thousand or more. He moved away, muttering as he went, and only a few grasped his last words:

"That is what it is; that was what it had to be. But that was not the way it will be painted for innocent children to learn. Loyal liars will slap the colors on great heroes and war-lords; outline their magnificent plans and wide-visioned leadership; make the era of war the birth of Life instead of the beginning of Death. So world war will start again and again; why not? What else can happen? Until men stop fighting because none are left to fight.

"And this in after ages will be the tale which Arachnid tells Amoeba about the incredible incident of Man and Earth. Nor will Amoeba believe it—for did not Man have brains?"

The police closed in, but the crowd began to become unruly and in the scuffle the old man disappeared.

It was then that Coypel had recognized Dr. Baldwin. Coypel and the classmates who met in 1914 had since often discussed that meeting. Indeed, before breaking up a clergyman had said to Coypel:

"Have you ever seen old Dr. Baldwin?"

"No, I thought him dead, but his son said not. He intimated that he was not well."

Cresswell broke in: "That young Baldwin is a son-of-a-bitch. He and his ambitious mother have tucked old Baldwin into some insane asylum so as to shut him up."

"I can't quite think that," said Coypel. "You know he was center of a new university system in this state—why there he is now!"

They stopped and stared. Soon they had the old man out of the hands of the police, and finding a quiet place sat down to inquire. The old man seemed quite rational. To Coypel's intense surprise he recognized him.

"This is Coypel, isn't it? Class of—"

"1899." It was incredible that the old man should remember a student of fifteen years ago. The others he did not recall. But he reminded Coypel of a study of Negro crime in which he was once interested.

"If you'll come home with me—"

"Home?"

"Yes—only a hundred miles or so, northeast. I have a cottage there, but sometimes I get a ride to Atlanta, when I have a word to say to the people."

Coypel got his car and although it was nearly sunset, thought it was wiser to drive directly to Tallulah Falls. They arrived about nine in the evening. They found a quiet cottage kept by an old and anxious colored woman.

"He ran away again," she whispered as she warmed up the waiting supper. "No, sir, he ain't crazy—just queer, and his son wants him to keep quiet and not to go to Atlanta."

Then later, when she said, "Mister, you got to help. The old man is harboring a Negro convict in the barn. He's a murderer and dangerous. You must help get rid of him for the neighbors is getting suspicious. Of course he is a protection for us. You see the crackers had begun to steal from us and annoy us. But not since that big black man has been here. He caught some of them and beat them, but they never got to see him good. Once the sheriff searched the premises. But he was hid too well. But he must be got rid of now, sir, or we'll have trouble."

Before Coypel could bring up the subject, Dr. Baldwin took him out to the barn and brought in the convict. He was a big black man, over six feet tall, and broad.

Old man Baldwin explained. "This man is a criminal; he has stolen, beaten and murdered. But I do not judge him. You remember what we concluded fifteen years ago? That the South was developing a real black criminal class. That it was investing in crime and making millions out of leasing convicts, and wholesale arrest of young and petty law-breakers. That it was turning back children into criminals who some day would prey on civilization. It's come true. Our jails are full of Negroes. It's mainly Negroes we hang and imprison for life. At least a fourth of our black workers are slaves of the state and likely to become hardened criminals for life.

"Now as of course you know, Coypel, the world is coming to an end and I am about to die."

Coypel started and said to himself, "Here comes the insanity." But Baldwin noticed nothing and continued:

"The Black Man—I do not know his name, I never asked—the Black Man has a plan. He proposes to burn Atlanta the moment this nation enters this wicked war. He will burn that city. He plans this as a sort of sacrifice of Fire to redeem Manhood. I asked him to wait until I warned the city and the world. This request he very courteously granted. Now the time approaches. I have warned the world and my message has been rejected. So the Black Man is leaving tonight. Later, in good time, he will return and together we will burn Atlanta."

The Black Man bowed gravely and stepped out into the night. Coypel gasped. Old Man Baldwin looked tired and spent. With brief greeting he walked back to the house and went to bed. Coypel reassured the housekeeper briefly and drove back to Atlanta.

The next morning he visited young Baldwin the mayor and told him all. Baldwin was more annoyed than ashamed. He explained the situation briefly and reassured Coypel. Yet within his soul John Baldwin was upset. Odd doubts mingled with the old conventional excuses. He said:

"I'm sorry, Coypel, you've been annoyed with this situation. You see, my father was always a little queer and after leaving his real life of teaching in Augusta he had become even more unpredictable and difficult to guide."

Coypel recognized this portrait of a man of original mind, difficult for reactionaries to understand. Baldwin continued.

"We found him unsuited to lead our new state educational program, and finally as his mind weakened we arranged to have him return and live continuously in his summer cottage which he had always enjoyed. We found a reliable housekeeper for him and thought all was well. Then came this extraordinary case of street harangues. We thought of confining him but have concluded it will be better to have professional keepers instead. We hoped that this would prove satisfactory. We certainly thank you."

The matter was dropped, but Baldwin began to wonder how wrong he may have been in the past. Yet on this he did not dwell long. He dropped the thought, for the other forces within him were too strong.

Just as the tensions of the world in 1914 threw mankind into insanity, so the strains in the heart of Old Dr. Baldwin thrust him over the thin line which leads to lunacy. And so, too, Booker Washington, as the world lapsed into universal murder, lost his grip on complete reality. He was, of course, always a lonely man; his first wife had lived but two short years and given him a daughter; his second wife had given her life to organizing Tuskegee and borne four sons, but gave him little of her time. His third wife was a statuesque, well-trained woman, who entertained his guests and made a good speech, but married him for his name and neither for his body nor soul. He had no recreations; no field of escape. For fifteen years he had been acclaimed but also cruelly attacked and blamed. Of the thousands whom he met he really knew few and believed in fewer. He was tense and full of fears and suspicions. He had few close friends and did not trust even them.

One night he was alone in New York; his secretary had been detained, his usual guards did not know his whereabouts. He spoke to a great hall of strangers in the suburbs and was, as usual, under tense nervous strain. He usually drank some whiskey before and after talking, and tonight perhaps rather more than his usual allowance of stimulant. When it was over, he slipped out and quietly wandered off alone in the night. He huddled in the noisy, crowded elevated.

Suddenly he wanted the companionship of women. He wanted to sit beside somebody he did not fear, somebody who was not spying on him, who had no complaints. He remembered vividly that evening spent with the jovial Charlie Anderson, who wanted nothing from him but political backing for a presidential job. It was a small, gay group somewhere on West Sixty-Third—11, 13, or 15?—It was so quiet and homelike. The women were white so they could not tattle to Negroes—they could not take him to task for not helping all the black folk of the world.

He wanted desperately to find one particular one again and for a moment know peace. He left the Ninth Avenue L and wandered along the dark 63rd street and searched the numbers in vain, when it happened; when that happened which all his hard life he had avoided, feared, hated—a white man saw him, hailed and cursed him:

"Kill the nigger; he's after white women!"

Washington turned, staggered, and ran toward the park, stumbled and fell. Next morning he found himself in jail. He never recovered. Two years or more passed. Everything was easily explained. It was at worst a mistake; at best a lost way. But Booker Washington never really recovered. In 1915 he died, but was never forgotten.

His secretary's assistant, a man who looked white and was hired for that reason, was bitterly disappointed at the catastrophe of Washington's untimely death. He had reached New York too late to be of use in guiding and protecting his employer. He lost his employment, but lingered in New York, seeking other work.

He kept haunting 63rd Street, until one night in desperation he found himself in a liquor saloon on Tenth Avenue. He was drinking steadily and wondering what he would now attempt on which to build a life. The Tuskegee job had been good and paid well; it brought him in contact with persons of influence. Now perhaps it would be best to go abroad where a drop of black blood was not of such cosmic importance as here. He pulled out his handkerchief and a letter in the pocket with it fell to the floor. The white man beside him bent to pick it up and noticed the address "Tuskegee, Alabama."

As the secretary started to thank him the stranger said with a foreign accent: "Your pardon, Sir, but do you know Tuskegee?"

"I live there."

The stranger hesitated and then said slowly, "My card, Sir. Perhaps you will have lunch with me sometime. I am interested in Tuskegee."

The secretary readily assented and gave the stranger his name and address. Then they parted. Three days later they met in a private room of one of the most noted hotels of New York. They shared a bountiful lunch. Then the German agent talked. Quite evidently he knew all about his guest: his bit of Negro blood; his work as assistant to Booker Washington's secretary; his present effort to find a new and suitable job.

"Why not go abroad?"

"I have often thought of that."

"There is no chance for a colored man in this country. Wilson has just seized Haiti. I have been reading this morning of a mob of thousands of men, women, and children publicly burning a Negro in Waco, Texas— Jesse Washington; perhaps he was a relative of Booker? At any rate you owe nothing to America and Germany needs you. We can use you right here and now; afterward you will find a home in the Motherland. Listen."

They talked together long hours and many days. But what came of the talks, few knew.

It was two long years before the solace of death came to Old Man Baldwin. For all the year 1916 he was confined in his home at Tallulah Falls under the brutal eye of a guard brought in from the State Lunatic Asylum at Milledgeville. The old man lapsed into compulsory silence.

In the spring of 1915 the great ship Lusitania, sailing in St. George's Channel near Ireland, shuddered and heaved. Its gilded magnificence of tapestry and gold, crystal and silver; the velvet of its carpet, the carving of its furniture and sweet music of its organs, bands and orchestras rose and dove into the grey and singing waters until straight down it dashed to the ocean's floor and mingled with the rusted ribs and bleached bones of the great Armada sunk four hundred years before.

In the White House, President Wilson, stricken to heart, sat very still. Only two years ago he had been elected president. A year later came the incredible World War. He swore he would never enter it. Here was his invitation. Here was more than invitation; it was brutal command, and he shrunk in the face of it.

He wrote a letter, a stern letter to "Wilhelm, von Gottes Gnade, Koenig von Pruessen, Deutscher Kaiser." The emperor replied, and other letters flew. Then, in 1916, Old Man Baldwin reappeared in Atlanta and spoke on the steps of the Capitol to a vast crowd:

"To the insane all the world is mad and only they are calm, logical and rational. They are the keen-eyed seers and unmoved prophets. Consider the record: the privilege of French nobility was wrong; the poverty of the 19th century factory workers was unendurable; Negro slavery was an anachronism; colonial imperialism and democracy are incompatible; yet the world fights valiantly for the Old; rages mightily against Socialism; strains every nerve to re-establish black slavery and now raises heaven and earth to retain the British Empire; and all because we are crazy, yet think others are—"

The keepers appeared with an ambulance. Baldwin was whisked back to the hills, put into a straightjacket where for weeks he lay silent. Finally he was allowed to sit up and walk about. He seemed quite normal until he got hold of newspapers by bribing one of the servants. On April 6, 1917, we the United States declared war on Germany. On April 7, Old Man Baldwin had tried again to escape but was caught, cruelly whipped and again confined in a straightjacket. His transfer to Milledgeville was decided on. The guards kept narrow watch. On May 18, President Wilson signed the Military Conscription Bill. On the night of May 20, the Head Keeper saw the Old Man preparing to slip away and was beside himself.

"Give me the slip again, will you, God damn you," he cried, as he tore off the Old Man's gown, "you whining old goat, I'll learn you." And he drew back his hard fist.

But silently out of the night there came a great arm that slithered around his fat neck and tightened, tighter and tighter, until the keeper, black in the face, with protruding tongue, slipped dead to the dewy ground. The black giant above him was naked, with face and body scratched, torn, and blood-stained. He was a ghastly, repulsive ruin of what was once a magnificent human being. His nose had been broken and one eye was gone. Scars crossed his face from chin to forehead. His skull was dented. One arm was twisted awry. Welts seared his limbs. His back was criss-crossed with salt-sifted gashes made by great whips. He had lost his fingers and toes. Yet he glared, unconquered and unsubdued above it all, and his voice roared up like a deep growl of unforgetting and vindictive hate. It was as though fiends had tried by unending pain to mutilate what was once a splendid man sculptured in grand lines and covered in velvet and ivory, with dark, half-dried crimson blood still dripping down. He muttered as he set the Old Man free and covered him with a clean white gown.

"Tomorrow Atlanta burns! Come!"

At midnight, beneath the half moon, they turned toward Atlanta. Dr. Baldwin spoke, half to himself:

"Yes, that will be just. Babylon burned, and Thebes; Rome and Chicago. But who are you?"

"I am the 'nigger' they lynched in Toccoa last night. Remember me?"

"Yes, of course. I hid you once. Are you dead?"

"Not yet. We both die tonight."

"Good! I am ready. I have long been ready. Atlanta is ripe for the flames."

Silent and swift the two moved, like wraiths beneath the moon, found a waiting wagon with mules and at dawn, May 21, 1917 they had covered eighty miles and sat on a flat black tomb in Oakland Cemetery, Atlanta. With interest the Old Man deciphered the family name of "Baldwin" on a stone of discolored marble. Then he saw the others: the yellow, ragged women who served the breakfast: chicken, cornbread, and cold water. The birds twittered and sang as they ate. Then a man, a neatly dressed brown man, rather small, said:

"Look beyond the railroad tracks. See? There thousands of poor Negroes live."

"Must we begin with the poor and black?"

"Yes, because the white fire fighters will be slow to help them. They'll let the hovels burn. We'll set the fires in a semi-circle, from east to west along Decatur. The south wind is strong —we prayed for it since midnight in Wheat Street Church which rises yonder on Auburn. Before the firemen begin to fear for the white homes north, the flames will roar over Ponce de Leon."

Low fanaticism burned in his voice as he poured oil on rags. The woman looked west:

"Wished we could start where that new public library is— they put my boy in jail for trying to borrow a book there. He never came back."

Old Dr. Baldwin mused: "Where Andrew Carnegie sits between Shakespeare and Aristotle—"

But the naked giant growled: "That's the stone-built business houses there. I helped build them. They won't burn. No—north, to the fancy homes where people live and laugh and scheme and gamble! Come!"

They moved across the tracks like ghosts in the mists of morning. They went to the lumber pile beside the Georgia railroad and poured kerosene over it. The wind rose wildly and carried the flame across the tracks of the railroad on which whites had often murdered Negro firemen. It first burned by the dozens of little Negro homes of one and two stories. The fire department came late and did not overwork to save the homes of "niggers." Then arose cries of terror. Here, there and yonder little flames arose, wavered, caught and spread until as the smoke piled up three hours later the rising wind swept it north.

"It's a warning," said a white streetcar motorman. "We was starting to kill people in Europe, and it wasn't right and God done sent this fire to say we'd better watch out."

"Oh Lord, Oh my God," screamed a Negro woman standing midway in a doomed alley off Auburn Avenue.

The world seemed on fire. The sparks from beyond Oakland Cemetery had leaped in the high wind across the Georgia railroad. Before the flames had died on Edgewood Avenue, Auburn was ablaze and the flames descended upon Darktown. Hundreds of old one and two-storied buildings melted; all of the property of white landlords who lived beyond on higher land; and the landlords were standing and calculating how much they had gained by paying insurance on the shanties which once covered the swept land that was still theirs.

But the dark tenants ran here and there, weeping and shrieking and wringing their hands, for they had lost all. Fire companies now rushed in from Macon, Augusta, Chattanooga and Rome, from Decatur, College Park, East Point, Marietta, Newnam and Hopeville. Three thousand soldiers marched from Fort McPherson and stood on guard. Bucket brigades were formed. Three churches disappeared before the flames, and then old Wheat Street Church fell. A deep groan went up from every Negro throat. They stood aghast and watched. Streets were filled with pictures, clothes, cabinets, chairs, while scores of people sank to the pavements and the gong of ambulances mingled with the ever-rising clang of firebells. In the midst of this, the black people stood and prayed.

"Oh my God. Oh my God. It is the world's end."

Then suddenly the landlords and the merchants to the North in the main city, the white agents and millhands, saw the flames rise like a crimson curtain and bear down upon them. The destruction of Darktown was as nothing to the destruction that now poured up the Boulevard and up Hilliard and across Houston and Jackson. Magnificent homes fell before the flames, and then the roar of dynamite shook the earth. Dynamite alone could save the larger city. All Peachtree trembled. All Piedmont was aghast; Druid Hills and Lenox Park and Brookwood Hills and Madison Park. Hotels, schools and hospitals stared with frightened eyes.

Betty Lou Baldwin stood on her front porch and looked with mounting terror at the great crimson cloud that loomed up from the southward. The roar of dynamite was like the blast of the great guns far to the west on the allied front. It tore down beautiful mansions and lovely gardens. It swept for fifty blocks from Decatur Street to Ponce De Leon Avenue. Five and one-half million dollars worth of property went up in smoke; three hundred acres and three thousand dwellings; forty-two stores and three hundred and fifty garages sank to ashes. All the firemen and policemen of Atlanta, all the soldiers from Fort McPherson fought the flames. All of the cities round about for one hundred miles rushed their fire-fighting engines.

Eleven hours the fires burned, from noon until midnight. In less than one and one-half hours the flames had swept from Forrest Avenue to Ponce De Leon, from the old woman who told of Judgment Day when Wheat Street burned, to the millionaires of Peachtree Creek. And then, slowly, all was quiet. Silently the fire glowed and smoked, and the cloud above the city mingled with the mist that always lay near Atlanta.

Some men say (others as stoutly deny) that in this red dance of fire, there floated at the front, a black and awful shape of One lynched and crucified, a black giant, blood-covered, in swirling smoke. As he crossed to the elegant homes of Peachtree Street he raised his terrible red arm, looked back and beckoned an Old Man in White. The Old Man followed. The wind tossed him about, his white gown billowed in flame and blood dripped from his crown of ashes. With outstretched arms he rose toward heaven, while the black man disappeared, twirled in a cloud of smoke. He threw his great dark arms athwart the sky as he staggered north and shrieked:

"I go to haunt the earth—hail little white Jesus—meet you in Hell!"

A whole square mile was burned on that sweet May morning, leaving ten thousand homeless people and ten million Southerners in doubt and tears.

Slowly the city staggered to its feet. It was the legend afterward that the city recovered and rebuilt itself, larger and more vainglorious than before. But this was not true. It was another city that grew on the ashes of the old; another set of owners and merchants who slowly but surely displaced the group that had lost. In the great gamble that spelled Business in Atlanta, wealth passed to other hands so quickly, so inexorably, that men were filled with fear and passion.

Civilization, culture, industry, was not a thing built slowly and progressively; it was a matter of sudden lurches, here and there, ready for the hands of those able to grasp, snatched from the weakened arms of those who faltered or met the unlucky chance of fire, storm and war. Atlanta grew again, but not for all Atlantans. Some lost irretrievably; some sank to poverty and crime; some sat in dull apathy; and some blossomed with new wealth and ostentation. Winter fell upon the city, wet, with streaks of snow, now and then with storm and drizzle; and then there seemed one fitting expansion of Atlanta's soul when Atlanta invited Billy Sunday to come.

He was then at the height of his career; a vulgar, loud-mouthed preacher, who yelled at God and scared the people with pictures of Hell and Death. A great tabernacle costing thousands of dollars was hastily erected on the Old Wheat Street circus grounds, where the ghosts of elephants, monkeys and giraffes screamed at the converts. Bitter cold came with December and January, and the building could hardly be heated; but thousands of people packed the tabernacle, and hundreds of converts, weeping and yelling, "hit the sawdust trail." But they were all white. No Negroes were admitted.

Meanwhile, the fire of Atlanta swept around the world. The United States was at war at last, after furnishing food and arms to both sides for three years. The demand for labor increased and Negroes poured North. Their coming was met by riots in East St. Louis, Chicago and even in Washington, the capital city; while the black soldiers at Houston, Texas, mutinied in resentment at Southern prejudice. Atlanta lifted up her head and squared her shoulders, for her new money-making. She sang: "Happy days have come again!"

CHAPTER III

WORLD WAR

One thing which gave Manuel great joy was the news of the Russian revolution. He remembered that the Russian serfs were granted freedom only two years before the American Negroes. Like an obbligato heard faintly and indistinctly above the turmoil of his own life ran this vast Russian tragedy: the death of Rasputin in December; the abdication of the Czar in the Spring of 1917 and in April a new Name, Lenin. Then in the Summer came news of bloody defeat and the strange parties, Bolsheviki and Mensheviki. Mansart welcomed Kerensky, tried to get some real news of Kornilof, but at last cheered the October Revolution.

In April, 1917, Dr. Grogman looked old and sad, as Manuel Mansart entered his office. He was, to be sure, past 75, but it was not his own death which he foresaw. It was the death of his school, of Clark University to which he had given forty years of his life. Now it was dying. It had done good work—everyone said that. But Booker Washington had said that industrial schools, not colleges, were needed and so the Methodist Senate, representing the rich Methodist North, had expressed regrets but they could no longer support Clark. The alumni protested, but there were no alumni millionaires. Even the few local well-to-do had been robbed and killed in the Atlanta Riot. So Dr. Grogman had hardly noticed the morning papers until Mansart mentioned the declaration of war. He smiled. He said:

"Now it will come again."

"What?"

"America will suddenly become aware of Negroes as human beings. In every national crisis that is what happens. There was revolt in Haiti in 1800. We were frightened. 'Stop slavery lest Negroes overwhelm America. Stop the slave trade and slavery will die.' But what of the 750,000 Negroes living right here beside them? 'They'll die out,' they said, they hoped; then they feared as they realized that they were building the Cotton Kingdom.

"Then the Negro problem was forgotten until in the twenties

43

the Kingdom grew and there came the question of what America was to be: Atlantic Coast or valley of the Mississippi, or the breadth of the continent? As it swept toward the Pacific there arose again unexpectedly the query: what of 2,000,000 Negroes and their work and the land they will work? So the Abolition controversy arose in which Americans tried desperately to avoid discussion of the Negro.

"Then came the Civil War. The 4,500,000 Negroes suddenly loomed large. But they cried, 'The war is not about Negroes. Let us not discuss Negroes.' Then the war became a war over Negro slavery and Negroes helped decide it; indeed in a sense the Negroes settled it. At the turn of the century, when Populism loomed, the political attitude of 7,000,000 Negroes became important and we disfranchised them by law so that they would count for nothing. Yet today there are ten million of us! Know what the nation is asking?"

"Yes. 'Shall we draft Negroes? Are they American citizens? Shall we train them as we do whites and put guns in their hands? Will they be loyal before German propaganda? Shall we put Negro officers over Negro soldiers? Shall we send them abroad to represent America and fight for us and tell foreigners how we treat them?' "

"Yes, my boy, that is the fear and questioning now sweeping the United States, and many are angry that this Negro Question should obtrude just at this time! The old pattern lives again. Well, it will, it must; it always will, until we are seen and treated as human beings." Crogman mused and then looked up suddenly. "It will touch you deeply this time?"

Manuel started; and for the first time realized the implication: his boys! Why had he not thought of this before? Or if he had for a moment, he had dismissed the idea. His children were so young—then he seized the newspaper—seventeen! My God, Douglass would be 18 this year and Revels seventeen! He hastened home.

The war took Atlanta first by surprise; and then suddenly the city found a new means for making money. Money began to pour into the South, especially to Atlanta for supplies and for cantonments. The city saw a chance to have a Federal camp practically within its borders.

Leonard Wood, seeking training ground for soldiers, chose a

site thirteen miles from Atlanta on condition that the city would furnish a water supply. It meant laying mains that cost $200,000. In a whirlwind campaign, Atlanta raised by subscription the necessary funds for piping the water and making other arrangements; and soon Camp Gordon, with all its spending power, was at Atlanta's gates. Thousands of soldiers swarmed about the streets.

Both Douglass and Revels, Manuel's sons, were drafted. In addition news came from Savannah that the younger brother of Mansart's wife, the only one now left at home to support her widowed mother, was drafted also. He was just twenty. Susan screamed:

"They're taking my babies to fight for their country; what country? They have no country; they are stuck pigs in a dirty pen!"

"Hush, dear!" whispered Manuel Mansart anxiously, afraid she might be overheard.

"Why did you make me bear children to die for white folks?" she moaned, and sobbing, was still.

Mansart soothed her. "There, there," he said. "It may not be so bad after all. Don't you see, we are now citizens of this country. The nation is depending on us as its sons. This means the end of segregation. A black man worthy to die for his country is worth living for it, too."

But even as he reassured his wife, Manuel Mansart was uneasy. It had been a strange decade from 1907 to 1917. He had been transferred and was getting now $1500 a year, which with his four children made his poverty more visible. His wife continually complained. She still wanted to move out of the South to the North and feel free; have a decent income to live on and a future for their children.

The campaign of 1912 had brought out the contradictions in the Negro's plight. Booker Washington, who had advised taking no part nor interest in politics, had long been chief political advisor to Roosevelt and Taft on Negro appointments to office and on Southern policies. Now in the North the radical Negroes, led by the bitter-tongued Forbes and the fanatical Trotter, were advising Negroes to vote the Democratic ticket and help elect Wilson as president. It was a shrewd move. How could the South react?

Then came reaction like a blast from hell; evidently a reaction of one piece with the reaction to Washington's Atlanta speech: enthusiastic acceptance of sacrifice and surrender; determination to make color caste legal, first in the South, now all over the country, next all over the world; the black and darker people must bow to White Supremacy.

It was a frightful prospect but it was real. A mass of bills, proposals and administrative acts poured not only into Congress but into the legislatures of the states. The movement was too broad and similar in subject and tone not to have been the object of wide, concerted and secretly plotted effort on the part of powerful interests. Mansart had heard before of world-wide conspiracy against the colored peoples. His grandmother, that ancient, curious hag, had even related in detail a journey which Colonel Breckinridge had once made at midnight out into the Sea where the mighty of the world had agreed on such a program. How she learned of it he could not dream. He had dismissed it as an old wives' tale; but here it loomed. Was it really true? Was there no chance for race equality or human democracy in the world?

Even as he racked his brain and worried, there came the faint rumble of disaster to all these plans against humanity. Naturally, he did not recognize the portents. Neither for that matter did the most reactionary of Negro-hating Southerners. They saw Europe again threatening war as she had periodically for years. They doubted if much would come of it. Least of all did they see or dream of any threat to White Supremacy. Certainly the South was safe for eternal white rule and prosperity, with the help of Northern capital.

The *Crisis* worried, but few listened:

"At the coming meeting of the peace societies at St. Louis the question of peace between civilized and backward peoples will not probably be considered. The secretary of the New York Peace Society writes us that 'Our peace congresses have not dealt in the past with the relations of civilized and non-civilized people;' and he thinks that largely on this account 'our American congresses have been more dignified and more influential than those held abroad.'

"We are not sure about that word 'influential,' but there is no doubt about the dignity of the American peace movement. It has been so dignified and aristocratic that it has been often most difficult for the humbler sort of folk to recognize it as the opponent of organized murder.

"At a recent meeting of the New York Peace Society the war in the Balkans was eulogized and applauded, and the president, Andrew Carnegie, stated that 'when we advocate peace' it is for nations 'worthy of it!'

"Such a peace movement belies its name. Peace today, if it means anything, means the stopping of the slaughter of the weaker by the stronger in the name of Christianity and culture. The modern lust for land and slaves in Africa, Asia and the South Seas is the greatest and almost the only cause of war between the so-called civilized peoples. For such 'colonial' aggression and 'imperial' expansion England, France, Germany, Russia and Austria are straining every nerve to arm themselves; against such policies Japan and China are arming desperately. And yet the American peace movement thinks it bad policy to take up this problem of machine guns, natives and rubber, and wants 'constructive' work in 'arbitration treaties and international law.' For our part we think that a little less dignity and dollars and a little more humanity would make the peace movement in America a great democratic philanthropy instead of an aristocratic refuge."

By 1914, years of imperialistic rivalry resulted in the inevitable clash. All the nations of Europe were at war. While fighting they needed food, clothes, munitions and cash. Their own industries could not supply the demand since their laborers were fighting. We could and we were quite willing to do it. Our machines began to run 24 hours a day. The plows on the countryside quickened their pace. We were willing to furnish materials, munitions, to either side, but soon discovered that because Great Britain was a master of the sea we would have to sell only to one side. We sold the allies ten million dollars worth of materials a day. We went to war in 1917 to ensure the repayment of this fortune.

It did not at first occur to Mansart that the war raging in Europe was going to touch this country or him. He had rejoiced when Wilson was re-elected because he had 'kept us out of war,' and his record on the Negro problem had been disappointing; yet he knew the organized forces that were trying to make caste based on color a part of federal law in the United States. But after all, this fight in Europe might have its influence on the United States.

When in 1917 there came the draft he was astonished and particularly overwhelmed when he realized that two of his sons were to be inducted into the army. There was little chance for exemption, which white students easily got. The South was torn by doubt about the war along the color line. At first, before war was declared there was a concerted move to exclude Negroes from the armed forces because of the danger of arming them, and on the ground that they were not really citizens. This was met by the decision of the Supreme Court in 1915, the first since the Civil War upholding the 15th Amendment. This was the first real triumph of the NAACP.

The South was slowed in its reactionary program, and then definitely alarmed by the German spy scare. It was not that the evidence of German tampering with the Negroes was at all clear so much as its logical possibility if the Negroes had sense or memories. No one could put his hands on actual proof, but that same and awful fear of racial revenge which haunted the slaveholders for two hundred years now stealthily crept again in the guilty consciences of ten million Southern whites. Finally, when the nation actually declared war, new phases and facets of the race problem appeared.

The South, by and large, had no particular stomach to fight this war with or for the North, but the Atlanta Draft Board found a way out, as did other draft boards all over the South.

"Let the 'niggers' fight," they said; and they put practically every colored draftee into Class A; while out of 815 white men called, 525 were exempted. This was a little too raw and the Draft Board was dismissed by the Federal Government, for unwarranted exemptions and discharges. Nevertheless, Georgia Negroes were far more largely represented in the army than Georgia whites. The Army, dominated as ever by Southern white officers, determined to draft the Negroes into labor battalions and not for bearing arms.

Lynching continued. From 1910 to 1920, from 52 to 99 Negroes accused of crime but never brought to trial, were murdered by white mobs each year; a total of 807 persons. On July 18, 1917, 15,000 Negroes marched down Fifth Avenue, carrying banners as a Silent Protest Parade against lynching. "We march because we want our children to live in a better land and enjoy fairer conditions than have been our lot."

The black nation arose so strongly in protest that it had to be listened to. The Federal Government, already bedevilled by its switch from an anti-war attitude to a pro-war regime, did not want additions to its troubles. It began to be sensitive to Negro delegations, newspapers and mass meetings. The segregation in government offices in Washington to which Wilson had assented on the insistence of his wife and the host of new white Southern appointees, had to be modified. Especially the question of Negro officers and Negro combat troops had to be faced.

In 1917, just as the Negro soldiers were being drafted, came the Houston riot in Texas. It stirred Manuel because it touched so many things in which he was interested. The 24th Infantry had been sent to Houston, Texas, in camp preparatory to going to war. For a long time colored soldiers had been a sore point in the South. They had rioted in Texas in 1906. This indicated armed resistance to segregation, insult and intimidation, and so far as possible it was arranged that there should be few sent South. Most of the southern states had disarmed and disbanded their colored militia. They had opposed drafting of colored men in this war. On the other hand, when there were profits in having soldiers, black or white, training in their midst, all were welcomed, but color discrimination continued.

When a Negro army regiment went to a southern state like Texas, either they had to be kept from exercising their normal rights as soldiers or the town had to change its attitude towards Negroes. Houston did not change. Houston was another poor white town, destined in time to outgrow Atlanta. It insulted the black soldiers in all traditional ways. It segregated them. It separated them from whites on streetcars and buses. It refused them service in restaurants and lunch stands. The soldiers, naturally, resented it.

Then, to make matters worse, the officers, instead of trying to change the manners of the town, disarmed the soldiers. Now a disarmed soldier is an anomoly and the thing didn't work, so that at last the inevitable happened. Some of the black soldiers stole out at night and shot up the town, killing 17 whites. This was followed with swift trial and almost no pretense at fairness; and quick, drastic and cruel punishment, with no attempt to identify the guilty soldiers. Thirteen soldiers were immediately hanged for murder and mutiny, forty-one were imprisoned for life, and forty others held for investigation.

The occurrence startled and angered the colored people. For years it continued to rankle in their minds; and to Manuel it was a matter of depression and despair. The colored people sought continuously to have the remaining soldiers dismissed from charges, and finally succeeded in freeing all the living, although the effort lasted over a decade.

A month after Houston, in Spartanburg, South Carolina, a colored regiment, member of the National Guard of New York State, was stationed. Noble Sissle, a colored composer and drum major, went into a hotel to purchase a newspaper and was cursed because he didn't remove his hat. The hat was knocked from his head and he was kicked out of the place. The soldiers started to rush the hotel and another Houston might have ensued. But the white commanding officer ordered the soldiers to camp, and the War Department rushed the regiment overseas where it became the first Negro contingent to reach the war theater.

Mansart's sons took their draft in different ways. Douglass was angry and outraged. He had already, as supplementary to his school work, begun to cooperate with Herman Perry in founding the Standard Life Insurance Company. He had made up his mind that he was going into the insurance business. He was bitter and outspoken.

"Fight for my country? What country? What country have I got? Land of Liberty? Land of Slavery is what they ought to name it! I won't go to war. I'll do anything before I'll be put into the army and be kicked around by white men!"

But Manuel pleaded with him. The war could not last long; there was absolutely nothing else for him to do. He must either go into the army or go to jail. A year's experience and he might come out physically stronger, and certainly with greater knowledge of the world. Why not go ahead and submit peacefully?

The reaction of Revels was different; he was younger but cooler and less emotional. He looked upon the scene about him with level eyes. He did not propose always to submit any more than Douglass, but he had more of his father's compromise in him, although it was of a different sort. He was going to see that he got ahead and that he did not get into trouble.

A third boy, John Sanders, the young uncle of Douglass and

Revels, living in Savannah, was of still another sort. He could read and write but had little further education. He was thin, tall and silent. He had worked steadily all his life but was not strong, and was slow in his movements and thoughts and feelings. For a time his mother had hoped he would be a minister, but he showed no interest and she could not afford to keep him in school. After the father's death, the boy helped keep the house going by odd jobs and by collecting and delivering the laundry which his mother and his sisters washed and ironed. His being taken by the draft therefore spelled calamity, but his help to the mother meant nothing to the draft board.

At first, to his mother his drafting seemed the end of the world, and then after desperate prayer, depths of despair, and heights of religious ecstacy, she saw in it all the hand of God. She was proud of her drafted son and the church folk round about her joined in praise. There was purpose in it and over it all. This was a Holy War. Black boys were soldiers of the Lord and fighting for the Kingdom. Emancipation for black folk must come out of this color struggle. Some would die, living sacrifices for the Truth; but John would not die.

"He could not die," the mother said within her soul. "He is coming back to lead his people." When she heard that he might be sent overseas she quickly took the long journey to his camp in Carolina and prayed with him loudly, to his silent embarrassment and to the unconcealed amusement of his fellows.

Then came the orders. With no chance to bid his mother good-bye, Sanders was entrained for Newport News and sent overseas. He never could remember consecutively just what took place in the next twenty-four months. It was always a sort of phantasmagoria of experiences, hungers, hurts and dead fatigue. Sick and miserable he was tossed across the sea, and his body landed in the unintelligible and inconceivable land of a strange language where nobody could understand or be understood. His lot seemed cast usually with the meanest and cruelest of ignorant, white Southern subalterns. He was ordered about with oaths and blows. Never in his life and experience had he dreamed of such treatment and humiliation. Never before, even in Georgia, had he stood so much or borne such insults. He slept in mud and worked in rain and dirt.

The French he saw only from afar. He had almost no contact

with them; or if contact came he had no power to speak to them or they to him. He sank into a sort of lethargy, trying dumbly to keep the rules; which meant he got little to eat and saw nothing of the beautiful land about him. His muscles, untrained to such continuous strain, left him at first dead tired after twelve, fourteen and sixteen hours of continuous lifting, hauling, shoveling and digging. At night he would crawl into his tent and sleep like the dead. He would eat the food dished carelessly out to him, whether palatable or swill. He made no resistance. His soul died.

He had landed just as a brilliant American general conceived a cosmic thought. It had long puzzled the American officers as to how they could make these Negroes who had come over with the crazy idea that they were going to be soldiers, work, and work enthusiastically as common laborers. The general launched the much advertised "Race to Berlin." The officers egged the Negroes on with bribes, prizes, privileges and threats and made them compete against each other ship by ship, to unload and load, lift, dig, fetch and carry. The poor black boys worked their hearts out so that white men could hate and kill each other in singular compensation. It was a horrible competition. It murdered and maimed men; but it fed and supplied armies.

Sanders seemed to live through these awful days without conscious or consecutive thought. He saw the white prostitutes guided into camp by the High Command on bicycles, and lay with some of them and then went to the waiting army doctors to be disinfected. He drank hot, raw liquor and would willingly have gambled had he not kept to the one determination of sending every cent of his pay home to his mother.

Moved suddenly up to the front to work with defensive weapons, he heard one night that thunder of the great guns which no one who heard ever forgot. He saw the stars falling from heaven and the earth shuddering with an impact of murderous force such as never wounded the world before. Almost deafened, he dragged on; and then heaven opened and in a blazing roar of light he was thrown headlong, blind and stunned. Later, years later it seemed, he was dragged through the trenches across mud-washed fields back into a camp where the terrible, crucifying lice were driven from his body; and finally, on the tossing misery of a ship, he started home. But he never arrived. They buried him at sea.

Ten thousand of his black fellow laborers were kept long after the Armistice to search over 500 square miles of the Meuse-Argonne battlefield and in rain and cold to exhume 22,000 rotten and stinking bodies of the American soldiers from this bleak hilltop, and then to re-bury them, in the new cemetery at Romagne.

From Atlanta, Douglass was sent into a Mississippi camp. He got into repeated troubles. He was in the guard house several times. He was knocked about by the white non-commissioned officers and then, with little warning, dumped on a troop ship and rushed to France in a colored company with white Southern officers. The hard-pressed French were screaming for soldiers.

This company was brigaded immediately into the French Army and rushed to the front. They saw the fighting front of war. They had a chance to appeal to the French over the heads of their officers, and while this did not settle matters it did make the situation more endurable, for the French needed soldiers and not argument. Douglass knew a little French and learned much more.

Once he was given leave and went into the town of Nancy. He found some pleasant white acquaintances and quite naturally escorted a pretty French girl to a public picnic. There he met one of his white Southern commanding officers. The officer ordered him back to camp. Douglass refused. He was threatened with court-martial but it was too near an impending engagement. The commanding French officer released him and the company went into battle.

Douglass was frightened but stubborn. He gritted his teeth and thrust his body into that flaming hell. Shuddering with tears he bayoneted young, struggling German boys and despised himself as he did it. A French officer rushed by, clapping him on the back and cried: "Famos! Il faut que vous recevoir le Croix de Guerre! En avance!"

Douglass staggered on, blind with blood and deaf with unendurable thunder. Then the mists suddenly cleared. Ahead a company of German Hussars came advancing like automatons of Fate. Beside him clustered a hundred black boys from his own company, but immediately ahead and between them and the Germans, scurried a bunch of their own white Southern officers. Both stared back, both stared ahead. Douglass saw distinctly that sneering officer who had ordered him home from Nancy. Deliberately he raised his rifle; deliberately the rifles of the other black boys were raised too; and then all fired: the Germans, the French and the black soldiers. Between the fires the frightened Southern white officers dissolved into bits of flesh and blood.

The war went on but the colored troops now were heroes. Douglass' company received the Croix de Guerre and were soon hurried home by the American High Command lest they become too popular in France. Douglass was among the first to march up Fifth Avenue amid the plaudits of the populace.

Revels Mansart had a different experience. He went to a training camp in Virginia and meticulously obeyed the rules. There was a good deal of trouble in the camp because the Negroes, especially those from the border and northern states, were bitter and rebellious. Revels did not rebel but there was something in his cold attitude that did not invite too much imposition.

When the colored officers' training camp at Fort Des Moines was announced, Revels, because he had given least trouble, was called in and asked if he wanted to go despite his youth. He showed no particular eagerness but consented, and found himself for the first time in the North and in a western state, and receiving training as an officer. He liked it but he was still wary. He did not believe that colored cadet officers would ever really be commissioned. However he was determined that if they were he would be among the best.

They were being trained as part of the new Negro division, the 92nd, as to whose fortune none could guess. There came difficulty about segregation when they went to town for amusement even in this Northern state. The commanding white colonel sent out a notice advising compliance with established race discrimination. The colored cadets resented this and talked about it, but Revels kept quiet and did not go to town.

Among the trainees were not only college men but a large number of older, regular army men who had served as non-commissioned officers with white line officers in the colored regiments of the regular army. They had learned to keep "in their places" and were openly favored for commissions over the younger and better educated Negroes. The feud between these two groups grew and was encouraged. Whites reasoned that such unrest might prevent any colored graduates. Even after the training was over, there was a pause and it was feared the colored cadets would never get commissions. But pressure was brought to bear on the Secretary of War by Northern Negroes. Delegations of prominent and influential Negroes waited on Secretary Baker. Baker was irritated and growled that he was not fighting this war "to settle the Negro Problem." A black man answered, "But you must settle enough of it to enable you to fight the war." Baker replied by commissioning 700 black officers.

Most of these were second lieutenants. There were a few captains, nearly all of whom were old regular army non-commissioned officers. Revels was too young for a commission. But he looked mature and his attitude pleased the commanding officer. He was made a captain and thus rewarded for keeping his mouth closed while others complained.

He went with the 92nd Division to France. No sooner had they landed than difficulties appeared. It seemed that there had been no hotel accommodations held for them at Brest. But with them was a colored officer from Louisiana who spoke French.

"We are holding certain accommodations," said the host politely, "but they were not assigned to this division."

"But yes," said the Captain, replying in French to the delight of the Frenchman. "Unfortunately there has been a mistake. These accommodations I assure you were meant for us."

The host yielded. In that way the colored officers moved into the leading hotel. When the American white officers came they found themselves without rooms and were not on that account reconciled to the situation. The friction increased. The 92nd was deliberately kept in the rear for a long time. They did not have the chance for training or to meet officers of the French Army. In fact, these French officers were warned officially by American liason officers not to fraternize with the Negro officers. "Il faut eviter toute intimite trop grand d'officiers francais avec des officiers noire, avec lesques, on peut estra correct et aimable, mais qu'on ne peut traiter sur le meme pied que des officiers blancs Americains sans blesser profondement ces derniers. Il ne faut pas partager leur table et eviter le serrement de mains et les conversations ou frequentations en dehors du service." The French did not always obey these suggestions of the Americans, but they could not altogether ignore them.

There were some lovely incidents, like the Negro bands. As one wrote:

"Tim Brimm was playing by the town pump. Tim Brimm and the bugles of Harlem blared in the little streets of Maron, in far Lorraine. The tiny streets were seas of mud. Dank mist and rain sifted through the cold air above the blue Moselle. Soldiers— soldiers everywhere—black soldiers, boys of Washington, Alabama, Philadelphia, Mississippi. Wild and sweet and wooing leaps the strains upon the air. French children gazed in wonder—women left their washing. Up in the window stood a black Major, a Captain, a teacher and I—with tears behind our smiling eyes. Tim Brimm was playing by the town pump."

At last, just one day before the Armistice the Negro troops were rushed up into the Argonne. Captain Mansart found himself and his company entirely ignorant as to where they were going, what they were supposed to do, and what the plan of battle was. Not only was he ignorant, but he suspected that the white field officers either knew no more than he did or cared less.

The Negroes went, an untrained, inexperienced mass, up into the hills and forests of the Argonne, and met withering machine gun fire. Mansart and other colored officers sent frantic messages to the rear for support or orders. They found the white colonel back in his quarters in hysterics, knowing no more of plans than the colored officers at the front. The battle line began to disintegrate. Revels was the last to return, but when he finally discovered headquarters he met a stern American general who had just appeared out of nowhere; and to cover his blunders he promptly ordered twelve of the colored officers, including Captain Mansart, to be arrested for cowardice and desertion in the face of the enemy.

The group was promptly court-martialed and all forthwith sentenced to be shot. Over the whole American army the story was broadcast that the experiment of Negro officers had been a flat failure and that they had proved inefficient and cowardly in line of battle. Certain white men of influence were sure that this would keep Negro officers out of the American army forever.

However, when this sentence came up for review difficulties arose. It was not easy to prove Negro incompetence without reflecting strongly on white field officers. The French, who had praised Negro soldiers with the highest decorations, could not be depended on to support such testimony as the Americans were eager to offer. There was no doubt but that the Argonne battle had been crassly mismanaged and probably the less said of it the better.

The disconcerted American leader got revenge. The Armistice was signed and the world knew it. However, it had not yet been officially proclaimed. The commanders of the 92nd Division deliberately ordered the colored troops into battle and they went. A hundred were murdered by German artillery twelve hours after peace had been signed. However, the black officers previously condemned to death were quietly shipped back to the United States and some months later were pardoned by President Wilson. The President had learned a great deal since the day he faced Monroe Trotter. But whatever faith Revels Mansart ever had in white Americans had long since died. Thus, Revels Mansart landed in New York in 1920 but he did not return home. He did not plan ever to return South. He was going to make his way in New York.

The entrance of America into the World War changed the outlook and plans of two Atlanta white men considerably. From his Princeton days, John Baldwin, son of Old Dr. Baldwin and Betty Lou Breckinridge, had fastened on politics as his career. Through political office he planned to use the power and wealth of industry to guide the state and the world. His connections with the Pierce empire made this a possible and attractive future. As a loyal Princetonian, he rejoiced when Wilson "kept us out of war," and was a bit startled when in 1917 we declared war on Germany. Of course, the provocation was great, but would war be good for business? He had been designated already in 1907 as prospective candidate for mayor, and became mayor in 1912. After that he could expect, if all went according to schedule, to go into the legislature and then governor, United States senator and—well, all was possible. But matters did not shape up as he had planned.

The reappearance of Tom Watson as a rabid rabble-rouser, the resurgence of the Ku Klux Klan and the new battlefront of labor, were making a situation which called for consultation and new tactics. Baldwin was now introduced to that government by secret clique which had characterized the South since 1876, and which under the disfranchising laws and the "White Primary" was now standard political procedure. By 1910, in law, custom and force the Negro was disfranchised practically in the whole slave

South. With disfranchisement, democracy disappeared and the primary for white voters only, replaced the legal election.

Big Business in Georgia had to consult and plan. A meeting took place in 1914 on a sea island in southeast Georgia, where a Northern millionaire had built a winter rest and sport resort. The meeting was informal and leisurely, with every surrounding of comfort and service. It was decided that Baldwin could best serve the causes in which they were interested by his activities in industrial and financial organization rather than in public office. He would therefore be held for a while in the background, while experiments would be tried. He would go to the Legislature, and on the basis of his being the son of the famous educator, Old Doctor Baldwin, he would guide a new state educational program.

This was thought very necessary. Negroes, aroused by disfranchisement and legal caste, must be mollified by yielding to their craze for education. They must be given enough schools of the appropriate type to stop their complaints. At the same time, the education of whites must be stepped up not only to supply skilled labor but also to encourage the rise of a cream of ability which could drain into the ruling classes. All this was fundamental for the future. Thus, John Baldwin had secured the appointment of Andrew Coypel as Superintendent of the Atlanta city schools. Later, after his term as mayor, he entered the Legislature and guided its most powerful committee.

He began to realize that it was not the figurehead who bore the title of office who had the real political power. At the council table of great corporations like the Georgia Light and Power Company, the Coca-Cola Corporation, and the Real Estate Board lay the real political control of the state. As John Pierce passed 60, he began to retire from active work and John Baldwin began to represent him on the powerful Boards of Directors. It was decided then that Baldwin would, for a time at least, work with John Sheldon as his active lieutenant. This was especially effective as Joe Scroggs began to emerge as labor leader and spiritual successor of Tom Watson. Baldwin was being considered for governor in 1918, but the war and our entrance in 1917 changed all that. Baldwin joined the services and went abroad as a captain, while Scroggs joined as a private.

Captain Baldwin was in France a year and returned as a major, and what was much more to the point, as a formidable candidate for governor. But in the election of 1920 it seemed wiser to let Congressman Hardwick, a flaming radical who could easily be guided, make the campaign against the Watson and Ku Klux forces, which he did and won; while Scroggs entered the Legislature. Baldwin now became Speaker of the House and put many irons in the fire.

In the post-war boom, he proposed incidentally to increase his personal wealth but also to make his state increasingly the center of industrial and commercial development. He encouraged Federal subsidies, the railways and the utilities; continued to invite openly and secretly capital from the North, and he furthered by every device of publicity the growth of his city. Atlanta became the commercial capital of the South.

There was for Manual Mansart both satisfaction and distress at this time. But he was most upset when just as the colored soldiers, including his sons, were returning from war there came what has been called the Red Year.

Just as in 1906, a decade of race hate had turned Atlanta into riot and murder, so on a national scale World War turned in America into Race War. On the whole, it was the worst experienece through which the freed Negro had ever gone. No one interested in the Negro, and no Negro, particularly those of education and standing, came out of the year 1919 as he went in.

It seemed to Manuel that he lived personally through all of the incidents since he was so familiar with the kind of conflict which so easily arose. In this awful "Red Year," there were 25 anti-Negro riots, prefaced two years before by the outbreak in Houston, Texas; then, in 1919, the murder in Long View, the astonishing uprising in the capital at Washington, the Chicago riot, the troubles in Knoxville and Omaha, and the attempt at slavery in Elaine, Arkansas, which he understood only too well.

In July, 1919, there were newspaper rumors of Negroes assaulting white women in the Capital. Mobs, principally of white sailors, soldiers and marines, ran through the streets for three days killing several Negroes and injuring others. On the third day when the hoodlums tried to invade and burn the Negro section, the Negroes arose, armed with guns and grenades. Numbers of whites and Negroes were killed and wounded due to the stern action which the Negroes took.

In the same month in Long View, Texas, several white men

were shot when they went into the Negro section of the town searching for a Negro school teacher who was accused of sending a release to a Negro newspaper concerning a lynching. A mob poured into the Negro section, burned homes, flogged the Negro school principal on the street, and ran several leading Negro citizens out of town.

There were other riots, in Knoxville, Tennessee and Omaha, Nebraska; and not simply race war—race hatred and sadism which made one of despair of civilization. They burned a human being in Tennessee in 1919. The local newspapers reported details:

"On one side was the road, 10 feet above the hollow into which the Negro was dragged and chained to a log. On the other three sides was a forest, the trees black with figures of men who had climbed into them for better views—"

"Ten gallons of gasoline was then poured over his clothing and a match applied. While the fire, starting at his feet, crept slowly toward his face a ten-year-old Negro boy was placed on the other end of the log.

" 'Take a good look, boy,' someone told him. 'We want you to remember this the longest day you live. This is what happens to niggers who molest white women.' "

"A woman screamed not to use gasoline. 'He'll burn too fast; he'll burn too fast,' she cried over and over again, and others took up the shout."

"Although he writhed in agony, the Negro made no outcry. Several hundred members of the mob crowded about, fighting for bits of his clothing and the rope."

"The Negro drank deep of the first sheet of flame and smoke and relaxed upon his hellish couch. When the body had been burned sufficient to satisfy the lust of the executioners, one man in the crowd cut out the Negro's heart, two others cut off his ears, while another hacked off his head."

"The flames and smoke shot high in the air, and the frenzied men cheered as their victim writhed in agony and then was stilled in death. "A Negro in an automobile drove close to the pyre, caught up an American flag and waving it above his head shouted: 'We're all through here, boys. Let's join the Germans.'

"He tore the flag to shreds and was immediately grabbed by a crowd of white men who attempted to rush him to the dying blaze where the skeleton still hung. Five policemen rescued him. He will be turned over to the Federal authorities."

CHAPTER IV

THE NEW ABOLITION

Manuel Mansart, the new supervisor of Negro schools in Atlanta, was having his first general meeting with his teachers and matters were not going so well. Manuel could feel the impatience, distrust, and resentment among these hundred or more persons. They were of all colors, mostly dark brown, but many of them yellow, olive, and some quite white. They were for the most part well-dressed, intelligent, but their countenances were either sullen or blank. They resented being under the authority of one of their own color, although they would have denied this, if put that way. It was bad enough being subordinate to whites but that was normal, and at least now inevitable. But it was ridiculous to be under the pretended authority of old John James; they simply ignored or even insulted him. They were glad when he died, or, if not glad, at least indifferent. But this upstart was simply assuming authority, or, if he had some authority which the new white Superintendent was trying to put into his hands, he knew the city would not back him. They proposed to sit still and see him fail. He would fail if they had their way, even if he ought to succeed.

Mansart knew all this. He knew that they were bringing to bear on him the resentment which they felt toward the whites but could not effectively express. He must somehow get their sympathy and cooperation by convincing them that they were all in the same boat with him and working for the same ends. He started with his proposals for improving Negro schools, but they had almost sneered. They had heard this stuff before. "The only way to any real improvement here," said one, "is a program like that of the new N.A.A.C.P." Some had heard of this new organization of Northern whites and Negroes. But one injected: "It grew out of the Niagara movement."

Mansart encouraged him. He had heard the name but really knew little of it. Indeed, he was bothered as he realized how little he knew of the inner history of the Negro group. "Tell us about it," he said, grasping for a topic of interest which would give some grip on this audience.

"Well, I had an uncle, a Washington lawyer, who was among the original twenty-nine persons who attended that meeting at Niagara Falls in 1905."

The evident interest of his teachers in current Negro events and their ignorance of Negro history gave Mansart a clue for further action. He got an increasing number of them to form the habit of meeting at his house and work out ways and means for a study of Negro history. There was no text-book in the schools and no such study laid down. But also, Negro history was not forbidden.

One evening Manuel Mansart was meeting in the home of one of the well-to-do teachers. Both husband and wife had long been in the puplic schools and their two children were grown and self-supporting. They could afford considerable comfort; a recently built home with lawn and flowers; a wide front porch with chairs and swings; front and back parlors, dining room and kitchen and upstairs four bedrooms and bath. The teachers were gradually getting used to these meetings with the colored supervisor. They were an innovation and marked an era of recognition of the colored supervisor as a person of power.

At meetings like this, contact and consultation was often very interesting. In this case, a son of the hosts was back from Europe and had brought a friend. Friends from New York had dropped in, and one said:

"I believe Harlem is destined to be the capital of Negro America."

"Why?"

"Well, it not only already has a hundred and fifty thousand Negroes, but it is a center of expression in music and art such as we never have had."

Mansart added, "We must consider the facts. In the beginning of the Twentieth Century eight of the nine million American Negroes lived in the South and the development there was decisive for the race. But on the other hand there had been drained off to the North since the Civil War and before, a mass of leadership and talent which made the black North vocal and active among Negroes to a decisive degree for racial leadership. Indeed, from this Northern group came much of Southern Negro leadership during Reconstruction. Northern Negroes lived largely isolated from each other, grouped in various Northern cities so that each group eventually contributed some peculiar gift for the total forward movement.

"Black Boston put reason into the Abolition movement; Black Philadelphia gave birth to an autonomous Negro church; Black Cincinnati, where Harriet Beecher Stowe wrote, became a center of underground encouragement of runaway slaves before the Civil War, and afterwards of strife to make free Negroes full citizens. Chicago first saw the Negro enter American industry on a large scale."

Then the first speaker continued: "But it was in New York City that Negroes developed the self-expression that first gained the ear of mankind. Back in the 19th century came the actor, Ira Aldridge, who played opposite young Madge Kendall. A Black Patti sang before a president, and a Black Swan sang before Queen Victoria. Then later in the century and over into the 20th, came the Sons of Laughter."

He continued at length because he had been studying in New York: "The unconscious or conscious effort on the part of the oppressed to turn the mood of the oppressor from wrath to laughter by skillful clowning or talented diversion is a resource as old as the Court Fool and the medieval minstrels. It was a conventional resort on the slave plantation and lasted over Emancipation. White players imitated it.

"The vogue of the black and blackface minstrels in the late Nineteenth Century gradually gave place to talented Negro entertainers who launched into music, drama, and the dance. There was Sam Lucas and the Luca family, and finally, fin de siecle, Williams and Walker, Cole and Johnson, and Will Cook. With them came extraordinary musical comedy, new dancing and 'rag time' evolving into 'jazz.' Here was something new and exotic done by black folk of genius. There has been no modern comedian like Bert Williams; there have been few entertainers like George Walker, long the best groomed man in New York. Seldom has the fairy dancing of his wife been surpassed. The vogue of this new Negro music and drama swept the town and fed racial jealousy. It brought a vogue of sneering references to Negro color and characteristics:

" 'All coons look alike to me!' "

One of the women teachers—rather cynical, who often spent her summers in Harlem, said, "Yes, indeed. But did you ever read what happened in Harlem in the midst of all this triumph of Negro entertainment? It was August 12, 1900. Arthur Harris, a young colored man and his wife, were walking along West 41 Street near Eighth Avenue, in New York City. It was near midnight and they had just left the theater in Times Square where Williams and Walker were playing 'In Dahomey.' Even from their balcony seats—Negroes could not buy places in the orchestra at that time—they could hear and see pretty well and were happy at the evening's entertainment.

" 'Wait here a moment, Honey, while I buy a cigar,' said Arthur, stepping into a drug store at the corner of Eighth Avenue. When he came out a moment later his young wife was struggling in a white man's arms. Harris jumped on the man and was struck over the head by a club. He drew his pocket knife and stabbed the assailant.

"The white man, Robert Thorpe, was a very popular policeman in plain clothes, and before he died he claimed that he was arresting Mrs. Harris for 'soliciting.' Harris disappeared and was never found. The funeral of Thorpe brought out a vast array of police and admirers whose desire for bloody revenge was loudly expressed.

"On the night of August 15, a furious mob of thousands of whites raged up Eighth Avenue from 27th to 42nd Streets, the heart of the Negro residential and business district. They beat Negroes on the streets, dragged them from streetcars and assaulted ihem. Those appealing to the police were in turn clubbed by the police. The mob called wildly for 'Williams and Walker!' 'Cole and Johnson!' and 'Ernest Hogan.' Waker barely escaped lynching and Hogan was hidden in his theater all night. All night the drunken orgy went on."

"Sounds mighty like Atlanta," someone volunteered.

"But it wasn't. These Negroes moved. They didn't take this risk lying down."

This meeting of teachers dissolved, but not before their interest in Harlem had been fired. Thereafter Manuel Mansart followed the subsequent development of Harlem with deep interest. He met later at Atlanta University a young white woman who was visiting the South.

Mary Ovington was among the many whites who was outraged at the inaction of Mayor Van Wyck over the riot. Mary was a beautiful young woman in her thirties. She was deeply interested in social work and had since her graduation from Radcliffe given much effort to studying the plight of Negroes. Most of her time had to be given to care of her elderly mother. But what time she could spare was now devoted to Negroes after the city and police did nothing, and no one was ever punished for the riot.

She talked to her friends about organized action and began to meet them regularly for consultation. In 1903 she had read the *Souls of Black Folk;* in 1905 she heard of the new Niagara Movement formed among Negroes, and the next year the *New York Evening Post* sent her to report on the second meeting of the Niagara Movement at Harper's Ferry.

The Niagara Movement was a burst of indignation from young Negro America at injustice and cruelty. In Boston, Monroe Trotter was put in jail for trying to heckle Booker Washington about his stand on Negro suffrage. It was at a public meeting in a Negro church and the younger Negroes were determined to put a stop to Washington's evasion and double-talk about the Negro's right to vote. There was nothing illegal about questioning a public speaker. It is not as usual in America as in England, nor in the East as in the western United States. There was no disorder. But the rich whites in the North were determined to placate the white South by teaching a lesson to Negroes who dared to oppose hand-picked Negro leadership. The church was crowded with an audience mostly of Negroes, which was unusual in Mr. Washington's case. But there was a goodly number of prominent whites there also, and the police had been alerted since the *Guardian* had announced that questions would be asked.

Trotter arose. He was stocky, yellow, with burning eyes. A shock of close-curled black hair covered his head and he spoke clearly in Harvard accents.

"Mr. Washington, will you please explain to this audience just what your stand—" He got no further. Police rushed in, seized him, struggling, and rushed him to jail.

The younger Negroes of the nation arose. Twenty-nine of them met at Fort Erie in Canada, opposite Niagara Falls, in 1905. The following year they met at Harper's Ferry where John Brown made his desperate raid.

"Trotter, Trotter?" asked Manuel. "Why, I've heard of him before."

"Of course, he was the one who faced Wilson and protested against segregation of colored civil service employees in Washington."

"And Wilson dismissed him and his delegation. Said they were insulting."

The Niagara Movement in 1905, when it came to implementing practically its program, ran into difficulties. Its real mission proved to be emphasis on an ideal, which was not new but had fallen into neglect and must be reemphasized. Negroes must believe in themselves and fight for equality. But how? The *Guardian* was the official organ of the new organization; and its editors saw its first object as attack on Booker Washington. Many agreed on much that Trotter and Forbes wrote, but their negative stand had to be widened by positive, constructive action. The Niagara Movement cried at Harper's Ferry:

"In the past year the work of the Negro hater has flourished in the land. Step by step the defenders of the rights of American citizens have retreated. The work of stealing the black man's ballot has progressed and the fifty and more representatives of stolen votes still sit in the nation's capital . . . Never before in the modern age has a great and civilized folk threatened to adopt so cowardly a creed in the treatment of its fellow-citizens, born and bred on its soil. Stripped of verbose subterfuge and in its naked nastiness, the new American creed says: fear to let back men even try to rise lest they become the equals of the white. And this in the land that professes to follow Jesus Christ. The blasphemy of such a course is only matched by its cowardice."

They met again later at Faneuil Hall, Boston, and in Oberlin, Ohio. Negroes like Kelly Miller sneered at this uprising and the great white world of editors and rich philanthropists raved at these "radicals," but the Negro world gradually closed ranks behind this movement.

In the first decade of the Twentieth Century, nearly a thousand Negroes were lynched in the United States. In other words, black men and women were seized by mobs of whites and publicly murdered without trial. One of the most brutal cases took place in the North in August, 1908, in Springfield, Illinois, where Abraham

Lincoln, the "Great Emancipator," lived, married, and practiced law from 1837 until he became President. In Springfield he lies buried.

In this town, a street-car conductor's wife accused a Negro of raping her. At the trial she repudiated this charge, and accused a white man whom she would not name. A mob began to attack Negro homes and shops. They lynched a Negro barber, accused of nothing; and an 84-year-old Negro, who had lived with a white wife for thirty years, was publicly murdered within a block of the State House. The State militia was called out. In all, two Negroes were lynched, four whites killed, 70 persons injured, one hundred arrests were made, but no one was punished.

This shameful occurrence aroused a group of young white folk in New York. William English Walling began by demanding a new organization to "finish the work of Abraham Lincoln." Around him began to cluster Mary White Ovington; Oswald Garrison Villard, grandson of the great Garrison; Henry Moskovitz, a Jew; and twenty other persons. They united in a call for a national conference on Lincoln's birthday, 1909.

"We call upon all believers in democracy to join in a National conference for the discussion of present evils, the voicing of protests, and the renewal of the struggle for civil and political liberty."

This conference brought together Jane Addams, William Dean Howell, Livingston Farrand, Edwin Seligman, John Dewey, Jenkin Lloyd Jones, and William Hayes Ward.

The new N.A.A.C.P., conceived by whites, had first to find a Negro following and next to decide on a program. The first almost wrecked the effort. Trotter and the black woman leader of the first effective anti-lynching crusade, Ida Wells Barnett, refused categorically to join. They distrusted the whites. But a majority of the leaders of the Niagara Movement recognized that white cooperation in fighting anti-Negro prejudices was absolutely essential. This was accomplished finally in 1910 when James Burghardt and most of the promoters of the Niagara Movement joined the N.A.A.C.P. and made the movement truly inter-racial.

This new organization included the radical Burghardt as its only Negro official, who for that very reason wielded disproportionate influence. Without him no inter-racial effort could succeed. With him, his radical ideas must be pushed. This Burghardt from the first insisted on, when he proposed a monthly magazine to voice the program of the N.A.A.C.P. The other officials hesitated. They not only feared the editor's ideas but they pointed out the cost. Burghardt assumed personal responsibility for this cost and in November, 1910, the *Crisis* appeared as a magazine of 18 pages. The magazine spread like wildfire, not simply because it was readable but because it was timely for a people emotionally starved in a crisis of their development.

From a circulation of 1,750 in 1910, it rose to 9,000 in 1911, 27,000 in 1913, and 100,000 in 1919. In ten years it sold ten million copies.

For twenty years, the *Crisis* made a fight on a program aimed at civil and political rights and social equality. Led by this propaganda and organized into local branches, the N.A.A.C.P. gradually succeeded in making the nation ashamed of lynching, and willing to discuss political and civil rights; but its propaganda also succeeded in bringing some considerable official opposition; but especially in scaring Big Business into action. Lynchings decreased from one a week to seven or eight a year. Also, through court cases and the assistance of well trained lawyers, white and black, the Supreme Court began to recognize the Negro as a free citizen.

The directing body of the NAACP contained, however, from the first, antagonistic elements: well-to-do whites with philanthropic tendencies; poor but radical Negroes demanding forthwith all social, civil, and political rights; a few socialists with Marxist leanings; and some middle-of-the-road liberals, including Jews. The elements who finally got control were whites who wanted to stop mob violence, secure civil rights for Negroes, and who admitted the necessity of letting Negroes work. But they wished to say nothing about social equality or intermarriage; they were strong believers in the rights of property, repudiated socialism, and had no sympathy with the labor movement. They wanted to build Negro rights into the law of the land by court decision.

Later, as the NAACP grew, Mansart listened to Burghardt as he described one of its meetings. It was in 1917. At 20 Vesey Street, opposite Trinity Church and looking on Wall Street, a meeting of the seven-year old NAACP was being held in the offices of the *Evening Post*. Eight members of the Board were present and the ninth came in before the meeting ended.

Most prominent was Villard, grandson of William Lloyd Garrison and also of Henry Villard, the railroad financier. Villard was always conscious of his birth and wealth, although a kind-hearted and honest young man. But he was rich and a powerful editor, and used to being listened to with deference. Today he came in with a rather curious proposal, and that was that the *Crisis* magazine, the new organ of the NAACP, hereafter publish not only its monthly list of Negro lynchings but also a list of "crimes which Negroes had committed."

This aroused the colored editor almost to fury. He refused to do any such thing. He declared crime was human but lynching was race discrimination. He said that Villard had no business to give orders to the editor of the *Crisis;* that they were both equal employees of the NAACP, and that he was going to edit the *Crisis* as he thought best, and not as Villard ordered. This disagreement disturbed the Board. It was unexpected and might disrupt the young organization, for Villard was chairman of the Board and it was expected that he would raise from his rich friends funds to keep the organization going.

But Joel Spingarn intervened. Spingarn was a young Jew, thin and handsome, who had in 1908 resigned his professorship at Columbia University in furious protest aaginst the mistreatment of old and respected Professor George Woodberry by the czar of Columbia, Nicholas Murray Butler. Spingarn gave up a life work and one which he much loved, but stood on principle. Looking around for new interests, this well-to-do young man had joined the Board of the NAACP. He threw himself into it with all his energy and devotion. Eventually he succeeded Villard as chairman of the Board. He had fled into this organization with enthusiasm to learn about a race problem of which he knew little. He brushed aside the lynching list as immaterial compared with the fact that the government was not appointing Negro officers in the opening war and he proposed to lead an agitation.

Villard thought that agitation was not proper; he knew President Wilson personally and promised he would "talk to him" about it. Pressure rather than open complaint was probably better. But everyone could see that Spingarn was going straight ahead with his proposals. Perhaps some faint anti-Semitism was entering here.

It was then that Milholland began to talk. Milholland was a **handsome Irishman who sometimes** preferred to be regarded as of

Dutch descent. He was a promoter of the new underground mail tubes and also from the first interested in the NAACP. He was a man of large ideas who sometimes after he had proposed them forgot to help to cary them through. Just now he suggested that the NAACP needed larger offices, a larger staff and better paid employees. This was true, but Villard sniffed.

"Where is the money coming from?" he asked.

Mary Ovington attended all meetings. Just now she was distubed because there were not enough branches. "We called ourselves 'national' but we were really just a little group working in New York City. We ought to do more about organizing groups throughout the country." She appealed to the secretary.

Roy Nash had just succeeded a paid secretary who had resigned, and was himself serving as an unpaid worker until a new secretary was elected. He was an enthusiastic and good-hearted young man, small of stature and willing to do a reasonable amount of work, but naturally he couldn't see himself travelling about the country, organizing branches for the NAACP. He did, however, propose the election of John Shillady as permanent secretary.

Shillady was a trained social worker with the ideas of modern social organization, but he must have a salary of $5,000 a year. This rather astonished the Board and they hesitated and argued. It indicated a branching out far beyond any resources then in sight. But finally the motion was passed, and with Shillady as secretary, James Weldom Johnson was chosen to join the staff as field secretary for the next year.

Charles Edward Russell, a solid intense man who could always be depended upon to bring up something which touched Marxism, was in attendance. He was a Socialist, as were Walling and Miss Ovington, and they wanted the colored people to move toward socialist ideals. But they got little encouragement for different reasons among men like Villard, Spingarn and Milholland.

John Haynes Holmes, the fiery young radical, was the only minister on the Board although Stephen Wise was interested for a time but at last discreetly ceased to attend. Holmes came into this meeting late and took part in the discussion. One felt his dynamic power. He agreed with Spingarn about the colored army officers. He agreed with Burghardt about not publishing a catalogue of Negro crime. He brought in a fighting, resisting spirit of which many were a little afraid. He deeply sympathized with Russia.

Outside of Burghardt, there were not many colored members present this afternoon. Sinclair was there, a Philadelphia black man, slightly obsequious as usual and with nothing very new in ideas. Dr. Waller, with his British accent was expansive and always interesting, but had not been able to get over from Brooklyn. He telephoned his excuses.

Florence Kelley, a big, substantial Irish woman, was not present. She was a well-known social worker and champion of the rights of shop girls and consumers. She sent in a note complaining of an article by the editor of the *Crisis* in which he had said that Negroes demanded the right "to marry anybody who wanted to marry them." Mrs. Kelley thought that this was much too strong and would certainly make enemies. The note was referred to the editor of the *Crisis,* who made no comment.

Nearly all of the Board meetings, like this one, were well attended, were interesting, with discussions that were often rather warm but seldom angry. Everybody believed that this eventually was going to be a strong national organization, but many feared the rocks which were ahead. Some of these were the distinct although latent opposition to the doctrines of Booker Washington on the part of some supporters, although others, like Villard, were close friends of Mr. Washington. It was agreed by all to avoid personal or bitter attacks on Washington. The omnipresent fear was of lack of funds to carry the organization on. Everyone expected that it would subsist on philanthropy. No one dreamed that eventually the colored members of the organization would themselves furnish the main support which the organization needed.

In this intricate intermixture of opinion it was difficult to form a labor program, especially with Negro leaders who knew nothing of Karl Marx and his philosophy. The nearest approach to unconscious Marxism was the Negro demand for the production of social leadership by the education of a "Talented Tenth"; but these leaders were not envisaged as workers but as thinkers, with no dictatorship over the mass beyond appeal to reason and right among an ignorant and inexperienced folk.

There met in the *Crisis* office in 1910, a number of persons of distinction interested in Negro labor, but frankly not in entire agreement with the editor of the *Crisis,* nor even with the general ideas of the NAACP.

Professor Seligman of Columbia, the most distinguished sociologist of his day, opened the meeting by saying:

"We are friends of the Negro and sympathize with your feelings as Negroes. We know that right here in New York you cannot buy a seat in the orchestra of a first class theater; that you cannot eat even in ordinary restaurants or stop at hotels; that when Miss Ovington recently attended a public dinner at which Negroes were present, the *New York Times* rebuked her; all this we know and do not extenuate. If you will and can fight this sort of thing we certainly will not oppose you. But personally we believe that the really important thing for the Negro today is not theater going or restaurants for the well to do, but jobs for the mass of workers. We have therefore formed the Urban League for opening avenues of employment for Negro workers. We do not oppose your program of agitation and appeal. You have a right to follow it but we want to confine ourselves to this humbler and simpler job, and we propose therefore to delimit the field of Negro help, so as not to engender opposition and dispute but to work in cooperation and harmony."

There was some argument.

"Of course," argued George Haynes, who had fathered the idea and was secretary, "we know that workers without votes in competition with voters are at serious disadvantage."

But Jones, destined soon to displace Haynes and give form to the work of the Urban League, interrupted:

"Nonsense, votes or no votes, we have got to fight the white trade unions and keep them from ruining industry with impossible demands; if the Negro helps rescue industry, industry will see that he survives and prospers."

The representatives of the NAACP said little. Many of them agreed with the Urban League idea. The editor of the *Crisis* said simply "Go ahead!" He foresaw what would happen if they tried to make scabs of Negroes. He also knew that these representatives of wealth and power must be placated so as not to attack the N.A.A.C.P., but let it go forward with agitation and radical reform. The two organizations thus started out in friendly recognition of each other's fields.

The inevitable happened. The rich employers and their friends who first dominated the League early came under bitter attack from the trade unions on the one hand, for furnishing Negro scabs to undermine union labor, and bitter answers from the Negroes regarding union discrimination; there was little effort at real united leadership toward combining Negro rights and the labor movement. It was many years before the Urban League sensed this fundamental dichotomy in its program.

But from the first it helped thousands of Negroes get work where otherwise they would never have been employed. What this meant to the general labor movement was another question.

CHAPTER V

HIGH HARLEM

Mansart soon realized that so far as American Negroes are concerned, progress was not what it should be. In the days after the First World War until the Depression, contradictory happenings highlighted their plight. New segregation laws were passed in Richmond and Atlanta; a German opera put on at the Metropolitan was changed so that no one would suspect that in the original the hero was a Negro. Students in the oldest colored college, Lincoln University, declared that they did not want colored teachers to replace white missionaries. Philadelphia Boy Scouts would not admit Negroes; and in the Episcopal and Catholic churches Negro priests were either excluded or admitted under difficulties. Hotels, north and south, persistently discriminated, and also theaters and residential sections. The disfranchisement in the South was untouched. In eleven Southern states not a single city or state appointed a Negro official. Many friends of the Negro, like Moorfield Storey and Louis Marshall, had died. Prominent Negroes like the dentist Bentley, a colored judge, and a Negro associate of Edison, all died practically without national recognition.

But the greatest occurrence of this era was the Harlem Renaissance; the sudden flowering above the music and dancing of the Sons of Laughter of a distinct Negro American literature and art centering in Harlem. It was foreshadowed in the half-hidden rebellion in the heart of a comedian like Bert Williams, who was never allowed to portray a man—only a "nigger." He said:

"I breathe like other people, I eat like them—put me at a dinner and I'll use the right fork. I think like other people. In London I am presented to the King, in France I have sat at a dinner with the President of the Republic, while here in the United States I am often treated with an air of personal and social condescension by the gentleman who sweeps out my dressing room or by the gentleman whose duty it is to turn a spotlight on me."

He was called our greatest comedian and compared, as indeed

74

he deserved to be, with those other great wits of the world, Shakespeare and Moliere and Mark Twain. In the bitter bleakness of a March day, fifteen thousand people thronged the streets at his funeral.

The strong and contradictory feelings engendered swelled to literary expression. First came the *Crisis,* beginning in 1910. Monthly and yearly for a quarter of a century it talked to white America as America had never been addressed before. It tore at hypocrisy and drove murder out into the open. It was fearless and factual and clear. It minced no words and apologized to no power. It accused and dared; it sneered, caricatured, and pilloried; it revealed and investigated. It was declared "bitter"—bitter and bitter again, after the fifteen years of soothing syrup from Booker Washington. It was fiercely attacked by great Americans in periodicals, in legislatures and on the floors of Congress. The influential Southern *Raleigh News and Courier* wrote:

"It is hard to tell which is the worst enemy of the Negro race— the brute who invites lynching by the basest of crimes, or the social equality-hunting fellow who slanders his country. Fortunately for the peaceable and industrious Negroes in the South, the world does not judge them either by the writer or the animal, and helps them and is in sympathy with their efforts to better their conditions."

The *Crisis* kept right on, with perfect English, unanswerable truth and rare restraint. Only once in 24 years was it even threatened with a libel suit.

But the *Crisis* became more than complaint; it was a vehicle of the human expression of a race. It printed pictures of prominent black folk; faces of cunning black babies and of almost all black college graduates who excelled. It printed poetry; it discovered poets; it published stories. Gradually, other journals joined the *Crisis*: *Opportunity* from the Urban League; Philip Randolph's socialist *Messenger* and the anarchist *Challenge.* The voice of the Negro became louder and more strident with novels and books of essays. After that blood bath of 1919, the West Indian poet, Claude McKay, burst out in Harlem with the crowning defiance:

"If we must die, let it not be like hogs!"

Clearly, a new nation was expressing itself; first and most clearly in poetry, as poets always precede a literature. Then came drama, descended directly from the older musical comedies and the new "Shuffle Along" and "Blackbirds." These were still for white folk, but there followed a new trend: a distinct Negro Theater, the Lafayette Players in Harlem, which brought hearers from downtown where Negroes were not welcome as actors or hearers. There followed the great experiment of interracial drama, the soul clash of black and white, with the Torrence plays, and Eugene O'Neill's "Emperor Jones." These plays increased race hate and threatened riots. A "Little Theater" in Harlem, backed by the *Crisis,* won second prize in a national contest with white American and British players.

It was in music that Negro genius was first recognized in America and in the world. All Africa sings and dances and the roll of her drums comes down the centuries from Egypt to the Gold Coast. Her music and rhythms were transported to America where they were re-born in new reincarnation. A Negro wrote: "Little of beauty has America given the world save the rude grandeur God himself stamped on her bosom; the human spirit in this new world has expressed itself in vigor and ingenuity rather than in beauty. And so by fateful chance the Negro folk-song—the rhythmic cry of the slave—stands today not simply as the sole American music, but as the most beautiful expression of human experience born this side the seas. It has been neglected; it has been, and is, half despised, and above all has been persistently mistaken and misunderstood; but notwithstanding, it still remains as the singular spiritual heritage of the nation and the greatest gift of the Negro people."

Negro music enveloped the United States. It came as slave songs in work and religion; it hummed in lullabies and dirges. It became Negro ballad and folk song in "My Grandfather's Clock," "Carry Me Back to Old Virginny," and "Listen to the Mocking Bird." It was imitated by whites and appears as "My Old Kentucky Home," "Way Down Upon the Swanee River," "Nelly Gray," and "Dixie." It was developed into "rag time" and "jazz" on the one hand, and became "Gospel Hymns" on the other. Then Negroes and whites began to build a new music on this foundation: Burleigh, Dett, Rosamund Johnson and Still. Great musicians from abroad like Dvorak conceived a New World Symphony on tihs Negro foundation; and a black boy from Mississippi conceived the "Blues."

Even into science Negro genius tried to thrust. But this was strongly barred; this was not individual effort but appointment to laboratories, with materials and instruments furnished. Turner in entomology had a European reputation, but his appointment to Chicago University lapsed when the head professor died, and Turner later died from overwork in a public school. Ernest Just, a great biologist, was held back by red tape at Woods Hole, the national laboratory. Just was on the path that led to Lysenko.

Negro writers in this century have published thirteen books which deserve to be called literature. Some, indeed, are recognized as such by white America, albeit usually without enthusiasm. Most are quite unknown or forgotten by whites and because of that not widely known even among Negroes. But all are great and under normal circumstances would be lauded as foundations of a real literature of a people. One book of self-revelation was widely acclaimed: there was a study of Harlem and one of Philadelphia; there was an exposition of the Negro family; there was a widely acclaimed biography; a probing into nasty Negro social depths, which whites liked; two good novels and two broad anthologies.

What did Negroes write? It's hard to say exactly. Stories, of course, to tell how the world seems to a black man and what he means to the world, like Chesnutt's "Wife of His Youth," where a handsome mulatto gives up the rich, beautiful bride he's about to marry, because his black companion of slavery suddenly returns to his life. Then one's own life is always interesting, like "Up from Slavery," and lives of other black folk—a long, long line. There were essays—short ways of saying what caste is, like those passages from "Souls of Black Folk."

There were the twenty-five volumes of Woodson's *Journal of Negro History,* preserving a past the white world was struggling to forget; there is the Negro's own story of Reconstruction, so long distorted. There are the long line of anthologies, Braithwaite's compilation of all American poetry which kept verse living when it tried to die; those of black poetry down to the splendid "Caravan." There is the Fauset cycle of colored Philadelphia; and Fisher's slight but precious vignettes; the Trombones of Johnson and Harlems of McKay; and many thoughts about Negro music, work, play, and sorrow songs.

Our actors blended with our musicians to make a splendid galaxy; from Sam Lucas to Will Cook, Rosamund Johnson and Williams and Walker. Maud Cuney Hare wrote and played its story. We went on the stage with Gilpin, sweet Florence Mills, great Robeson and young Richardson. We burst into vocal song with Hayes, Bledsoe and Anderson. Finally our fingers moved in painting and sculpture; Tanner who put the Bible in color, Warrick who wrought "The Wretched," and Elizabeth Prophet carved while Scott and Aaron Douglass did their frescoes, and Barthe his sculptures.

In the new Little Theater which the *Crisis* opened in Harlem in 1927, in the same building as the new Schomburg library of Negro Americana, there was a recital of Negro poetry. Negro children from the public schools, some dark actors from Broadway and several writers themselves took part. A hundred colored people in the auditorium decorated by Aaron Douglas listened breathlessly, while Charles Burroughs named the readers and the poems.

There came first grim realization of just what Negroes faced in America:

"To be a Negro in a day like this
    Demands rare patience—patience that can wait
In utter darkness. 'Tis the path to miss,
    And knock, unheeded, at an iron gate,
To be a Negro in a day like this."

A dark girl expressed apprehension as to the ultimate end:

"O Earth, O Sky, O Ocean, both surpassing,
    O heart of mine, O soul that dreads the dark!
Is there no hope for me? Is there no way
    That I may sight and check that speeding bark
Which out of sight and sound is passing, passing?"

A little golden girl incongruously talked of dark despair:

"The heart of a woman falls back with the night,
And enters some alien cage in its plight,
And tries to forget it has dreamed of the stars,
While it breaks, breaks, breaks on the sheltering bars."

A tall black boy expressed bitter disdain for the oppresssor:

"The painted beauty sings thy songs.
The lavrock lilts me mine;
The hot-housed orchid blooms for thee,

The gorse and heather bloom for me,
   Ride on, young lord, ride on!"

Then from a small brown girl, doubt and determination came
forth:

"And it's oh, for the white man's sad neglect,
   For the power of his light let go;
So, I know which man must win at last,
   I know! Ah, Friend, I know!"

James Weldon Johnson, thin and sallow, recited his own lines:

"There is a wide, wide wonder in it all,
That from degraded rest and servile toil
The fiery spirit of the seer should call
These simple children of the sun and soil.
O black slave singers, gone, forgot, unfamed,
You—you alone, of all the long, long line
Of those who's sung untaught, unknown, unnamed,
Have stretched out upward, seeking the divine."

Three young boys recited in unison:

"Symbolic mother, we thy myriad sons,
   Pounding our stubborn hearts on Freedom's bars,
Clutching our birthright, fight with faces set,
   Still visioning the stars!"

Claude McKay arose in the rear and recited:

"O Kinsman! We must meet the common foe;
Though far outnumbered, let us still be brave,
And for their thousand blows deal one death-blow!
What though before us lies the open grave?
Like men we'll face the murderous, cowardly pack,
Pressed to the wall, dying, but—fighting back!"

From the *Crisis* was read a poem published in war time:

"These truly are the Brave,
These men who cast aside
Old memories, to walk the blood-stained pave
Of Sacrifice, joining the solemn tide
That moves away, to suffer and to die
For Freedom—when their own is yet denied!

O Pride! O Prejudice! When they pass by,
Hail them, the Brave, for you now crucified!"

Burroughs read Jean Toomer's "Song of the Son"—Toomer,
grandson of a black Senator:

"O Negro slaves, dark purple ripened plums,
Squeezed, and bursting in the pine-wood air,
Passing, before they stripped the old tree bare
One plum was saved for me, one seed becomes

An everlasting song, a singing tree,
Caroling softly souls of slavery,
What they were, and what they are to me,
Caroling softly souls of slavery."

Frank Horne reads from his "Chant for Children":

"Hannibal . . . Hannibal
Bangin' thru the Alps
Licked the proud Romans,
Ran home with their scalps—
'Nigger . . . nigger . . . nigger . . .' "

Langston Hughes, laughing, brilliant, and beautiful, sang:

"Bathed in the Euphrates when dawns were young.
I built my hut near the Congo and it lulled me to sleep.
I looked upon the Nile and raised the pyramids above it.
I heard the singing of the Mississippi when Abe Lincoln
    went down to New Orleans, and I've seen its muddy
    bosom turn all golden in the sunset.

I've known rivers;
Ancient, dusky rivers.

My soul has grown deep like the rivers."

Arna Bontemps, with sad, brown face, recited his "Nocturne":

"The golden days are gone. Why do we wait
So long upon the marble steps, blood
Falling from our open wounds? and why
Do our black faces search the empty sky?
Is there something we have forgotten? some precious thing
We have lost, wandering in strange lands?"

Countee Cullen, with his round face, dark and shy, read in a low voice:

"I doubt not God is good, well-meaning, kind,
And did he stop to quibble could tell why
The little buried mole continues blind,
Why flesh that mirrors him must some day die,
Make plain the reason tortured Tantalus
Is baited with the fickle fruit, declare
If merely brute caprice dooms Sisyphus
To struggle up a never-ending stair.

"Inscrutable His ways are and immune
To catechism by a mind too strewn
With petty cares to slightly understand
What awful brain compels His awful hand;
Yet do I marvel at this curious thing:
To make a poet black, and bid him sing!"

And finally a visitor from Philadelphia read from his poem:

". . . I was raised
By God to know my calling. It is this:
 To set my people free and make that world
Where black men live a safe and sure retreat
For all the friends of freedom everywhere.
It is not, then, to make one race supreme
That we must fight, but to make all men free.
Whatever government gives hope of this
Has my allegiance . . ."

Few Americans read these poems or pondered them; few whites; few Negroes. The reaction of middle class Negroes was illustrated in a Harlem liquor saloon. Someone was mentioning Countee Cullen and Claude McKay. The man in the center of the bar squirmed and glared. He was big, brown, and well-groomed. He demanded a refill and muttered:

"I'm as broad as any; but tell me: what the hell do 'niggers' want with poetry?"

The West Indian down at the end, pleasantly happy with his fourth, responded, "Right—abs- slutely right, Man. Damn right! And fudder more what we want wid roses? An' ef yo' as' me, whut we want wid de Moon? Fac' is what do we *want?*"

But the well-dressed man had left with a look of supreme disgust on his carefully shaven face.

This Harlem Renaissance was an abnormal development with abnormal results. It was not a nation bursting into self-expression and applauding those who told its story and feelings best, but rather a group oppressed and despised within a larger group, whose chance for expression depended in large part on what the dominant group wanted to hear and were willing to support. This, then, was but a part of the true, uninhibited message, and there was consequently offered prizes to those willing to distort truth and play court fool to American culture. Even this situation produced a bit of Negro literature but nothing complete. For a real literature demands truth and real feelings and not submission to what others want to hear, especially when most of these "others" hate the ground on which these black artists walk, and pay well for any caricature which tickles their own false and cheap ego.

It was all an extraordinary effort which met American prejudice head-on and was beaten back by the concentrated efforts of white editors and booksellers and then, at last, by the world Depression.

So there was the beginning of a Negro American literature, but not complete. There were young geniuses who flashed and died like smothered candles or falling stars—Bohannan, Cotter, Larson. Others who died dumb, like starved souls and murdered spirits.

But Negro effort must have a stage to play on, a physical center to live in, and that it lacked in New York. And in New York the Negro Renaissance was born. To accomplish this came the battle of Harlem led by a black real estate operator, Phil Payton. Negroes needed homes; sweeping up from Wall Street, Fifty-third Street was overcrowded. Many of the better class Negroes had gone to Brooklyn and thence later spread out to Long Island. But Payton saw that the best living space in Manhattan was in Harlem.

Harlem in 1900 was a place of brownstone fronts, polo, racing, and Saratoga trunks. Then the building speculators moved in. By 1910, Harlem around 135th Street had been overbuilt by gamblers in land and housing. Whole blocks were half filled or empty.

"Mr. Towns," said Payton in 1910, "I can fill your vacant tenements."

Towns, a white Harlem "realtor," was facing bankruptcy and had to listen to his black visitor, although he plainly showed his dislike.

"Fill? With what?"

"Negroes."

"What? I haven't time—"

"Listen. I can bring to Harlem this year Negroes enough to fill every empty flat you own and they'll pay you more rent than whites do!"

Towns stared. He saw escape. He hated the path, but after all, black money was as good as white.

"Go ahead," he shouted, "but remember, money talks!"

The battle began. Blacks moved in by thousands. Whites organized and protested. Whites threatened, but blacks paid high and higher rents. It was dimes against dollars but dollars lost. Banks foreclosed mortgages and refused loans, but Negroes bought the property with higher interest and bonuses. A black church moved up from mid-Manhattan and bought twenty blocks at a single deal.

Whites moved out and laid down deadlines—125th Street, 145th Street, Seventh Avenue, Eighth Avenue. One by one these battlements sagged and fell. A great insurance company sold to Negroes a whole street of its select homes, planned by Sanford White. The Negroes held Harlem. The white mob dared not enter.

A new Negro life began to blossom. Black folk worked, laughed, whored, and gambled; but also they sang and danced and stringed their instruments, and their music rolled around the world until Europe, Asia, and Africa knew Negro music and Harlem.

One singular expression of the Negro soul was the Pageant, "The Star of Ethiopia." It was first designed in 1913 to celebrate fifty years of Emancipation in New York. Then, in 1915, it was repeated in the capital, Washington. In 1916, it celebrated the One Hundredth Anniversary of the African Episcopal Church. Finally, in 1919, it was given in Hollywood Bowl.

The story of the pageant covered 10,000 years and more of the history of the Negro race and its work and suffering and triumphs in the world. This was the message of its 1,000 actors:

"Hear ye, Hear ye! Men of all the Americas, and listen to the tale of the eldest and strongest of the races of mankind, whose faces be black. Hear ye, hear ye, of the gifts of black men to this world, the Iron Gift, and Gift of Faith, the Pain of Humility and the Sorrow Song of Pain, the Gift of Freedom and of Laughter, and the undying Gift of Hope. Men of the world, keep silence and hear ye this!"

A white woman in government service said, "I can hardly think of any way in which more of beauty and inspiration and information could have been brought to us. It was one of the most beautiful things of the kind I had ever seen, and the most beautiful I had ever seen in Washington."

Then came the plight of Africa which turned the thought of Negroes back toward Africa, a matter of which none of the whites in the N.A.A.C.P. were thinking, and from which most of the Negroes were by hereditary culture-patterns opposed to considering in any way.

The editor of the *Crisis* thought differently, and the *Crisis* during the war had become the most powerful part of the NAACP organization, being entirely self-supporting and having an income of $78,000 a year compared to $43,000 received by the main organization. The editor of the *Crisis* believed, as did numbers of American Negroes led by a group of Philadelphia Negroes, that the Congress of Versailles should try to settle the problems of Africa. The NAACP was willing that the editor of the *Crisis* should explore such possibilities if the *Crisis* met the expense. Also, the NAACP suggested that at the same time the editor might investigate the treatment of American Negro soldiers in our army, concerning which there was continual complaint.

So the *Crisis* went to Europe after the Armistice, without backing from the NAACP but with its blessing. The result was momentous. Burghardt asked the American authorities for permission to hold a Pan-African Congress in Paris to petition the Peace Congress. The editor reported:

"I first went to the American Peace Commission and said frankly and openly: 'I want to call a Pan-African Congress in Paris.' The Captain to whom I spoke smiled and shook his head. 'Impossible,' he said and added, 'The French Government would not permit it.' 'Then,' said I innocently, 'It's up to me to get French consent.' 'It is!' he answered, and he looked relieved.

"With the American Secret Service at my heels, I then turned to the French Government. There were six colored deputies in the French Parliament and one was Diagne, an under-secretary in the War Department. 'Of course we can have a Pan-African Congress,' he said—'I'll see Clemenceau.' He saw Clemenceau, and there was a week's pause. Clemenceau saw Pichon, and there was another pause. Meantime, our State Department chuckled and announced that there would be no Congress, and refused Negroes passports. England followed suit and refused to allow even the Secretary of the Aborigines Protection Society to visit Paris, while no South African natives were allowed to sail.

"But there were six Negroes in the French House and Clemenceau needed their votes. There were 280,000 black African troops in the war, secured by the efforts of one of these deputies. Before these France stands with uncovered head. The net result was that Clemenceau, Prime Minister of France, gave us permission to hold the Pan-African Congress in Paris.

"If the Negroes of the world could have maintained in Paris during the entire sitting of the Peace Conference a central headquarters with experts, clerks and helpers, they could have settled the future of Africa at a cost of less than $10,000.

"As it was, the Congress cost $750. Yet with this meagre sum a Congress of fifty-eight delegates, representing sixteen different Negro groups, was assembled. This Congress passed resolutions which the press of the world largely approved, despite the fact that these resolutions had paragraphs of tremendous significance to us, such as:

" 'Wherever persons of African descent are civilized and able to meet the tests of surrounding culture, they shall be accorded the same rights as their fellow citizens; they shall not be denied on account of race or color a voice in their own government, justice before the courts and economic and social equality according to ability and desert.

" 'Whenever it is proved that African natives are not receiving just treatment at the hands of any State or that any State deliberately excludes its civilized citizens or subjects of Negro descent from its body politic and cultural, it shall be the duty of the League of Nations to bring the matter to the attention of the civilized world.'

"Colonel House of the American Peace Commission received

me and assured me that he wished these resolutions presented to the Peace Conference. Lloyd George wrote me that he would give our demands 'his careful consideration.' The French Premier offered to arrange an audience for the president and secretary of the Conference. Portugal and Belgium, great colonial powers, offered complete cooperation."

In 1921 a Second Pan-African Congress was held on a larger scale. There were 110 delegates from 26 countries and a thousand visitors. The Congress sat successively in London, Brussels and Paris. Jessie Fauset wrote:

"The dream of a Pan-African Congress had already come true in 1919. Yet it was with hearts half-wondering, half fearful that we ventured to realize it afresh in 1921. So tenuous, so delicate had been its beginnings. Had the black world, although once stirred by the terrific rumblings of the Great War, relapsed into its lethargy? Then, out of Africa, just before it was time to cross the Atlantic, came a letter, one of many, but this the most appealing word from the Egyptian Sudan: 'Sir, We cannot come but we are sending you this small sum [$17.32] to help toward the expenses of the Pan-African Congress. Oh Sir, we are looking to you for we need help sorely!' "

We had been invited to Brussels by Paul Otlet, Father of the League of Nations, and Senator La Fontaine and had been helped greatly by M. Paul Panda, a native of the Belgian Congo who had been educated in Belgium. The Congress itself was held in the marvellous Palais Mondial, the World Palace, situated in the Cinquantonaire Park. We could not have asked for a better setting.

British, French, Belgian and German periodicals commented:

"Every white man present must have been amazed at the revelation of power and ability."

"One could not fail to be impressed with the sense of potency and possibility."

"The educated Negro has become vocal. He has tasted some of the fruit of the tree of knowledge, and has been asking himself questions—questions, some of which even the white many may find it difficult to answer."

This Congress said:

"The experiment of making the Negro slave a free citizen in the United States is not a failure; the attempts at autonomous government in Haiti and Liberia are not proofs of the impossibility of self-government among black men; the experience of Spanish America does not prove that mulatto democracy will not eventually succeed there; the aspirations of Egypt and India are not successfully to be met by sneers at the capacity of darker races.

"This is a world of men, of men whose likenesses far outweigh their differences; who mutually need each other in labor and thought and dream, but who can successfully have each other only on terms of equality, justice and mutual respect. They are the real and only peacemakers who work sincerely and peacefully to this end.

"Surely in the 20th century of the Prince of Peace, in the millenium of Buddha and Mahmoud, and in the mightiest Age of Human Reason, there can be found in the civilized world enough of altruism, learning and benevolence to develop native institutions for the native's good, rather than continue to allow the majority of mankind to be brutalized and enslaved by ignorant and selfish agents of commercial institutions, whose one aim is profit and power for the few."

At the very time that the Pan-African Congress was convening in London and Brussels, there was another series of meetings sitting in New York under the leadership of Marcus Garvey. William Pickens reported to the NAACP on these meetings.

"That low barn-like hall was packed with thousands pouring in from a street parade. They were uniformed in crimson and green. There were Black Cross nurses, the African League banners and songs."

"And Garvey himself, what of him?"

"Not impressive at first—short, stout and black, but fiery, dramatic and earnest. It was not so much the man as the message; a new black world over against the dominant white. And the method? Commerce and trade; a Black Star Line in a city where the White Star Line was high finance. To this Garvey added deftly the shadow of brilliant ceremony—an Empire of African titles, knights and ladies; veiled references to himself as King by the Grace of a black God. It was fantastic and yet tremendously impressive. His following must be in the hundreds of thousands; perhaps a half million.

"Did he have any money?"

"He certainly did. He collected millions between 1920 and

1927. He threw it around with no sense of its value and cost in the sweat of his fascinated disciples. He bought ships. He published books, periodicals and newspapers. When he fell it was on this waste of money."

Garvey was a demagogue with a core of sincerity, and deep color prejudice against whites and mulattoes; not so much unscrupulous as totally inexperienced. He wasted and lost thousands of dollars of the wages of the poor. But he aroused a consciousness of Africa and of the dignity of the black race among West Indian peasants and spread it in the United States. His thesis was based on independent statism for black folk and industrial and commercial development by black shippers and traders along conventional current lines of white commercialism. His plans were balked by lack of any African base of operation and by his own ignorance of trade and finance.

This might have been remedied in time by experiment and patient effort. But Garvey was not built for this and doomed his own ventures by extravagance, rodomontade, and breaking United States laws. He was jailed for misuse of the mails in 1925, but pardoned by Coolidge and deported to Jamaica in 1927. He died in London in 1940, forgotten and neglected.

And so it was that in Harlem after the First World War, the American Negro, in a burst of brilliance, achieved his greatest step toward self-expression and organized fight for freedom. He stretched out his hands toward Africa. As a result, today there exists in nearly every African province, a National African Congress, founded on the example of the Pan-African Congresses, and in some cases inspired by the memory of Garvey. On these the fight for African freedom is being waged.

In the United States, opposition to the NAACP in the South was shown by physical violence which the white secretary encountered while travelling in Texas. He was thrown into utter confusion by this startling phenomenon of violent opposition to social reform. He resigned and eventually went insane.

The executive direction then passed into the hands of Negroes. A staff of five was gathered which worked well for a while. One was genial and accommodating; another energetic but selfish; a third proved a "me, too" man who followed the prevailing wind; the fourth was an honest but impulsive orator, and the fifth a lively preacher. This team led the organization through the war period and into the aftermath. The Negro secretary was forced out by the ambition of his assistant.

But the NAACP was too well-grounded in its ideals and methods to let personalities ruin it. Hard work in organization, progaganda and a systematic collection of funds followed. The honest and efficient handling of money brought the NAACP to new prosperity. Particularly it brought the miracle of mass support for an organization which from the start had assumed that it must depend for survival on alms from white philanthropy. Some whites, to be sure, gave considerable money in the aggregate, but from 1910 on the NAACP got its chief and increasing support from the mass of Negro laborers, who themselves were earning wages far below the average of the nation.

"Who would be free, themselves must strike the blow!"

Pressing problems re-arranged themselves and had to be faced. There was the matter of legal redress which must become something more than individual legal defense. This, however, called for more funds than were available. The matter of civil and political rights must be pushed, but in what direction? Lynching was scotched although lower court injustice remained and increased. Should segregation be opposed as such or only where advisable? They must stand for civil and political rights but not for a moment surrendering social equality. One white man was irritated at this continued reference to social equality, and was with difficulty retained in the organization. Still another white man was a lawyer, and protector of wealth, who as a diversion, conscious or unconscious, insisted on a purely legal program.

Thus the NAACP also hesitated in its attitude toward the labor movement. Its leaders knew well that the area, where practical planning was really needed, was in the matter of industry; the question of work and decent pay for Negroes. But here the NAACP was reluctant to take a stand. Its direction consisted of white and black, rich and poor, employers and workers, investors and socialists. Only one member of the staff continued to press this point.

In 1924, this member induced the annual conference of the NAACP to appeal to the American Federation of Labor:

"For many years the American Negro has been demanding admittance to the ranks of union labor.

"For many years your organizations have made public profession of your interest in Negro labor, of your desire to have it unionized, and of your hatred of the black 'scab.'

"Notwithstanding this apparent surface agreement, Negro labor in the main is outside the ranks of organized labor, and the reason is first, that white union labor does not want black labor and secondly, black labor has ceased to beg admittance to union ranks because of its increasing value and efficiency outside the unions.

"We thus face a crisis in interracial labor conditions; the continued and determined race prejudice of white labor, together with the limitation of immigration, is giving black labor tremendous advantage. The Negro is entering the ranks of semi-skilled and skilled labor and he is entering mainly as a 'scab.' He broke the great steel strike. He will soon be in a position to break any strike when he can gain economic advantage for himself.

"On the other hand, intelligent Negroes know full well that a blow at organized labor is a blow at all labor; that black labor today profits by the blood and sweat of labor leaders in the past who have fought oppression and monopoly by organization. If there is built up in America a great black bloc of non-union laborers who have a right to hate unions, all laborers, black and white, must eventually suffer.

"Is it not time, then, that black and white labor got together? Is it not time for white unions to stop bluffing and for black laborers to stop cutting off their noses to spite their faces?

"We, therefore, propose that there be formed by the National Association for the Advancement of Colored People, the American Federation of Labor, the Railway Brotherhoods and any other bodies agreed upon, an Inter-racial Labor Commission.

"We propose that this Commission undertake:

"1. To find out the exact attitude and practice of national labor bodies and local unions toward Negroes and of Negro labor toward unions.

"2. To organize systematic propaganda aaginst discrimination on the basis of these facts at the labor meetings, in local assemblies and in local unions.

"The National Association for the Advancement of Colored People stands ready to take part in such a movement and hereby invites the cooperation of all organized labor. The Association hereby solemnly warns American laborers that unless some such step as this is taken soon the position gained by organized labor in this country is threatened with irreparable loss."

The Federation of Labor did not respond to this appeal and the NAACP did not push it further. Philip Randolph in 1925 formed an organization to promote unionism among Negroes with Morris Hillquit on the advisory board. This effort died. Then Randolph delimited his field and organized the colored Pullman porters. He secured partial recognition from the A. F. of L. and finally full admission to the Federation of Labor in 1937.

But these lone pioneers little knew the size of the forces of colonialism. One American told the story. Major General Smedley D. Butler described, in picturesque language, his work as guardian of American Big Business interests in foreign lands:

"I spent 33 years and four months in active service as a member of our country's most agile military force—the Marine Corps. I served in all commissioned ranks from a second lieutenant to major-general. And during that period I spent most of my time being a high-class muscle man for Big Business, for Wall Street, and for the bankers.

"I was a racketeer for capitalism. . . . I helped make Mexico safe for American oil interests in 1914. I helped to make Haiti and Cuba a decent place for the National City Bank boys to collect revenues in 1915. I helped purify Nicaragua for the international banking house of Brown Brothers in 1909-1912. I brought light to the Dominican Republic for American sugar interests in 1916. I helped make Honduras 'right' for American fruit companies in 1903. In China in 1927 I helped see to it that Standard Oil went its way unmolested.

"During those years I had, as the boys in the back room would say, a swell racket. I was rewarded with honors, medals, promotion. Looking back on it, I feel I might have given Al Capone a few hints. The best he could do was to operate his rackets in three city districts. We Marines operated on three continents."

CHAPTER VI

THE NEW EDUCATION

The dinner which Mrs. Van Rensaeler was induced to give the Chinese ambassador was most interesting. Wu Ting Fang had proven to be a great social attraction in America; his gracious manners; his old world culture and his curiously frank but always intriguing conversation were widely commented on. Then, too, his costumes, that mandarin's gown, with its priceless silk and lovely and intricate embroidery gave an exotic finish to his personality. The ambassador had expressed interest in the problem of Negroes in America. "I have been quite curious to know just how your effort at emancipating slaves turned out. In China, from age to age, either the enslaved died out or became a part of the master class. What's happening here?"

It was determined to have present at the dinner, Lyman Abbott, the leading New York protestant minister, and Hamilton Mabie, editor of the widely influential weekly, the *Outlook*. Oswald Villard, grandson of Garrison, the abolitionist, must be there. Not only was he liberal by birth, but his other grandfather represented Big Business. It was significant that this Villard not only had married a Southern girl but was president of the new emancipation movement, the NAACP. Also, he was a close friend of Booker Washington.

"Ah yes, yes, indeed," murmured Wu Ting Fang. "I shall be glad to meet this Mr. Washington."

The dinner took place in the old Fifth Avenue homestead of the hostess. There were a dozen guests and naturally none were colored. Characteristically the guest of honor noted this and remarked upon it. He peered about:

"Am I right," he said, "in assuming that none of you have Negro blood? I had looked at least to meet that friend of yours, Booker Washington." He looked at Mr. Villard.

Mr. Villard explained the social conventions—

"Yes, yes," replied the guest. "But when the NAACP succeeds in its mission will Negroes be asked to dinner?"

"You have put your finger on one of our main difficulties,"
answered Lyman Abbott.

"I see, I see," responded the guest. "You are not sure how
much emancipation you want. Of course, of course, that is natural.
I am most interested. Something of the past I know. Your slaves
revolted as all slaves eventually do—"

"Oh, no; our slaves were quite docile."

"Indeed; but how about Toussaint and Gabriel; Vesey, Nat
Turner, and 200,000 Negro soldiers in the Civil War? But never
mind that. Since then, I believe you had high hopes that the
Negroes would die out, unable to stand competition of the whites.
Are they dying duly?"

"Most certainly not."

"How thoughtless! I note the lower classes are often that way;
they seldom do what is expected of them! And then you planned
to re-export them back to Africa. That I hear was dropped because you needed their labor. They became serfs, without votes or
justice. So to preserve civilization, here is the NAACP. What does
it propose to do?"

Hamilton Mabie laid down his fork and leaned forward.

"The fact is, Your Excellency, this second decade of the new
century has brought us face to face with decision. The Negro is
here to stay. If he remains a second class citizen, disfranchised and
lynched, we cannot maintain our democracy. Therefore he must
be raised."

"Or," said the guest, "be allowed to raise himself."

"There lies the trouble," said Villard. "William English Walling, a Kentucky white man, resented a lynching in the birthplace
of Abraham Lincoln and called for a second emancipation movement. I joined and promised to raise funds for the movement
among my wealthy friends. Mary Ovington, a social worker, urged
that we ask the help of Negroes themselves and Henry Moskovitz
brought us the views of liberal Jews, and was later joined by the
Spingarns.

"Then came trouble. Dr. Abbott and Mr. Mabie looked on
Booker Washington as spokesman for Negroes and I largely
agreed. But I was willing to invite to our councils the more
radical Negro group. The Boston contingent led by Trotter and
Ida Wells Barnett refused to cooperate. A less radical group
joined, but to my disgust they came to lead, not to follow, to

tell us, not to listen. Through the *Crisis*, they took over the policy of the NAACP and demanded not only equality before the law for Negroes and the right to vote, but as they brazenly proclaimed, 'every right which belongs to an American citizen.' "

The guest of honor smiled. "This was going too far for you?"

"Not perhaps too far, but certainly too fast."

"It was crazy," interrupted Mabie. "This land naturally must keep law and order. As a democracy it is bound to let those persons vote who reach a certain standard. But Americans simply cannot assimilate Negroes—they just cannot."

"But I am told you have assimilated several million, of whom your Mr. Washington is one."

"That was due to slavery. It has now ceased."

"And to keep it so you refuse to invite Negroes to dinner. And Negroes agree?"

"Wise Negroes do. Others foolishly demand social equality."

"And if and when they rise to equality, won't they continue to insist? Won't they marry those who want to marry them? This, my friend, can be stopped only in one way. Prevent this rise to equality and restore slavery whatever you may call it. Otherwise, face the fact: in a century you'll be octoroons." The diners were silent with disgust, but the suave guest continued unchecked. "You will find before this century dies that stopping the rise of a determined people is a hard job. We Chinese know, and we are still learning." The ambassador leaned back and sampled his champagne again, and belched openly and without apology. He waxed philosophical:

"The fact is you Americans may look forward with a certain complacency to the next two hundred years. Your rather coarse and hard faces will acquire some of the soft curves of Africa and what is more important, your distressing lack of what the Chinese regard as good manners will receive touches of Negro humility and graciousness which I'm sure you all realize is desperately needed.—Yes, of course," and Wu Ting Fung arose courteously with his hostess, and bowing to take her arm, strode majestically toward the drawing room.

The Chinese ambassador was too great a gentleman to pursue further a subject which he saw was proving embarrassing to his hosts. The rest of the evening was devoted to a most interesting examination of the history and deeper meaning of Chinese art. Mrs. Van Rensaeler was deeply gratified.

His Excellency, Wu Ting Fang, was determined to have a heart to heart talk with Booker T. Washington. He began next morning, but learned to his regret that Mr. Washington had just died.

With the death of Booker Washington, the white South began to gather up into its own hands the direction of Negro education. Negroes themselves, except one in the influential position of Washington, could have little educational leadership. Disfranchised, they could not make the Southern states support decent Negro public schools. Philanthropy, chiefly from white Northern churches, still helped. But after the First World War this source of funds began to die away, partly because of the increasing cost and partly because of the call of other causes, but also because tne new South stridently promised to assume the burden of Negro schools provided southern advice and direction replaced northern. But for this the South asked a price: northern gifts must be handled by southern whites and white education must take precedence over Negro in time and cost.

This was the educational reasoning behind the Booker Washington "Atlanta Compromise": the white South would direct all schools, black and white; the white South would handle all or most gifts to Negro education and would direct all educational policies. All this planning had not worked out as well as northern philanthropy had hoped.

On the other hand, all the Negro organizations—the NAACP, the Urban League, the great church organizations—continued to stress better Negro education, and this unanimity was a direct descendant of the educational crusade following the Civil War. The public schools were admittedly bad; there were few high schools. Higher education depended still almost entirely on private philanthropy. When the Federal government began to appropriate funds for state colleges, especially in agriculture and industry, the pressure on the South to share these funds equitably with Negroes increased. Most of the Southern States began to establish colored state agricultural and mechanical colleges, but with wretchedly inadequate funds. Negroes, forming over a fourth of the Southern population, got less than a tenth of the appropriations. A dominant Southern white philosophy was that educational facilities should be measured by ownership of property. The rich should have good schools; the poor, bad schools or none. This was heritage from slavery. It was modified after 1880; the whites should have the better schools because they pay most of the taxes and have better brains; Negroes should have schools, but schools suited to their needs and these needs corresponded with the demands of white employers for profit. Here the popular Hampton and Tuskegee philosophy saw eye to eye with Big Business. But white artisans and the labor movement opposed this kind of Negro education as well as Negro public schools.

Then came the demand from Negroes for equal educational facilities, at least in expenditure of federal funds. The Federal land-grant funds of 1862 went entirely to white schools in the South; but in 1890 a further grant allotted a small share to Negro schools, which necessitated the furnishing of buildings by the states. Several Negro Land-Grant colleges were started, varying widely in efficiency. By the time of the First World War, there were 17 such colleges and they shared, albeit inequitably, in the Federal funds given thereafter. Under Northern pressure, and because of increasing Negro agitation, these Negro colleges, supported in part by federal funds, had to be improved.

It was considerations like this, added to what he thought were the much greater needs of the white colleges, which moved John Baldwin to undertake a complete reorganization of the educational system of Georgia. John Baldwin never became governor of Georgia. After the First World War there came unexpected developments. Tom Watson, after his fierce anti-Negro campaign which helped bring the Atlanta riot in 1906, had gone into retirement for a decade in disappointment and frustration. But in 1920 he appeared again upon the scene to run for United States senator. He had dropped the Negro, was half-hearted in fighting for white labor, and fulminated against Jews and the Catholic Church. At the same time, the Ku Klux Klan was revived and business began that miraculous upsurge which ended with the crash of 1929.

John Pierce, banker and mouthpiece of Big Business, talked with Baldwin:

"John, I had always pictured you in a successful political career—governor, and senator; perhaps even higher. Now I doubt. In this next state campaign we need a rabble rouser like Tom

Hardwick. He can sweep the state and we can handle him. Meantime, your role is in business; there you'll have more power than any official. We're facing a tremendous era. Power to help guide it will be in your hands."

Baldwin demurred as did his mother and wife. But Pierce prevailed. One matter, however, Baldwin managed to guide, especially since it accorded with the plans of Big Business, and that was the rehabilitation of the state university system. This he could guide from his powerful position in the Legislature.

The old university, once presided over by his father, was well enough in its way, but needed revamping and expansion. It must be made part of a state-wide industrial development which would especially include the Atlanta Institute of Technology and a new liberal arts college in Atlanta with modern professional schools. These new institutions might replace or complement the University at Athens; agriculture and some other branches of science might remain there.

Finally, higher Negro education must somehow be fitted in, if for no other reason than to retain Federal funds for the state. Moreover, there had got under way a Negro demand for trained leadership which could not be stemmed. There was no use today in trying to tell Negroes that all they needed was skilled or half-skilled workers. A mass must be led, and Negroes no longer trusted whites as leaders of their race. They did not even trust Negro leaders like Washington, who did what whites wanted done. It was a peculiar complication that at present the Negro private college, Atlanta University, was actually the best college in Atlanta; while a poor state school in Savannah was the state-supported Negro institution. The head of this branch was called Principal of the Colored A & M, and spent most of his time distributing among his white trustees and merchants such favors in spending and purchasing as his institution's small income would allow.

Baldwin's first step toward his educational program was to secure ample state funds for the white Institute of Technology in Atlanta, to be supplemented by donations from corporations interested in having gifted young men trained for their factories, mines and business. At the State University in Athens, a new College of Agriculture on a large scale was given appropriations by the Legislature.

After this, Baldwin called in Coypel and rather suddenly offered him a position which would eventually make him Chancellor of a new University of Georgia.

"My dear Coypel, there is one anomaly in our Atlanta educational system, which I am sure has struck you as it has many others, and that is that the only first-class college in the city is the Negro Atlanta University. We need a great college for whites. Such a college can become an integral part of a state system, comprehended under a re-furbished University of Georgia. I am glad to say that at last such a system is in sight. Northern finance has promised us a nest egg of five million to establish a college in this city to be known as Fulton University. This institution, along with the Institute of Technology, Agnes Scott College for Women, and the University at Athens, will be united into a new State University. With these in time will be incorporated all the other higher schools of the state, white and black.

"All of this is for the future. What I want to offer you now is the position of dean of the University of Georgia, and later the presidency of Fulton University when it is started. Meanwhile, I want you to act as head of a powerful and well-financed committee of the proposed University System. You will also be appointed to the present University Board of Regents and to the trustee boards of most of the colleges of the state. You will have suitable offices, and a home in the suburbs for your family. Your real work will depend on legislative action which will be pushed as rapidly as possible."

Coypel had by this time become thoroughly uncomfortable in his job as Superintendent of Atlanta city schools. This was not the small, precise, well-ordered program which he had been able to carry out in Lanark. It was a big, sprawling mess, and while he had made the schools of Atlanta very considerably better than they had ever been before, it was not yet a good school system and he knew it. With the pulling and hauling in the city, the various special interests, the people who wanted positions for their friends and favors for their enterprises, agitators like Scroggs, and with the over-shadowing industrial empire—well, with all this he could not see his way to a fine, complete educational job. He was especially irked by the small progress made by the Negro schools because of small funds. He was ready for a change.

Baldwin sensed this and he made his offer of a new position

attractive. Here, withdrawn from the center of strife in a big, brawling metropolis, was a chance to start a fine educational job and to build practically from the grouhd up.

Coypel hesitated. It was not a real job but the prospect of a vast one. It was the beginning of a plan yet to be worked out. For assured success it called for a man of wide reputation and proven ability in educational work. Coypel was a small man with only local renown. He had concepts; he was widely read; he felt he might in time measure up to this great opportunity. He knew what a great State University in Georgia might yet mean to America. But could he start this great enterprise? And would Baldwin and the forces supporting him really give him a chance or were they merely pushing him forward as a stopgap, holding on until some great educator was willing to take on the real job, backed by real organization and large funds?

Coypel finally said Yes because there was nothing else to say. He did not want to remain in his present job. He would try this new one. If he failed or if it failed him, he could go back to his flowers in Lanark. He had already made overtures. He even felt a glow at the prospect of failure here. He said:

"But remember, Mr. Baldwin, that I may fail. First of all, my preparation for conducting an educational organization for a great state and indeed of a region is painfully narrow. What the masses of this state are interested in and must be educated for is first earning a decent living."

"Good," said Baldwin, "and that is just what we want."

"Yes, but that is not all we want. We want these people to know just what the life is and can be which they are preparing to live. The Institute of Technology can teach weaving, building electric motors and bridges, but what can a college teach about Life, Love, Tolerance and Dreams? I don't know and I accept this job because I know so few others who know more or as much as I."

"Let it go at that," laughed Baldwin. But Coypel interrupted: "And now, about the Negroes?"

Baldwin smiled. "I knew you would bring that up," he said. "There again I have plans. What we have now is a mess. The old Booker Washington program has not worked. We can't confine all Negroes to cheap common labor. We can't reserve a well-paid aristocracy of labor for whites. Mass production and Negro colleges have changed all that. Negroes are slipping into skilled labor and white-collar jobs; whites are falling down to common labor. Both will be forced sooner or later into a common labor union movement. Very good; we've got to seek out a new program.

"First as to Negro higher education: it's here to stay. There are four or five private Negro colleges. All depend on philanthropy which is fading away. There are three state colored industrial schools, none of them efficient or getting enough money. We are going to cooperate with Northern philanthropy to consolidate the best private Negro colleges into one university. Meantime, by action of the State Board of Education and legislative appropriations which are already certain, we are uniting all the Negro state schools into one Negro State Agricultural and Mechanical College with new buildings and equipment.

"Our ultimate aim is to unite both private and state higher training for Negroes under single state control; but that we're not yet announcing. What we'll try right off is to increase appropriations for white education to five million a year; and Negro appropriations to a half million. That is not fair, I know full well. But it's three times what the Negroes are getting now and it's all and perhaps more than I can get today. Tomorrow we may do better but never in our day can we expect Georgia to do for blacks what she does for whites. Meantime, we're ready to appoint Manuel Mansart principal of the new State School.

"Now, as I said before, Mr. Coypel, this isn't justice. But it is as much as the state dares to do just now. If the black school does its job, it will be getting a million in ten years while the whites will be getting, well, at least ten million."

"I accept on one condition," said Coypel. "It must be 'President' Mansart, not 'Principal.' "

"Accepted," answered Baldwin after a pause. "But, Mr. Coypel, remember this: whatever the title, it is largely empty; you as representing the white university are going to be the real head of the colored college with Mansart as your assistant and under your orders. On no other terms can we get money for this program. Let Mansart wear whatever title he wishes, the real head of this institution is you."

Coypel was silent. If he had spoken he would have said that Mansart would have complete power so far as he was concerned.

But under what other white man likely to succeed him would this be true? He was Mansart's only chance. He said nothing more.

The State Board of Education began the establishment of the new Negro college in Macon by buying a private Negro school which had been run by missionaries of the Northern Baptist church and served as a high school for the colored community. It had a good location with about fifty acres of land and three buildings, once substantial but now needing repair. The governor appointed a Board of Trustees and in a subtle way the New Education began in Georgia.

One of Mansart's first problems was that of preliminary housing for the college. It was too soon to consider a complete building program but a beginning must be made. There was already on the old campus one building which had been used for forty years for recitations, assemblies and administration. It must be largely rebuilt or entirely discarded. There was one old girls' dormitory and a president's home. Mansart and Coypel after careful consideration decided for the present to repair the main building, rebuild the dormitory and make the residence serve as Mansart's home with room for a small number of men students.

Later the whole problem of suitable buildings on a scale suited to the growth of the institution could be faced. There is, of course, no standard of cost for school building and particularly buildings for schools in the South adapted to Negroes. In fact, the only matter that received careful and prolonged attention was usually how much the white contractors could make in profit out of the state appropriation. Such appropriations for colored schools had been very popular in the past and much sought after by white trustees.

Coypel and Mansart had talked over the matter rather carefully, and had decided on two policies: first, the permanent buildings were going to be well planned, and secondly, the contracts were going to be carefully drawn. Before, however, anything had really been decided on or even the size of the legislative appropriation made definite, Mansart had a visit in his office from one of the trustees. He was a local Macon white man, not one of the cotton aristocracy, but he had been expanding in business and making considerable money in various ways.

Mr. Sykes was in a hurry, and greeted the president by his first name. This Manuel had some time ago decided was of little real account. The only difficulty, of course, was in the case of being thus addressed in the presence of students. Perhaps that could later be arranged. He would talk to Coypel about it.

Mr. Sykes brought out a paper which was the contract for an administration building, along with plans. Mansart looked at it with astonishment but gave no sign of what he was thinking. Evidently Mr. Sykes was going to jam through a contract quickly and get his profit settled. Evidently, too, Sykes was insinuating himself into the space between the white president and his colored representative. Mansart was expected to be flattered by this recognition of his authority and once his assent was gained, Coypel could be handled as he did not seem too strong.

Manuel took the paper and began to study it carefully. "Thank you very much, Mr. Sykes," he said. "I will look over this matter and consult about it."

"That isn't necessary at all," said Sykes, "and, er,—I'm in a hurry. I want to get this settled; the lumber business is facing a fluctuating market and we must make our decisions immediately."

"Well, of course, Mr. Sykes, but I would not want to decide anything before I had put it before the trustees and consulted—"

"Listen, Manuel, it isn't necessary for you to consult anybody. You and I are going to settle this thing and settle it right here. Now, let's have a clear understanding. As the best known local member of the Board, I propose to take a leading role in running this institution."

Manuel paused a moment and looked out the window. He made up his mind slowly. Then he said, "Mr. Sykes, I'm afraid you and I are not going to agree."

"We'll either agree, Manuel, or you will lose this job."

"All right," said Manuel, "then I'll lose it."

Sykes stared at him in astonishment. He knew, of course, that he was being a bit high-handed. Coypel and the trustees might object if he pushed this thing through too fast. But he had not expected any opposition on the part of Manuel. He leaned forward.

"Of course, er, you understand, President Mansart, that you're going to get a reasonable cut—"

Manuel pretended not to understand the implication at all. "Of course, of course," he said, "Mr. Sykes, I shall get my salary, I hope, regularly, but—er—let me be plain. I do not want to appear stubborn or anything of that sort, but this contract is not going to be settled today or any day soon until I have a chance to think it over and consult with the authorities and with my friends."

Sykes sat back in astonishment. Slowly he arose. "All right, boy," he said, "apparently you are making your choice. And let me tell you, you're making the wrong one. Good day."

For some time Mansart heard no more of Sykes. But he knew he would hear. The main building and land-buying program had not yet come up. When it did, there was no doubt but Mr. Sykes would be on hand and a crucial battle would have to be joined.

This was, as of course Manuel knew it would be, only the beginning of a series of encounters. Everything that was done for the school or bought for the school was carried out on the supposition that the smallest possible sum would be paid for materials and work, a large part of the remainder would go to the contractors or the white merchants, and a small amount of graft would be handed to the president. That had long been the rule in state schools, and especially Negro schools.

Word got around. The white merchants now made up their minds that they probably would have to give a little larger share to the president than they had planned. They didn't like it, but after all, these were new times, Mansart was stubborn and they must yield.

Even beyond this it occurred to several of them that perhaps this upstart was proposing to take over the whole of the graft from this new venture for himself, in which case he had better be warned. It was for this reason that the next week one afternoon a small, self-appointed committee called on Mansart representing the grocery firms where the school would buy its food, the bookstore which would furnish textbooks, and the large repair shop which might do a good deal of work for the school. They were quite polite. They addressed Manuel as "President Mansart," and after they were sure that the doors were closed they got right down to business.

"Now, President Mansart, there will be, as you know, large profits in furnishing this school. We can understand that you may want a share more favorable to yourself than is usual. But don't get any ideas. You are not going to be the sole one to profit from the business of this school. Let's have that understood—"

Manuel interrupted. "Gentlemen, you quite mistake me. I not only am not going to be the only one profiting from school business, but no one, so long as I am president here, is going to get anything more than the proper current recompense. That is to go solely to the person who furnishes us the best goods and services. I do not propose to take anything in any way beyond my salary."

The six men each in his own way laughed in Mansart's face, and gave him to understand that it was quite unnecessary for him to rehearse any such fairy tale. There wasn't a single school in the state that was run that way and there wouldn't be and that he was crazy to think that they believed he had any such project.

They talked a long time and the more they talked on the less the participants understood each other until finally the white merchants laid down a pretty clear statement.

"If you try anything smart in this case, Mansart, you are not only going to find yourself out of a job, you might find yourself pretty dead." And they got up and left.

It was not a pleasant project, but in time Mansart's firmness and integrity established certain business methods so that he was able with Coypel's cooperation to get more honest contracts.

On the other hand, in the matter of labor, the question could not be so easily settled. White union labor insisted upon its right to do union work at union wages on buildings put up on the campus. And colored laborers, because they were excluded from the unions, were to be deprived of work on what they regarded as their own school. This was a source of continuing friction, and here Mansart waged his fiercest battles. There were no unions among the colored carpenters, masons and plasterers in Macon. There had been in the past, but these unions had been broken up and put out of business by the new white unions who had united in a city center.

The head of the city center soon came down to warn Mansart concerning the relations of colored people and particularly on the proposed training of his students to work in the building trades. He could have all the so-called industrial education he wanted to, in cooking and house service, but there was to be no training in masonry, carpentry or plastering; no one of his students was to do work of that sort even though the work was for the school, and no colored workmen could be hired on school contracts. That was the decision of the unions and that was going to be carried through. Now, if he wanted to get on in his position he had best understand that.

"But my dear sir," argued Mansart, "one of the reasons for this school, the original reason, was particularly to train Negroes in the trades. You know quite as well as I that most of the work in the building trades in this city used to be done by Negroes."

"Yes, we know, and because we do know, it's going to be stopped. The skilled trades hereafter in the South are going to be confined to white men. No matter what Booker Washington or anyone else said, we are not going to have our wages dragged down by cheap 'niggers.' "

"But," interjected Mansart, "that's just the point. If Negroes receive good training and are admitted to the union they will make just as good union members as white people, and help keep wages up."

"They don't know nothing about unions," answered the men. "They couldn't keep a promise to save their necks. And if they did, and kept wages up, we still don't want them! Nope, they're not going to be admitted to the unions and they ain't going to work!"

"It seems to me, gentlemen," retorted Mansart, "that you are going against the whole trend of the times, and that you are attempting an impossible thing. If there is a body of labor fitted for this work and yet not admitted to it, it will become your competitors by underbidding. You are asking for the very thing that you are trying to prevent."

"Listen, Mansart, you needn't keep up this kind of talk. There ain't going to be no Negro skilled workers on any school jobs. Get that into your black head. Good day."

Here was the threat of mob law and aggression from poor whites who envied the colored students the beautiful campus and good buildings which were expected; from the rich who wanted good servants rather than lawyers and doctors would come added opposition. Here Mansart determined to make a fight. He had to; this was an open and conspicuous matter. If colored masons and carpenters were not employed on colored school work, if no Negroes were hired, this would arouse the Negroes of the state. Moreover, here Mansart could get sympathy from both races; from whites who wanted Negroes kept on the job so as to keep wages down; from the Negroes compelled to keep these skilled jobs or sink to the inadequate wage of common labor.

In 1920, Manuel Mansart became the president of the Georgia

State Colored Agricultural and Mechanical College at Macon. He held this position from 1920 to 1946, over a quarter of a century. It became his life work. In this era between the first and second world wars, Manuel Mansart developed his theory of life, of what it was and how it should be lived.

Manuel hoped that his sons would unite and help him in his new career. But Douglass preferred remaining in Atlanta at present to help Perry in the insurance business. Eventually, he was still determined to live in Chicago. Meantime, he would come to Macon regularly and see if he could help. Revels was determined never again to live in the South. He was studying law in New York. Bruce was about to enter college. He would go to Macon, but was not sure what eventually he would want to do. Just now, most of his time went to football. Sojourner did not count although she seemed interested in music.

Manuel tried to get some broad grasp of the world about him at this time. He took the *Crisis* and read each word each month. The new emancipation centering in the North was really pointed at this Southern world where Mansart lived and where the results of emancipation must be worked out if at all. Mansart looked around him. In the world of Manuel Mansart of that time there were separate churches and separate schools. On the whole, the neighborhoods were separate, although not completely. The kind of work which the colored people and white people did differed in general—the colored people doing the more subservient kind of labor and service. When it came to the government, the colored people had little to do with it. Their contacts were brusque and formal and consisted of paying taxes and obeying ordinances. The policemen had attitudes toward the colored group which they did not have toward the whites. In white stores, there was a certain separation and subservience in the way in which colored people were waited upon. There were separate seats in the streetcars and buses, the colored people filling up from the back or indeed standing, while the whites filled up from the front or left empty seats which the Negroes dare not occupy. There was, of course, separation in the railway depots and trains; although once in a while a well-to-do colored man would ride on a pullman, usually being assigned one of the end seats. In the depots, the whites were sold tickets at their windows first, and then the agent turned to the window opening into the colored waiting room. Often, there was no time for them to buy tickets and if they did not get them, they had to pay extra on the train.

In public, it was the white people that gave the orders and the colored people that took them. This was not always so; but anything else was regarded as unusual and exceptional. One expected to see colored people as laborers, porters, public servants of variour sorts, janitors and scrubwomen; while the whites were merchants, officials, policemen and foremen, and if engaged in labor, working in separate gangs or on separate jobs. Colored and white artisans were usually separated, sometimes by job, sometimes on the job.

There were certain happenings that were of interest to colored people and not to white people, so that a sort of world of colored news and white news and gossip grew up. Usually, the colored people knew more about the general facts and gossip of the white world than the whites did of the colored world, although this was not always true. There were Negro newspapers, usually weekly. The history of the past was separated, there being a history of the colored world written and unwritten, and a general history of the white world which both worlds shared.

The colored world around Manuel tended to be a larger and more complete unity. The neighborhood organized itself for various local purposes like adorning the streets and fixing playgrounds and visiting the schools. There were united protests to the authorities about clearing the streets and garbage removal, and sometimes about the actions of the police or their absence.

Then, in larger matters concerning the city there were Negro agitation for appropriations to their schools, and for the few and bare parks, or perhaps for admission to the public parks. Beyond this came the state and the attitude of Georgia toward its colored people, the work on the legislature, not so much to get it to do things for Negroes as to keep them from various kinds of new oppression. The legislators seemed continuously to forget that one-third of the inhabitants of the state were Negroes; that black workers were an asset and not merely a cost and liability.

The attitude and thought of the Negroes of Georgia was illustrated as early as 1899 by their protest to proposed disfranchisement. Twenty-four prominent Negroes wrote:

"We, your petitioners, understanding that there lies before your honorable body, a bill known as the Hardwick bill, designed to change radically the basis of suffrage in this Commonwealth, desire respectfully to lay the following considerations before you.

"It is a solemn moment when a free community proposes to change the fundamental form of its Government, and especially to determine what voice its citizens shall have in the conduct of its affairs. Such changes and decisions, affecting the very root of democratic institutions in this country, ought not to be undertaken and carried through without careful deliberation, wise forethought and a broad and statesmanlike spirit of justice.

"Especially is this true in Georgia today. The future prosperity of our State depends upon the preservation within her borders of peace and security, good government and the impartial administration of law. Whatever tends to excite strife and restlessness, or opens the door to unfair dealing, or spreads the sense of injustice among the masses of the people is unwise and impolitic.

"It has come to be the concensus of opinion in civilized Nations that in the long run government must be based on the consent of the governed. This is the verdict of more than three centuries of strife and bloodshed, and it is a verdict not lightly to be set aside. Nevertheless, the Nineteenth century with its broader outlook and deeper experience has added one modifying clause to this, to which the world now assents, namely: that in order to take part in government, the governed must be intelligent enough to recognize and choose their own best good; that consequently in free governments based on universal manhood suffrage, it is fair and right to impose on voters an educational qualification, so long as the State furnishes free school facilities to all children.

"To these principles, we, as representatives of the Negroes of Georgia, give full assent. We join heartily with the best conscience of the State, of the Nation, and of the civilized world in demanding a pure intelligent ballot, free from bribery, ignorance, fraud and intimidation. And to secure this, we concur in the movement toward imposing fair and impartial qualifications upon voters, whether based on education, or property, or both.

"Nor is this, gentlemen of the Legislature, a light sacrifice on our part. We Negroes are today, in large degree, poor and ignorant through the crime of the Nation. Through no fault of our own, are we here brought into contact with a civilization higher than that of the average of our race. We have not been sparing in our efforts to improve.

"Notwithstanding all this, so far as the Hardwick bill proposes to restrict the right of suffrage to all who, irrespective of race or color, are intelligent enough to vote properly, we heartily endorse it. But there are two features of the proposed law against which we desire hereby to enter solemn and emphatic protest. These are:

"First. The so-called 'Grandfather' clause, which provides 'That no male person who was on January 1st, 1867 or any time prior thereto, entitled to vote under the laws of the State wherein he then resided, and no lineal descendent of such person shall be denied the right to register or vote at any election in this State by reason of his failure to possess the educational qualification provided for in this paragraph.' And

"Secondly. We protest against the clause which restricts the right to vote to those who can read AND UNDERSTAND a clause in the Constitution; and which allows the local election officers to be the final judges of this 'understanding.' We firmly believe that the exceptions in the first mentioned clause are wrong in principle, unfair in application, and in flat contradiction to those very principles of reform upon which the whole proposal is based; while the second clause is a direct invitation to injustice and fraud.

"We know that there are among our white fellow-citizens broad-minded men who realize that the prosperity of Georgia is bound up with the prosperity of the Georgia Negro; That no Nation or State can advance faster than its laboring classes, and that whatever hinders, degrades or discourages the Negroes weakens and injures the State. To such Georgians we appeal in this crisis: Race antagonism and hatred have gone too far in this State; let us stop here; let us insist that we go no further; let us countenance no measure or movement calculated to increase that deep and terrible sense of wrong-doing under which so many today labor."

A general thought and action and stream of consciousness coursed through the colored world. It was still remembered what a thrill went through the dark people when Jack Johnson defeated Jim Jeffries; how white mobs broke out here and there, and white newspapers sternly warned Negroes not to be too "uppish." The whites rejoiced and the Negroes were sad when Johnson ran

athwart the law. But the Negroes knew this was simply because
he had married a white woman. Then came the "Birth of a Nation," that splendid new effort at moving pictures which unfortunately centered on the race problem and aroused the passions
of the mob. Negro audiences shrank at that wild ride of the Ku
Klux Klan to rescue the white girl. They knew just what the white
world was thinking.

The Pan-African Congresses in Europe in 1919 and after
scarcely interested Mansart. There were, however, several persons,
ministers and teachers, who took the trip to England, France, and
Belgium to attend the second, in 1921, largely because of the
novelty of traveling abroad, but also because of interest in Africa
and the feel of a tie between the American Negroes and their
African cousins. When they came back, there were some speeches.
One delegate told about the meeting in the largest city in the
world, and especially of discussion and dispute in Brussels, where
the Belgians were afraid that American Negroes were trying to
put radical and rebellious ideas into the minds of the Congolese.
It was, however, in Georgia a minor matter and aroused but
passing interest.

The matter of taking part in politics always interested Negroes
and divided them. There was an incident in Louisville where in
order to issue bonds, in this case for school purposes, a majority
of all the citizens and not simply of the whites, was required.
This made Negroes in several Southern cities realize the power
that they had, and in Louisville they proceeded to defeat the
bond issue, which kept the city from spending money for public
schools. The reason, of course, on the part of the Negroes was
because the money was going to be spent almost entirely for white
schools. In the future, this political tactic was destined to play
considerable part in the South, and Manuel gave attention to it.

CHAPTER VII

THE WHITE BLACK GIRL

Down in Louisiana, since the 17th century, the Du Bignons had been a mighty clan. Great land proprietors, owners of droves of slaves, wealthy and aristocratic, their plantations stretched down the delta and up the Mississippi as far as Vicksburg.

The present head of the clan, Hortense du Bignon, was known as Mère Du Bignon. She was an imposing woman, nearly six feet tall, broad and grandly proportioned. Her olive-skinned face was marked by a prominent hooked nose. Her black eyes were brilliant and sparkling, and her head covered by a piled mass of silk-white hair. Her mouth was thin and straight, her hands and feet small, her whole carriage that of an aristocrat of the old school. She boasted that her family was descended from the high nobility of France before the peasantborn Napoleons and even before the traitorous house of Orleans. There remained a dagger in her heart because there were others less beautiful, less rich, and less aristocratic who sneered that there was other blood in her veins; that it was indeed royal but that it came from a thousand years of rule among black chieftains of West Africa.

There were white Du Bignons; there were black Du Bignons; and there were Creole Du Bignons who were neither black nor white, whose name and race gossip bandied but with peril. Even imperious Mère Du Bignon had been smeared behind her back but far behind for more might have spelled death. Many were the stories of this clan: once, in the forties, a splendid Governor Du Bignon had married a homely wife of high birth and vast wealth. Her black maid was a full-bosomed woman of velvet beauty whom the governor loved. The wife found them together in his bed and that night she set upon the woman; next morning the wife was found dead in a pool of blood. The maid was seized, but the Governor ordered her release and declared himself the murderer although none believed him. At long last, he was acquitted by the courts. He killed the wife's brother in the ensuing duel. The black woman continued to serve him to the end of his days. But who

would dare to say in the veins of the woman who was now at the
head of the Du Bignon clan there was a drop of the degraded blood
of Africa? No one, to be sure, to Mère Du Bignon's face, but some
sneered and giggled behind her back.

She was born in 1816 and had married a cousin at the age of 15.
There had been two children: Claire, who married Colonel Breckinridge; and a boy, Maurice. Maurice had never married but,
according to the custom of Louisiana gentlemen, had taken a
slightly colored concubine and from her had one daughter, born
in 1853. It was this girl, Marie, whom Colonel Breckinridge saw
in 1868 and whom Mère Du Bignon was castigating for not being
willing to "go white."

This brought out the contradiction in the masterful old woman's
character. She knew perfectly well that there was black blood in the
Du Bignon clan. In earlier years it had been openly acknowledged,
but in later years just as fiercely denied. She herself despised the
blacks, had no faith in the possibility of their ever becoming civilized men. But on the other hand, she was willing and even eager
now and then to excuse a "touch of the tar brush" in particular
individuals, as for instance, in Marie.

But Marie, a singularly beautiful blonde, had fallen in love with
a man also colored, and flatly refused to obey her grandmother's
order to give up acknowledgement of her colored blood and pass
as white. She and the young man, a handsome, olive-colored boy,
finally married and lived in New Orleans. Their daughter eventually married a white planter from one of the Du Bignon plantations at Delta, on the Mississippi River, opposite Vicksburg, and
went there to live. They had a daughter in 1870, named Marie after
her grandmother.

On the neighboring Breedlove plantation, a little black girl was
born in 1867 who soon became the companion and child nurse of
little Marie. Marie was not yet old enough to realize differences
of race. She did not know that two physical characteristics especially, set American Negroes aside from their white fellows and
seemed to most of them the most terrible of afflictions and the
most certain insignia of inferiority; and that was the color of their
skin and the texture of their hair.

Now to Marie, Sarah's skin was beautiful. It was delicate and
soft, very dark brown almost black, and had a sort of sheen and
texture so that Marie loved to touch it. At first Sarah shrank from

this and thought Marie was making fun of her. What else could she think? She was born into a world, and destined to live in it a half-century, which despised her color and not only declared but believed deeply that this color was an indication of inborn inferority. This Marie could not understand. But to Sarah it was axiomatic. Everybody thought this, everybody said this. All standards of value assumed that black folk were the least of human beings. At this Marie laughed. But to Sarah it was no funny matter.

In Sarah's case, however, the thing which tremendously intrigued Marie and that eventually became the life work of Sarah, was Sarah's hair. It was not as most people assumed, intrinsically different from the hair of white persons. It was simply flatter in cross section, much flatter than that of straight Mongolian hair and considerably flatter than that of ordinary European hair. This meant that it curled, not in large slow curls like white people's hair, but in little quick curls of close and small diameter, so that it appeared as a cap covering her head. That meant it was more difficult to keep clean, to comb, to arrange in any way.

Sarah's mother, when she could find the time from her work in her fields, used to spend a great deal of time over Sarah's hair, since it was unusually long and thick. She carefully washed and dried it, and then she oiled it and brushed it until it was pliable, and finally braided it into tiny little braids, so that the mass of braids covered Sarah's head like a curious and exotic crown. All the plantation people admired it tremendously. But this hair dressing took a long time, and when Sarah's poor old mother lay down the burden of her work and worry, of her cringing and bowing before her white bosses; when she died, Sarah for a while struggled in vain with her thick, recalcitrant and unyielding mass of hair, and then began to neglect it, brushing it once in a while with the old brush that her mother had left, but never washing it nor cleaning it, since many of the old women told her that in that way she might catch cold.

"My mother uses a curling iron," said Marie. "I should think you might do something like that."

"But," argued Sarah, "it would have to be an iron with more than one prong. And then, too, the hair and scalp will have to be carefully cleaned, which is awful hard with hair so thick and curly. I ain't got that time. I think I'll cut it off." But she did not.

Sarah was ten and Marie six when they first met and became

close friends. In the next few years Sarah, young as she was, began to keep company with one of the black field hands, Jeff McWilliams, who was sixteen and felt himself quite a man. They often took little Marie along with them on their excursions to the woods picking flowers and fishing it in the river, and as Marie approached the age of ten and Sarah that of 14, Sarah revealed that she was going to leave the plantation, marry Jeff and go to Vicksburg to live. Marie was inconsolable, but it turned out as Sarah planned and Marie's last service was to wash and comb and braid Sarah's hair.

So across the river and into the great city of Vicksburg the child bride and her young husband began their married life. It was easy for Jeff to get work down at the docks. They lived a simple and happy life, and had one daughter. Then suddenly came tragedy. There was a row on the docks when the black stevedores began to make wage demands and several of them were shot down by the bosses without argument. Among them was Jeff McWilliams. So that at the age of twenty, with one child, Sarah was a widow.

She began to support herself by taking in washing, but it took hard, long and continuous work to support herself and baby at the small wage which white people were willing to pay for their washerwomen. Her hair was in her way. It caught the steam from the tub and the sweat from her skin and stood up in a great, unwieldy mass.

"Why don't you cut it off?" said her neighbors. "I wouldn't be bothered with all that stuff. There ain't no way of taking care of it."

But Sarah hesitated. In spite of her own distaste for her hair she could not forget the admiration of Marie. And so she tried in her few leisure moments to begin to do something with the hair. First of all it had to be kept clean, and she began washing it with soap and water. That made it dryer and more brittle. Then she put oil upon it to soften it. Then someone again suggested that just as the white people used a curling iron to take the ugly straightness out of their hair, she might use one to take out the excessive curl. But the single iron which could be used on straight hair could not easily get at the strands of this close-curled mass; until at last Sarah happened to think of using several irons set in a comb, and with some difficulty she got such a comb made. This was so successful with her own hair that after a while she was able to give up some of her washing and ironing now and then and take care of the hair of her neighbors. But of course the difficulty was that they had little time to give to this and less money to pay for it.

Finally a neighbor suggested that she go to some place up the river where colored people were more prosperous and had more paying jobs and that there she could find more customers for her method of hair culture. She set out for St. Louis and in that thriving city where she began again to wash and iron, in 1890 she met a man named C. J. Walker. Walker had ideas of business and business development and he became interested in what she had done to make her hair more presentable. He helpd her get a more suitable comb made and particularly he and she went to work on oil preparations for the lubricating of the hair and the cleaning of the scalp.

Colored people in America were always sensitive of their skin color and the texture of their hair because these differentiated them from their fellows in appearance and were used as a measure of superiority. There early came, therefore, attempts to color the skin in various ways as human beings always have done, but this was not very prevalent among American Negroes because it was so easily detected and brought a great deal of criticism from the group itself, of Negroes as being "ashamed of themselves."

The matter of hair, however, was different. In the first place there was not such an exact difference in the hair of whites and colored people as the slaveholders used to pretend; that is, the Negro's hair was not wool and the white man's hair was not silk. They varied in gradations from so-called straight hair to the curly or almost crinkled hair. There came, therefore, efforts from earliest times on the part of both white and colored people of all races to change the texture of the hair by cleaning it and heating it and making it straight or curly. The Egyptians had spent much time at this.

After a while, Sarah got quite a clientele of customers, and in 1905 set up a business of making hair preparations and using the straightening comb. After her husband's death she travelled from door to door. She met some opposition, but on the whole her business prospered and developed. Some of the ministers frowned upon it. They said that since the Lord had made colored people's hair as it was they ought not to try to change its texture. They ought not to be "ashamed" of it.

By 1910, Sarah had set herself up in business in St. Louis and had then begun to travel about the country. She was on her way to becoming a business woman who had started a new profession. She had by that time gotten some answers to the objections. She pointed out that men shaved and spent considerable time at the barber shop; that they improved their personal appearance with tailored clothes, and that it was the business of human beings to look as presentable as they could and that this was no affront to the Lord.   She travelled to various cities, demonstrating her work and working on customers, until another idea occurred to her. Instead of acting as a travelling maid what she ought to do was to center her work in little shops so that just as washing and ironing was going to the central laundries, so the maid-service which colored people needed could go into beauty parlors. She bought a barn in St. Louis and erected a manufacturing establishment and she began to open beauty shops in Pittsburgh, Boston, Philadelphia and other places until soon she found herself making money and looking forward to a prosperous life.

In time, she hired a lawyer to give her legal advice; a business manager to help her in her enterprises; and within a few years she was not only a rich woman but had established a new line of work for young colored women who did not like the slavery of house service and who could be independent and respected in their own shops. Despite the opposition of churches, despite the fact that colored newspapers for a long time refused to carry her advertisements and that most colored people, while they resorted to her business shops, were ashamed to confess that they were having their hair straightened and arranged, there arose this new branch of work which gave Negroes an income and a chance for economic development.

Marie remained on the Du Bignon plantation opposite Vicksburg and married one of the local boys, a thin and rather ineffectual octoroon. She gave birth in 1900 to a girl baby who was christened Jean. The couple and little daughter moved to St. Louis where the man thought he might make a better liivng. But he began to drink and gamble and Marie, refusing to appeal to her great grandmother in New Orleans, got in touch with her friend Sarah, now known as Madame Walker. Sarah came immediately and took charge of the family.

Jean then had an extraordinary, almost inexplicable life. From her early childhood she had known few persons and led a quiet life, with enough to eat and to wear but nothing to waste. She lived on a plantation with colored and white folk. She had always felt herself instinctively and complacently "colored," not because of any visible color but because both her parents frankly talked of their Negro descent. And yet she was continually getting into curious difficulties.

There were the white children across the road whom she met when she came to St. Louis with her parents. They were inventive and jolly. They brought new games and new experiences; and then suddenly they discovered that she was "colored" and accused her of it. She flared at the accusation. She couldn't understand of what she was accused. She had never deceived them or misrepresented herself. Her neighbors were of all colors—black, brown, yellow, white. Her father and mother were "colored" even if they were white. What was there to reveal or disclose? And moreover, she said shrilly, standing her ground in tiny dignity, "What if I am colored? Whose business is it? I am glad I am colored. I hate white folks."

They threw mud at her as she ran screaming away. And then, curiously enough and to her utter perplexity came difficulties on the other side. Colored children avoided her or called her names. She had often to be especially introduced and vouched for. She had to be careful, so careful of their assumption that she wanted to be "white" even if she wasn't. If she went out, as she grew up, with a crowd of colored children, there was always the officious attempt of some white person to separate her from them, until she had to shout the truth angrily; and then the whites seemed to become viciously bitter.

Then the father disappeared and Marie, on her deathbed, gave Jean to Sarah. If Jean had been perceptibly "colored," Sarah would have been only too happy to adopt and keep her as her own along with her own daughter; but this was inadvisable as well as dangerous. White authorities might accuse her of kidnapping a white child, and colored folk would certainly ask if there were not enough poor black children in need of a home, without Madame Walker's getting a white brat to pamper with the money they spent with her.

Madame Walker was well acquainted with the history of the Du Bignon clan. She immediately wrote Mere Du Bignon in New Orleans and first saw the head of the family. Mère Du Bignon child, and that the child was beautiful and white.

Thus it was that at the age of 10 Jean Du Bignon came to New Orleans and first saw the head of the family. Mere Du Bignon looked her over and liked her, with her chestnut hair and blue eyes. Since she showed no trace of colored blood, the old lady determined to take her in as her own great granddaughter. But little Jean showed some of her innate stubborness. She didn't want to be white, she wanted to be colored. White folks were not nice, and colored people had always been very lovely to her, "specially Sarah, who is in the hair business in St. Louis."

Mère Du Bignon stormed and sent Jean to the white school nearby, where Jean promptly upset the routine by her extraordinary notions and actions. But she did study and learn, and by the time she was ready for high school even Mère Du Bignon was ready to send her away. And to make her decision complete she sent her to the "Damyankees" in New England, where she was to be prepared for college, although for what end Mère Du Bignon did not know. At any rate the brat did not belong in New Orleans.

Every year in summertime Jean returned to her great grandmother. It came to be a most interesting and revealing companionship. Although Mère Du Bignon would hardly have acknowledged it, she lived the whole year for the joy of receiving Jean during the summer. The girl went through the high school triumphant. Then she entered Radcliffe College which had become an adjunct of Harvard.

Here Jean had curious experiences. As a girl from a Northeastern school she had companions and most of them were determined to get high marks and make Phi Beta Kappa. On the other hand, no sooner was her name learned than the Southern girls were in a twitter; she must be from the well-known New Orleans family and would be a strong candidate for the most exclusive sororities, especially as she had sufficient money and wore her expensive clothes well. But Jean was not easy to approach and claimed St. Louis as her real home. But the aristocratic girls, North and South, continued to court her, and a number of eligible young Harvard men tried to date her, until Jean got annoyed. She had come to college to learn and not to dance. And she made up her mind to get matters straight without delay.

They were all in the Radcliffe lounge after dinner one day, pausing for a bit of gossip. The main topic became, to Jean's disgust, why she had refused the bid of a Cabot to the Tech prom.

Jean pleaded a psychology exam. Then came the inevitable gossip about New Orleans society and that famous Mardi Gras at Mère Du Bignon's.

"Of course, Jean, you must know Mère Du Bignon."

"I certainly do; she is my great-grandmother."

A chorus of awed comment arose, but Jean continued: "But you see, I am from the colored Du Bignons."

This bombshell cleared the room and filled the two campuses for days. Even the Dean of Radcliffe thought it necessary to intervene.

"Pardon me, Miss -er -Du Bignon, but do you think it was wise or—necessary thus to reveal your colored blood?"

"Why not?"

"Well you see, facts are facts; American race prejudice cannot be ignored and you must realize that hereafter your position here may be embarrassing."

Jean faced her and blazed, "All right, then let it be. I'm going to lie neither for you Northern hypocrites nor to Southern rebels. I am colored and I don't care a damn who knows it. This, Madam, I trust finishes the subject."

It did so far as the college officials were concerned. They would not even consider disciplinary action on account of her language. But in the student body it was a topic never to be forgotten. Jean had, with all her experience, never dreamed how vital "color" was in American life. She found herself compelled to face everything from studied neglect to actual violence as, for instance, when she felt called on to slap a man's face in front of the John Harvard statue. The reason was never explained.

Her whole contact with the student body slowly but subtly changed. Instead of the crowd of well-dressed and perfumed girls who used to rush to greet her every appearance, she could now walk the whole length of the campus alone, which was a privilege after an inspiring lecture. Idle young men no longer got under her feet when she went to the post office or the Co-op. Students not only did not eagerly seek her notebooks, but also when quite unconsciously she turned to her neighbor for consultation the neighbor was often gone.

But not always. Slowly other students whom she did not remember ever having seen before would greet her diffidently or wait for her at the lecture hall door, or on the long walk. She began to realize to her amusement that she was collecting a new set of friends and acquaintances and that her earlier criticism of the shallow caliber of the average student must be revised. For the most part she was relieved and went at her work with new zest. Sometimes she was rather lonely and at a loss for someone to talk to, or angry at some awkward insult. But when she began to pick her companionship she discovered a wealth of friends.

There were even some men, usually from the west, who really wanted to talk with her in public without venturing into indecencies. Once she deliberately walked with a black male student across the campus. But he was evidently so uncomfortable that she did not try this again until her senior year. Then she escorted a crowd and soon had as many whites as blacks.

Becoming interested in history and sociology she was also attracted by the new experimental psychology which was being built on the work of Freud. She had discussed her studies with her grandmother during the summers, and the grandmother, despite her predilections and her deep belief that women had no business in college, found herself increasingly interested in what Jean was doing and thinking. Nevertheless, after graduation Mère Du Bignon expected Jean to come and live with her; but no, Jean wanted to take her Doctorate. Mère Du Bignon was aghast. She did not know what a doctorate was or what it was for. She only knew that no lady in her experience had done such a thing, and what on earth would Jean do after she became this kind of a doctor?

"I'll tell you what, grandmother. I think I want to study races of the world and their relations, and I think that the United States is undoubtedly the best place to do that. Here we've had a long and most interesting contact between whites and blacks."

To which Mère Du Bignon replied that you could not have contacts between men and beasts. That the whites had dragged the Negroes up as far as they could and now they were sinking back to where they belonged. The discussion continued off and on during Jean's visit. Then at last came time for decision.

It was in New Orleans in 1918, in the French quarter south of Canal Street. Behind beautifully wrought iron gates lay an old mansion. In the blooming flowers of its garden, sitting in an old armchair, was a massive woman, tall, old, beautiful, with silver hair piled on her head, with dark traces of moustache on her lip.

She was weeping and swearing, clasping with wild abandon in her arms a young woman.

"Sapristi," she yelled, "sacre nom de dieu! Mille tonerres, imbecile, cochon! Why must you go? Why will you act like an idiot?"

The girl answered patiently, with a calm face on which perhaps was the shadow of a smile. "Now, grandmother," she said, "what's the use of going over all this again? You know perfectly well why I must go. It is because I want to be a human being, and not a pampered fool. There is no life for me here. I am neither white nor black. I do not object to this, but most people do. I am going, therefore, to make my own way. I am not going to stay in this peculiar, anomalous and crazy position."

"But," stormed the old woman, "there is many a person here in New Orleans with as much black blood as yours, passing as white. Why shouldn't you?"

"Simply because I do not want to. I am interested in this matter colored people because they explain the whites."

"But you can work with them here."

"No, I cannot. Here I am neither one nor the other unless I entirely desert the one. I won't do that. There's no use yelling and screaming about it. You know that my mind is made up and that when I make up my mind I usually carry my intentions through."

"Yes, yes, I know it only too well. You are determined to make a fool of yourself. What I ought to have done was to marry your grandmother off when she got these crazy notions and sent her north or to civilized France. But I let her hang around here until she got big with your mother. And now, after you have twined yourself in and around my heart you are deserting me. Well, go, and God go with you."

Suddenly Jean realized how old Mère Du Bignon had become.

"Grandmère," she suddenly stopped and asked, "How old are you?"

"None of your damned business," blurted the old woman truculently; and then characteristically, added: "I'm going to die soon, Honey, and then the vultures will gather."

Jean started back to her chamber which was in the far reaches of the vast house where she could have quiet for study. She had been planning to write Chicago University for entrance to the Graduate School this Fall. But now what would she do? How about money which hitherto Mère Du Bignon had furnished readily? Would she offer it now? and if she did should she accept it? Should she leave the old woman here, alone with her awful family and hangers on?

She had little time to consider because the very next day, unflinching, Mère Du Bignon looked Death straight in the face. She lay in her great bed swathed in lace and silk, with streaming hair and ravaged face.

"Send for Jean," she gasped, "Send for that white bitch!"

But the relatives milling about, sent no word to Jean. Why should they? The old harridan might alter her will at the last and leave what little was left of the Du Bignon estates to this proud darky. And there was little enough left from the bankruptcy of this once vast barony. So with one voice they answered, "Yes, grandmère,—at once dear Maman," and vicious as they were, without the chamber hissed, "Forget it; let that nigger never know."

Mère Du Bignon wept and raved: "The ungrateful devil—cochon noire. I'll cut her off with not a penny, my Jean, my beautiful hateful Jean."

But Jean came. The colored retainers saw to that and relayed the message to her at once. She came, rushing hastily through patio and hall, pushing the angry relatives aside. The old woman glanced up and smiled.

"Jean, Jean my darling, I'm going. Two things. Give me your hand; bend over me. Slip this ring on your finger and shove this envelope up your sleeve. This is what I leave you. I wish it was more, much more; but it's stuff that can be turned into cash. There would be no use of putting you in my will. They'd upset it toute-de suite. Take these bonds to Huey Long—he's nothing but a cracker but he's the only one I trust. He knows of you." She sank back exhausted, but roused herself as Jean straightened up: "One thing more, now, and don't fail. Have you heard? The Bishop of Uganda is in town. He preaches tomorrow in the Cathedral. He is from Africa. I owe Africa much. I want him to shrive me!"

"But Grandmère, he—he's black."

"Nonsense, no Bishop could be black. Do as I say and quick, before I die." Mère Du Bignon whispered her last command: "He will come here; the Archbishop will bring him to give me the last blessing and usher my soul into heaven. Do you hear? Give him my orders!"

Jean flew to the Archbishop's palace. There was hesitation and questioning. But even the Archbishop could not question the command of Mère Du Bignon. The black Bishop of Uganda came, with the white Archbishop of New Orleans. With altar boys and waving of incense, with low song, he entered the great and ornate chamber of death, in cloth of gold, alb, surplice and mitre. The great lady lay still wtih closed eyes, her silver hair outspread, her jewels gleaming, her silk and lace-embroidered gown sewn with silver and gold, her hands covered with rings, her face hewn grandly in the last marble pallor of death.

As the tall dark bishop intoned she opened her black eyes. They widened and stared; she gave a frightened whisper:

"Sacré nom du nom! Le Saint Sauveur est noir! By my Faith and Salvation, of this I never dreamed; forgive me Almighty God!" And Hortense Du Bignon died in the ninety-ninth year of her stormy life.

Jean did not attend the funeral; she knew how imposing and crowded it would be and what efforts would be made to thrust her aside. Instead she packed her belongings and sought the office of Huey Long, the busy State Railway Commissioner. He knew of her, expected her, and welcomed her breezily. He mentioned the dead woman with deep respect and then asked of Jean's plans.

"I think grandmother was a little insane on the subject of Negroes," said Jean. "The blacks really, you know, are doing some extraordinary things and if they had half a chance they'd do more. But it is not simply of blacks and their relations to whites: I am thinking of blacks as human beings and whites as human beings and the way in which they contact each other. And I want to work on that."

Huey Long expressed more sympathy than she expected. He said, " 'Niggers' are rising. Never doubt that. Go on and study. Teach 'em. When you're ready for a job, consult me."

At one time he had told Mère Du Bignon of the Negro school that he was promoting in Louisiana.

"I'm going to make it the biggest damn 'nigger' college in the United States," he said.

"All right," Mère Du Bignon had said, "give my granddaughter a job in it."

"What? A white woman in a colored school?"

"Oh, she has a touch of the 'nigger' in her and feels it more than anything else."

Now he examined the bonds Jean brought. "They're good; but sell them now. Don't wait or the Du Bignon clan will be after them like a pack of wolves. Here, turn them over to me. Sign this. There'll be at least $10,000 to your account in Chicago tomorrow. Leave tonight."

Jean left. She was easily admitted to Chicago University and secured her doctorate in Sociology in 1921. She wrote Huey Long and he gave her a letter of commendation to the head of the Negro College he was promoting.

It was thus that Jean went over to Southern University for a visit. She asked the principal to recommend her to a school. No, she did not want to teach at Southern. That was too near New Orleans. Very good. He gave her a recommendation to President Mansart of the new Georgia State College; merely writing that she was "colored" and not mentioning how slight her color was. He emphasized the fact that she was a Doctor of Philosophy and that she wanted to teach but would help in his office as stenographer and assistant, if needed.

Mansart seized the opportunity quickly, writing out a telegram and carrying it to the telegraph office himself lest it might otherwise go astray or cause professional jealousies on his staff.

A quick reply came naming a date which he forgot. Today he remembered and wished to God again that he had some secretarial help. He was telling his woes to his son, Douglass, who was just returning to his study and job in Atlanta after a weekend with the family. Mansart always hoped that Douglass would sometime decide to join the school and take over some of the administrative and clerical work. But Douglass was too wrapped up with his insurance business in Atlanta. He did not think much of hiring this Du Bignon woman.

"Too damn much education, especially for a woman and for secretarial work. You need a smart business woman and you'll have to pay her plenty."

"But I could never get permission to pay a secretary more than six hundred dollars, and what teacher knows shorthand?"

Soon Jean was in a cab wheeling toward the station. She took a seat in the parlor car and was hardly settled before Huey Long came blustering in, short, stout, with uncombed hair, clothes rather mussy, and a loud voice.

"I want the drawing room," he yelled. The porter tried to mollify him.

"Commissioner, we just didn't have one left. But after all, the ride isn't long."

"Oh, all right. I'll sit here." Then he saw Jean. "Hello. I know you. Yes, you're Jean Du Bignon. Yes, yes, I remember all about you."

The girl smiled. "I am gratified, Mr. Long. I have just started out on my life pilgrimage."

"That so? Where are you going?"

"To Macon."

"And what are you going to do there?"

"I'm going to work in the new colored state college."

"Well, well, well! Damn fool thing to do! But I'm interested to see you doing it. You know, we've got to pay more attention to this 'nigger' question. Know where I'm going now? I'm going to Baton Rouge. I'm going to stop off there to see one of the smartest colored men I know. He's got a school there, you know, the school I wrote you about, Southern University.

"I've just been looking over Howard. We've got to give money to these Negroes, build up their schools and build them up. One of these days they're going to vote. I'll be glad when the day comes. You tell the fella that runs that school—what's his name—Mansart?—yes, yes, I've heard of his name. You tell Mansart to go to the new governor or the man who's slated to be the next governor, Scroggs. Tell Scroggs I said to give his college next year ten times as much money as he's giving this year. Tell him it will be an investment that will pay."

And so he ran on for an hour until they came to Baton Rouge, talking loudly and waving his hands. Then he got up and cried, "Well, so long Jean. Good luck to you. Good bye."

And so Jean Du Bignon rode on to Macon. In Macon she was expected, although Manuel Mansart really knew little or nothing about her, least of all had he any idea that this colored girl who had applied for a secretaryship and was so unusually well-equipped, was of Negro descent to be sure, but so white that none would have suspected her descent.

She expected most of the difficulties which she met. She had come in on a pullman train and was naturally mistaken for a white person. She asked the cabman to take her to the Negro State School, and he being sure that she had been somehow misled, took her to Sykes, the member of the Board of that school who was best known in Macon. Sykes received her with great politeness while the cabman waited outside. Unperturbed, Jean told him that she was the new secretary to President Mansart of the colored State College and had asked to be guided there, although the cabman, evidently by mistake, had brought her here.

Sykes immediately told her that a white girl could not be secretary to a Negro, and she explained patiently that she was a "Negro," smiling a little as she said it. His air immediately changed. She was used to that. He sat down slowly, and his manner assumed a little truculence as he looked her over appraisingly, with lowered eyelids.

"I think I could arrange to give you secretarial work."

"But I have a job."

"Yes, I know, but that isn't suitable for you and, er, I can afford better wages than that school can."

"Thank you, sir, very much, but I have already given my word and I'm going to keep it." She rose. "Can you tell me how to reach the school?"

He hesitated, but there seemed nothing else to do.

"Well, of course, a white cabman can't take you there, and I don't know where you can find a Negro."

"Very well, I'll try," she said, and walked out. She then had a talk with the white cabman. He finally promised to drive down by the square where a colored cabman might be picked up. This was arranged after some bargaining, and the charging of a fee considerably larger than was legal. Finally, about four o'clock, two hours after arrival, Miss Du Bignon walked into President Mansart's office.

To all appearances she was white, tall and slim, well poised, with a humorous cast of countenance and soul. The President rose and came forward politely. It was not often that a white woman came to his office, but he was always careful to treat them with consideration.

"Yes, madam," he said, "what can I do for you?"

Douglass stood with his back toward them, looking out the window.

"I am Jean Du Bignon," said the girl pleasantly.

The President stared at her and Douglass whirled about and stared, too. Jean stood easily and thought to herself, "well, here we go again." She explained that she had come in answer to the offer that he had made to give her a trial as teacher and secretary.

"Yes, yes," said the President, "but I—I of course assumed you were colored."

"I am," said Jean patiently, and waited.

The President sat down. Douglas glared resentfully, and the girl still stood. Then Manuel came to his senses.

"Why, of course, of course. Sit down, won't you? I—frankly, Miss Du Bignon, I—I didn't know—you were so white. I—I don't know whether we really could use you."

"Why not?" said Jean. "There are lots of white people with Negro blood."

Douglass bridled. "Well, why don't they go on and be white, then," he said. "We've got plenty of colored girls who need work."

But the President had gotten hold of himself by this time. "Miss Du Bignon, if you want to try, I'm going to—er-let you. I'm not sure that this is the kind of work that will interest you."

"I'm sure it is," said Jean. And she told him about her conversation with Huey Long.

The result was that with the almost open opposition of Douglass, Miss Du Bignon was soon installed as President Mansart's secretary, with the vague promise of a class in Sociology "as soon as practical." She had an assistant, a good-looking young colored girl who resented her presence from the start; and an untrained student clerk. She took hold of a situation that was plainly a mess: many letters unfiled; some correspondence unanswered, and even a part of it unopened; office equipment missing, typewriters old and shaky. She studied the situation, tried unsuccessfully to get on pleasant terms with the other office help, and then went and sat down and had a heart-to-heart talk with Manuel Mansart.

He appreciated it. It relieved him immensely. She touched on just the problems that he knew had to be attacked. The office had to be re-organized, there must be one or two new and modern typewriters, and other office machines. There must be a system of receiving visitors and protecting the president from chance callers. There must be a system of filing.

Then, leaving the office of the President, Jean Du Bignon went up to her little room and had a talk with herself. The room was small and neat; it was sparsely furnished with bed, washstand and bureau. The walls were painted white and were without pictures.

But the wide window looked on a beautiful stretch of yard, unkept but with natural glory of grass and vine and wild flower. Across it went an almost continuous stream of humanity; student, teacher and worker, and all colored. Jean sighed luxuriously; it was such a relief to see color, unconfined, free, content. To glimpse seldom if at all, the bloodless, straight features of that dominant world in which all her life she had been imprisoned, no longer set about her in unsmiling superiority. She felt at long last free in her own world. She sensed no incongruity in the fact that her face was white; she was only keenly aware that the people she wanted, to whom she felt nearest, were now about her and that for and with them hereafter she was to work. She was not unconscious of the fact that these her people would not automatically or easily accept her, veiled as she was in a hated color of skin. Already the President's son had rejected her. But this she cast aside gaily. Acceptance would come. She would make it and it was the natural thing, for race was not color; it was inborn oneness of spirit and aim and wish; and this made this school her home; her very own.

CHAPTER VIII

THE SCHOOL BECOMES A COLLEGE

The difficulty with the position which Manuel Mansart now assumed was that it had no precedent in the South. Most Negro colleges were headed by white Northerners and supported by Northern alms. The few private schools supported by colored churches had Negro presidents but were of small importance. The new colored state schools had nominal Negro principals but the real authority rested in the hands of the white trustees, usually represented by some local white man. The new colored state colleges now arising in every Southern state had Negro presidents but they were usually, in law or in custom, subordinated to the presidents of the corresponding white schools. The integration was not complete for fear of the federal funds involved but so far as possible the colleges were run as subordinate parts of the main white institutions. Gradually, however, a change was coming. A type of Negro administrator was arising who was quite as capable as the white presidents and sometimes better educated. He tended to become an independent president of a really separate Negro college.

What Baldwin had planned in the case of this new and more important state Negro college was that Coypel, of the University of Georgia, should be the real head and Mansart his assistant. But Coypel from the first had other plans and when he had demanded the title of "President" for Mansart, he meant that Mansart should exercise the power of his position. In this, Coypel was within his rights and was following the wording of the state law; the trustees decided the allocation of funds, and Coypel signed checks, but Mansart as president planned expenditures and reported directly to the state. It was soon clear who was really running the school.

How now should this Negro with unusual power and influence be treated? He could be called by his first name and treated as Negroes in general were treated. But this might cause some white contractor or merchant to incur his enmity. It was this question that confronted the chief city book seller as he confronted Miss Du Bignon and demanded to see Mansart immediately. Miss Du Bignon was very courteous.

"Mr. Stearns, you will understand that President Mansart has a lot to do, a good deal more than any one man can attend to, and he cannot receive anyone at any time."

"I must see Manuel now," answered Stearns, and he went on in. Evidently one of Miss Du Bignon's first big jobs was to take up the Stearns problem. She told Manuel about Sykes and his offer of a job to her, and Manuel told her about the building contracts.

"Now, I hope I'm not intruding," said Jean, "but, Mr. President, in order to do your work properly, you must assert yourself. Stearns wants to sell us books and to talk this over at his own time. Barclay has certain teachers whose appointment he wishes to push. There are several men who are looking for contracts. Most of these men call you by your first name and burst into your office at any time they choose. This must stop. It degrades you in the eyes of your students and colored constituents and it ruins your work. Will you put this matter of appointments in my hands?"

Mansart hesitated but finally assented. He knew that this apparently minor matter might be serious. Jean went ahead and put a lock on his door which she could manipulate from her desk. Stearns returned the next day. He ignored her but could not open Mansart's door.

"What's the matter here?"

"I am."

"What?"

"I'm afraid you did not hear me say that the President is busy."

"I want to see Manuel now—"

Miss Du Bignon put on her best and coolest manner and looked Mr. Stearns straight in the eye.

"Listen, Mr. Stearns; you can't see him, because I say so. When you do, you will address him by his title and not by his first name. If not, we'll buy our books hereafter in Atlanta. If you do not believe this, try it out."

"Listen, young woman, let's understand each other. I like Manuel. I am giving this school good bargains—"

"True, and we know it. But one bargain you refuse to give and that is the respect which is due a State official, and without which he cannot do his job. We'd rather pay more for books and less for insult."

They looked at each other. Mr. Stearns was no fool. He was in fair way to make good profit off this school and this woman might wield more power on both sides of the color line than he suspected.

Some chance colored visitors wanted to walk in on the president in the midst of his work and were stopped by the pleasant and firm Miss Du Bignon, and sometimes went away quite mollified even if they did not see President Mansart at the time.

It took considerable time to install these improvements and innovations, but within a couple of months the office was transformed. The former chief clerk had left in high dudgeon, and this presented a new problem to the office because she was related to alumni of the school and to prominent colored residents of Macon. But Jean met that problem partially by hiring a young black girl who had real ability and who had been overlooked in the search for help.

New filing cabinets were in place, new typewriters were bought, and in Mansart's own office mail was opened, read and answered, for the most part the same day it was received.

This was but one kind of difficulty with which Jean must cope and she realized it. She must not only help organize and systematize the general college administration, but in so doing the hindrance due to her color or lack of it could help in some cases and in others hinder. She must visit the city now and then. There she would meet difficulties, in stores, in elevators, on trains and on the streetcars.

Had she been black she would have encountered difficulties of one kind. Invariably, she was taken for white and then other difficulties arose. It was almost bitterly resented when she made known her drop of Negro blood. It was always a puzzle as to how to do that. If she went into an elevator the men took their hats off. Should she tell them that they were making a mistake? That, of course, would be silly; but she felt like it sometimes. If she went into a store, the clerks were all obsequiously at attention. In her personal shopping there was no difficulty about trying on shoes or hats or gloves or coats, but then sometimes, inevitably, she had to let them know. Perhaps most often this came in giving her address. Streets and localities had racial identities in most of the stores.

"Where?" a clerk would ask sharply, stare at her and perhaps leave the "Miss" off her name when he wrote her address.

In stores when they learned she was buying for the Negro college, she must always be on guard against being cheated, against being sold one grade of goods and having a cheaper grade delivered at the same price. She was always pressed to buy more than she intended and continually offered bribes, either gifts or discounts or actual money. There was no use getting angry; she would calmly refuse or in emergency call in the proprietor. Occasionally, the whole matter had to be referred to President Mansart. Gradually, however, the stores learned that they were dealing with a level-headed woman whom it was profitable to treat honestly.

On the streetcars, she usually tried to sit in the middle; but even then there would be difficulties. Perhaps she would sit down deliberately beside a black woman and the conductor would try to make her move. Or, perhaps a white man would offer her his seat in front and she would refuse, to his confusion. Once or twice, when she was sitting with colored men, chivalric white men tried to rescue her from their proximity or escort. Sometimes it was very funny. Sometimes it was near tragedy. She bought a small car as soon as she could, and realized why so many Negroes who could hardly afford it, owned cars.

It was a most puzzling world, and yet she liked life, and the curious thing was she wanted to be colored. The more she saw of white folk, the more she liked Negroes. She knew whites and understood them. She was not at all torn by a desire to be white. She did not hate her black blood; she loved it, because she had loved her grandmother, Marie, and her friend, Sarah.

Jean's trouble came not entirely from whites; they flared from blacks most unexpectedly. On the campus, she spoke to everyone she met. The students took this as a matter of course; the teachers always let her speak first, which she easily did. But in the city, this was sometimes difficult; in the welter of white and black faces and with the whites taking her for white and cordially receiving her, the blacks on the contrary were suspicious and resentful, and too ready to assume that she wished to ignore them. With the best effort, she now and then failed to recognize some new colored acquaintance.

Once a man, a workman on the campus had passed before she

realize who he was. When she saw him next on the campus, she started to apologize but he flared:

"You damn nigger, ef you don't wants to know me when youse white, jes forgit me when youse black."

She forgot him but never mentioned the incident. He neither forgot nor forgave, and assiduously spread the gossip that the "Du Bignon woman" wanted to "pass." This was annoying and could not be met—it could only be lived down.

On the other hand, the advances of white men never ceased. Deliberate approach by white men was difficult to avoid and yet if not stopped might be so serious as to cause the President trouble if not to require her dismissal from the work which she knew she was going to enjoy. Ownership of women was standard pattern in the white South. It was limited by the social standing of the white woman and the knowledge that infraction of this code might mean death. White women of ordinary status must fend for themselves, protected by white public opinion and the white police. Colored women must depend on their men, who also might in turn become themselves the attempted aggressors. In the case of a colored girl, too white to be distinguishable, the plight was doubly dangerous: so much so that sometimes flight was the only alternative.

In New Orleans, the power of the Du Bignon clan was strong enough to protect even its colored clients. But in Macon, Jean had been in residence scarcely a month when a young white man openly spoke to her on the street. He was handsome and in cadet uniform. He passed but a casual word which bystanders would hardly have noticed but which Jean knew to be an invitation to meet him down the street. She paid no attention to it and went up the street and then returned to the college by a round-about route. The next week, the same man waved at her from a sheltered store entrance and again she paid no notice. Then began a series of phone calls to the office followed by written notes, becoming more and more frank and professing "love" and firm determination to meet her. Finally, on the street she appealed to a policeman, which sent the young man sauntering off. But soon she realized that this was a mistake, for the next day this policeman leered at her. Later, he handed her a paper which she thought was an official notice of some sort—perhaps for wrong parking of her little Ford. But it proved to be a violent love note from the cadet, demanding a rendezvous next Saturday along a well-known country road.

This was serious. She did not dare yet to tell the President. There was nothing he could do without endangering his own status and the institution. She had been making careful and discreet inquiry through students whose parents worked for leading white families. She learned that the Cadet was Captain Sparks, of a well-placed and wealthy family. He was affianced to the Christie girl, leader of the younger Macon white smart set. He was headstrong and wild, else he never would have ventured on this dangerous flirtation. He was too often drunk. For this very reason, he must be stopped or he woudl be dead and she hopelessly compromised. She made up her mind quickly. Taking his last note she got into her car and drove directly to the residence of Miss Christie. The girl came down quickly, smiling and holding out her hand—

"I've forgotten your name," she began.

Jean did not take her hand but said, "You do not know me and I must apologize for this unwarranted intrusion, but I felt compelled to come. I am Jean Du Bignon and I am colored."

The smile faded and a puzzled look came on the girl's face. She hesitated, but Jean continued before Miss Christie could decide whether or not to ask her to sit or indeed what to do.

"Miss Christie, I am in a terribly embarrassing position and I hardly know how to begin to tell you. But the fact is that I have just had this note from Captain Sparks and from what I hear you ought to see it."

Miss Christie read the note and froze. The blood left her face and flooded back. Jean stood quite still as the girl crushed the paper and went to the window. She stood there for a couple of minutes. Then she returned with herself in complete control. She looked at Jean coldly.

"How did you get this?"

"It was handed me by policeman Monaghan."

"Where?"

"On Main Street before Klieg's stone."

"How did you know it was from—Captain—Sparks?"

"I have received other notes,—and he has spoken to me."

"Where do you live?"

"I work at the Negro State College." She paused but the girl said no more.

Jean turned and said, "I am very sorry. I realize that this is but the prank of a thoughtless young man; but I am compelled to protect myself. Good day." She left.

When she returned to the college, she went to the President's office and told him the whole story, giving him the other notes received and a schedule of the phone calls. He listened and read the notes.

"This is serious," he said, "but I am not sure but you did the only possible thing. We'll wait."

The next afternoon a tall, rugged white man, erect and well-dressed, entered the president's outer office. Jean was at the desk and arose.

"Can I help you, Sir?"

"I am John Christie. Are you—" he paused, "Jean Du Bignon?"

"I am."

"You called on my sister yesterday and made serious charges —very serious."

"Yes, sir. I have just told the facts to President Mansart. Will you talk to him?" She ushered him in. The president showed him to a seat.

"I am sorry for this, Sir, more sorry than I can say. Miss Du Bignon has just told me the facts."

"Who is this girl?"

"She is an excellent person with a good education. She has been here six months. She came with good references and has become indispensable in my work. Yet the college comes first and if you demand her withdrawal she must go. But such a course would be unfair. I should hate to take it."

"But, damn it, Mansart, what can be done? This is my sister. Sparks is a — gentleman. Can I—"

"Pardon me, but Miss Du Bignon is a lady despite her drop of black blood. This affront to her was no fault of hers—"

"Are you sure of that?"

"I am absolutely certain."

"Very well. Call her." When she entered, Christie said abruptly: "You say that you received this note from Sparks?"

"I received it from Officer Monaghan."

"You have had other notes?"

She handed him several, which he read.

Then he said, "Very well. this must come to a final settlement. Do you know this place that he has pointed out? Have you been there with him?" He hesitated, "—or anyone?"

"No," said Jean. "I have never been there. I know in general where it is. I have seen it in driving."

"You have a car?"

"Yes, it's outside."

"I want you to meet him there."

Jean hesitated. And then she said frankly, "I am afraid."

"You need not be. We, I and my sister, are going to be near. I want you to drive there, get out and speak to this young man. Then we will appear."

Jean hesitated and looked at him and at Mansart. "This," she said, "is asking a great deal. I do not know whether it would be wise to follow your advice, but if the President wishes I will. The hour that he has set is 6 o'clock. It is 5:30 now. Shall I go?"

"Yes." Mansart sat down heavily.

She went out and got into her car rather numbly. Was this the end of her career? It might be the end of her life. She drove slowly along the roads, up the hill and down, to the rise that looked toward the river and the meadows, and then around the corner. For a moment she stopped. Then she drove on. In the twilight she saw him standing by the big oak, just off the road. She drove up, stopped, got out and faced him. As he started forward she stiffened, and he saw the grimness on her face. Impetuously he cried:

"Darling! Sweetheart! Don't look so tragic! I knew you would come. Listen to me!"

And then came the voice behind him. "Perhaps first, Jack, you had better take this back, so as to be free to talk." And Miss Christie handed him the engagement ring. He turned and looked at her and paled. Then he whirled upon Jean.

"You damned bitch!" he said. But there came another voice.

"That will do, Sparks. You did write that note? You did make this appointment?"

Sparks looked at Christie and his face went dead. "Yes," he said.

"Then," said Christie, "if you are not out of this town tomorrow morning, I am going to kill you."

Sparks turned and left.

Jean trembled a bit as she climbed back into her car. Christie said, "You may follow us back to the city."

But Miss Christie said, "Wait, I will drive with you." And she got into the car with Jean, while Christie drove ahead.

"I am sorry," she said. "I am very, very unhappy. I want to talk to myself, alone." Jean did not wince at the implication but drove slowly and steadily, while the other car rushed ahead. The girl sat straight and aloof and talked in a low monotone.

"I am that most unfortunate of human beings, a young rich white woman living in the South. I do not know whom to call friend. I do not know who is telling me truth or falsehood. I do not know the difference between good and evil.

"I am bound hand and foot. I am guided and advised; I am watched and criticized. I am told what to think and what to do and how to look. But of myself I know nothing. I am alone in a lonely world. My parents are dead: my father died re-fighting the Civil War; my mother died trying to keep rich; my sister lives in perpetual boredom leading society. My brother never lived— he dressed. And me? I eat, I drink, I dress, I play cards. I am waiting not to be given but to be sold in marriage. I have been trained to seek men like Heaven and fear them like Hell. Are all women like that? Is this the horrid lot of all? I was told that Love was Sin or Salvation. I have just seen it was only cheap Lust. I want to die. I would God I could die now!"

They came to the white pillars of the Christie mansion. Her tall brother, impeccably dressed, stood awaiting her. The car stopped. Without a word the young lady got out and took her brother's arm. Neither looked back. Wordless, they turned and walked up the flower embroidered path. The black butler silently opened the great front door.

Gradually, by 1924, Manuel Mansart came to be a respected official of the State of Georgia, whose position as president of a college was recognized. There was much to be settled as to the policies of the institution, but these matters were now settled by frank conference in which the black president was listened to with courtesy.

First of all, there came a great deal of argument with teachers, students, trustees and the public as to the courses of study which this Negro school should offer. At first, there was strong and loud talk from the trustees about the industrial training that Negroes must have and the waste of higher training. Said a member of the legislature at the first meeting of the Board:

"What we want in this school is the teaching of work: preparing Negro boys and girls to carry on our work well, intelligently and carefully."

"What work?" asked Mansart.

"All sorts of work."

"Masonry, carpentry, machinery, use of metals, textile spinning and weaving, chemistry of soils and foods—"

"Oh no, no. White workers will do such things. I mean cooking, cleaning, sewing, plowing, harvesting."

"But all these they know now in practice. They shrink from this work because it is paid almost nothing and the conditions of work are bad. This work could be better done if the workers knew how to read and write and cipher well; if they studied physics and chemistry so as to handle food and soil, and if they learned of commerce and markets."

"Negroes don't need all that. Education of that kind spoils a field hand."

"Then why have schools for Negroes at all?"

"Well, if you ask me—"

The Governor interrupted: "Nonsense. The worker, white and black, needs education. He must read, write and count well. Then he must know something of modern science. After that, most of them should enter industry."

But Mansart insisted: "But what branches?"

A merchant said: "I should say first of all the building trades which for ages they have done well in the South; then agriculture —modern, scientific agriculture; housework on a high level with machines; science—"

And Mansart added: "With high wages and decent treatment."

But a white politician asked: "What will the white trade unions say to this?"

So it went on until in the end, finding themselves in contradiction and paradox, the whole matter was tossed back into Mansart's hands to work out as he could. Manuel brought into the next meeting of the Board a statement as to costs. What it would cost in machinery and shops to train students for agriculture and stock-raising, for the building trades, to teach cooking and housekeeping, sewing and cleaning. He explored other trades, cotton spinning, weaving, embroidery, metal work, carriage building, automobile repairs, shoemaking and shoe repairing, tailoring, and a dozen other things. Two objections immediately leaped to the fore, as Manuel knew they would. First, the cost. They couldn't afford all that land and money. And then, secondly, interference in the domain of white trade unions.

Notwithstanding the fact that Negroes had long been prominent in the building trades, the trade unions now among the whites were determined that state money should not be used for training Negro carpenters, bricklayers, or plumbers. So that, after all the fuss and fury, about the only thing that came out of the industrial training program was cooking and sewing, so as to furnish competent cooks and maids for white households. At least this was what the Trustees had in mind. Even agriculture must wait until the school could buy and equip a farm.

Thus, the difficulty about subjects of study was the question as to whether these boys and girls were to be trained to do only what they were doing at present, and do it more efficiently; or be trained for future work which they hoped they might do. It was not altogether a matter of the humble status of their present work, but the fact that this work was not enough really to engage their talents and especially that it was wretchedly paid; and of course, in addition to that they wanted not simply to be laborers, servants and nurses; they wanted to enter the professions as lawyers, doctors and teachers. They felt that they could do this kind of work.

If, however, their colleges trained them for that now, they were training them for a possibility of employment which might not materialize in some time; and at the same time, they were depriving the surrounding white folk of the South of their laborers and their servant class and their cheap wage. It was really a rather tremendous problem, including the practical questions as to how much should be spent on laboratories of physics and chemistry, what time should be given to history and sociology; should there be courses in music and drawing, and so forth and so on.

The trustees were pretty stubborn. They wanted a very strict and narrow program. But there again the only thing that was agreed upon was that the cost for equipment for any course was going to be considerable. The result was, as Manuel knew it would be, the Board came to no final conclusions and repeatedly left the matter to be worked out by himself and President Coypel of the State University in such a way as would necessarily result in considerable deception and camouflage. In the long run, the college would have to adopt the traditional college course of studies and only be careful not to put too much stress upon the humanities.

When it finally came to the regular subjects of study, Manuel very easily could show that if children were going to read and write, they had to be taught by teachers who knew something about reading and writing. If they were going to learn history, they had to have teachers trained in history and the best trained were none too good.

So that after a while and after a great deal of argument, Manuel was able to put into the institution the curriculum of a modern high school and in addition that of a college suited eventually to train men and women who could enter life and the graduate schools of the North. But all this took a long time and it was difficult to accomplish.

His problems were the problems of all schools and all colleges, but they were emphasized in his case. This was a school subject to all sorts of criticism. Criticism from the whites because they thought it was attempting to do too much or even the impossible. Criticism from the Negroes because the work was not really well done or was not aimed in the right direction. Many a midnight headache Manuel carried to bed over problems of this sort.

One of the difficulties about Negro industrial schools was that those Negroes who knew industry did not know manners. They were not the kind of people whom you wanted to put in control of students. They were often dirty, they usually used bad grammar; they were not used to associating with well-mannered people. It was much more difficult than one would think to get a man who could teach shoe repairing and also really occupy the place of a teacher of youth. But even beyond that, the kind of young colored man and woman who offered themselves to teach Latin, history, literature, mathematics, was not always the sort of person that Manuel wanted. He wanted a well-bred and well-mannered person who knew the world and its amenities; who knew how to sit at table, how to walk; who talked good English easily; who led his pupils into the green pastures of the modern world. If he laid too much stress here, it was because the white world criticized the black world so strongly just here.

He knew, of course, that he was asking from his teachers more than he himself could furnish. And yet he had ideals. He had been taught by well-mannered New England people. He had seen something of such folk in the North. He wanted his pupils to have the advantage of this. But, unfortunately, the ambitious and the pushing among the younger colored people, those who had gotten through college by hook or crook, who had gone to Northern institutions but had little contact or little opportunity to know the finer side of life, were the ones who got their degrees and offered themselves for teaching. They were apt to be cocky and careless. Their English was atrocious. Their manner of dress was careless. They had the disadvantages and the bad manners of all poor, struggling people who had come up from the depths, and he had a hard time choosing between them.

Sometimes he got another sort of young colored person; now from an old and well-bred colored Northern family; now from a Southern colored family of the house servant class; or even blood relatives of white aristocrats. But in these cases, the teacher was more than apt inwardly to despite both his job and his students. He could not forget what meager facilities the school had and how poorly trained the students were. He might feel so far above the colored people around him as to resent the task of always working with them and being hemmed in by their destiny. Such teachers acquired a sort of contempt for themselves which infiltrated into them from their continual environment. It became difficult for them to get on with each other and recognize each other's abilities and peculiarities.

Particularly was there difficulty with the wives of the teachers. They came from all sorts of strata. A pretty girl would be picked up and married by a young professor and prove to be about the last person to enter into the social life of a college faculty. A smart girl would be too critical; a poor housekeeper would set a bad example. All the time, quarrels were arising, difficulties, demands for appointment of such and such persons, and dismissal of others. It was enough to drive a president mad. Moreover, his choice was not free because of the number of persons who needed jobs and the friends who pushed them.

Mansart faced a certain opposition among educated Georgia colored people who saw this comparatively unknown upstart coming to the head of a school which was to be the chief Negro school of the State, and receiving a higher salary than most colored teachers or even other Negro college presidents. He had to be careful of them because this colored public opinion and atmosphere was powerful. After all, this institution belonged to the colored people of the state. They had a certain vested right in the work which it offered. So that all sorts of persons pushed their sons and daughters and their acquaintances for appointment and could not see why Manuel hesitated in cases which seemed to them so obvious.

"That gal of mine," said old man Moses, "has got a good education, and it sure cost a lot. I sent her up North three years, and now 'stead of giving her a job of teaching English, you bring down a Northern Negro. This school belongs to us. We don't want no high-falutin' outsiders coming in and getting money taken from taxes we pay. I wants that my gal gits the job an' gits it now!"

The discipline in the school brought endless and difficult problems. The school body, even more than the teachers, represented all levels and kinds of culture. There were some who came from families which for generations had had manners and some wealth. There were others who had crawled straight "out of the gutter," or out of equally bare and filthy plantation cabins. There were those who were lazy and slow and those who were impudent and quick. It was extremely difficult to apply the same rules, the same treatment and the same punishment to all these differing individuals.

Of course, the sex offenses before everything had to be watched and curbed and routed out. This was difficult in a country where for generations both white and black had had little discipline and less decency in the matter of sex. The social intercourse of boys and girls had to be watched and curbed in ways that Manuel hated but had to follow. One spinster who early had charge of girls came to him in a dither:

"Mr. President, I saw that boy Joyce kiss Mamie Saunders right on the steps of the dormitory. They should both be expelled."

Mansart wanted to commend Joyce's taste but he patiently argued that all caressing could not be stopped nor was it absolutely undesirable; and then next year he tried to get a new matron. But this was not easy. Persons of education and manners did not want this kind of job with its low pay, indefinite duties and embarrassing tasks. The code of social intercourse, therefore, was a rather singular patchwork, and its enforcement was always unsatisfactory.

And then, the matter of money and accounts raised all sorts of questions. Students who could pay their bills promptly, did not, through carelessness or something worse. Students who would have paid, had no money or it came irregularly. What should be done when such accounts accumulated? After all, it took money and it took a lot of it to run the school. The students, as a matter of fact and as Manuel could show his Board, paid a large proportion of the cost of their education, but the rest must be had; appropriations from the Legislature were hard to get, and it was difficult to show a people who had been systematically robbed that they should regularly pay bills owed to thieves whose fathers had bilked them.

The scholarship problem was also difficult. It was hard to make some students realize that studying was serious, and that it really did make a difference as to whether a student received 50 per cent in his marks or 75 per cent or 90 per cent; that the difference, although difficult to come by accurately and subject to all sorts of mistakes, and sometimes actually meaningless, nevertheless was an attempt to measure the degree of application, of knowledge and of understanding; and that they were in school to accomplish something in this line and not merely to play around with dreams. There was always the complaint of students who thought they were marked too low and perhaps were; of parents who knew that their children were not getting academic justice, and the much more serious complaints of those who were slow and dull and got their work only by struggle that brought blood; and the other sort of bright, careless and impudent students who would not work when they could, or did not think that studying was, after all, worthwhile.

In 1921 and later, there began a sign which encouraged Manuel a good deal, and that was the interracial work. A number of people, some of them connected with churches, others with social agencies, began to emphasize the fact that colored people and white people in the South did not meet each other as normal human beings. They met as servants and masters, in stores and in business and economic relations; they saw each other from the opposite ends of street cars and glimpsed each other on trains; but they did not attend the same schools or churches. They certainly did not meet under circumstances where they could talk about everyday life and humanize their relations.

A number of groups therefore were formed here and there, called "interracial," to get acquainted with each other. The movement began in Atlanta, after the riot of 1906, but did not last. Now it was revived. Theoretically, this effort was all right, but practically it had its difficulties. A few colored persons met white persons under entirely abnormal circumstances. What were they going to talk about? What was there in common in which they were interested? Most of the things of which they would like to talk involved differences and even violent differences of opinion. The schools, for instance; the question as to whether Negroes should attend white churches; the whole question of the relations of the Negroes to the police; and jobs and so forth.

If one were not careful, an interracial meeting would be an interracial fight. To avoid this, the interracial meetings tended to become innocuous, if not in a certain sense dishonest. When Manuel attended one he met, perhaps, a principal from a white school. He tried to say something pleasant and the principal tried to say the same thing. The result was that usually they said almost nothing. Then, there was always the man who from good or ill motives said the wrong thing and the untrue thing. Some colored men told the whites that colored people were quite satisfied with their own churches; that they wanted their own schools so as to have their own teachers; that the schools were on the whole in a prosperous condition and that they wanted to thank this white man or that man for what he had done in some racial difficulty.

So too, the whites on their side put themselves out to praise certain colored people whom they knew for actions which colored people had taken or had not taken. Thus, mutual admiration societies came into being, and while most of the people went away gratified that nothing unpleasant had happened, everybody knew that very little really had taken place and that the objects of interracial conference had not been accomplished. It thus became one of the problems which faced Manuel and his fellows to see how this kind of meeting begun so auspiciously and with such good will could be really made to accomplish something.

Real organization began at last among the women in the white Baptist and Presbyterian churches and under the leadership of Will Alexander and Mrs. Jessie Ames. White Southern women began to join and protest against the imputation that rape was always the reason for lynching; they looked into the matter of Negro education. They got money for propaganda. A central organization was formed, held meetings, began to get an endowment and issued literature. Mansart saw here a real beginning and tried to keep in close touch.

Music united all human beings, especially the Negro folk songs. In 1923, the works of Coleridge Taylor, especially his "Hiawatha," were performed in part at the new colored college with a great deal of interest. Some white people attended, but this brought up the perennial quesiton as to where they were going to sit, as to whether seats should be reserved for them; and how much special attention they should receive. It was not altogether a popular move. It was of interest to know that here was a Negro in England who was being given the best opportunity to become a great musical composer, and there was a question as to how far opportunities in a larger degree should be given to American Negroes. Among Americans Mansart was aware of a new impulse, of a distinct emergence of an American Negro literature and art.

CHAPTER IX

PRESIDENT MANSART

From the first, Mansart found startling contrasts between his work as a principal of a public school and his position as president of a state college. A colored school principal had very little real power. He was under the continuous scrutiny and direction of the white city superintendent of schools and his freedom of choice and action circumscribed by the attitude of his corps of teachers and the colored parents. They had direct contact with the superintendent and with other influential persons in the city. So that between his teachers and the school hierarchy of the whites, the colored parents, and the students, the principal amounted to little more than a chief clerk or an errand boy, and a representative of the impact of white power over black folk.

Mansart and his colleagues in colored state colleges in other Southern states evolved a subtle philosophy and method of work. They said little, they did not protest publicly, but quietly and persistently they kept pressing on, often winning victories, but staging no celebrations, never boasting but always insisting.

This concerted effort arose first by individual effort with little consultation. Then the presidents began to visit each other as they travelled, using each others' homes as hostels, in the absence of hotels for Negroes. Finally they formed a national organization of Negro Land Grant Colleges and here, more in personal contacts than in official action, they evolved a course of procedure.

Thus, as president of a state school, Manuel Mansart became a real center of power. The white South had never evolved a code of control for this new Negro entity. The Negro college was therefore a microcosm of the world in which he lived, and was as unmolested by the outer world as was possible for any group encased and dominated by that world. In this area, the city police entered only occasionally; the other white people practically only by invitation, and the president was the resident ruler.

Mansart soon realized that here at last, in the South, he escaped the recurrent threat of the mob. The whites were always armed and ready to cow and kill the blacks; to chase a runaway, to capture a rebel. After the Civil War and emancipation, the small town became the capital of oppression, with an armory, white militia and courts; here reigned lynch law and the mob rode north, east, west or south at the slightest provocation. In the city, the white police were always at hand with white armed citizens always ready to lend a hand. Only in the black slums, unlighted and unpaved, with ruins and hiding places, did the police walk warily and seldom, and always in couples or squads, while white firemen let the blaze burn or pillaged the homes. Here, the peaceful Negro was free of the white mob, but unprotected from the black thug. But on Mansart's campus, the dark dwellers were safe; no white man dared to invade this sanctuary and swagger and kick. Here swarmed a group of husky, red-blooded youth, with great eyes too easily filled with hate; white police could be called but they brought warrants, walked warily, and watched; they were careful to follow the forms of law. When once the luckless student was safe in jail, they could beat him up at leisure. But the police were seldom called and very rarely was a student arrested. Here was sanctuary from the white mob.

The president ruled over a physical kingdom. It was situated near the center of the state of Georgia, on the outskirts of the city of Macon, and his realm consisted of fifty acres which, with a few old buildings, had once been the campus of a colored private missionary school. This was, of course, to be only the beginning of the school. In a few years, a large tract of land suitable for a campus and farm was to be purchased. This would involve hard work and negotiation, not only with the legislature but with white real estate interests. But something must be worked out if the college survived. Manuel knew that once established, the surrounding land would be more available for purchase.

He ruled over a constituency which began with 500 students and teachers and eventually increased to over 2,000. For this constituency, he legislated. Of course, there were limits to his making of laws and rules—the limits of the state laws, the customs to which the state officials were used, especially in interracial matters; and certain special enactments made by the trustees. But the trustees were not an ever-present body. As a matter of fact, they met officially only twice a year and their executive committee hardly more than once in three months. At first, they were inclined to interfere in all matters, but as time went on and the school progressed, they interfered less and less.

If teachers were hard to choose and appoint, the trustees were even harder. In the first place, theoretically Manual had nothing to do with the choice of trustees. That was the perquisite of the Governor. The Governor worked through Coypel, and Coypel was advised by the State Board of Education and the University Regents. But especially the well-to-do whites of Macon looked upon the colored school as something which they could use for their own advantage, but when they sought to bring pressure on Coypel, they were invariably referred to Mansart. Just because Manuel, however, did not have a vested right to advise in the appointment of the trustees, he could work all the more sedulously for their selection. And in this he was backed up carefully by President Coypel, of the State University. So that by words dropped here and there, by pressure of all sorts, Manuel got a number of excellent men appointed to the Board.

He was not successful in all cases. Some scoundrels and grafters found their way to appointment. But on the whole, as time went by, the Board improved in character, and after a while by hard maneuvering and pressure a few colored men were appointed to the Board. They were not exactly assets, but they established a principle. Having gotten the appointment, they were apt to be all the more obsequious to the white members of the Board, and Manuel could often count on their voting wrong even when some of the white members in whom he had least faith would vote right.

Manuel found this Trustee Board, in the long run, was increasingly under his domination. As he began his work, it was a Board already set up by the Governor. It had a number of local white dignitaries and had, of course, no colored members. But these were all busy men and Mansart had only to satisfy them, to be let alone. Moreover, he found that when there was a vacancy he could not only advise but, after a few years, his advice was usually taken. So that when he had been in his position ten years, the Board was practically a Board which he had appointed.

Thus, his power to legislate, to make the laws and rules of this little realm increased tremendously until it had few limitations, and those the broader limitations of racial policy and expediency. He not only thus made the law but he carried out the law. He was the executive, and the spending of money came to be increasingly a matter of his planning and carrying out; and while checks were actually signed by state officials, they in time signed such checks as Mansart asked them to, and finally Mansart himself signed most checks with Coypel's co-signature. Appeal, of course, could be taken from his decisions, from his recommendations as to appointment and dismissal of teachers, from his laying out of courses of study, from a dozen and one different particular questions. But as time went on, appeals became less and less frequent until the teachers began to understand that he had the power of appointment and dismissal and that there was little use trying to go over his head.

Thus, he was legislature and executive and he was also judge. His decision in matters of discipline was practically final. His settling of disputes between departments and persons had limited appeal. He decided matters of salaries and tenure, and when the Legislature interfered, as it did now and then, he was the one who spoke for the college. Of course, all these results and this power developed after long years of trial and failure. Always, over and above him presided public opinion, and a peculiar public consisting of white and black, employers and laborers, parents and students.

While Mansart's relation to his trustees, his students and teachers, and also toward the merchants and contractors, seemed in line of reaching normal relations, his contacts with white labor were still to be considered. He knew the local labor situation pretty well. But the national labor problem he did not know, and was puzzled as to what to do. He wondered just what the situation was in the country at large. He went to talk it over with President Coypel. Coypel was ignorant of labor developments during the 20th century. He had understood that what was often called the "Atlanta Compromise," arising from Booker Washington's speech at the Cotton States Exposition, was an understanding that Negroes were to be trained for work and not so much stress put on higher education and politics. Now here were these labor unions practically telling Mansart that he couldn't use skilled colored on his own school work, and that he couldn't teach skilled trades. It really seemed ridicuous. Coypel mentioned the matter to Baldwin.

Baldwin explained. "Listen," he said, "the nation is having trouble with the labor unions, as you must know. The whole Tuskegee program, as we conceived it, was not so much to advance

Negroes as to repress white union labor. For a while, all tried to make alliance with white union leaders. Employers' trade associations and the unions signed wide agreements, and perhaps you have heard of the Civic Federation formed in Chicago in '96, which became a national organization in 1900. It discouraged strikes and recognized labor unions and so forth, and had some powerful people as members of it; ex-president Cleveland, John D. Rockefeller, the labor leader, Samuel Gompers. But white northern labor got ambitious, strengthened the unions, and we had to start out on a fight to smash them, and we're going to do it. But this will take time; and because of the political power of the white union men in the South, we cannot yet bring forward black skilled workers as their competitors."

"But," interrupted Coypel, "why should you divide the working class into two competitive parts? Why not let them form one union?"

"Because," said Baldwin, "that's just what we don't want. The reason we are going to educate the Negroes is to make them rivals to the white workers and keep down wages."

Coypel scowled, and the conversation that afternoon did not continue long. But both Coypel and Mansart began to watch the development of the labor world, the formation of the National Association of Manufacturers, the beginning of the open shop propaganda, and particularly that dreadful occurrence in Ludlow, Colorado, when to force the open shop, thirty-three people were killed and over a hundred wounded in a battle which lasted fourteen hours. The Miners Union lost. Manuel particularly began to read what the muckrakers were dragging in, and to realize the significance of the battle between capital and labor which was beginning in the United States.

The more subtle psychological problems which Manuel Mansart faced as president of the colored state college were of extraordinary variety. First, and overshadowing all, was the question of interracial attitudes. He was occupying an unusual position. Never before in Georgia had a Negro had the legal right to expend so large an amount of the state funds. He was a state official, and had power and responsibility. At the same time he was a Negro, and he was expected to act as a Negro. He was expected to show a certain humility and obsequiousness in the presence of white people of any sort.

Now if this attitude was carefully thought out and arranged it need not be difficult. But if not, it could be devastating. He set himself therefore carefully to meet white people courteously, but not cringingly. To raise his hat, especially when he addressed a white man, entered white homes or public places; to say "Sir" in addressing white people of any position; to be very careful to thank any white person who did even ordinarily courteous acts.

His family, particularly his sons, resented this. As an Atlanta school principal he had to be careful that they did not, like so many young Negroes, rush in the opposite direction and be deliberately impudent and discourteous, at least as far as they dared under given circumstances. He knew that his sons and other colored boys avoided meeting white people under any conditions where they had to show courtesy or even ordinary human sympathy.

All the more, in his present position, he had to do this. He did not like it, but it was not a question of "like," it was deeper than that. It was Duty; unpleasant—often irksome—but Duty. Then, there were certain things that called for curious thought and reflection. Take, for instance, the matter of an automobile. He needed a new one, especially for the many errands that he had and for the time that he must conserve. And since he would give it hard use, he needed a good one. But he must be careful. If he purchased an expensive automobile, he would be liable to criticism from white and black, and perhaps something worse from whites. It would probably be wiser to get an unobtrusive car of the cheaper sort, and then buy another when that broke down. This was the wisdom of the serpent. It brought tears akin to oaths from his sons, but he followed it out.

Other family and social complications followed. His wife began to attend the new Madame Walker's hair-dressing shop and to spend money there. He was very much upset. He called it foolishness and vanity and lack of "race pride." It showed she "wanted to be white." She retorted that no one more than colored men admired straight hair or elaborate hairdressing, and that moreover it was none of his business and that she was going to continue to go to the hairdresser.

This did not come up in the case of his daughter because Manuel had only one, and Sojourner was not a bit interested in hairdressing; but Bruce and Roosevelt Wilson, his pal, had a good deal to say about it with regard to the girls they associated with, and the general proposition of making oneself attractive. Finally, this matter of hair culture made considerable disturbance in the school. The girls wanted to go to the colored hairdressing shops in town, which the president regarded as very unwise. But if that was not allowed there ought to be arrangement for home hair-dressing in the dormitories, in the basement or in their rooms; and a good deal of serious discipline arose from what should have been a small matter.

It was just then that his wife decided that she wanted to join the new Episcopal church. This was a small mission church for Negroes just established by the fashionable white Episcopal church, and it had already attracted some of the upper class of colored people. Naturally, it was looked upon askance by most of the working black folk of the town.

Susan Mansart was tired of the noise and demonstration of the Baptist church in which she had been born. She wanted for herself and children something a little more respectable and reasonable. She wanted to be among better dressed people who used better English. She did not understand why it was anybody's business what church she attended. Manuel had to argue long and carefully.

"You see, Susan, we occupy an unusual position. We must not seem to be ashamed of their old customs and ways, and try to put on airs. In one sense, of course, our religion is our private business, but in another we are expressing the feeling of the whole community and that feeling must stand by the old beliefs and the old customs.

"The great mass of Negroes are Baptists and Methodists. Moreover, these churches are theirs, founded and organized by themselves. The others are churches of the whites. We have got to stick to our people."

Susan was outraged, and the result was a rather bitter quarrel in which Manuel had to exert his authority rather peremptorily because he realized that probably nothing would hurt him more at just that time than to have his wife and children desert the Baptist church and join the new Episcopalians.

There was another kind of problem which came from his intercourse and rivalry with Negro officials in other institutions—presidents of one or two of the smaller Negro colleges in the state, and with several of the large institutions outside the state. They ought all to work with a certain harmony and unity of aim. They did not. They were suspicious and jealous of each other. There were several who Manuel knew wanted his job and were scheming to get it and had a fair chance of accomplishing this unless he deftly watched his step. There were those occupying positions in his school and other positions in and outside his state who were only too ready to ostracize him and to succeed him whenever there was the slightest opportunity. He had to be extremely careful of those men, to realize their peculiarities, their ambitions, the particular difficulties which they, too, were facing, and try out of this rivalry to get a certain unity of purpose and concert of action, which was difficult.

By 1924, Mansart saw a problem approaching which he knew would cause trouble. It was now high time for a permanent campus with appropriate buildings to be planned and erected. A large tract of new land must be bought and this would raise the eternal question of the permanent location of a colored community and its relation not simply to white communities as distributed at present but with regard to white residential sections which real estate interests might have in mind.

Mansart knew well that this time the cormorants, as represented by Sykes, would be in force and carefully organized. Since his first encounter, he had had no further trouble with Sykes. But Sykes was still on the Board and was well-to-do and widely known. He had been influential in the beginning in having the Negro college established in Macon. Now, the matter of the general distribution and character of the college buildings had to be settled and Manuel felt that here would lay the real test of his administration.

He determined on his course of action; ample and suitable land must be purchased; the buildings must be good, substantial and pleasing; they must be convenient and well-placed; and he himself must have the right of consultation and final agreement before anything was settled. Again, there must be open and careful contracts drawn for supplies and for all dealings, especially with local merchants. And finally—and here Manuel set up his banners—there must be some colored skilled laborers hired on all building operations. Here was the real fight and here must be no surrender.

Mansart was first worried over the question of land. The college needed not only land for a campus, but for future growth and for the school farm so long discussed. The main city lay to the east. Between the city and the college was a semi-slum area settled by colored workers. This was owned by white landlords and Mansart was sure Sykes and his friends had picked this out for sale to the college at an exorbitant price. It was not large enough and would bring the campus nearer the city. To the west lay an old neglected plantation, but no one supposed it could be bought, least of all for a Negro school. It was the property of an old planter family, the Claytons. There were six hundred acres of field and forest, never divided and now in possession of an elderly woman who had always refused to sell an acre. But Mansart knew she was now old, sick and in financial difficulties. He talked to an ancient Negro retainer and then to her lawyer. There was but one other heir, a captain in the army during the world war. He needed money and was now willing to sell. There were at present no white residents near who might complaint, although no one knew what the future might bring. Sykes was quite well aware of the plight of the Clayton plantation. But his plan was to wait for the mortgages to become due and then buy the place in at auction for a song. He planned a suburban development here which would bring millions. For this, the Negro college must be pushed back from the main road and Sykes must get hold of the mortgage, which he had not yet been able to do. Mansart, unaware of the Sykes plan, quietly arranged the deal and talked in a general way to President Coypel. He thought he was ready for the July meeting of the Board.

There was a large attendance at this meeting: the new Governor, President Coypel, John Baldwin and two members of the legislature to watch expenditures; four merchants and industrial leaders, two colored men and President Mansart—twelve in all. First of all, the long established racial taboos must be observed, but as unobtrusively as possible. Mansart and the colored Trustees lunched in the President's home; Baldwin, Coypel and the whites were served separately in the State dining room attached to the Cooking School, so the colored students might exhibit their abilities. After lunch all the trustees assembled in the President's office. All had lunched long and well and were now in a hurry to rush through the "business."

Sykes, of Macon, now took charge. To Mansart's astonishment, Sykes exhibited a complete plan of the new college campus with buildings all located. The colored slum district was to be bought.

There were smaller plans of the separate buildings with details. The Governor seemed quite familiar with these plans, the costs, and the contracts which had, it seemed, been all but signed. Sykes closed:

"I have gone over these plans from time to time with the Governor and President Coypel, and of course with President Mansart. I think we can now take final action."

The Governor indicated his general assent and President Coypel looked surprised but said that since President Mansart approved he would make no objection. He wondered if Mansart had finally yielded to "inducements," and felt strangely disappointed.

Sykes laughingly interposed to add, "The local merchants and the Trades Union City Central have asked the college to accept from them a Buick sedan for the use of the President and his teachers on college business. I now move—"

Mansart interrupted: "I would like a word." Sykes frowned and the Governor consulted his watch. But Mansart was undisturbed in mien although despairing in soul. He said slowly: "I regret to say that I have never been consulted on these plans; that I see now for the first time the land, buildings and laying out of the campus which others have apparently decided on. I am not for a moment questioning the legal right of others to make these decisions, but I am saying that if this is going to be your method of procedure I will have no part in it as president or as office boy."

Sykes leaped to his feet with red face. "Do you dare to call me a liar?"

"No, sir, I did not say you were a liar. I did say, and I repeat, that what you said about consultation with me was untrue—"

"If you dare—"

The Governor intervened. "Gentlemen, gentlemen! Let us have order. I understood, Mr. Sykes, in our conferences, that you had been in constant consultation with President Mansart on all these plans."

"Yes, sir—"

Mansart calmly interrupted Mr. Sykes, contrary to all racial etiquette.

"That is not true. I beg Mr. Sykes' pardon, but he has doubtless forgotten. Once, when I first became president, Mr. Sykes came in with plans for the administration building all drawn up for my immediate acceptance. I refused and laid the matter before you. New plans were adopted and this building erected. Since then, no plans have been laid before me or discussed by Mr. Sykes or anyone else.

"Moreover, gentlemen, there is a major matter which must be considered before details of buildings and contracts can be gone into. That is the matter of land. These plans call for the purchase of 100 acres. This is not enongh if we are to have the farm which you have voted for. It will also displace a large number of colored laborers and bring the college nearer to the city with no chance for further expansion. In accordance with your previous vote, I have been trying to secure option on six hundred acres, sufficient for campus and farm, and I have succeeded. Had I known of Mr. Sykes' activities I would not have proceeded with mine.

"Moreover, I will not accept an automobile nor a go-cart from anyone who expects to profit from contracts. Finally, gentlemen, unless Negro laborers have opportunity to help build this Negro school, I will immediately resign. Evidently, gentlemen, here is a case where I as your executive official have been deliberately ignored. I am not too sensitive over this, but as you know if I am president, I must be so treated. If I am not, you should choose a man whom you trust."

The President walked out of the room. It was a bold thing to do, but Mansart knew he had no alternative. Sykes was known as overbearing and greedy. He had not dreamed that the farm next to the campus was in the market. Also, all knew that if Sykes recommended a piece of land it was because he had an interest in it. Few regarded it as good policy to have the Negro college expand toward the city.

On the other hand, to ask a white Trustee Board to side with a colored president against a rich and influential member of the Board ordinarily would not succeed. It was a bold risk, but as Mansart saw it he had no alternative. Behind him stood President Coypel. The governor would not likely oppose these two men. Moreover, local Macon jealousies ranged a number of other trustees against Sykes. The matter was really settled when the trustees learned that Mansart had actually secured option on the 600 acres to the west.

Mansart's forthright stand on employment of Negro labor ranged solid black opinion back of him and no small part of that white opinion which wanted cheap labor. Finally, Sykes was so surprised at this unheard of public rebellion of a Negro that he now made the mistake of losing his temper. He swore, called Mansart a damned impudent "nigger," and threatened immediate resignation unless his plans were accepted forthwith.

The Board did not stay much longer. Many of the members of the Board were pleased to have this Negro do what they did not dare. Sykes was getting too bold and regarding this school as his private oyster. They could not afford to take the side of a Negro against him, but if the Negro dared to speak up for himself, let him go ahead. They finally voted 7 to 4 to accept Sykes' resignation with regret, and to retain the services of President Mansart. The Governor was disturbed. He said, aside: "You've put us in a hell of a hole, Mansart, but I don't blame you."

The fact of the matter was that this quarrel split the white constituency both about land and labor. Big Business wanted black labor in the skilled trades. White trade unions could not insist on the closed shop on Negro work so long as they would not admit Negroes to the unions. Sykes would be getting too much gravy from this deal to suit other business men; and if the whites could blame a stubborn Negro for all this, it cleared their skirts.

The colored college prospered. Its new buildings were well arranged and well built. Working in conjunction and partially under the supervision of the State University, the contracts were carefully let and Mansart inspected all work. Eventually, the Trustees decreed that Negro skilled labor must be used where competent and available. The white unions did not dare fight this; but they admitted as few Negroes as possible to as few kinds of work as possible, and none to white unions. So there were no Negro plumbers, roofers, or metal workers on the buildings; but there was a fair number of bricklayers and masons and a few carpenters.

Gradually, the workmen came to respect this quiet and polite black man who knew his business and managed to get his way. After one or two dismissals and corrections of various sorts, the mass of workers settled down and did a good job. The buying was carefully conducted so as to gradually exclude the grafters, but still Mansart had very gently but very firmly to impress it upon white salesmen and merchants that he did not want a rakeoff and that he must have first class goods.

There were two unexpected results of the new land and building program; one was that the colored people living to the east of the campus got a sudden opportunity to purchase at very reasonable rates the homes for which they had long been paying exorbitant rents. Mansart planned a building and loan company to help them. Secondly, and to his surprise, his son Revels, now just beginning the practice of law in New York, asked to spend the summer at the college to work on a brief. Mansart arranged to take him on as watchman, and nourished the hope that once here he might decide to stay. Macon needed a good colored lawyer.

Slowly, he began to get better teachers. They were still poorly paid. His own salary was twenty-five hundred and the usual salary for professors was twelve hundred; but notwithstanding that, he gradually got some very excellent material. He waited a long time before he could get the right kind of matrons, and especially women who knew girls and boys; but he succeeded fairly well. In this way, the enrollment steadily increased until he had two thousand students who paid in over a hundred fifty thousand dollars in cash each year, a figure that astonished the state authorities. In fact, although this was not published, the Negro students paid a larger percentage of the cost of their education than the whites. Coypel chuckled over this fact and told Baldwin.

After some hesitancy, athletics were allowed and a good football team organized. It was excellent publicity and it paid for itself, but Mansart was not quite sold on it.

Manuel Mansart continued to read the *Crisis* magazine. He regarded it at first as rather sensational and complaining. But he was attracted by its news, notes and facts, its historical references, and at last it became a regular part of his reading. He was careful, however, not to have it lying around too conspicuously when the trustees or white visitors came. One article he read tonight. It was written by "A Tired College President," and it said what Mansart felt:

"I am tired tonight. All day I have been working on curriculums and catalogues. The rating Boards all over the country tell me that our curriculum does not have enough calories of this and too many calories of that and no Vitamin D. I have tried to argue with them to no avail. I insisted that if I can get a few good teachers who can introduce the pupil's little mind to a few elemental things, to arouse in him a little curiosity, he will, him-self, select the right ingredients for a proper intellectual diet. But they say no. So I must make a new catalogue embodying many nice new changes, for if I do not, they will not recognize our college and freshmen will not come to us.

"I am tired tonight. All day I have been wrestling with problems of administration. All my time is taken with problems, policies, personalities. Meanwhile the Negro youth waits at the cross-roads for someone to tell him which way to go. I have no time to tell him. I have no time to teach him anything. I take a little time off now and then to tell him he is not as good as I was when I was young and that he is on his way to perdition. But he knows I am not telling the truth. I wish I had a little more time to spend with the youth, to know him and to let him know me.

"I am tired tonight. All day I have shipwrecked my brain trying to reconcile the various theories about what is the best thing for the masses of my race. There are so many fine theories—all very good, of course. I once mustered up enough courage to tell them one little thing that I thought would be nice for them to do—to go away down in the country and to stay there for a hundred years or more—to make a little home down there and to make employment for themselves and their children forever.

"But the great Negro leaders squelched me. They said I was denying the Negro his fundamental right, as an American citizen, of the utmost freedom of movement—to live where he pleases and to do whatever he desires."

During these long, weary months and years no one was more conscious than Manuel Mansart of the invaluable service which Jean Du Bignon was rendering him, the college and the race. She was indefatigable and uncomplaining. She kept herself in the background, asked no recognition and yet foresaw every contin-gency. His mail was answered promptly and far more thoughtfully than he could have done; his visitors were met, detoured and often satisfied without a personal meeting. The newspapers and maga-zines were marked and placed before him, and now and then books of interest appeared on his desk. Facts and figures were found for him miraculously and, above all, whenever he had time or wish, Jean Du Bignon was ready to talk, to advise and to en-courage, and she showed the result of study, wide reading and clear thinking. She could talk, but also she could keep still and listen. Of course, she had little time to teach, but the little she did set the students on edge, and once or twice when she lectured, the school, faculty and students, and the town crowded in, except the whites who kept away only because Jean absolutely forbade segregation in seating. The President did not intervene.

Above all, Jean helped in Mansart's family life; to buy new furniture and furnishings, to advise in buying clothes, to hire house service which Susan had not dared to ask. This made meals on time and more appropriate food. Bruce, Sojourner, and Douglass when there, joined more regularly in the family group, and now and then there were guests and even small evening parties. Yet, Jean's help was rendered so unobtrusively that no one noticed it in particular, and especially Susan and the family felt no interference. But Jean was often a tired and lonesome worker. She roomed in the dormitory and ate with the students.

Mansart would have liked to make Miss Du Bignon dean of the institution. He needed to decentralize power and share the increasing burden of his work. But a reliable and trustworthy subordinate was not easy to come by. There was envy and jealousy about him. There was every temptation to deception and trading between races and groups. Looking about him in the college and in the state he could not be sure of a young, vigorous and honest man who seemed to him suited to handle this role. Jean could do it; but she was a woman, which, in the South and among Negroes, was distinctly against her. He dare not attempt such an innovation at this time.

There came with this thought the consideration of the Negro group in general. There had been a time when to himself the American Negro had appeared as a chosen people, a group dedicated to the emancipation of the dark and tortured people of the world. As he grew older, he realized that this was an exaggeration. Negroes were not exceptional in soul and sacrifice. They were just human. They had all human frailties, with some of the lower and meaner emphasized by what they had suffered. They were still a cramped and degraded people and he could not expect from them immediately the help he needed and which the world needed for salvation.

So, too, the whites about him were not born devils. The ruthless greed and sadism which encompassed them covered human hearts and decent desires. He must help them; he must try to uncover the best and loose the decency within. It was hard and his doubts ran deep, yet the example of Coypel alone sustained his faith. He would work steadily on and hope.

The matter which underneath all most distressed him was his family. The children were now approaching full growth and walking out into the world with an assurance and force that was frightening. Douglass was a man who proposed to arrange the world as he thought best for himself. Revels was in New York pursuing his determined, dogged way. Bruce was still at home but preparing to leave and instead of the other boys' grim assurance, he was going carelessly and fearlessly into a world of which he knew nothing.

To Sojourner, Mansart had paid little attention until almost by accident he discovered her love of music. Once in a while, they sang together and both loved the Negro folk songs at which the rest of the family laughed. Often, as they sang, Sojourner found that she could accompany him on the almost unused piano. Mansart determined that he would cultivate this strange child's music when he had time. But now he was worrying about the boys and wondering how he could induce them to join him in his work for the college.

His wife had at last escaped the drudgery of housework and the fear of poverty. But in the place of fatigue and worry, there was little upon which she could fall back. She had never read much; she disliked sewing, she found no joy in gardening or music. She did, however, love her youngest son passionately and concentrated all her fear of the future on him. She spoiled him utterly and instead of Bruce uniting his parents, he further estranged them, so that Mansart found little satisfaction in his home despite its new cleanliness and order.

Always, outside and beyond the school and its problems swirled the problems of race and nation which Mansart could not ignore. As he looked back, occurrences which at the time he had hardly noticed, now came back to insist on attention.

The election of 1920 made it clear to the Negroes, especially through an article and chart in the *"Crisis,"* how far the rotten borough system in the South, based on flaunting the Negroes as citizens and not letting them vote, gave increased power to the South over the North; and this repeatedly was brought up as an argument for enforcing the 14th amendment, showing the injustice of the political situation in the South.

Also, in 1920, the year that Manuel became President, 60 Negroes were lynched. It would be difficult for an outsider to realize what lynching meant to the American Negro and how the number of lynchings served as a sort of barometer to his hope and despair. No reliable records were kept before 1882, and even those afterward were not thoroughly established. In fact, every Negro knew that killing of Negroes by mass murder was a long-ingrained habit in the South.

The lynching record hovered always over Mansart. It was a sort of thermometer which he was glad to see fall from 65 a year to 18 a year in the first five years of his presidency, and then it rose again and hovered between 10 and 30. He was glad to read about the great meeting against lynching in New York.

He was particularly pleased to see the push toward education among Negroes steadily rising. Negro college graduates rose steadily from 400 in 1920 to 700 in 1925. Most of these, of course, came from Southern colleges. But the number of Negroes in Northern colleges nearly doubled between 1920 and 1925. This showed how strong the impulse toward education persisted.

In the year of Mansart's inauguration came the case of Sergeant Caldwell, at Anniston, only 150 miles west of Macon. Following a dispute with the conductor of the streetcar, Caldwell was kicked from the car. As he was about to rise from the ground, the conductor and motorman of the car advanced on him with weapons in their hands to attack him further. Caldwell drew his revolver and killed the conductor and wounded the motorman. He was arrested by civil authorities, although he was a soldier and subject to military trial. He was found guilty of murder and sentenced to be hanged.

The case was fought through the various state courts of Alabama, in which the branch NAACP was aided by other Alabama branches and the national office. After reversals, the case was carried to the United States Supreme Court. Caldwell lost and was hanged. As he died he said:

"I am being sacrificed today upon the altar of passion and racial hatred that appears to be the bulwark of America's civilizaiton. If it would alleviate the pain and sufferings of my race, I would count myself fortunate in dying, but I am but one of the many victims among my people who are paying the price of America's mockery of law and dishonesty in her profession of a world democracy."

CHAPTER X

THE FIRST-BORN

Douglass Mansart, of the 371st United States Infantry, smiled grimly in 1919 when his unit was separated from the French and hurried down to the de-lousing station. He realized that Negro troops were going to be gotten out of France just as quickly as possible. Otherwise, being part of the French army they would have a chance to meet and talk with the French and the result might not be pleasant for the reputation of America. So the troops were de-loused quickly and almost before they realized it, they were aboard ship and on the way to the United States.

It was a pleasant and restful voyage, although somewhat crowded, and the reception in New York was astonishing. These were the first troops from the front after the Armistice, and as they marched up Fifth Avenue, the ovation was deafening. Douglass went to Harlem, to a small and not very convenient hotel on 135th Street and there found two letters. The first was from his father:

"My dear son,

"I thank God that this will find you back from the front alive and I hope well. We all send love. I am in good health and your mother is pretty well, although not as strong as I could wish. You know that Revels is still in France. Bruce is here and rather uncertain, and Sojourner as shy as usual, although her interest in music is increasing rapidly.

"I write this specially to urge you to think of the future. There seems to be a pretty good chance of something unusual happening to me, and I want you to be a part of it. I wish you would hurry home and finish your college course at Atlanta, then perhaps go north for some post-graduate work, and by that time I may be able to find a place, and an important place for you.

"Meantime, while you are in college, Perry tells me that he can use your services in insurance as he did before the war. That will help you with pocket money and give you experience.

"Let us hear from you as quickly as possible.

163

"With all our love,

Your father, Manuel"

The other letter was from Perry. Perry told him that the insurance business was booming, that already the Standard Life Company had spread into most of the Southern states and that he was going soon to spread out into other ventures. He was willing to give Douglass a good chance if he wanted to become a modern, well-paid business man.

> "Then, too, you must have heard how the West is booming. Of course, the Standard has not yet gotten North, but the Negro population of Illinois has tripled in the last ten years and it is going to be one of the great centers of Negro development."

When the Standard Company entered Chicago, he wanted Mansart there to take a prominent place in its spread. He was awaiting a letter with anxiety.

Douglass thought over these two letters. He answered his father quickly, saying that he would be home sometime in the fall, but that meantime he was going to make a visit to Chicago, which he had long wanted to see. Perry he did not answer. He had made up his mind that he did not want to live in the South permanently. He could not endure a "Jim Crow" world. He had glimpsed in France something of freedom without a color line; he had made up his mind that Chicago was the place where he wanted to live and work. And therefore, after looking around New York a little and being not altogether satisfied with what he saw, of discrimination and carelessness, gambling and extravagance, he took the train late in July, indulging in a Pullman berth, and went to Chicago.

It was Sunday morning, July 27, 1919 when Douglass landed at the La Salle Street Station and made his way on the Southside Elevated to 29th Street where he found an apartment house which had been made over into a colored hotel. The accommodations were not bad, the food was very good, the crowds and noise a little unsettling. Douglas lounged about, had a good dinner, and then late in the afternoon walked out and made his way toward the lake which looked beautiful in the late afternoon. He could see that the shore was thronged with bathers, and he noticed that there were black people and white, but the whites congregated pretty well toward the north and the black people toward the south.

Then, rather suddenly there was commotion. He could not see just what had started it. But soon white and colored people were fighting; stones were hurtling through the air, angry cries arose and people began running. He moved back and out of the way, but all that afternoon and long into the night he could hear the fighting, shrieking and cursing; and men with bloody heads, black and white, moved along the streets.

Monday morning was ominously still. And then, late in the afternoon, the streetcars began to be attacked. Trolleys were torn from the lines; people, particularly Negroes, were driven from the cars, and shooting and fighting began, back from the lakeshore and toward the west. It seemed to Douglass that again he was back at the war front, particularly when during the night he could see from his hotel window autos rushing to and fro with flashes of gunshot.

There was a pause again Tuesday morning, and Douglass began to think of leaving the city; but from noon to midnight there came a strike on the streetcars which made it impossible for him to get to the depot; and there was fighting down in the Loop, where stores of white businessmen were attacked and black men killed.

On Wednesday, the militia came, marching bravely through the South Side; and rain, sheets of dark, muddy rain which poured down and cleared up the blood and, mingled with tears, cooled the hot and murderous city.

Probably nothing could have been more unexpected to Douglass Mansart than the riot. He knew of race, riot and murder in the South. One of his first and unforgettable experiences had been the Atlanta Riot. He knew, too, in a general way that sometimes something like that happened in the North. But that one of the great cities of the West could for a week give itself up to murder, race hate and disorder, was absolutely unexpected.

When the rioting stopped, he sat around for a few days and saw what was being done to explain and understand the gruesome happening: the count of thirty-eight dead bodies; the search for unknown murderers who were never found. The crowning anomaly and disgrace was seventeen Negroes indicted and four whites; three Negroes convicted and two whites! Douglass climbed onto the train going south and sat there in bitter disillusionment. This was Justice in a modern, northern American city. And here was more of what he was to expect, because on the Illinois Central which he had boarded, he was sitting in a "Jim Crow" car which boldly started out from Chicago and traversed the North in open defiance of the law.

He was going back to Atlanta, at least for a time. There he would study and work and plan a life. But he knew perfectly well at what that plan was going to aim. He was going to get enough money and power to be free, here in the United States; or, if necessary, outside this country.

Frankly, he did not find his family particularly interesting. Home was crowded as usual, and he increased the crowd. He roomed with Bruce and, after two years apart, they were strangers. Revels had not returned. His mother was, as usual, busy, querulous and complaining. And of Sojourner he saw almost nothing. He did, however, learn of his father's new appointment as president of the new colored State College at Macon, which pleased him.

One of his first jobs was to go and see Perry. And he was really astonished at what Perry reported.

"Sit down," said Perry. Douglass laid his bundle of books on the table and sat down. Perry rose carefully and laid the books aside and picked up the Bible that was under them.

"Never put anything on top of the Bible," he said, solemnly.

This seemed almost too smug; but Douglass soon forget it. He was soon telling Perry about what he wanted to do and Perry was telling him of Standard Life Insurance Company, which had nearly 23 million dollars of insurance in force and was taking in over a million dollars a year. It was operating in eleven states. Douglass did not hesitate; he accepted a job as one of the Georgia supervisors, and without great enthusiasm enrolled at Atlanta University to finish his college course, with the understanding that he might have to be absent on account of his work a good deal of the time.

Very gradually but completely, he guided his actions so as to adjust himself to the South. He avoided all unnecessary contact with the whites. He was careful when downtown about brushing against them, about going into stores where Negro trade was not wanted, even about asking for information. He did not cringe nor apologize. He found that a calm, unsmiling look warded off much thoughtless aggression.

He began to see that the whites in a certain way were afraid of Negroes. They did not usually, thoughtlessly or deliberately affront them unless the Negro seemed of the cringing kind, or unless the white had a crowd behind him. Looking a would-be white aggressor square in the eye usually brought compromise and withdrawal in attitude. Of course, one must act circumspectly. One must withdraw, also, as soon as the spirit of aggression subsided. Quietly, one must walk away if possible. What the whites feared most was that other white people might see them yield to a Negro. For Negroes, yielding in itself was the part of wisdom in many cases. In this way, Douglass avoided trouble with the whites.

Douglass took careful note of the political situation. His father's new state school would probably become the colored state university with a considerable income. Federal appropriations would make this compulsory. But it would be subordinate to politics and Negroes had small weight in the political organization.

Manuel wanted his eldest son to get a thorough classical education, then to train himself as a teacher, become one of his teachers and his eventual successor in this school. This did not appeal to Douglass at all. He didn't want to live in the South, he didn't want to teach school, and indeed, if the truth were known, he didn't want to be a Negro. The only way of escaping the penalties of being black was to make money, and he proposed to devote his life to that. He told this to his father, causing him a good deal of uneasiness. However, he kept in touch with the school in Macon, often spending weekends there and consulting with his father.

Manuel had hoped that his sons, especially the two older, would soon become his assistants in planning and running the school. In anticipation of this, he had neglected the organization of his office, and as a result it grew into a mess as his work became more complicated and far-reaching. He needed trained assistance.

With the present help that he had taken from the student body, with two or three clerks from the outside, things were not going satisfactorily. These colored girls had had no opportunity of seeing how an office ought to be run, had had no standards as to work and accuracy. They were good-hearted, they had ability; they simply did not know. Manuel told Douglass of the applicant from New Orleans whom he had accepted and hoped would fit in as a sort of administrative assistant; she would be familiar with the technique of large institutions and at least for a time be a substitute for the work he had hoped Douglass or Revels might do.

Douglass was rather repelled. He did not believe it was the business of girls to go to college or to become, as he put it, over-educated. Still, he admitted that this seemed a well-trained girl and that she certainly could be used at this institution. He agreed with his father that she ought to be tried. They continued to discuss the future career of Douglass and were not reaching real understanding or agreement.

When Jean Du Bignon actually arrived, there was added to Douglass' distaste for over-educated women, his further recoil from white colored folk. He assumed they were patronizing darker folk and taking work with them because they could not get other work; or for other ulterior motives. Since it was inconceivable to him that anyone would not pass for white if he could, he could not imagine this woman coming to work here by choice. He greeted her briefly and left for Atlanta forthwith.

An occurrence which greatly influenced Douglass in Atlanta was meeting John Mitchell, Jr., of Richmond, Virginia. Whenever any colored business men came to Atlanta, Perry always entertained them and introduced them to his young men. Thus, when Mitchell came in 1922, his fame had preceded him. He was a bank president and the only Negro member of the American Bankers Association. John Baldwin noticed him sitting in one of the meetings and inquired about him.

Perry had just organized the Citizens Trust in 1921, and he was eager to talk with Mitchell. For this tall, gaunt, yellow man had a sort of free arrogance and independence which fascinated Perry. Mitchell was directing his business ventures toward solving the Color Problem.

John Mitchell, Jr. was born in 1863 on a plantation near Richmond. He graduated from the Richmond Colored High School, taught in the colored public schools, and was a reporter on a local colored newspaper, "The Planet." This paper carried an editorial protesting against the proposed replacement of Negro school principals in Richmond by whites. The editorial caused the school Board to dismiss a large number of male Negro teachers, including John Mitchell. He thereupon became editor and finally owner of "The Planet."

In 1890 he entered politics, becoming boss of the old Jackson ward where the bulk of the Negroes lived and which for a time held the balance of power in municipal politics. Then he became prominent in the Knights of Pythias and was chosen head of its Womens Auxiliary. In 1900, he gave up his political leadership, and organized the Mechanics Bank in 1902. This bank did business for poor people. Of its 1600 savings accounts, two-thirds were under $100. It financed a cemetery for colored people, since they could not lie beside the dead whites, and were relegated to untended stretches in the rear of white graveyards. It made loans to small businsses and gave mortgages to buyers of small homes—all useful but risky. It was mixing profit and philanthropy, which white banks avoided.

But Mitchell went further; and this proved his undoing. In Richmond, as in most Southern cities, theaters and the new cinema were a thorn in the side of Negroes, especially the educated and well-to-do. They were allowed to sit only in the top balcony, where often they could not hear, see or be seen; the surroundings were dirty and crude, and there was no protection against hoodlums who rather enjoyed this freedom to annoy the "darkies." Mitchell, resenting this, let his prosperous bank, in 1922, buy the Strand Theater in downtown Richmond, well-known to white theater-goers. Mitchell announced his intention to open this for Negro patronage.

The whites were affronted. They refused to recall that the white population was not supporting this place and that quite naturally the blacks long deprived of decent entertainment, wanted to take it over. "No!" said white Richmond, and offered Mitchell a good sum to re-sell it. But Mitchell, arrogant and confident, said "No!" brusquely and went ahead with his plans. Then he attended the bankers' meeting in Atlanta, and there Douglass met and admired him.

But John Mitchell reckoned without the tie-up between the State Banking Department and Business. When he hung up on the telephone conversation between him and the Commissioner concerning his bank's carrying of too much real estate, the Commissioner went to work, and despite a half million dollars of assets, closed Mitchell's bank just as he returned from Atlanta.

Mitchell fought back, writhed out from under a criminal charge and bankrupted himself, even to selling his prized Stanley steamer auto, to pay every cent of his bank's debts! Bank and theater disappeared and John Mitchell died a pauper in 1925. Douglass was startled. He began to assess Perry's business ventures with a wary eye.

Other things equal, he would have liked to help the Old Man in the State College. But other things were not equal. Political power for Negroes was not entirely absent in the South, but it was indirect. If his father's tie-in with Big Business, in the person of John Baldwin, could be strengthened, there was a possibility that Negroes could break into the White Primary and help rule the state against the trade unions, the farmers and poor whites. Not that Douglass liked or trusted the whites; he hated them, and especially despised the poor whites. But self-interest might bind the rich whites to forward-pushing Negroes for mutual advantage. In that case, and with enlarged appropriations for the school, there was a chance for a lucrative career for him in some connection with the school. Not in teaching—the study for that took too long and it never was well-paid; but as business manager or administrator of some sort.

All this, however, was questionable. His father was no politician. He was too soft. He was always yapping about "his race" when he knew full well the Negroes would sell him out for a song. Moreover, Douglass doubted their real worth; they were too ignorant and unreliable. He was not going to sacrifice his chances for them. At present he was giving most of his time to Perry and insurance. It paid fairly well.

For the future, Mitchell's collapse alarmed him, but Perry reassured him. Mitchell was on the right track but had kept no proper white contacts. He had let the poor whites gerrymander him out of control of his Negro city ward and kept no close connection with the white banks. He ought to have played along with the Banking Commissioner, sold the theater for a profit, etc. Now he, Perry, had a much bigger scheme which was sure-fire. He then disclosed his plan for land and housing; his laundry and printing ventures, his contracting and building interests, and his bank to finance all this.

"You see, the whites will get a hand in this and yet we run it. I tell you it's a gold mine."

Douglass still had doubts but decided to stick with Perry a while longer. Eventually, he would go to Chicago where business was booming, either to represent Perry's company or to join Pace and Gibson whom he knew and who had just formed an insurance merger. He was sure, as they were, that well-paid northern Negroes with votes would eventually support better Negro business than poor, disfranchised Southern workers.

On the other hand, white capital naturally favored Negro capital. In 1900, there were four small Negro banks with a total capital of less than a half million, but by 1920 there were thirty-five such banks with a capital of 10 million dollars. They were, of course, completely under the ultimate control of the larger white banks. The real significance of Negro banks lay in the fact that in a score of Southern towns the savings of thrifty Negroes were in places where the white financiers could use them in any way they wanted to, and even seize them without too much difficulty, if such seizure was profitable or socially desirable.

It was easy, therefore, for Standard Life in Atlanta to get the money which it needed to capitalize its various enterprises, even beyond the cash which was pouring in from its insurance business. One of the pressing problems of Negroes in cities like Atlanta was the matter of housing. The old pattern was for Negroes to rent small cabins, flimsily built, with no modern conveniences. If, having ambition beyond this, the better-paid Negroes tried to build, there was the question of decent sites. If they bought a good place from white people the surrounding whites began to complain and even to riot. If they tried to buy land by themselves they found themselves crowded out by noisy or unpleasant factories or businesses.

Perry realized this. The attempt to improve Negro housing in the 4th Ward of Atlanta by individual initiative had failed. The Negroes were hemmed in by jealous white residents and the business expansion of Atlanta. The Great Fire wiped out some of their slums and better districts, but they could not secure capital to rebuild.

It was here that Perry came to the rescue in a rather astonishing way. First of all he was faced by the problem of what he could safely do with the million dollars cash that was coming into his hands annually from the insured. If he put it into white banks he would get, of course, a very small return, not enough to pay for the part of the expense which this income ought to stand. On the other hand, how could he invest it himself? He could not go into the market where he might so easily be cheated. But it occurred to him that he could build houses for colored people, which they needed, and that they would pay for them. Perry therefore turned aside from the old 4th Ward and went to the West Side, around and beyond Atlanta University, where values were low because of the Negro college. Perry used some of the funds of the insurance company to organize the Service Realty Company. He paid out more than $600,000 until his company owned at one time most of the property between Simpson and West Hunter, stretching a mile, with several hundred acres.

For two years, he did a vast real estate business selling property on the time payment plan to colored home buyers. These could be financed only by mortgages and the prospective home owner with a small amount of cash would have his home built by Perry's Service, Engineering and Construction Company according to their own plans and specifications. The mortgages usually landed in the Standard Life Insurance Company and the remainder of the price was accepted in the form of a second mortgage.

In 1923, the Standard Life and others purchased the Odd Fellows block, paying a large part in cash and assuming mortgages for the rest. Then, in order to facilitate the financial transactions, the Service Company took over a small colored bank which was about to fail and organized the Citizen's Trust Company, opening offices on Auburn Avenue.

The most spectacular deal was eventually made with the City of Atlanta. In 1919, the colored people organized and defeated a bond issue because they could not get the city to promise them new schools even if bonds were issued. In a former bond issue of three million dollars, the Negroes got only one small school. They therefore defeated the proposal of 1919 and the city admitted in 1922 that the amount invested in Negro school property was too small to obtain results. The state was receiving at this time $666,000 from the federal government, and $60,000 from private sources for schools. It had therefore to make some move, and in 1924 it promised the colored people that if they would vote a bond issue they would receive five new schools to cost $1,200,000. They kept their word, although most of the bond money went for white schools and nothing was done for Negro schools until all the white schools were finished.

When the Negroes thus held up the city on the bond issue and compelled them to build for the first time a Negro high school, Perry offered them a site for the very reasonable sum of $40,000. It was a good piece of land and well worth the expenditure. The city therefore put up a good Negro high school on the land which

Perry sold to the city, and citizens placed before it a replica of the Tuskegee statue of Booker Washington "lifting the Negro."

This did not, of course, settle the Negro school problem. In the Negro schools there were 12,500 pupils and seats for less than half of them. Most of the children received from two and a half to three and a half hours instruction a day. In general, the state was spending ten times as much on its white schools as on its colored schools, although the colored people were more than a third of the total school population.

The Negro capitalism now arising was on a different level from the tremendous white leviathan which encircled it. The white financial world could by world-wide banking facilities transfer investments from failing to earning enterprises, let the loser flounder and disappear, while the Captains of Industry went on to higher profits. For this reason, the general money market was rigged against investment in real estate which was not easily transferable. To Negro investors, on the other hand, real estate was the basis of property and investment. Big Finance could at any time push them into bankruptcy, as they did in John Mitchell's case in Richmond. Soon the shadow of this loomed over Perry and the Standard Life in Atlanta.

Perry kept expanding to best the squeeze. He had control of several hundred acres, stretching a mile to the west. He built the Howard Junior High School for the city at the cost of $400,000, and for a private theological school he put up a $200,000 building. Two drug stores were started, and a job printing establishment which did catalog work for the colleges and all the printing for Standard Life. There were other large but vaguer plans: a Farm Bureau, a coal mine in Tennessee, and a Foundation for gifts to Negro schools. About 1924, the reserves of the Standard Life Company were found by the State officials to be impaired and it was necessary to increase the stock. Stock was sold for $250,000 cash. But this cash was paid not by colored people but by whites who began thus to get a grip on the Negro insurance company.

Douglass did not understand this intricate financing at first, but as he studied it he got frightened. By 1925, the grip of white business settled more firmly. The Realty Company deeded its properties to a white company, the Southeastern Trust Company, in trust. The Standard Life itself was merged with the white Tennessee Company. The Tennessee Company gutted the Standard

Life of all its most valuable securities. The Southeastern Trust Company foreclosed and secured a majority interest not only in the Service Company but in the Standard Life. And thus, into the hands of the whites disappeared a colored insurance company with paid up capital of $250,000 and over $30,000,000 worth of insurance in force, and $4,000,0000 in assets.

Colored people were incensed at this development. Women wept and men swore vengeance. There were rumors that machinations of white secret societies had brought about this collapse, but as a matter of fact it was all due probably to the current growth throughout the United States of dreams of unlimited wealth, and the encouragement of wild business methods, which looted the pockets of the poor to swell the profits of the rich.

Douglass began to study economics and business, and on his weekly or bi-weekly trips to Macon, he discussed labor and business with his father; and he began to talk now and then with Jean Du Bignon whom he discovered to his surprise knew considerable about the matter and was neither condescending nor apparently conscious of color.

He was still determined not to stay in the South. The whole "Jim-Crow" system, the discrimination, the method of life, was something that he would not accept. Moreover, he wanted to live better than he was living, with a fine home, a wife, children and luxuries. And when he thought about a wife he began at first unconsciously and then more and more distinctly to think of Jean Du Bignon. His talks with her, however, never reached personalities. She talked about the world market, international trade, and mass production. She had books on these subjects, and read them and loaned them.

"So you're going into 'business'—I thought it was insurance?" she said.

"What's the difference?"

"Business is for profit; insurance is for people."

"I'm for profit. People can take care of themselves."

"I'm sorry—people need so much."

"So do I. I need money."

"For what? You have enough to eat and wear and a good place to sleep."

"I need a house, well-built and furnished, with servants; a car, good food and wine and a well-filled purse; a well-dressed wife and a couple of kids in a good school; and trips abroad now and then, in comfort."

She looked at him speculatively. "And something worth living for?"

"That'll suit me very well."

"I wonder!"

Jean was especially sympathetic with the white labor movement. Here Douglass was antagonistic. He had no sympathy with white laborers. And his father, Mansart, joined him in this. They both regarded white laborers and particularly poor white Southern labor, as the enemies of Negroes. Douglass stuck to that point of view and he and Jean had several hot arguments.

As the Negroes continued to pour north Douglass rejoiced, but Jean was apprehensive. They must not become scab labor, she warned. But that was exactly what Douglass wanted them to become. Unconsciously, his interests were with employers and not with laborers, and he was glad that the Steel Strike had been lost. He attributed, rightly, riots such as that in East St. Louis to the enmity of white labor, but he would not admit that unless Negroes joined the white unions they had no chance to rise in the industrial world.

"What if they wanted to join white unions," he cried. "The unions would not let them in. They had not admitted them in the case of the Steel Strike."

It was in vain that Jean pointed out that the prosperity of Negro business and of the country was being built on dangerous ground. There was revolution in Eastern Europe and even the phenomenal rise of such a business as Coca-Cola in Atlanta was not setting a pattern which Negroes could afford to follow, and of course as it was, they were not allowed to follow it.

The fairy tale of Coca-Cola early attracted Douglass and made all Atlanta, if not all the South, more or less crazy on the subject of profit. When Jean first mentioned it, Douglass was not prepared to reveal his ignorance. Manuel, however, spoke up:

"I remember well when I entered the high school of Atlanta University in 1890, Professor Webster warned me not to drink Coca-Cola. 'It contains dope,' he said. I was astonished and looked my disbelief. But, in 1906, Mr. Rucker sued the company under the new Pure Food Law. Rucker was a handsome brown man with laughing eyes who was Collector of Internal Revenue for the State of Georgia."

"And what did the government do?"

"The government seized the kegs and then the company changed the formula."

"Well, then, it's all right."

"Well, it isn't poison. They use caffeine instead of cocaine."

"They seem to be making plenty of money with it."

"They certainly are. If ever prohibition was a God-send to any-body, it was to the purveyors of soft drinks and drugs in the United States."

Manuel remembered vividly one of his conversations with an old Negro. They were walking along the Chattahoochee River one day in silence, when they began to talk about it. The old man was ninety years of age, yet walked firmly and lightly mile after mile. A truck loaded with Coca-Cola passed them and Old John gazed after it.

"It minds me of the Chattahoochee," he had said. "I have seen the Chattahoochee where it was small and narrow. Here, in the Spring it's a flood."

"So is Coca-Cola," Manuel had said.

"It looks like the Chattahoochee; the same color."

Suddenly they stopped and stared down in the stream.

"I knowed him back in '86," said the old man. "He made a headache medicine for people to drink in drugstores; half sugar and half water, with dope. He called it Nerve Tonic." He added: "And even back there folks said it had about it 'a smell of poison.' Then Candler took it over into his drugstore, and now comes prohibition."

It was a case where a patented soft drink which cost little or nothing was sold at a standard low price on a large scale, and that scale increased by fabulous advertising until, as a source of wealth, there were few companies in the world that made greater and more continuous and more certain profits. But the extraordinary thing about the whole fantastic creation of this business was that it was getting something for nothing. By mixing sugar and flavored water, and spending a million dollars a year in advertising, the sale of the drink had gone up by leaps and bounds, especially after prohibition. From 25 gallons manufactured in 1886 it leaped to ten million gallons thirty years later. The syrup was sold to the bottler for a dollar a gallon. Out of this the bottler could make five gallons of drink and sell it for 5c a pint. The profit was enormous—perhaps 200%.

Revelation of the methods of a great business institution came to Douglass slowly. It was not nearly as intricate as he had supposed. But the point that puzzled Douglass for a long time was why people bought it. They liked it, of course, but why didn't somebody else manufacture just as good a drink and sell it for 3c or 1c? They could still make a profit. He mentioned this to Jean and was ashamed to be shown his ignorance. She went on to point out that this was one of the worst cases of misuse of our patent laws, although there are thousands of others. Laws which were made to protect individual genius and secure to inventors the fruit of their inventions are now used to protect monopoly and keep the public from enjoying methods and inventions which cost little or nothing but can be held against the world.

Coca-Cola had been made into a monopoly by the extraordinary number of decisions, ranging from local courts to the Supreme Court of the United States. As a result neither the word Coca-Cola nor any word that sounded like Coca-Cola could be used by a rival company, even if their drink contained cocoa or the cola nut; and this in spite of the fact that Coca-Cola itself contained neither of these ingredients. No bottling company could manufacture, deal, sell, use or handle any product that was a substitute for or imitation of Coca-Cola if it wished to handle Coca-Cola. The company even went so far as to try to stop manufacturers from coloring their products brown. They did not quite succeed in doing this, but up until 1940 they made it impossible for any drink but theirs to be called "Cola," or to use any labels that looked like the Coca-Cola label, or bottles of the same shape. Astute and well-paid lawyers had thus built up practically a complete monopoly, and the company was vigilant to prosecute severely anybody that tried to infringe upon their legal rights.

The result was that a group of men got the right to sell sugar and water with a certain amount of coffee in it at a fantastic profit, and nobody could compete with them. The manufacture spread over Georgia; it spread over the South; it was re-organized so as to make the original owners rich several times. It became a national corporation and did international business. It was sending goods to North and South America, Europe, Asia and Africa. Thus the rivulet of medicine was turned into a river of soft drink which looked not unlike the Chattahoochee where it originated, and out of it rolled minted gold. Millionaires were made south and north; colleges endowed, real estate handled, and a tremendous economic empire reared, for a share in which people are still scrambling, and which had more real political power and social influence than any state government in the South.

Then Coca-Cola went into international politics. It became a substantial part of the Marshall plan. It was forced on Europe and sold in England, France, Germany, Italy and Spain. Its capital became a part of the vast capitalistic enterprises of the world. Its officials became almost public officials.

Before all this, Douglass stood astonished and intrigued. The more he learned the more perplexed he became. If this was a specimen of Atlanta business, what about the other things? He began to realize the link between business and politics. He sensed the role which the State College might play. Searching the tales of the past, he reminded his father that the school for Negroes which he headed was not upon a sound foundation because of the lack of political power among Negroes.

Mansart reminded him that the men who had formed the Odd Fellows organization, that is, Davis and Henry Lincoln Johnson, were also politicians, and that while the Negro did not vote in Georgia and was excluded from the white primary, nevertheless the state government was influenced and guided by the national government, and in the national government the Negroes were powerful. They had a good deal of influence with the election of Harding and his administration, and kept it up during the administration of Coolidge. They had kept control of the state organization of the Republican Party, and while these Southern Republicans were disfranchised largely in the counsels of the party, nevertheless their vote in the national committee was often decisive as to candidates. Therefore black Georgia still wielded political power.

Then Douglass got down to cases. He reminded his father of the utterly unfair division of federal educational and other funds between the races. He showed that whereas Negro colleges in the South should be getting four million a year, they were receiving less than a million. Manuel smiled.

"We know this well," he said. "President Coypel has been regularly forcing up our appropriations with this threat."

"But at this rate it will be a hundred years before we'll get justice."

"Unless," said Jean, "we bring the labor movement to our aid before that."

Douglass sneered as she offered her opinion, as she was apt to do while the two were talking. She tried to say that they must not lose sight of the labor movement and the white trade unions of the South. Douglass was disgruntled.

"And why notice them?" he said. "Their power is waning because of the increased power of the farmers, and one of the difficulties with my insurance company is that the black artisans cannot get work and are kept out of the white artisans' union. Under this leader, Scroggs, they are excluded more than ever. Look at the plight of the black firemen, for instance, not to speak of the men in the building trades."

"True, true," admitted Jean. "But you see, that is bound to change. In the North, it is changing and changing rapidly. The white laborers beset by company unions and injunctions were beginning to realize that they must admit not only colored workers but the white workers engaged in mass production."

But Douglass reminded them of what was happening to the unions and how strong the fight against them and especially against the closed shop was.

"No," said he, "I am against union labor. I am going to fight it here and in the North. Here your only chance, father, is to get the wealth of Georgia back of this college, and in the North where I'm going to work I am going to do all I can to get the Negroes to fight the white unions."

But as he stayed on and took his summer vacation before leaving for Chicago, despite himself he became more and more intrigues with Jean Du Bignon. His interest in her, however, was personal; hers was in his thought and the fact. She was continually arguing, especially on economics. He was a bit peeved to realize that she wasn't thinking of him as a person but as a set of opinions.

Nevertheless, looking her over with an appraising eye, Douglass made up his mind that after he had gotten a good start in Chicago he would probably come back and marry her. It would be a good investment. She was white, she would insure light-colored children. She could be very, very ornamental with some money spent upon her. Yes, that was what he was going to do. He did not mention the matter to her. He could see that the idea had never occurred to her. But that made no difference. Some women were that way.

Jean, on the other hand, was quite unaware of Douglass' thoughts of her personally, but she liked to talk to him. He was a foil to her sharp thinking. On most subjects, they quite cordially disagreed. She taxed him for his ultra racialism and he taxed her for being ashamed of what little of the race she represented. She promptly denied this by saying, "If so, why should I be here?" He countered by asserting that she knew very little of what colored folk like himself had to endure, and she reminded him that he had one great advantage; that people knew he was colored when they saw him; that in her case they had to discover it. And that often made things doubly unpleasant. On the other hand, outside of their bickering they found much in common in books to be read, in general questions to be discussed. They became sort of embattled friends.

He was especially astonished when she mentioned Madam Walker casually and said that she knew her. "Indeed, she was my foster mother." She told him the story of Sarah Breedlove and Jean's mother, Marie.

"She died a millionaire, just as I got my doctorate at Chicago. I had visited her the summer before in her beautiful twenty-room mansion at Irvington-on-the-Hudson, with sunken gardens, a library and a great organ." Jean paused reflectively. "I rather wanted to stay with her. She asked me, but we both knew that her daughter and I would never make it together."

"What did she do with her money?"

"She helped Negro organizations in various ways, the YMCA and the YWCA, and types of social work. She had spread her business over three continents; her factories turned out 34 products, and in the United States alone there were 25,000 of her agents. She had worked hard and long, and on May 25, 1919, in her lovely home on the Hudson, amid a thunderstorm, she died."

After her death it was learned that she had made efforts toward making her business more than a source of private profit. Two-thirds of the profits of the business she arranged were to go to charities. Here, Jean pointed out it probably did not occur to her that the profits might be more logically and ethically divided among her own workers; but for them she left a theater and beautiful office building and a good wage scale but no pensions or tenure. Her profits were put under the control of trustees and were to be distributed annually mainly to Negro enterprises, but not wholly to them. The City of Indianapolis and some white concerns shared in her bounty. Other organizations came to do the same kind of work that Madam Walker was doing, but she was always looked upon as leader and peer, and every year there was a pilgrimage to her grave in Woodlawn Cemetery, New York.

Meantime there was looming in 1926 a decisive political campaign in Georgia. Watson was dead and with him went the last dim hope of Populism. Coca-Cola had its Georgia representative in the Senate, and the candidate for governor of the state stood for the last of the old planter aristocracy, having married a Colquit. Eugene Talmadge was leader of the white farmers and candidate for Commissioner of Agriculture. The trade unions, under the leadership of Scroggs started forward, encouraged by the example of Huey Long in Louisiana. Scroggs became candidate for Commissioner of Labor, supported by the labor movement, working in the white primary but threatening an appeal to the popular vote. It bade fair to be a bitter and close fight.

Scroggs began his agitation long before the election. He appealed to the workers. He borrowed the slogan, "Share the Wealth." He attacked the utilities and the monopolies. He appealed to the poor and unemployed and he berated the Negroes. He not only had behind him the rank and file of the American Legion, but he also had the Ku Klux Klan and other secret societies.

The governorship was safe in the hands of Big Business. But it might happen that the white farmers and white labor would increase their political power. In that case, Negroes should seek alliance with labor. There was small chance of recognition by the farmers since Watson's career. But surely union labor should know that the Negro laborer must be recognized. If not, and white union labor triumphed in this election, Coypel would undoubtedly resign and Mansart's college would be starved to death.

In the question of what ought to be done, Mansart and his son Douglass were in aboslute disagreement. Mansart's idea, which he cautiously advanced, was that in some way Negroes ought to get in touch with Scroggs and see if they could not gain at least some sympathy for the plight of the colored people, not simply in education but in employment and on the farms; perhaps they might make him understand that black folk are a part of the worker whom he is trying to defend. Douglass furiously disagreed.

"That ignorant cracker," he said, "understands nothing and never will. He is simply a confirmed 'nigger' hater. To crawl to him would be to inflate his contemptible ego. Moreover, we are representing not the slums and hoodlums of our race but people of education and talent who sometime, despite Scroggs, will have wealth and power."

Jean Du Bignon, after a long and similar argument with Douglass, dropped in quite casually to chat with the President. She thought his plan had something to it.

"Why don't you talk with Coypel," she said.

Mansart took a trip to Atlanta. Coypel said frankly that he did not think that any attempt to approach Ccrokks would be worth while and it might mean a great deal of humiliation. "But," he sighed, "it might be worth trying. You have a chance that is denied me. I can't ever approach him."

Douglass threw himself into the campaign. The Negro's right to vote was only nominal. The white primary practically exclude them. Nevertheless, he attended political meetings and expressed himself plainly. Some of his sharp attacks on Ccroggs were applauded by the white capitalists and got into the white newspapers. In the meantime, Mansart determined to talk to Scroggs. Scroggs had his headquarters in a leading Atlanta hotel, and Mansart called him up.

"Who did you say you were?" growled Scroggs.

"Manuel Mansart, President of the Colored A. & M."

"What do you want to see me about?"

"I want to talk over the campaign and your position, Mr. Scroggs."

"You know my position and you know I am against 'niggers.' But come over, Manuel, if you want to. I will see you."

So Mansart went to the hotel and walked in the front entrance and went to the desk. People stared at him.

"What?" said the clerk.

"I have an appointment with Mr. Scroggs."

He telephoned up. "All right," he said, "there is the elevator."

But the first elevator was full and the man at the second elevator waved him away. The third was the freight elevator. Mansart went up on that and had an interview with Scroggs. It was a curious setting. Scroggs had never before sat down to talk with an educated Negro. When he had addressed one, it had been to yell at him with oath and vituperation. He was, therefore, at a peculiar disadvantage—how should he address this man, who was not a man in his opinion and yet who had been to school and doubtless knew more in some ways than he did. He decided that if the "darky" tried to put over any damn high jinks, he'd get the bawling out of his life.

But that was just what Manuel had no intention of doing. He was expert in white psychology. It had been his life study. And while he knew less of poor whites than of rich, yet the poverty of Negroes taught him much of what misfortune did to human beings of any hue. He was therefore quiet and deferential, and careful to use plain and simple English.

"Mr. Scroggs," he began, taking the initiative so as to put Scroggs at his ease, "I come from a family of poor, ignorant working people. My father was born a slave, worked as a field hand, and when he was murdered, was at the head of a union of stevedores. My mother washed dirty clothes to give me an education, and I became a teacher. My people need teachers to cure the ignorance so longed forced on us."

"And which you then forced on white people who can be educated, which most of you can't."

"We did not deprive you of schools. We voted schools for all. It was the planters and employers who gave you poor schools and us worse. These masters, Mr. Scroggs, are too often the enemies of us both. And it ain't smart for you to give them more power by cutting the labor vote in two."

"You won't vote with Labor. That's why we disfranchise you."

"You don't disfranchise us, you just hand our power to vote to your enemies; and we go north and vote."

"Yes, and you vote against Labor."

"Of course, when Labor deprives us of work. Mr. Scroggs, we got to eat. To eat we must work. If you won't let us work for union wages, we must scab."

"We'll kill you first."

"You've already lynched a heap, Mr. Scroggs, but we're not all dead. You can't be rid of us! Why not let us work with you for your good as well as our own?"

"And try to marry our girls? We'd rather die!"

"Nonsense, Mr. Scroggs; it's not the workers who chase women; it's the rich who take our women, yours and mine, for playthings. If we had good wages at decent jobs we'd soon stop that. Has any Negro ever tried to marry your daughter?"

"Ef any damn 'nigger' so much as looked at her, I'd kill him!"

"Well then, what are you afraid of? No black man will marry a white woman unless she wants him."

"That'll never be."

"So that boogey is gone. Now, Mr. Scroggs, instead of making us cheap labor for the rich, why not let us both be well-paid workers for ourselves?"

"Because there ain't enough work for all and we'll never starve while 'niggers' grow fat."

"Mr. Scroggs, there's plenty of work for all; plenty. If you become governor, try to make Negroes intelligent by giving them schools, and make them supporters of Labor by giving them the vote!"

"My God, do you suppose I could get my followers to swallow that?"

"Why not? Tom Watson did and if he had stuck to it we might have had a decent South today. Moreover, unless eventually you let Negroes vote for you, the employers will let them vote for them and kill the Labor Movement."

"My God, 'nigger,' you know who just told me that same thing?"

"Who?"

"Huey Long. I don't believe it—but it bears thought. I'll think it over. And by God, Mansart, maybe you've said something. Shake my hand. It's the first time I've ever took a 'nigger's' hand; it may not be the last. Goodbye—and thanks, thanks."

Mansart found the freight elevator after a long wait. During that wait and on the way down he thought over that talk. A year ago, he would not have spoken like that. He would have defended the rich employers or at least excused them. And he would have voiced bitter charges against the poor whites. Yet, what he had just said he had come to believe, and the reason arose from his talks and arguments with Jean Du Bignon. In these arguments, he had usually disagreed with the thesis which he had just confidently voiced. Face to face with a poor white, who he could see had suffered and toiled for what he believed, suddenly Mansart saw and believed much which he formerly had vehemently denied.

Instead of being a despised Negro, facing a hated lyncher, he became a man who had had some education and opportunity, who lived in comfort and respect, with much control over money and power; and he was facing an ill-dressed and hard-pressed man who writhed under the results of toil, deprivation and pain; who was desperately fighting his way up and trying to drag up with him his family, friends and race; and who regarded Mansart as a cause of his disasters. Mansart had to placate, ignore and explain. He silently thanked Jean for the ability to do this. He walked slowly out the side door, and met his son Douglass face to face. Douglass glared, and then without a word walked away.

The next morning in Macon, Douglass confronted his father. He was in a cold, bitter rage. He told Mansart that he was thoroughly ashamed of him; that he had lost the respect which he had once had because he had found out that his father was a coward and a lick-spittle, an Uncle Tom and a white folks' "nigger"; that whatever he had accomplished for this state school, and he may have accomplished something, he had paid too much for. He had bought it at a price which was the betrayal of the manhood of his race. For a person in his position to ride up on a freight elevator and beg crumbs from a professional low-born "nigger"-hater was the last straw. He, Douglass, was leaving the South forever.

Mansart listened and made no answer. He said simply, as Douglass went out: "Good-bye, my boy, and good luck!" And then alone, he bowed his head upon the table and his shoulders shook.

Jean, on her way to her morning work, met Douglas and he told her briefly what he had discovered, what he had said, and what he was going to do. She made no answer but there was no smile on her face. He paused for a moment and looked at her.

"I am going North," he said. "I am going to Chicago. I can't stand this situation here. It chokes me. I am going to be free. And when I have made good I am coming back to ask you to marry me, but not until them. And I want no answer now. Good-bye."

She stared at him but said no word. Then she went into the office and went quietly about her work, saying nothing to the man with bowed head whose shoulders had suddenly become still when he heard her entering. Some minutes later, she asked him quite casually a question about certain routine matters, and he answered with equal casualness, and later left the room.

Jean knew that Mansart's attempt to conciliate poor whites was not the sole reason for the decision of Douglass to go North. He was afraid of the future of Perry's enterprises; he was excited by the immense industrial boom of the nation, led by the North; and he had received an offer from a new Negro insurance venture in Chicago. Together, these reasons were stronger than his father's effort to placate Scroggs. At the revelation of his marital intentions, Jean was both astonished and repelled. It was not the first time that men had taken her assent for granted to plans on which she had never been consulted.

So Douglass went to Chicago and accepted a position with the new Supreme Liberty Life Insurance at a better salary than he was getting in Atlanta, and with bright prospects. He began work carefully and hard. At the same time he was convinced that working for a salary would not bring him the money he was set on having. He must look forward either to quick promotion in this company or to other means, for Douglass was convinced that American fortunes were no longer based on pennies earned and saved but on grasping what men called "The Big Chance," and not ignoring it when it swept into view.

Binga and his new bank intrigued him and he spent much time consulting him. Binga introduced him to the Johnson Brothers. They were wealthy, educated, well-bred Negroes who were starting Negro business enterprises of various sorts. When Douglass inquired into the source of their large and seemingly inexhaustible funds, he found they were at the head of the Chicago policy racket. Gambling was being carried on widely in Atlanta and New York by colored men and white, and one profitable branch was the policy racket, where poor people bet small sums like 5 cents and 10 cents a day on the chance of a certain number turning up in some public report. When the number turned up, they were paid from $1 to $500. It was a gold mine for the manipulators, and he was not surprised when he learned that the Johnson brothers were at the head of the policy racket in Chicago.

On the other hand, these were educated men. They had interesting families and beautiful homes. They gave very intriguing entertainments. Not only that, but they were pushing Negro business. They had started a department store on the colored South Side. They manipulated real estate and various other enterprises; and they hired young colored people at good wages who often could get no other employment but menial service, and who would rather be a clerk at thirty dollars a week than a house-worker at fifty. They looked Douglass over with appraising eyes and made up their minds that he could help, and one of them had a talk with him.

One said, "Mansart, I don't like gambling. It's a dirty trick, and I'm taking money from children. But listen to this. If I didn't take it, somebody else would, and in nine cases out of ten they'd be white people. When they got hold of the money, they'd use it for white people. Colored people wouldn't get any chance at it. Now, we're making money, we're making plenty of it. But we're using it in part to employ colored people, to give them a chance. We need smart young fellows like you. Of course, we're taking big risks. We may get in jail any minute, and the control of the racket go over to somebody else. In the meantime, however, we're making hay while the sun shines, and even suppose we do get in jail, when we come out we'll come out as rich men."

Nothing further was said at the time, but Douglass knew that the unusual confidence was really an offer to him. He made no answer but he began to think hard, and he "went into politics." That is, he joined political clubs, attended meetings, and came to know the bosses. He saw how Chicago politics was tied up with business enterprise, which reached up to railroads, factories and industrial combinations. But up there was no entry for Negroes.

On the other hand, politics also reached down, away down to lower methods of money-making, like peddling dope and organizing prostitution. He rather held back from these. They involved danger from the police, and they were a little nasty. It wasn't absolutely a matter of difference of principle, it was a question as to just how far a man was going to let himself down. To take a penny offered you on impossible chances was one thing. To provide youngsters with poisons and sell girls, that was not simply something else, it was something a great deal lower. Douglass Mansart determined to avoid that phase of business. On the other hand, he wasn't going to betray those people who did go into it, or play the heavy moralist when talking about it. He simply wouldn't reach down to those depths. But Policy?

It was perhaps a contradictory argument and drawing of rather tenuous lines, but Douglass Mansart asked no one else's opinion. And he went further "into politics." In the campaign of 1928, to the astonishment of nearly everybody except the Johnson brothers, he became alderman.

CHAPTER XI

THE BEAUTIFUL BROWN BOY

Naturally, one of the first problems which faced Manuel Mansart as President of the colored State University was the matter of athletics. Personally he knew little about them. He had taken almost no part in games while in college, and although he had later attended a few games between colored schools, he had not been particularly interested because he did not understand the rules.

His first reaction was to keep athletics out of the school. It was distracting and costly and led to complications. Whatever educational value they might have could be better obtained by real work. But he soon realized that this was impractical. The games occupied too high a place in the minds of the students, of the graduates, and of the public, black and white. So that they must be arranged for.

But another thing that both pushed and retarded him was the interest that his son, Bruce, had in football. Bruce, born in 1903, was 17 when Manuel became president of the state school. In the high school, he was an excellent quarterback. In college, he became the chief player of the football team, and soon was giving most of his time and attention to football. In his general studies he hardly obtained passing marks and these mainly because his father was president. He was captain of the team and arranged a schedule with Atlanta University, with Tuskegee, Fisk, and half a dozen other schools. A rich white trustee of the school gave $100,000 for a new stadium. It was early in 1924, when Bruce was 21, that the great game with Atlanta University took place in Atlanta. Everybody hoped that by 1925 the Macon stadium would be ready.

Manuel was disturbed. He wanted Bruce to begin to think of his life work as he would probably graduate the next year. But Bruce was indifferent. He had been a favorite of his older brother, Douglass. Together they played, read, walked and fished. They had certain secret plans for the future, which included, on Bruce's part, an electric factory capable of extraordinary feats; and on the part of Douglass, the amassing of an immense fortune by a huge department store where the factory output would be on sale.

Bruce was fifteen when his brothers went to war, and he was very lonely and distraught. Naturally, he could not play with a mere girl, especially if she was silent and shy like Sojourner. A laboratory for physics would have been heaven, but the colored high school had no apparatus and the private collection which Bruce could amass was very unsatisfactory. Games he liked, for he was quick and wiry and could run swiftly. In baseball he was a good shortstop, but in football he soon became expert. Between football and his private experiments in electricity, his life was passed.

He was a charming young man of medium height, seal-brown skin and handsome, with beautiful eyes, long curled hair, soft voice and gentle manners. His very indifference, with its consequent utter unselfishness, made him a universal favorite with girls and boys, men and women. His mother worshipped him and spoiled him in every possible way. His father could not bring himself really to discipline him. Even the white world felt his charm. He had none of the churlish resentment and antagonism of most young Negroes and did little courteous actions quite unconsciously, that disarmed the whites and brought out curious mutual warmth of feeling.

Once, when he was only 12, he met Zoe Coypel quite by accident. She was ten and had just moved to Atlanta. She had as yet little consciousness of race, and while he had much more, he quite forgot it at the sight of this radiant girl with corn-colored hair and deep blue eyes. She was starting to cross the crowded highway with the same abandon she had always exhibited in her little Carolina home town. He darted out into the traffic, lifted her lightly in his arms and laughingly set her back on the sidewalk. She looked up breathlessly, and for a moment both stared into each other's beautiful eyes. Then, horrified, Mrs. Coypel caught up and seized Zoe.

"Baby, aren't you ashamed of yourself! Get out, boy! Don't you ever dare touch a white girl!"

It was over in a second. It was not forgotten for ten long years.

Simultaneously with the Atlanta game of colored teams, there took place the game between Georgia Tech and the University of Georgia, a matter of bitter and long-standing rivalry. It would have been wiser not to have the two games scheduled the same day, but Manuel had not thought of this and since they were playing at separate ends of the city there was no reason to believe it would lead to any clash.

Of course, the colored teams must be particularly careful, and so far as possible keep to their side of town. This was carried out without difficulty, except at the very last moment when partisans of both teams approached the Union station at almost the same time. The state school had been triumphant over Atlanta University, and Georgia Tech over the University of Georgia. The colored team was marching up Mitchell Street with a crowd of students; the white team was approaching the Union Station from the other direction down the same street. There was no need for them to meet. The white team could have passed into the front of the depot which was the entrance for white folk; the colored team would enter the side door where Negroes were supposed to go. But both crowds thoughtlessly or carelessly or impishly surged out of bounds.

There was plenty of time before trains would leave. The Negroes overflowed past the depot along Mitchell to Whitehall, singing and cheering. The whites deliberately rushed past the depot down Mitchell almost to Friendship Baptist Church. Then, turning back, both became entangled and intermixed. The whites, according to custom, were in many cases drunk. The blacks had drunk little because of ground rules and vigilant white police, but they were enthusiastic and self-assertive. There was no call for anything more than some good-natured pushing and shoving, but this was the South. Here Southern tinder was ready to flash into flame.

It was due chiefly to the playing of Bruce Mansart that the colored State College had triumphed decisively. He was the hero of the day and led the march to town, to finish the celebration and to accompany the pretty girl, Sarah Linton, whom Bruce had escorted to the game. He had met Sarah when the Mansart family moved to Macon. She was cream-colored and good-looking, without being strikingly handsome. She was good company, sensible and capable. She had just opened in Macon one of the Madam Walker's hairdressing parlors, and on the question of allowing the girl students to attend her shop, she first came in contact with President Mansart and his family. She was courteous but insistent.

"You see, President Mansart, it is not easy for a colored girl to get respectable employment in Macon, outside house service."

Jean Du Bignon entered the lists and told of little Sarah Breedlove, her mother's friend. She related how rich and famous Madam Walker had become.

"Really, it is a saga of business for human improvement," she said.

Susan Mansart, the President's wife, backed her fiercely, and enjoyed the encounter. He asked Sarah's company to the football game, and they both enjoyed the trip. Bruce and Sarah were therefore in the lead of the mass of students marching in gala attire, with banners flying.

Leading the white students were Zoe Coypel and the captain of the Tech team, handsome and a little drunk. Zoe Coypel had become a sort of college widow. Coming to Atlanta at the age of ten, she had grown up as the darling of Tech campus, the prettiest of all its children, the best dressed, and encouraged by her mother in all sorts of gaity and social exploits. The mother was in her glory. She had money to spend by using most of Coypel's salary. She had a home which was beautiful and a center of social activities. By the time Zoe was twenty, she apparently could have married any of the eligible students or young men of the campus and city.

For a while, she was closely associated in all social events with Lee Baldwin, the son of the banker. Lee Baldwin, then 16, was too young for thought of marriage but was already "in society." He was gay and irresponsible and soon became dissipated and unscrupulous. Zoe's mother had almost forcibly to separate them. They were going much too far, even for her very liberal standards. Zoe then flirted here and there with undiscriminating abandon, and at the time of the football game, she was engaged to the captain of the Tech team.

Southern tradition was that the colored people should always yield the sidewalk to the whites; but in common practice, tradition was not always called upon to act. In this case, however, on account of the crowd, somebody must step off the sidewalk if the two groups were to pass; and quite naturally the whites did not propose to. Also, almost as naturally, these young Negroes were not at first disposed to yield. But custom was strong, and as the two groups stopped and glared at each other the colored students back of Bruce and Sarah slowly and silently gave way and passed into the street.

But Bruce stood facing the whites, holding Sarah behind him and backing up against the inner wall of stores. There was left passage enough for the whites, but they were flushed with drink, trimuph and racial arrogance. The young football captain especially, triumphant in sport and escorting the loveliest girl of the campus, could not for a moment think of yielding an inch to a black boy, especially one as lithe and handsome as Bruce, who took the opportunity to look straight into Zoe's eyes. She looked back and then shrank into her escort's protecting arm. She was a dazzlingly beautiful girl, daringly dressed, and used all her life to having her own way. In her presence and as her escort, no human power appeared strong enough to induce the captain of the football team not to show off his muscular and racial superiority.

It was all momentary, and yet might have passed harmlessly until the inevitable word passed: "See that damn 'nigger' crowding Zoe off the walk!" There was a scuffle and an oath, and in a minute the captain and Bruce were rolling in the gutter, clawing and striking.

It was then that the white police moved in, led by Officer Branigan, a fat and leisurely sergeant. As a disciple of Scroggs and a born "nigger hater," he realized that here was racial trouble where he need not hold his punches. In a moment he had brushed the crowd aside, seized Bruce by the neck and pulled him away. Wildly the boy lunged and struck the officer square in the eye, and the large and rather corpulent man stepping back, stumbled and sprawled in the gutter.

His fellow policemen launched themselves on Bruce. He was pounded, torn and thrown into the Black Maria which appeared with a shriek. A dozen black students were also arrested but none of the whites. The black students were quickly released, except Bruce. Once in the city jail, Officer Branigan took off his coat, rolled up his sleeves, and with the help of his fellow officers beat Bruce until he was insensible.

Bruce was never again the same person. The several broken bones healed quickly. The scar under his eye almost disappeared, only to pulse and glow red in excitement. He soon looked nearly the same, but he never was. His spirit was twisted, his disposition soured. There was a headache that never left him, always hurt, and at times changed from faint discomfort to a piercing flame that drove him half insane.

President Mansart had not attended the game and heard of the trouble from a telephone call to Macon which Sarah Linton made just before she boarded the train. He immediately telephoned President Coypel and hurried to Atlanta. Together they went down to the jail. Bruce was a sickening sight and both he and Coypel were terribly moved. Mansart was calm but never forgave himself for not accompanying the team to Atlanta. He did not enjoy football games, and while he knew it would be wiser to go he had let his work hold him.

The boy was made comfortable and taken to a little colored nursing home on the West Side. In a few days, he was arraigned in court. A truculent lawyer, determined on making an example of him, asked for a chain-gang sentence. The magistrate wanted to agree, but he had had a telephone call from the governor. He came to the bench angry, and drummed his fingers while looking at Bruce.

"Nigger," he said, "you were lucky that you weren't lynched; and I ought to send you to the gang for a year. But since the policemen gave you a good beating, I am going to let you off with a fine of five hundred dollars."

Then, turning to Mansart he said, "What's your name?"

"Manuel Mansart."

"Well, Manuel, you will pay this fine now or I will send this boy up."

Mansart signed a check, which the magistrate refused to receive. They had to wait until the bank sent the cash.

From this incident, Bruce never recovered. In after years, Mansart often wondered if there might not have been some permanent head injury, but this at least was not certain. But the spirit of the sensitive, delicately-tuned boy was broken and his whole character changed.

Policeman Branigan declared that Bruce threatened, as he passed out of the courtroom, that he was going to kill Branigan someday; but this was forgotten in the excitement and distress occasioned by the whole incident. Neither the whites nor the blacks liked the occurrence. It was like the sudden revealing of hidden volcanoes that could fill the air with fire and blood, as once before in 1906.

Mansart was more shaken by this incident of Bruce than he ever confessed. It seemed to him that the firm foundation upon which he was building racial advance and comity between white and black showed itself horribly unstable. Susan Mansart, his wife, never really recovered from Bruce's predicament. She had not been well since the birth of Sojourner, in 1907, and in the last ten years had moped about her housework with frequent but seemingly not important illnesses. She had given up her social life and concentrated upon her children, and particularly upon Bruce. She hovered over him, often to his annoyance and resentment.

Soon Bruce made up his mind that he could stay no longer at the institution. He insisted on going West. He would live with friends of Sarah Linton in Birmingham and work at radio. He would write. His mother pleaded but he left. When he left his mother fell really into some sort of decline, losing flesh and giving up interest even in her home. Her religious life intensified. She took to careful attendance upon church and prayer meetings and thought she saw visions. Once, in the middle of the night, she woke Mansart and said with low intensity:

"Something is wrong with Bruce. I know it."

He pacified her by promising to get in touch with Bruce, since indeed they had not heard from him for a long time. In about two weeks, he received a letter from Bruce, from Kansas City, with $100 enclosed. It had but a few lines, but this money was to buy a present for his mother. She was pleased and hoarded the money, but she was not pacified.

"He isn't happy. He is in danger," she said.

During the next two years, letters came from Bruce from Birmingham, St. Louis, and Kansas City. He was well. He sent presents. But he said little, and he never returned.

Jean Du Bignon, watching this family tragedy with sympathetic eyes, conceived a plan. What the President and his wife needed was a new home, comfortable and modern. Part of their trouble was living in crowded and uncomfortable quarters and almost total lack of pleasant and relaxing surroundings. This was one of the penalties of Mansart's position. He was from the first afraid of spending money on himself. He chose without complaint an old house, already in desrepair, which had long encumbered the campus. He had it patched up and was himself as comfortable as he had ever been. Susan, his wife, also had never lived in a modern home. She was unused to the new gadgets and scared at the cost. Manuel did not exactly limit her spending, but he did not encourage it and Susan tried to spend no more than they had spent in Atlanta.

Jean pointed out that the new building program for the college had started. The new athletic stadium would open an unused part of the campus which now ought to be laid out for future development. The Board talked the matter over. Certainly, new dormitories for both men and women were needed. The Administration building should no longer try to house lecture rooms, but there should be a building devoted to recitations and laboratories. Finally, Presiaent Coypel exhibited plans of a residence for the President, which Jean had talked over with him and for which he had secured estimates. Manuel protested weakly, but the Board approved of the whole plan, to be added to the master plan already adopted.

The residence, on insistence of Coypel, came first, and Jean tried to get the interest of Susan but without great success. Susan had few suggestions and seemed actually frightened at all mechanical contrivances. She hesitated at a gas range, frowned at an electric refrigerator, and at first stubbornly refused a vacuum cleaner. Manifestly, a housekeeper, in addition to the regular help, was indicated, and accordingly Jean arranged that at least a part of the upkeep of the house of the president should be a college expense. Then she searched for a suitable woman to put in charge.

So at last, a ten-room house was finished, with porches, bedrooms, guest rooms and three baths; a large dining room and breakfast nook, and a fully equipped kitchen, a study, a music room, and lawns with shrubbery and flowers. But poor Susan looked on it without interest if not with distrust. She had too long been satisfied with a roof which did not leak, a wood stove with enough fuel to cook a full meal, and one bathroom. She never enjoyed the new home, for before it was wholly ready there came news from Bruce, and his mother simply closed her eyes and died.

President Mansart had walked into his office one morning and found Sarah Linton waiting for him. At first, he could not place her as she arose in her black dress and greeted him with sad eyes. Then he remembered, and instantly thought of Bruce. This was the girl who had been Bruce's closest companion and he knew she had kept in touch with him, and it was with her relatives and under an assumed name that he had stayed in Birmingham. He welcomed her to his inner office and waited for her to speak with apprehension. She began quietly:

"Bruce is dead," she said. Then, after a moment of silence, she continued: "He was hanged yesterday in Kansas City."

Mansart somehow felt that he had already known of the death and feared the shame of the end. For a moment he saw everything that he had built up begin to tumble about his ears. But Sarah Linton quickly reassured him:

"Bruce went to Birmingham at first. He found work in the shop of an electrician at laborer's wages with frequent lay-offs; but with the willing connivance of his employers, he got work at a bench and learned much of the trade. Eventually, the white workers sensed that a Negro at low wages was doing a good deal of the regular artisan's work and they resented it. He was discharged, but his employers found him work in a non-union shop at lower wages than whites earned, but at regular electrician's work.

"Finally, his new shop was in open conflict with the unions. Calling mob law to their aid and securing the cooperation of the American Legion and the Ku Klux Klan, the union men staged a riot which resulted in a free-for-all fight. In the end, Bruce found himself on the chain-gang under his assumed name with a six-months' sentence."

Sarah had gone to him and with her relatives tried in every way, on the one hand, to make him submit to the hard work, cruelty and insult of this slave labor; and on the other hand to secure a cutting down of his sentence. She was having some success when, for insolence and infraction of the rules, Bruce was mercilessly whipped. That night, he escaped, shooting the guard who had whipped him squarely through the forehead with a pistol that Sarah had smuggled to him. Together, they had concocted letters to be mailed from Kansas City to his people under his real name, while he had left her without word of his plans.

For more than a year, Sarah heard nothing of Bruce. After a time she had word of him from a jail in Chicago, whence he had written. She went to him immediately and from his lips pieced together the story of his wandering. From Birmingham, he had gone to Memphis and again found work in a non-union shop in a city where the unions were weak. As he was put to work of greater variety and bought books for study, he began to enjoy his work.

His headaches lessened in frequency, and confidence in a future returned. But not entirely; always, as he felt the headaches returning, he knew that there was something he must do, that he had sworn to do; and when the pain beat him toward unconsciousness he knew just what it was: he was going to kill a policeman and rape a white girl. He just had to or he could not live.

Then, in time he became more normal. He worked hard, read carefully and slept regularly. He experimented. His fellow workers got on with him. He was likeable and, as a lone Negro, not too conspicuous. Little discriminations in toilets and even meals were ignored, although some whites grumbled.

Then came the organizer from the North and talked of a union. For the first time Bruce heard of the philosophy of labor unions, which so far had only meant to him exclusion of Negro workers; and realized that they were not just designed to deprive Negroes of work. He told the organizer he was willing to join. The organizer included his name in the first list. Then came the protest:

"We can't have no 'niggers' in our union. Bruce may be all right but others will pour in. We can't make no exceptions. Take Bruce north and give him a job there."

Bruce heard of this and waited for the organizer to approach him. When he did not and the organizing proceeded, Bruce went to him.

"I hear the whites don't want me in their union."

"That's so, Bruce."

"Can't I do the work?"

"You're the best man on the job."

"Well, I don't exactly like to leave the South; it's my home and I don't relish running away, but I don't want to be in the way of progress here; if you'll get me a job North, I guess I can stand the snow."

The organizer looked uncomfortable. "Tell you the truth, Bruce," he said, "They don't admit colored boys to the Electricians' up there, either. It's a damn shame. But you see, lots of Southerners have gone north; and besides, most Northern whites, don't like colored people much as equals."

Bruce was angry. "All right, then, I'll stay here and scab!"

The bosses were glad to have him and wanted him to get other Negro electricians. But Bruce knew of none. So matters moved on until the union was strong enough to strike. Then came the pickets, and Bruce crossed them. He was set upon and arrested and thrown in jail. The bosses settled the strike on union terms, but left Bruce in jail. When Bruce was released he went to St. Louis. He had a good kit of tools, a little money and a considerable library of books. He thought of setting up a small repair shop, but he lacked enough money. The only work that offered was bell-hop in a hotel.

This opened up unaccustomed vistas. He had before this seen nothing of the idle, spendthrift rich; knew little of indulgence in alcohol or gambling by the poor. He was soon carrying liquor to guests and drinking with his mates. He began gambling. He cared little for drink and got but moderate excitement in dice. Yet, he needed companionship; he might increase his savings, and could not appear to hold himself above his fellows.

So he lived on carelessly but with increasing uneasiness and lack of interest. He was always astonished at the futility of others' lives. The business men were always hurrying out so as to come back and get drunk. His fellow workers, too, were often drunk nights and living miserable days, and seemed either broke or riotously extravagant. There was a big, florid white woman, rich, over-dressed and often drunk. She threw her money about and flaunted her jewels and yet was never happy. Often, he saw her in tears or furiously angry.

One day he found the woman's handbag. He knew it by sight and went to her room to return it. She was not in. Then, instead of searching for her he hurried to the dinner served for the help knowing that if he were late he'd get little to eat. Then, with the bag stuffed carelessly in his side pocket, he went back upstairs to the lobby, and seeing the woman in the center of an excited crowd —which was not unusual—he went up to her and handed her the bag. An ominous silence fell on the crowd. She took the bag roughly, while a policeman seized Bruce and clicked handcuffs on him.

She cried out, "No, no; let him go; they're all here!"

"Are you sure? Look carefully." She turned out the hoard of gorgeous jewels on the floor where they gleamed like a galaxy of magnificent stars. Then carelessly she swept them together again. "I tell you they're all there. Let the boy go. Here." And she thrust out a bill.

The policeman was still suspicious. "Where'd you get the bag, 'nigger'?" he asked.

"I found it on a chair on the lounge."

"That's right—there's where I had it—"

"What did you do then?"

"She was not in her room and I went to supper."

"And found you couldn't hock them so you brought them back. If you listen to me, Madam—"

"I tell you, let him go. Here, boy," and she again thrust the bill into his hand as the handcuffs reluctantly fell away.

Sick and bitter, Bruce moved away and the Bell Captain slowly and unobtrusively followed.

"How much did she give you?" he whispered later. Then he whooped. "Five dollars! And them jingles worth at least a hundred thousand! My God! Listen, boys." And they crowded about and jeered beneath their breaths: "Honesty is shore the best policy—for saps!" cried one.

It was a day later, after work hours, that the Bell Captail approached Bruce again.

"Say, Bud, ain't you a mechanic of some sort?"

Bruce told listlessly of his work as an electrician. The captain eyed him calculatingly.

"That office safe where she keeps her jewels when she ain't drunk, that ain't so hard to open, is it?"

Bruce looked at him and he at Bruce; then both turned away. Bruce brooded. He had once assumed that good work was wanted and well paid in the sense of furnishing a living and the joy of creation. Then he found that men often were not allowed to do what they could do but must do what they disliked in order to eat. But even so, if they worked hard there would be a chance in time to do their own work. But no, no; hard work sometimes resulted in nothing and even brought suspicion and danger. Why not then steal instead of dig? Danger? What was Life but Danger? Wrong? What was Right?

So he waited until the Bell Captain returned at night with two white men, well but plainly dressed and quiet. They came straight to business: "The hotel safe contains generally considerable wealth: jewelry, valuable papers, bonds, some cash. There is ample opportunity to get at it. But the stuff once removed would be difficult to cash in on."

"What would you want to open the safe and turn the contents

over to us?"

Bruce had thought it over. "Two thousand dollars, cash!" he answered. They agreed. It proved very easy. Very early one morning in the slack season, Bruce opened the safe and his confederates took the contents. They gave him two thousand dollars in small bills. That night he left for Macon.

He slipped quietly into the city and went to Sarah's home. He looked worn and wild. He smoked incessantly and devoured the *Atlanta Constitution* which Sarah always had. He read only the society news, and searched for the name of Zoe Coypel. Suddenly Bruce was on his feet.

"Loan me your car."

Sarah looked doubtful. "It's late, Bruce—near midnight. I'll need the car tomorrow afternoon for calls."

Bruce turned his eyes on her. "I'll be back before noon."

Sarah sighed. In a moment he was flying up the street with open throttle. Early next morning he rode out Peachtree road, Atlanta. He hid his car in the woods beyond the Point and waited. About nine a car passed. He recognized young Lee Baldwin. Two hours later Zoe came in her small roadster. Bruce saw her tiny red hat and golden ringlets. He stepped directly in the path of the car. She swerved quickly and came to a halt. He stepped on the running board. She looked startled at first and then sat proudly beautiful, with something of insolence and pity in her look

She whispered. "Once when we were children and I first saw you I thought you were the most beautiful boy on earth. I could have loved you, and in a decent world we might have worked with God. It was never possible, it never will be." Deliberately she raised her fingers and touched the grey lock in his hair. He recoiled angrily, but she continued whispering: "You won't touch me; you can't, you're too decent."

"Get out of the car," he said in cold, impassive anger.

"I won't. Get down, you fool. There'll be a car along any minute." Then she continued slowly. "Bruce, I know what you feel and what you've suffered. I once told my mother that I loved you and was going to run off with you. She was aghast and furious. Said you were a dirty 'nigger' and that decent little white girls never could look twice at you. She gave me the first real beating I ever had. I was concsious of you for the next ten years, but never saw you again until the day we and the football coach collided and that policeman beat you. I almost fainted. I was sorry—terribly sorry; but what could I do?—Here's a car—get down and look at my tire." The car passed, unheeding. "Now, go."

He wavered and gripped her hand. "I was going to rape you," he blurted. "I was going to force you to yield to me in revenge for the hurt and horror done me; and then I'd kill that cop—"

She stared in terror and pity, hesitated and stammered, "Nonsense, Bruce, don't be a fool. You can't hurt me, you don't dare; you don't really want to. If you did, you'd be lynched and I'd be shamed for life. —There's another car. Step back behind the tree." The car passed. "Now Bruce, dear Bruce, please go." And suddenly putting her arms about his neck she kissed him.

He trembled and the tears rushed to his eyes as he clasped her while his heart hammered. He drew her toward him gently. For a moment she resisted and then yielded, her body softened and molded itself aaginst his. Her arms bound him closer and closer until their lips clung. She sobbed as she whispered:

"O Bruce, I think I have loved you since I first saw you, since you took me in your arms and carried me across the street. I have tried to love others. I have made believe, but always, always it was you—the velvet of your skin, the witchery of your eyes, the deep, loving, beautiful You that slept within your soul and mine. But it was useless from the first. God and the World was against us. I know I must not even think of you; you knew you dare not think of me. We were torn apart and sent to Hell just for this glorious love of ours. Go, Bruce, go, run and never come back—"

Then he felt her stiffen suddenly in his arms.

"Careful," she whispered. "A cop. He is hiding across the road."

Bruce was suddenly sane. "Slip down into the grass," he whispered. "Lie still. I'll circle around."

The morning was deathly quiet save for the twitter of birds and tinkle of waters. Making wide and noiseless detour, Bruce, peering back from the far side, could see the policeman creeping slowly and very carefully toward the spot where Zoe lay. He knew every bulge of that gross body. He saw him unlimbering his revolver; then he leaned over the girl. She stared coldly up into his face and never moved a mucle. The policeman leered and fumbled at his pants when Bruce raised a thick knotted hickory log and struck with all his might. Brains and blood spattered ten feet away.

With no sound, Zoe slipped to her feet and into her car and

in a moment was gone. Another moment Bruce lingered and harkened. No one passed by. Then, Bruce too was gone, and by noon drove into Sarah Linton's yard in Macon.

He spoke hardly a word and would not eat. For a moment, he stared at her sorrowfully, stroked her hair and took five of the dollars in the pocketbook she handed him. He was in a strange mood, such as she had never before seen him in. He was at once elated and calm. The old fear and bewilderment was gone and in its place a grim firmness. He talked a bit. Promised to send an address and return all he had borrowed, and to write to his mother. Rather tenderly he asked pity for all the trouble he had caused her. He might never see her again, but she would hear—she would hear. Just before the late train went, he slipped quietly away.

That night he was in Columbus and next day in Anniston. There, in a cheap lodging, he lay all day long and thought. He felt at last free. He had paid the vow which for two years had held him like a steel vise. That policeman was dead and the white girl —she had passed from a hated obsession and had become a lovely memory; but dead, or never, never born; never born. Now, at last, he could live. He would work hard; he would show the world what lay in him, what dreams he had and what plans he would make real. Crime? He had done no wrong. He had but avenged justice. They would not find him; that he never feared. He would seek work, any work. By night of next day, he was a porter in a factory. He hardly heard what wage he was offered.

Soon he was again on the road. This time he went to Kansas City. He was trying to persuade himself that the vengeance which his mandhood absolutely demanded was now settled and that he was going to begin an honest life under his own name. But this was going ot begin an honest life under his own name. But this was far harder than he had dreamed. Not only was his ability for hard work decreased but his desire for it was changed. He saw the whole world out of bitter eyes. He tried to work but his body was too weak. He tried to get employment in electrical work and radio but there was the old difficulty of union opposition, low wages and casual employment. Then a new scheme sprouted in his fertile brain. He could no longer do regular manual labor. His body was too weak, his headaches too frequent. But he could plan; he could scheme. He had certain theories of electricity. He had read of the cosmic ray and the fissure of the atom. With sufficient leisure he might give himself to a life of rest and thought.

There was one way of making money which he had neglected, and that was gambling. He had been in the midst of it since he left Macon. Everybody gambled in some way. What was business but gambling? He would work out a system, add a few thousands of cash to his savings and retire. After a good rest and perhaps sojourn in a hospital, he would start life with Sarah.

He began to study games and probabilities, and to frequent gambling joints. But Kansas City was small potatoes for real gambling, even if he could have penetrated the white places, which of course he could not. He went to Chicago. Soon, he knew where the big games were and soon the gamblers sensed that a new operator was in town. He played conservatively and by system, and he began to make money. He was watched. Many were sure that he was a professional and was cheating. But he was never caught. With many ups and downs he was, after six months, in sight of his goal. He was also the spotted victim of a set of thieves and murderers. He began to feel the strain.

That night, as he drew the last two thousand dollars into his grasp and put it leisurely into his wallet, he felt the headache coming. He turned slowly and refused a third time to give the losers another chance at satisfaction. He was afraid he might drop into a coma. He turned to the toilet, slipped through its window and fled without hat or coat. By morning, he was back in Kansas City and in the quiet retreat where his belongings, including his savings, were safely hidden. He added his last winnings and dropped into the torpor of burning pain.

How long he lay he never knew, but long before he could move he knew the thieves had found him. He did not move but watched under half-closed lids. They searched long and tirelessly with eyes on him, but it was in vain. Then they decided on torture. It was a risk they knew, but they simply could not discover the money they knew must be there. A bullet from that pistol of Bruce, which had already taken two lives, rang out. A man dropped dead, two others leaped out the window, and Bruce gathered up and pocketed his money.

He found himself in possession of five thousand dollars. But he was not in possession of himself. He had neither the physical energy nor the mental brightness to go on with his plan. He was tired, lonesome, discouraged. He felt himself beaten by life. He knew he was through. He arose and dressed carefully. Then he summoned the police and ordered breakfast. He was going to make no further effort.

When the police came, he confessed not simply to the murder of the man on the floor but to the murder of the white guard in Birmingham and his escape from the prison. He also told them frankly that there was a third murder but the time and place of that he would not confess. The trial was swift and decisive. He was sentenced to be hanged. It was then that he wrote to Sarah again and she left her shop and rushed to him. She pleaded with the governor. He was sympathteic but showed her that nothing could be done. Here was a cold-blooded, self-confessed murderer, a man broken in strength and ability early in his manhood. He gave promise of nothing but a life of crime. The only concession she could get was the possession of his body. There was no sign of any money.

That body lay now embalmed in the establishment of an undertaker in Kansas City, still under the assumed name. Mansart left that day for Kansas City, simply saying that he had heard from his son Bruce who was desperately ill in the West. From Kansas City, without appearing himself, he had the body shipped to Chicago to be received and cared for by his son, Douglass. Douglass, through an undertaker friend, had the body carefully re-dressed with signs of violence eliminated, and then Mansart telegraphed to Macon that his son Bruce was dead of pneumonia and that he was bringing the body home.

Jean Du Bignon, in charge of the president's office while he was away, and overseeing the new buildings, had one visitor who intrigued her. He was an old black man, very apologetic and humble. He had something "very important" for the president's ear alone. He was sorry the president was away. He would wait. No? Well, he would return. He returned again and again. Finally, Jean told him that the president would be delayed. Would he not better tell her what he wanted? He hesitated, evaded, and finally eagerly warned her not to let the President dig up the old and hitherto unused stretch of land where once the Claytons had lived. He worked for the Claytons; they were "his people." Old Miss Nancy was the last survivor and his present mistress. He warned and pleaded. The State didn't have no right to take this old plantation and Miss Nancy ought never to have sold it. The land was haunted. The result of building on it would "Be turrible! Turrible! There would be death and destruction!"

CHAPTER XII

THE SECOND SON

Revels Mansart, even as a boy, had few enthusiasms. He could work hard, he had a clear, incisive mind. His feelings he kept subordinated. He talked little. His experience in the army emphasized these traits, especially that horrible interlude when for six months he was unjustly under sentence of death. He became silent and cynical. He made up his mind that life was a fight and particularly a fight with white people, in which the thinker who was not burdened wtih scruples had a chance to come out ahead. He determined that he was going to become a lawyer and eventually sit on the Bench. He was going to work, not for humanity nor for "his people," but for Revels Mansart. Not with exclusive and silly selfishness, but simply to make it possible for him to have a decent life in spite of American color prejudice.

In order to have this, he must have education and position, and he must have money; particularly, he must have money and a good deal of it, so as to get his education in college and in law, so as to maintain a position in a law firm, so that he could choose his clients and make a reputation; and finally, to become a judge and live with limited work and with the comparatively few things which he really enjoyed. He had no strong sex appetite. He did not care about showing off. He would like a good automobile and chauffeur. He would like a well-attended home. He would like to have books and see pictures and hear music.

The education of the Mansart children had emphasized being unselfish, not lying, nor cheating, nor stealing. Yet much of this moral teaching was nullified by the example of the surrounding white world.

Then, suddenly, his entire outlook whirled and turned in a new and fantastic direction. It happened this way: when he was pardoned and discharged by the army court-martial, he met, as he left the portals of the New York City Jail, that same young white Colonel who was in charge of his regiment in the Argonne, and who had so miserably failed in his duty. It was Mansart who had found him hiding in the rear and in tears. The Colonel begged his pardon, and freely acknowledged his own deficiencies. Mansart was not impressed, but tried to be courteous and soon left him. He saw him again at the court-martial in France, and realized that even under pressure, he was making his complaint against the colored officers as light as he could without putting too much of the blame for the fiasco upon himself and his white colleagues. Mansart discounted all this and forgot the man. Now, at the door of the jail house, when finally freed, this young Colonel Wright appeared suddenly and grasped Mansart's hand. At first, Mansart did not recognize him in mufti and stared at him.

"God, Mansart, I'm glad you're free. I could never have forgiven myself if you fellows had been shot," he said. Mansart saw actual tears in his eyes. He had never before in his life seen a white man weep over a Negro's misfortune. He grasped Wright's hand and murmured, "Forget it!"

"You must come home with me. It's all arranged. Hey, folks!" And he drew Mansart toward a group. There was the elderly father and mother, four young men and a beautiful girl. They were all grouped about a carriage with a span of horses. They greeted Mansart pleasantly and before he had time to make up his mind, he was in the carriage and sitting beside the girl, who was the Colonel's sister. Impulsively and with a perfectly natural display of friendliness, she seized both of Mansart's hands and said:

"We're so, so glad! I thought I'd die with indignation when Jack told us about you. We've moved heaven and earth to help, and now you're here and free! You must stay with us a week until you've rested. Jack says your folks are all in the far South, and of course you've no place to stop except a cold hotel. You will stay, won't you?"

The father and mother seconded the invitation courteously. Mansart could not quite find himself before he had assented and was flying northeast, toward Connecticut. When at last he was alone in a simple white bedroom, whence he could see the acres and buildings of the farm, he tried to collect his senses. He was tired, very tired. He was exhausted by three years of extraordinary experiences, full of insults, pain, fear and work. He had faced death in many forms, and now, when all faith in the white world had gone, he was suddenly welcomed with a cordiality such as he had never experienced even among his own family and race.

Particularly he, who had almost never looked twice at a woman of any color, had been welcomed with every exhibition of enthusiasm by a beautiful young white girl and pressed by her family to be a guest. Of course, he could not stay. These were not his people. He must hurry away and finish his education and begin his law study. Naturally also, he could not act crudely. He had met French gentlemen and ladies and sensed as never before in his life what breeding demanded. Then, suddenly he remembered the four men who had come along with the family. They were not relatives but, as he later gathered, fellow officers of the young Colonel. Two were from neighboring New England states, one from the Middle West, and one—of all things—a Captain Clayton, from Georgia. They were courteous, but as he now remembered, there was no cordiality in their welcome, rather surprise. No, this was an impossible situation and he must go as soon as possible.

But he reckoned without Mary Wright. She had heard of the Argonne, when it occurred, and was deeply touched by the plight of the Negro officers. Moreover, she frankly liked Revels. He was so quiet and austere, held himself erect but he was so weary and tried so hard to act normally in strange surroundings. All of her life she had heard of Negroes, for her grandparents were Abolitionists. But she had seen few black folk and these from afar. The few she had met were poor and ignorant and a bit bizarre. She had never met a colored person of education and manners. Mansart's smooth brown skin fascinated her, as did his soft Southern accent intertwined with French. She was aroused to instant indigation and defense when she overheard the young officers talking to her brother.

"Oh, it's all right, Jack; you did the right thing under the circumstances. But don't forget that 'niggers' are 'niggers' and always will be. You can't welcome them into the family or you'll regret it."

"But you can welcome them into your army," flashed Mary, "and let them die for a country that was never theirs." Next morning, Captain Clayton, from Georgia, left and Mary did not urge him to stay. But when it came to Mansart, she simply would not let him go. Her parents were a bit amused, but Mary had always had her way. Her brother was at once glad and uneasy to note Mary's interest. He had been too deeply hurt by lhe Argonne incident not to want to see something done by his family to atone. The parents noticed nothing too unusual. They had always championed colored people and were rather pleased to have, for the first time, a Negro in the family. They treated him exactly like a son.

To Mary dawned a new and exciting experience. She was twenty and had never before met a man whom she could think of as a lover. The neighborhood boys were much too everyday to be thought of as husbands. The out-of-town suitors, and there had been several, all seemed of one pattern, which she did not like—smart, overbearing and presumptuous. She wanted difference, adventure, a cause, and a hero to lead it. She found all this suddenly in Revels Mansart. But he made no overtures, no response.

For the first few days, such a thing as love between him and a white girl, simply never for a moment entered his head. He had been brought up to regard racial intermixture as the crime of white men or, in a colored man or woman, as cowardly betrayal of their people, a miserable crawling after those who despised you. Of love and sex, he had had no experience with colored girls, and in France had recoiled from the prostitutes whom the army furnished, and made no advances to other women. He prided himself as one who never intended to surrender to the slavery of married life until he was rich and settled. He had never experiencd affection or caresses from mother nor sister, nor any other woman.

The sympathy and effection of Mary, her close and intimate understanding, came like a sudden revelation, and the day when, almost by accident, he touched her hand, and found her nestling in his arms in utter surrender, with her golden hair falling over his face, he as well as she were ready for the accolade of heaven.

Her brother Jack was too astonished to speak as he came upon them. Then his anger burst like a flame. He would have murdered Mansart then and there, but Mary towered before him in such wrath as he had never seen.

"Yes, I love him and we are going to get married. And what will you do about it?" she screamed. But Mansart left that night without food or baggage. He just staggered into the night and grovelled in utter abasement. He caught the midnight train to New York and awoke in the morning to find Mary calmly seated beside him with his bag and hers. She would not let him talk until they were in the depot restaurant and there they talked in low tones for two hours.

Mary put the matter tersely and clearly. Evidently, she had thought long and carefully. His objections, she said, were idiotic.

He was a grown man. She was a woman. They were not criminals. They were healthy and clear of mind. They both knew their own minds. This was a free country and what demanded more freedom than the love of one person for another? The only possible hindrance to their marriage was the fact that other people would not approve of it. Very well. They need not marry colored people if they did not want to. She did want to and that was that.

Mansart pulled himself together and argued calmly. He loved her. Never had he dreamed that he could love a human being as he did her. He shrank from no sacrifice nor suffering for her. But he did shrink and with horror from what he knew she must suffer if she married him—the public insult, the loss of old friends and making no new ones, the hostility of police and employers. How would they live? What would they do for a living? How could they ever earn enough to live like people? And what—he gulped as he said this—"What would be the fate of our children?"

Mary was unmoved; she even smiled. "Revels, dear, I'm no china doll. I can face hurt and pain if I must. What I cannot do is to surrender without a fight my right to freedom and happiness just because ignorant and bigoted Americans are determined to guide my life. No, Revels, I want you for my husband and the father of my children. If you don't want me or don't dare to be yourself, I can take the next train home."

Of course, there was but one answer possible and they began to plan. They would get a marriage license and hire an apartment. They would get married. Revels had what he had saved of his army pay. He would soon get a bonus. Mary had a thousand dollars in her own bank account and five thousand in bonds left her by an aunt; she had her part of the family property. Revels would go to college and then to law school. Mary would get a job. So off they went into the world.

The next year could only be described as a combination of Heaven and Hell for the young couple. They were passionately in love with each other and by that token sensitive and frightened at any sign of unhappiness or hurt and each too willing to blame themselves as the cause. Both knew about American color prejudice: Mansart from life experience; Mary from conversation and reading. But neither quite dreamed of how far it could go in a case like theirs; both thought they could ignore it or turn their backs against it. But as an evil, aggressive, cruel and resentful cloud of hate and hurt from which there was no escape—of this neither of them dreamed.

First, there came the difficulty of finding a home. Colored tenants in Harlem did not welcome a white neighbor; white tenants nowhere would welcome a colored man. Rents were higher in Harlem than elsewhere, but Harlem was near City College where Revels matriculated. Two poorly lighted rooms were found at $50 a month. The task of keeping them clean and clear of vermin was hard. The surroundings of folk and scenery were bad. The food in the Harlem stores was poor and dear, consisting usually of goods unsaleable downtown.

Revels had to work hard to keep up and insure his baccalaureate in three years. He toiled night and day. Mary sought a job. But even a white girl, with no skills, either worked for next to nothing, or, if pretty, was offered work by men who expected to sleep with her. Beyond this, whenever the fact of living in Harlem was learned, she was under suspicion, and when it was learned that her husband was black, she was either dismissed or her very beauty and comeliness was a lure for procurers. When they went out together, matters mounted often to unendurable insult. Everybody stared; stared and often commented aloud. She was set down as a prostitute and her husband as a pimp. Once they were arrested and several times policemen truculently questioned them. Colored women sniffed and white women were sometimes openly insulting. Virtuous matrons withdrew their skirts, and missionaries openly proselyted and were more incensed to learn that she was married than they would have been if she proved a street walker. They had no friends, none to speak to. Once Mary accosted her colored neighbor:

"Why do you dislike me so much?"

"People like you should let our men alone."

"Like me? What do you mean? I am a wife and love my husband. What is wrong about that?"

The woman stared, but said no word. Mary missed human companionship; she had always been neighborly and used to making friends on the street, in stores and in buses. To Mary, then, a friendless, retreating world came as a startling surprise. She soon learned to expect no courtesy from white folk, particularly if she was connected or classed with Negroes. But it struck her like a blow when the colored women of her neighborhood and even apartment house, seemed to resent her. One day she turned on the woman next door as she refused to respond to Mary's cheery "Good morning." Mary walked right up to her and said:

"How have I hurt you?"

The woman hesitated and started to speak when her husband came along. He scowled and both turned away. Yet, the very next night, as Mary ran into the man again, he asked her to step aside and when she did he deliberately made overtures to her. She felt sick at the stomach, but she said no word of this to Revels.

Gradually, they stopped going out in public together save on rare and necessary occasions. Revels stopped because he knew that at some affront he might be guilty of murder; it shattered him to see her insulted. Mary stopped because she sensed his distress and knew no way to make him disregard what was usually nothing but bad manners and the American desire to step on the helpless. But from whatever motive, they began to go out together seldom. Then, in compensation, Mary tried to make the home attractive. It was a hopeless job, from noise, dirt, cold and heat and the landlord's neglect.

Recreation together was difficult. Theaters were too expensive; movies in Harlem were dirty and crowded and downtown visits took time, involved rides on the subway and sometimes ran into discrimination. They listened to the small radio at home when anything worth listening to appeared and they sang together; Mary with her lovely soprano and Revels with his low, fine bass, when he was not too tired.

Gradually, too, the increasing cost of living made it necessary for them to review their financial position. Revels would have been hurt to the heart to have her sell her bonds for his support. His two thousand dollars and her thousand might, if stretched, last a year or eighteen months. But what after that? What of the other years in college and in law school? Mary insisted that they must sell her bonds. But Revels pointed out that even this would scarcely see them through, while it would advertise their failure to family and friends, and then they must think of the starving term which any lawyer faces—especially colored lawyers. He undertook to do work at night in a restaurant down on the East Side. He did not mind the work, but he could ill afford the time from his hard schedule. When some of his professors learned that he was married, **they dropped all desire to help him and at least one went further** than this.

Mary found work in a clothing factory, alongside Puerto Ricans who talked little English, with long hours, frequent layoffs and low wages. Revels writhed and the strained nerves of both led to some quarrels and misunderstandings. Then, always in deep abasement and with cruel regrets, they made up and clung together closer in soul and body. But Revels grew thin and silent; Mary was often sick of mornings—more often than she let Revels know. He, being silent and introspective, suffered more than she suspected. The dishwashing made him sick, and of nights he lay very still beside her when, as more and more frequently he could not sleep.

Then came the end. They had been gentle to each other as Mary left for the day. Perhaps Revels was more silent than usual, but there was no word of disagreement, and he remembered afterward the last long kiss she left on his drawn mouth. That night when he returned at midnight, she was not at the door with her sweet smile. There was no response to his ring and repeated call. Then, on the pillow he saw the letter and he knew. It was what he had expected and feared with a nameless dread.

"Dear Revels:

I am leaving for good. It was impossible from the first. Goodbye. God keep you."

It was typed and signed by a sprawling "M." For a moment he wondered where she got the typewriter, and then he remembered the factory. He uttered no word or sound. He gathered up his clothes and books and packed them in his suitcase and under his arms. So far as he thought clearly, it was to escape so that she could never find him. It would be so like her to repent and come back. He must never allow such a fatal sacrifice. As she had written, "It was impossible from the first." He must hide. He must leave this apartment and transfer from City College as soon as possible. He staggered away in the night. He never saw Mary again.

Revels transferred to Wesleyan College, in Connecticut, where by scholarships and the hardest sort of study, he not only succeeded in forgetting his marriage and its ending, but regained his health and got his A.B. in 1923. He got a scholarship for the Columbia Law School and began his law course. Only once did his past sorrow find him again. He received a letter forwarded from his old address, asking him to answer an application for divorce from Mary Wright Mansart. He wrote immediately assenting to all demands.

Then he drowned himself in work. True it was that the pain within again tore his soul. He knew now that a last hope lurking far down within was dead, and forever. He put every thought of his past out of his mind forever. He deliberately hardened his heart. What he wanted was a chance to earn a living which really could be called a living. He did not propose to crawl through life on his belly. If his nation and his times would not give him a living he was going to take it. He was going to take it carefully, even if it involved crime; but take it he would.

What white people did to each other was not always clear. But what they did to Negroes was all too open—they lied, stole and cheated, not only with impunity but with public approval. Revels therefore would never steal from his own folk or cheat them. He might not always tell them everything, but what he said would be true. With white people on the other hand, he had no such compunctions. He frankly began to explore how he might earn a living at the expense of whites with no moral scruples as to methods.

The first thing he sought was money. His father did not have much and there were other children. Douglass was taking care of himself completely through his business enterprise. Bruce seemed rather crazy, but he might find himself. Sojourner—she would probably stay home. After all, he did not see much of her and did not think much about her. She was an ugly little nonentity.

He borrowed $500 from his father to help him pay his way through law school. This was rather a difficult thing for his father to arrange, but Revels promised to repay it and Manuel knew that in time he would. Then Revels sat down to figure out how he was going to make some real money. It was impossible for him to get a money-making job and at the same time study and practice law. There was no use thinking of house service or work in hotels or work as a pullman porter. They called for hard service, and they paid almost nothing beyond support. Above all, they left no time for his profession.

As he was in his senior year in law school, there came one gleam of light. He knew that students who maintained high marks had a chance on graduation to be taken into the office of some judge of a high court, either state or federal. This gave experience and led usually to a junior partnership in a good firm. Of course, there stood the color line. Could he surmount it? Probably not, but he was going to try. He got high marks by studying day and night. He made the law school *Review*. There was the annual prize essay. His paper was certainly among the best, but the dean, from Mississippi, called the professors together. "Gentlemen, most of you have marked Mansart as highest."

They agreed and several made comments on Mansart and his work in general.

"Yes, yes," said the Dean, "but of course you know, gentlemen, that there is no absolute scale on which an essay or a man's work can be marked. Now, there are reasons which make it unwise for this school to overemphasize the work of a Negro. You know that. Even if he wins, no reputable firm will hire him. Would it not then be wisest on our part, and avoid controversy, if we let Mansart rank second or third rather than first? In the long run, it can make no difference." The professors dispersed, but one returned later and reduced Mansart's mark, so that he stood third. Of course, Mansart eventually heard the truth. He was not surprised. "Merit cannot win if it is black," he said.

He then frankly faced the question as to whether the various illegitimate ways of making money held any promise. Frankly, he doubted if any one ever got rich honestly. Of course, some methods of accumulation were worse than others. All were bad. Gambling, the buying and selling of prostitutes, the seeking of graft through politics, and other kinds of manipulation he shrank from. The policy game brought in a lot of money, but despite his cold and cynical nature, Revels couldn't see himself taking pennies from the black poor on such a game of chance.

Outright stealing from whites appealed to him as justice. But it is doubtful if he would have delibertaely planned anything of that sort had it not been that he met Captain Clayton again. He had first met this young white Southerner in France. Clayton had an inborn dislike of Negroes except as servants. He hated them as fellow-officers, but when asked to testify against the accused Negro officers in the Argonne, he flatly refused. He had been there himself and knew just what had happened. Mansart thanked him and shook his hand. It was the first time Clayton had ever taken a Negro's hand.

Then Revels had met him again at Mary Wright's home.

Neither liked the other but both held the other in a certain respect. Revels was astonished when Clayton walked into his office. It was in 1924. Revels had just been admitted to the bar and had established an office with two fellow students, a Jew and an Irishman who had been in practice two years. They had gone into partnership because they were all in the same boat. The only kind of law practice easily open to them was defense of petty criminals. But they needed money for clothes, board, rent, while they awaited more lucrative practice. They opened an office and waited.

Each had his specialty—the Irishman was the glib pleader; the Jew was the keen analyst. They needed a careful and accurate man for research and Revels gave promise of being such a man. But business was very slow. The prospects were not encouraging.

A day or so before Clayton appeared, a man had come into the office and asked specifically for Revels. This was the first time a client had done this. Usually, the few clients who called asked for a "lawyer" and if given a choice quite naturally took one of the young white men. Revels' recognized value came later in looking up the law and drawing the briefs. This was clearly understood from the start. To have, then, a stranger ask for him was a bit astonishing, until Revels saw the man. Of course, a poor colored man—then he noted that the man was an East Indian and not an American Negro. This was unexpected, for Indians usually avoided Negroes for fear of being identified with them and suffering their disabilities. This man was not well-tailored, but as soon as he began to speak he revealed that he was well-educated—probably in England, and his story showed that he had sought out Revels Mansart deliberately.

"In fact, I asked at the law school for a young colored attorney of ability," he said. "I am an Indian merchant, from Calcutta, where I was interested in the manufacture and export of jute. During the war I became a partner in certain European cartels which handled war material. This paid very well indeed, until the United States entered the war and seized the valuable assets of this cartel in this country. My own loss will be great—indeed, I face poverty—unless I can recover title to these assets. They are in the name of my former associates who were French and German. I have every reason to believe that they are making settlement, and, as white men often do, freezing me out. Legally, the matter is complicated and I must be very careful in any move I make. I want, therefore, the best legal advice. I cannot afford the best known, nor the most expensive; but my case is good and you have been recommended. I have come to you and brought all my papers. I firmly believe that my case is sound and if I win I will divide my gains with you on the most liberal terms."

Revels and his partners considered the case. They poured over the papers and searched the law and precedents. There was a chance to win, but it was faint and they were opposed by shrewd lawyers and big money. Moreover, those on the opposing side represented the very corporations which the firm hoped sometime to serve. On the other hand, if Revels wanted to take this case, it might be a chance for him. His partners liked him and he had ability of a high order. But they had begun to realize that a colored law partner was not wise. Here was a way out but they would not force him. If he chose to take the case they would suggest that he go it alone. That is what Revels decided to do. He saw the whole situation quite as well as his partners. He took the risk.

It was arranged that his partners should move to new offices, while Mansart stayed in the old. He must now redouble his efforts to pay rent and eat while working on the case of the Indian. It was at this time that Captain Clayton called. Revels was alone. Evidently, Clayton was rather uneasy and did not look too prosperous. Finally he blurted out the object of his visit:

"Mansart, your father is head of a Negro college in Macon. That college has recently bought a plantation of 600 acres which once belonged to my grandfather. I wonder if you ever heard of the Clayton treasure?"

Mansart thought a while and then said, "No, I do not believe I have!"

Clayton explained. "It is a story of the gold reserve of the Confederate states being buried in the outskirts of Macon after the surrender. And also," he added, "I know just what was buried and where. If I could get hold of it by myself I wouldn't be here; but I need help in getting it."

Mansart did not move nor show any particular astonishment. He simply waited. Clayton hesitated and then plunged on. "I'm at the end of my resources. The family fortune is gone to hell, nobody is left except an old aunt who lives on the platform in the outskirts of Macon, and one of our old retainers, an ex-slave. My aunt for years has postponed excavating this fortune because of deep conviction that all the heirs of those who took part in this venture must be found and consent. None have been located and now the critical time has come, since my aunt and I were offered a good sum by the State and had to sell before I could lay plans. I have in my possession a detailed statement of just what the Clayton treasure was, and I'm going to show it to you. No one outside of our family has ever seen it before. Here it is."

Revels reached for the document and read it. He read it with increasing astonishment. Frankly, he didn't believe it. It was an old letter on bond paper, in which Captain Clayton's father asserted that his father and several fellow officials before the surrender at Appommatox had taken a considerable part of the gold reserve from the Confederacy (which was never large and at the time amounted to perhaps $50,000, said the document), had taken this, packed it in a small beer keg, and smuggling it away from Montgomery, had buried it on his own Macon estate as their joint property. This estate had now been bought by the state for Mansart's college, and new buildings for farming were about to be built on it.

"If we let things go on," said Clayton, "in excavating they may run across this keg of gold."

And Revels echoed in his own mind,—"if it is there or if it ever has been there, or if this is anything more than a crazy legend." Still, the paper looked genuine. The man who wrote this believed what he was writing.

"Now," said Captain Clayton, "if you should go down to your father's college and settle there for a few months, I could put you in touch with the man who knows just where this keg is buried, and that man is the black ex-slave who is still working for my aunt. I have been keeping in touch with him, and lately he has written me frantically saying that the last landmarks are about to be moved, that we have got to dig up this keg now, that is, within the next few months or the college or the state will get it. I am asking you, if you will go in with me to recover this money?"

Revels considered. It occurred to him that here was a chance for him to get free board, and time for working on his case. On the other hand, this necessitated a return to the South at least for several weeks, and there he would find no law libraries open to

Negroes and no chance for legal consultation. Still, he could take books with him, have others sent, and he could stand Southern caste for a time if, of course, Clayton would pay the expense. And then, without beating around the bush, he said,

"How much is there in this for me?"

Clayton considered. "If the full amount is there, I should be willing to give you—" he hesitated— "—a thousand dollars."

Revels did not wink an eye. He simply folded up the papers and handed them back to the captain. "I am not interested," he said.

The captain fidgeted. Then he said, "Five thousand."

"It's a deal," said Revels. "But you must advance expenses."

"How much?"

"A thousand dollars."

"I haven't got it."

"Well, $500. That's the least. If not—"

Clayton counted out the money.

"And the balance?"

"When the gold is in my hands."

"No, the keg."

"Very well, the keg."

They went to work studying the map which accompanied the letter. Clayton kept the map but promised to let him see it again in Macon.

Revels wrote his father that he had taken a case which required study and concentration. He would like to do some intensive work that summer and he wondered if he couldn't have a little shack out where the new building was going on and bring down his books and study there. His father was overjoyed and said that it could be arranged easily. He could be made a sort of night watchman, with pay. So a short time after, Revels, in a dilapidated, second-hand car, drove into Macon. On that long ride, Revels determined to take at least half that treasure if he found it.

It would be wrong to think that Revels Mansart was by nature a thief. He was far from that. He hated theft. Not simply because it was dangerous but because it was cowardly. Because he wanted nothing that did not belong to him. He wanted to stand on his own feet nad make his own living. He was satisfied that under ordinary circumstances he simply had no chance to make a living as a lawyer, or, one might say, he had no chance to make a living that really could be called a living.

Here he saw a chance. He was under absolutely no obligation to this Southern white officer. He knew that the officer despised him and only came to him because he saw no other way out of his troubles. He was willing to trust a Negro because he believed the Negro would not dare try to cheat him, and if he did could easily be checkmated. Very well, he'd co-operate. He'd more than co-operate. He'd cheat and steal if necessary, because he was going to have an opportunity to do work that he knew he was capable of doing and he was going to do it well. So he simply stepped into this venture knowing exactly what he was going to do, what it involved, of possible crime and wrong, and what he might suffer for attempting it.

Before starting South, Revels had gone to the library and made a careful study of beer kegs at the time of the Civil War. Then he went to a theatrical property maker and told him quite clearly what he wanted: a beer keg of the standard size current in 1860 and supposed to have been kept in the ground ever since. The artisan stared at him and shook his head. It was a pretty difficult job. He doubted if he could do it. But he tried, and after several weeks a battered old keg was the result, which looked convincing. Then, before it was closed up, Revels calculated what a certain amount of gold would weigh. It would not, of course, be fifty-thousand dollars worth. Suppose he assumed that this thing was really true and that there was a gold hoard there. It might be $25,000. How much would $25,000 in gold weigh? Having ascertained, he put inside the keg an equivalent weight of sawdust and lead. Then he and the property man worked days to make this keg look as though it had lain 60 years in the earth. The result was not perfect, but plausible. Then he packed the whole thing in a trunk surrounded by law books. And it was with this equipment that he arrived in Macon.

The family welcomed Revels warmly. Douglass came down from Atlanta and spent a week. Soon, Revels was ensconced in a temporary shack near where the bulldozers were about to begin work. He arranged his simple furniture, stacked his books, was given a revolver and installed as night watchman. He ate with his family and remained an undemonstrative acquaintance. He met Jean Du Bignon.

On the third night of his arrival, an old black man slipped into his hut. It was the old Negro who was supposed to know just where the keg was buried. The Negro was secretive and frightened. He admitted that several people in the past had tried to get him to dig for the keg, but asserted that he had deliberately misled them. Now, Captain Clayton and his old mistress had ordered him to dig. He was ready to do it because he was under obligations to the Clayton family. They were "his people" and had been kind to him. But this was a fearful task. There were dark powers guarding the Clayton treasure; death and worse than death! Revels looked him over reflectively but made no comment. Finally, he said dryly:

"Very good. Where is the thing buried?"

The man revealed the map, but would not part with it.

They met next night out in the fields where the uneven ground heaved itself into mounds beneath old trees, boulders and remnants of half-ruined buildings. The old black man laid out an area in a half-hidden hollow, where a great oak rose a hundred feet; and indicated fifty square yards where he declared the keg must be hidden five or six feet beneath the ground. Revels later moved his hut and re-erected it near the tree, but not too near. The job of digging for the keg was evidently going to be difficult and strenuous, but Revels looked over the ground, read again the letter which he had carefully copied from Clayton's, and looked at the map which the old man carefully guarded. He said to himself, "This could be true. If it is, I am going to help get this money and I am going to keep more than the share which Clayton is willing to give me. On the other hand, if it is not true, I lose comparatively little."

Then began the nightly digging. It was a pretty hard job and left little time for study. They worked about four hours each night. After nearly a week's work Revels was quite willing to give up. They tried carefully to keep the evidences of their digging concealed. Nobody had seemed to notice anything, but they would have to hurry. The builders and surveyors were approaching this spot. Then came the find. They struck wood nearly seven feet down.

The old man did not know what to do. It was getting late and they had less than an hour before dawn. First he wanted to leave the thing in the ground until the next night. Mansart shrugged his shoulders. "Of course," he said, "somebody else might run across it." That was true. So working desperately they got the keg out and up and into the cabin. Then came another difficulty. The old man did not want to leave it alone with Mansart. Mansart said nothing. Soon the rattle of milk carts was heard. The man had to go. There was nothing to do but to leave it. So reluctantly he left. Mansart went to bed. And as he suspected, the old man crept back a half hour later to see if all was well. Then, finally, he disappeared.

When dawn came Mansart got up and compared the keg excavated with his taken from one of his trunks. They were not really alike. The one he had made was slightly larger, and of course the one they had dug up was much more dilapidated. Yet to note the difference called for much longer examination than they had been given. So without hesitancy, Revels made a bundle of the keg which they had dug up, wrapped it in oiled paper and in a blanket, removed the books from the trunk and put the keg in it, covering it with books and clothing, and closing and locking it.

Then he went back to the keg which he had substituted and began to work on it, with dirt and stain and the tools which he had ready. He made it look more like the old and dilapidated keg. It would, he was sure, pass casual inspection. But of course when it was opened it would be all too clear that this was a new and not an old keg. This risk he must take. He covered the keg with a blanket, went to his bath and breakfast and then came back to study.

As he half expected, during the next day Captain Clayton dropped in casually. He was taking a last glance at the old plantation, he explained. When he was alone with Mansart in the darkened room he hurried to examine the keg and seemed satisfied but nervous. He said that he was going to have an automobile ready sometime after midnight, and that the old man would come and carry the keg down. He would like to have a wheelbarrow which he could take along with him so as to leave no incriminating evidence. Mansart waited, and then finally said:

"And the check for $4,500?"

Clayton said impatiently: "I will have the check tonight."

Just after midnight the old black man was back, palpitating. Cautiously, they slipped the keg onto the wheelbarrow. It looked authentic and the old man showed no bit of suspicion as perhaps a more experienced person would have. They sat down to wait.

"Shall we open it?" asked Revels.

"No, no!" cried the old man, aghast at the mere mention of such sacrilege. "Marse Clayton will be at the gate with his car at two in the morning, prompt!"

Revels lay down and slept soundly. The old man watched nervously. He hardly moved his eyes from the keg. Revels had seen to it that a wheelbarrow was handy. They were at the gate at two, and there was Captain Clayton and his car. They started to load the keg, when Revels spoke.

"I believe you have something for me, Captain."

The Captain hesitated, as Revels expected he would. "You know I have nothing now."

"Then I must trust you for $4,500, with nothing to show for it?"

"Here is my note. It will be cashed as soon as I realize on this. Come, we must hurry."

Revels said nothing. It was coming out exactly as he had expected. If Clayton had paid him as promised, he in turn would have divided the treasure half and half. As it was, he would keep it all. Revels turned and walked slowly back to his hut.

The next morning he awoke early and began to review his position. If there had been a gold hoard, he had it, while Clayton and the old black were rushing away with the false keg which he had prepared. He began to figure out just what they would do when they found the deception. First of all, he was not going to run away. He was going to take his trunk, substitute it for another, and send it quietly by express to safe hands in New York, finishing the summer here with his study. If Clayton charged him with deception, he'd have to prove it, and how could he? If he offered to pay his note, Revels would demand half the contents of the keg which he must open in the presence of Revels.

While he was lying here considering his position, there came a clamoring at the door, and one of the workmen rushed in to tell him that an old black man had been found dead just outside the gate, his head horribly smashed. He had been identified as the old Clayton servant. Suddenly, Revels believed he saw Clayton's plot. He had killed the old man to destroy the evidence, and it might look as though this murder had been done by Revels.

But Revels became cold and careful. When the police came he told a straight story. Yes, he had several times talked to the old man who had an idea that there might be a treasure buried some-where on this land. He himself took no stock in this kind of thing, but it seemed that Captain Clayton, who knew the old man, did, and he suspected that they together had been trying to find the treasure. He himself had seen the old man once or twice on the grounds, but not within the last two or three days. If, recently, any treasure had been found, probably Captain Clayton was now on the way North with it.

The police were immediately sure that what had happened was that Clayton had dug up the treasure and run away with it, killing the old man in his escapade. There was clear evidence of digging not far from the hut, and yet digging was beginning all over this area. At the same time, the police were in no position to push this. Clayton was from a prominent family; they had no proof against him. After all, the murdered man was only a Negro. Of course, this young colored college upstart looked suspicious, but they had no way to test the matter. His father was in good repute.

Revels knew that ever afterward he would live under the apprehension, sometimes strong, that his crime might catch up with him; that he might be indicted for theft. But he did not on account of that hesitate in his work or forget his determination to do a good job for the world. He simply calculated that this was the price he had to pay for the privilege.

He quietly returned to New York and to his old offices. Mansart had had funds enough from his Southern trek to keep the rent paid and now he hired a clerk. What would happen when his money ran out?

Reprieve came suddenly and unexpectedly. The case of his Indian client had been carefully prepared. But the final decision lay in the hands of the Federal government and that could be indefinitely delayed and might easily be adverse when it came. In any case, it would involve more politics than law. Then, one afternoon, he was asked down to the Custom House for consulta-tion. Here they found the litigants on both sides, including the Indian merchant. He seemed to have reached complete understand-ing with his former partners, and they with the Governmet. The meeting was brief, polite and cordial. In the end, a paper was passed to the Indian and all left the room save him and his lawyer. He showed Revels a draft for $100,000.

"Sir," he said, "I am obliged to you beyond words. Here is the draft for the money. How shall it be divided?"

CHAPTER XIII

JUDGE REVELS MANSART

Revels Mansart sat quietly in his office for days and weeks. He was careful to make no conspicuous expenditure. He dressed neatly but cheaply. He had a small flat in Harlem on Edgecombe Avenue. Here, he took breakfast; his meager lunch was brought into the office. But at dinner time, quietly and with circumspection, he dined at good restaurants, including the one where he had once washed dishes. His bank account was kept small but his practice was growing substantially. The keg with its supposed treasure of gold was well-hidden, but he had never opened it. He spent little money. When not in court, he sat in his office and worked at his law books. The weeks dragged into months. And then, at last, the man he was waiting for, Captain Clayton, came.

He entered the office truculently and sitting down, glared at Mansart. Revels said quietly: "I was expecting you." Meantime, he looked him over. The man was poor, ill, badly-dressed and nervous. He was evidently addicted to alcohol and perhaps to drugs.

"Expecting me?" he growled. "Why?"

"I was waiting for the payment of your note for $4,500."

The man almost shrieked. "You stole the money from me. You know you did."

Mansart was quiet. He said: "When and how? I saw you put into your car the keg of stuff which you said was Confederate gold."

"It was nothing of the sort," yelled the man. "It was lead and sawdust, and the keg was new."

"So you say," answered Mansart quietly. "Then why did you kill the poor old man and make it look as though I might have done it?"

For some time the man was silent. Then he said, "Tell me, Mansart, honestly, didn't you get that gold?"

Mansart answered quietly, "No."

The Captain almost whispered, "My God, I don't know where I am or what. I tell you, and believe me it's true, there was nothing in that keg worth anything."

"Why did you kill the man then?"

"I had to. He thought it was gold, and I thought so. And you knew, damn you, you knew it wasn't."

"Yet you said it was," said Mansart.

"It wasn't," screamed the man, "and I am penniless and sick."

Mansart waited a while, then said quietly. "So the thief is asked for bread by the murderer who tried to pin crime on him."

The man stared "What?" he said. "But I can't pay. I have nothing."

"You never planned to pay even if you had got the gold."

"All right—so I didn't; so I didn't care if you hanged. But I am starving."

Revels sat still and thought carefully. If, as he had always planned, he got the key and opened the keg before this man and found it full of gold, the man might claim it all and put Revels in jail. If the keg had no gold, still the Captain could accuse Revels of theft, show the evidence and sue him. There was but one safe way and that was to buy the Captain off without surrendering evidence or even admitting he had it or had ever seen it.

Moreover, this gold, if there was any gold, did not belong to the Captain; others had just claim to share in it. But, in truth, who really owned it? The men who stole it or the extitnct government that gathered it, or the slaves who earned it? Here were several nice questions; and here, too, was a broken, starving derelict who had given him money when he needed it most and from which in a sense he had started his law career. Revels arose and went slowly to his safe, opened it quietly and took out an envelope. From the envelope he extracted a receipt.

"Sign it," he said.

"Sign what? And why?"

"Sign this receipt. In settlement of all demands."

"I'll be damned if I will," said the man.

"You'll be damned if you don't," said Mansart, as he extracted slowly five one thousand dollar bills from the envelope. "Listen," he said, "you gave me the chance to steal. I took it knowing just what I was doing. But while I was trying to steal, I won a case in court which gave me support until I was able to get a paying practice, which I am living on. I have never received a cent from your grandfather's hoard, if it ever really existed. But I am going to give you something to live on; in turn you must protect me from future blackmail. You must sign this release from all claims. If you do, here is $5,000. If you don't, go!"

The man glared and slumped. Then, with trembling hands, he signed the receipt. Revels summoned two clerks to witness the signature. The Captain arose almost staggeringly. He said, "Five thousand for perhaps fifty."

Revels answered, "Five thousand for perhaps nothing, with a murder thrown in."

Captain Clayton went out the door and closed it. For a long time Mansart sat staring at the wall. He never saw the man again.

Gradually, Mansart began to live better. He enlarged his office. He furnished it well and put more comfortable furniture in his three-room flat. He ate more for lunch. He now dined regularly at one of the best restaurants in midtown. At first, the waiters hesitated at seating him. He found his own seat. Then, for a time, the waiters seated him, but toward the back. His demeanor was quiet and well-bred. His tips were large. At last, he came to be treated as a welcome guest.

Then, as time went by, his work became better and better paid. He chose his clients and his cases carefully. Only those involving real knowledge and interpretation of the law were accepted. He absolutely refused cases involving petty crime. Judges began to note his knowledge and research. Revels Mansart became a recognized lawyer and joined, at its request, a well-established white firm.

Then, Mansart began to think of the future. He proposed to ascend the bench. There had been few colored judges in New York, but those few had done pretty well. Mansart proposed to be the next one appointed. He proposed also to get married. He allowed here no sentiment to enter. This was not a question of love but of business and comfort. A public man must have a family for appearance's sake, for entertaining his colleagues, for maintaining a home. He deliberately refused to remember that such a person as Mary Wright had ever existed.

He had long noticed in the building where his apartment was, a colored woman who was a teacher in the city schools. She was good-looking and well-bred; evidently she had had good training both in family and in school. They met now and then in the elevator and he could see that she was careful of any appearance of encouraging advances or even acquaintanceship on his part.

He liked that.

On the other hand, she was always alone. He was sure she must be lonely, one of those women always on guard, as colored women must be. They had two fronts of attack, white men and colored men. They must be doubly careful. And Joyce Green was aware of this. She rather admired this quiet colored man who said nothing and yet was courteous. She made inquiry and learned of his standing as a lawyer. He seemed as lonely as she, and yet she was startled and a bit annoyed when he said one night as they both came down the elevator:

"I wonder if you would mind having dinner with me."

She turned on him, also affronted, and then said: "Why did you ask me?"

"I hesitated, but there seemed little likelihood of our ever meeting socially. I know few people. I do not go to church and have joined few organizations," he said. "Somehow, I thought perhaps you might be as lonely as I am. I do not wish to be offensive, but dining alone all the time does get on one's nerves, don't you think?"

She paused and said, "Yes, I do think so. I shall be glad to dine with you. But may we have clear understanding from the first?"

"It is quite unnecessary," he said. "What you want to tell me is that this consent to come to dinner with me means absolutely nohting more than what it actually is."

"Precisely," she answered. And they walked together to the subway. He took her to his favorite restaurant in midtown. He knew it was expensive and that for this reason her suspicions would again be aroused. But the dinner was good. She put the burden of choosing it on him. She refused wine. But it had been a long time since she had tasted so tender a filet mignon. The salad was well mixed, the vegetables fresh and well cooked, and when it came to dessert she ventured to order crepes suzettes, and was glad to find that he was not surprised.

"You have been in Paris?" he said.

She told him of her study there, and at last felt relaxed and almost content. She had become a teacher in the New York City schools. She was now teaching History in the Wadleigh High School. It had been long since she had had opportuinty of talking with a companion who was of her own feeling and class. Her fellow teachers were all white.

The proprietor of the restaurant and the waiters looked her over speculatively. They were not used to seeing colored women in that restaurant. She was dressed well, very well, and yet not showily. She was a well built and good-looking woman, and well-bred. Her skin was golden brown and her hair curled affectionately. Her voice was low and her gestures few. All things considered it was a very successful dinner. It must have been costly, but he carefully concealed the check from her. Nor could she be sure as to the size of the tip.

This was the beginning of many such dinners, and one or two visits to the theater. And then at last, when she was beginning to feel that this must stop before she was compromised, he spoke frankly and asked her to marry him. She did not beat about the bush nor hesitate. She simply said, "Yes." He said nothing about love. He made no promises. He mentioned briefly his former marriage to a white girl and showed her the papers of divorce. She made no comment except one question.

"Were there any children?"

"Oh, no," he answered quickly. And then paused, because he had never thought of such a contingency. "There were no children," he added, and yet hesitated as he spoke. Of course there was no child. Had there been he would have known; but would he? Then he put the thought aside. He expressed no objection when she mentioned her desire to continue teaching. She sensed that he would rather she did not, but he did not say so. At any rate, she was determined. What would she be doing—nothing but housework?

As the years passed, both found this a rather successful marriage. They rented at last a larger flat on Washington Heights, with five rooms. There they lived quietly, not extravagantly, but expensively. In 1930, there came a tragic incident. She was late returning from school one day and when she came she brought with her a boy of about five years. He was a good-looking boy and bright, light-brown and curly. She explained: this lad's mother had been in her classes for two years. She died suddenly in giving birth to this child. The father was unknown and a grandmother took care of him. Mrs. Mansart had contributed to his care and looked out for him.

Last week, the grandmother had died and left the boy with questionable neighbors, one of whom had been arrested for stealing yesterday. The authorities had notified her, hearing of her interest in the child. She had hurried over and—"Well, here is the boy!"

The child looked at Revels a moment, greeted him pleasantly and then began to examine the apartment which he soon found of great interest and had many questions, including the sudden and rather startling one:

"Why can't I stay here, Auntie? I like it."

Mrs. Mansart looked upset and hurried the child out. Revels stared out the window. Later, Mrs. Mansart started to search for some way of finding him a permanent home. She asked her husband to examine the law. He had the boy given a thorough physical examination; looked up the facts about the mother and tried in vain to find the father. He examined the laws of adoption. Finally, one night after dinner, which the boy had enjoyed tremendously and kept the conversation from lagging a moment, Revels faced his wife when she returned from putting the child to bed.

"My dear," he said, "you'd rather like to keep the kid, wouldn't you?"

His wife almost gasped. Then she came slowly over to his chair and dropped on her knees beside him.

"Revels," she said, "that would be more than anyone should ask of her husband. But I shall probably never have a child of my own, and that poor girl and this child have gripped my soul. If you would—if you could let me take him, I—I—there would be nothing I would not try to do to repay you."

He looked at her whimsically—"Even to love me?" he said.

She twined her arms about his neck. "Even love you," she whispered.

He was glad to have her suggest that this young one should be adopted and renamed Revels Mansart II. The boy was quite happy and indifferent to the small matter of a name. Then Mansart, to relieve any anxiety she might have, told her in general about his income and savings. But she knew they were well-to-do. She gave up teaching to devote her time to the child.

His appointment to the bench came. He paid $10,000 to the Democratic machine and his election for a ten-year term was called a great triumph of the fight against the Color Line. He was gradually recognized as one of the best magistrates of the city.

Their social life was limited. A few of his white colleagues invited them to their homes, but not many. A few they invited to theirs, and always the occasions were enjoyable. The food was well cooked. There was not much strong drink, but some carefully chosen light wines. There was conversation and music. The evenings passed pleasantly. But there were not many such occasions. For the most part, they furnished their own enjoyment; at home with reading, and visits to theater and concerts.

It was not at first a romantic union but it was satisfactory. He had his work and gave most of his time to it. She made him and his comfort her career. They seldom exchanged caresses, but they were friends, and increasingly became good, loyal, loving friends. She remembered one night when she put her arms on his shoulders and said, "My regard for you, dear, is more than the emotion which men call love. It is respect, deep respect."

He gave her a disturbing answer. He said, "I am not quite respectable, Joyce. My country would not permit me that privilege." But he did not explain further, and wisely, she did not at the time ask.

After the adoption of the boy, this life was changed. He was a source of increasing interest and entertainment; and also of anxiety. They made their home his center, with his friends often dropping in. They saw less of each other alone, but drew closer and more sympathetic just because of that.

Yet, Mansart was not content. He had always assumed that discrimination against his race was based primarily on ignorance, incompetence and bad manners. Not wholly, of course, for his army experience had revealed something beyond this. But that was war. This was normal life and he was a judge in the greatest city in the world, and a good judge.

What galled and cut him to the bone was the fact that he was still an outsider; that always, no matter what his accomplishment or position, a colored man was not counted as a man. He was, for instance, never considered for admission to any social club. Now, that meant more than denial of natural ambition or of comfort in eating or loafing. It meant denial of the democratic process. One did not get well acquainted with people of influence and knowledge. One did not hear that great current of unpublished news and opinion. One could not get hold of private information or secure the personal influence which was often so necessary. Club life in any great city is of tremendous importance, and this was denied Revels Mansart and it would be denied him forever. No matter what his accomplishment or character, one had simply to be told he's a Negro. That settled it. He was not black-balled. His name wouldn't even come up for consideration.

Even in professional relations, he was apt to be forgotten or ignored or discounted. People did not consult him or even think of him in matters where he was really expert and experienced. In the more purely professional associations, he was either absolutely excluded, as was true with the American Bar Association; or, if finally he pushed his way in, he was still alone, uncounted, unthought of.

If a colored man of standing found himself in social contact with whites, he faced embarrassment unless he was very circumspect. He might adopt a certain ingratiating sycophancy, or an attitude of humble expectancy; he might have a fund of funny stories, or listen with rapt attention to anything the white man might say. Or, he might have to deal with the real difficulty, namely, that it was not easy for either to find common ground for light conversation. If with lawyers, he did not want to talk shop—but if not, what else? The weather? Golf? Family problems? Hardly. The difficulty was that the black man might share work with whites, but not play; profession, but not life; in most things that interested them most of the time, they were strangers. For instance, women? Taboo for both.

Then, at times, Mansart found himself in peculiar embarrassment. Once he walked across a room to greet a colleague, one who had always been cordial, indeed had even gone so far as to introduce his wife. Today, as Mansart approached, the man started to turn away; then he turned suddenly and blurted out: "Mansart, I met you yesterday right on Fifth Avenue. You wouldn't speak. I know you saw us and my wife remarked your action." Mansart flushed darkly and grasped his friend by the arm.

"Please—please sit down here a while and let me explain if I can." The lawyer saw that the situation was serious and he seated himself, wordlessly.

Mansart choked and started off:

"Collins, perhaps you will not understand this and it's hard for me to talk. When a colored man meets a white friend in public, on such a thoroughfare as Fifth Avenue, he does not know just what to do. If he greets him pleasantly, especially if he is with friends or, worst of all, with his wife, he may deeply embarrass this white friend. He may put him on the defensive or in some extreme case he may ruin a career. If the colored man waits for recognition first, he puts an unfair strain on his white friend. Already, his friend has stretched a point and challenged public opinion in meeting him as an equal at all, and in regular business surroundings. To presume on this and greet him publicly and socially, to drag in his wife, to butt into a rendezvous for a cocktail or lunch—that is unthinkable. The wisest thing is for the Negro to avoid such meeting—quickly to turn a corner; to stare into a window. In the case you recall, I saw you plainly but too late to avoid your notice. I myself was aghast. It was a hell of a dilemma! Can you understand, Collins?"

Collins stared and went pale. "My God, Mansart, is it as tragic as all this?"

They did not discuss the matter but, of course, both Revels and his wife knew that she was in even a more precarious social position than he. She could not expect the very ordinary courtesies extended to women. If a colored man rose in the streetcar to give her a seat, that was unusual. If a white man did it, it was epoch-making and even a bit suspicious. She not only must not expect courtesy, but she must not appear to notice that it was not proferred. She must withdraw and stand aside as much as possible until it became a matter of principle, and then when she pushed herself forward she must be prepared for contemptuous looks, if not open and vocal insult.

If in casual company, Revels and his wife adopted an attitude of quiet self-respect or aloofness, the whites, puzzled and offended, withdrew and left early. Naturally, as time went by, inter-racial friendships arose over trifles—adjacent backyards, the democracy of children, the unity of misfortune. Often, however, even then, neighborhood gossip, friendly warning, disapproving glances, turned an interesting white woman away, warned an enthusiastic white man to be "careful," or separated old friends. But not in all cases; in a few, gradually, real friendships across the color line persisted.

The adoption of a son brought further difficulties, as his wife knew better than most folk. The public schools of New York were bad, unless one lived in some exclusive section with the best equipment and selected teachers. In Harlem, the meager number of school buildings were overcrowded by the regular colored inhabitants who were average workers and servants but increasingly overwhelming by poor, and ignorant migrants from the South. If they all had been more evenly distributed among the mass of New York people, they would not have seriously lowered the cultural average of the city level. The Negro children would have learned manners and habits and the white children would have learned human sympathy. As it was, the public schools of Harlem were no place for Mansart's boy.

All these things and attitudes subtly transformed the character of colored people of the status of the Mansarts. It made them harbor, unconsciously, an inner bitterness. It made them more or less deliberately unpleasant in their associations with their fellows. White people of status got in the habit of avoiding colored people, of starting no incidental and natural conversations on street cars or in the street. If they did not absolutely avoid sitting beside colored people in public places, they certainly chose to sit with them last. They looked around carefully to see if there was any other place to sit. All this made the social life of the Mansarts a very, very unpleasant thing.

On the other hand, there were difficulties about their social contacts with Negroes. They must avoid seeking it to such an extent that they voluntarily segregated themselves. If they walked into a streetcar and there were two vacant seats, one beside a white person and one beside a colored person, they would take the seat beside the white person. Not, as one might think, because they preferred it; they didn't; but because they were sure that it was expected of them to occupy a seat beside a colored person. The colored man or woman beside whom they took a seat, too, would also be affronted if they thought that this person felt that he must sit beside them, when they really would rather sit elsewhere. It was a complicated and difficult sort of situation but it was always hovering in the back of their minds. It always conditioned their life and thought.

They had difficulty in securing help in the home. Colored folk did not want to work for colored folk; it emphasized their own failure to rise to independence and marked them as inferior to inferiors. It marked them in the eyes of the whites; it marked them in the eyes of Negroes. They believed that their colored employers must despise them and were too ready to resent any suspicion of superiority. Often, they charged Negroes more wages than they charged whites; more often, they flatly refused to work for Negroes.

The matter of living quarters at last brought illumination to Mansart's life. He wanted better schools for his boy, better police protection and better street car services. Mansart wanted to live better, with good treatment assured and the latest household appliances, with the best city services. He would have preferred quarters in one of the new type apartment houses but the delays in securing one, despite his influence and that of his friends, angered him. He knew what it meant. Then he turned to thoughts of a single dwelling in the suburbs. He learned at last of a beautiful house for sale in Westchester and determined to buy it. It was going cheap in the low market. Even here the purchase must be indirect to avoid resentment.

Also, his wife asked, "Can we afford it?"

It occurred to Mansart then that this was the time to tell his wife frankly of his financial status and of his great transgression. He arose, got his bankbooks and showed them to her. Then he said, "I've something else to tell you and show you." He told her of the keg of gold. She listened and was long in commenting. She had long known that he had never been entirely frank with her on money matters. He was always generous but never frank. At last she said,

"How much is the gold worth?"

"I do not know," he answered. She stared at him. She was already planning its return.

"You mean—"

"I mean I've never opened the keg. We'll open it now."

He led the way into his office which looked down over the shimmering length of Manhattan. On a new safe which, somewhat to his wife's surprise, he had recently had installed, he began to turn knobs until it opened, revealing not the usual shelves and cubbyholes but one large compartment filled by a large sealed package. Together they took the heavy package out and began to unwrap it.

"This is the keg," he said, "which holds the Confederate gold reserve, stolen and hidden in Macon on land now occupied by my father's college. I went South to help Clayton get it, but I distrusted him, stole it from him and brought it to New York, giving him eventually $5,000 as quit claim.

"I put it in storage, determined not to open it unless I could not build a law practice without using it. I found I could, due to that first lawsuit which I won with the brief I wrote while in Macon. I have never felt the need of money I could not earn until now, when I want to buy this Westchester home. It is right that Confederate gold, even if twice stolen, should pay for what anti-Negro prejudice makes me buy."

She pursed her lips. The outer wrappings were at last removed and the old beer keg stood naked and crooked before them. They began to pry at the top. It proved a tough job and took a long time. At last it yielded. It split and cracked. The musty smell of cotton lint arose from the solid dark grey mass which filled the keg. Some four inches of this packing was taken out before they reached solid matter. It proved to be a thick bolt, a foot long and rusty. Revels scraped at the rust, but it was solid iron. Then came more cotton and other smaller bolts and pieces of iron scrap, but no gold. They searched and scraped for hours without a sign of gold. All they had was cotton and iron and rust. At last they sat back and looked at each other. Revels began to laugh.

"I don't think I ever really believed in this gold. It was a fantastic tale. And yet, it has furnished me a sense of security for many years. I have felt able to wait, to take chances, to refuse cases, because I thought I had a fortune in reserve, even with the dim doubt that always haunted me. I suppose I would not have dared to marry without this belief. Then, too, there was that other feeling that whatever success I had attained never rested on theft.

"I would have hated that. Not from mawkish morality in this immoral time, but from pride in my own ability. Of course, even now I do not know about this keg. Was it all a lie from the start or was it a real theft and double-crossing with me as the final dupe? That was a fearful day when the slave-built Confederacy fell. Many a high-placed Southerner faced stark poverty for the first time in his career. Many a man lost all faith in his fellow man, doubted his life beliefs and looked at a fearsome world which he did not know.

"There was undoubtedly cheating and stealing and murder. Men stole for themselves and stole from each other. What gold reserve there ever was in Montgomery, who had access to it?— Who took it?—Who knows? Perhaps, Clayton's grandfather got hold of it; perhaps not. Perhaps somebody stole it from him—

perhaps. At any rate this will o' the wisp has now flown forever."

"Thank God," said his wife. "Now we need not buy in West-chester!"

"Not too fast. We still can afford it, I—"

"I doubt it. Remember your re-election comes in a few years. You'll need money for that. And again, I'm thinking of Junior."

"That's just the point! Surely the Westchester schools will be better than Harlem!"

"In some ways, of course. In others, they will face him wtih race and class problems. He is twelve and entering high school in new and unexpected circumstances. From being first and envied among poor colored children, he will be last and an outsider in a new world. The teachers will resent a Negro in their classes. The parents will rage and complain. The students, just at the cruel age of adolescence, will leave him outside of their thought and action. They will crucify him."

"He will fight!"

"He will not fight, unless it is for something he regards as worth fighting for. The company of whites or their approbation would not just now seem to him of any importance. A physical laboratory, experiments, machines, especially airplanes—these would be of im-portance. But social contacts? For that he'd never fight. He's just leave! Let's stay where we are!"

CHAPTER XIV

THE HOMELY BLACK GIRL

Sojourner Mansart was an unhappy child, unhappily conceived and welcomed to the world with tears and protest. She shared in this welcome. She was inordinately shy, and ashamed of herself. She was, to be sure, not a pretty child, but thought herself much worse looking than she was. Her skin was soft and dark brown. Her teeth were perfect, and her eyes beautiful when she did not close them against the world, as she usually tried to do. Even her features were not really unpleasing, but exaggerated in a racial type which the world about her despised and ridiculed. Her hair was strong and tightly curled and she gave it little attention. She was thin, almost scrawny, and it was not so much that she could not use her low voice as that she so seldom tried.

She was always slipping away and even hiding. She was late at meals. She was slow at work, and the family began to take her at her own estimate. The boys jeered and joked until they found how easily her eyes welled with tears. Her mother ostentatiously neglected her and her father, when he remembered, overdid his efforts to be nice, which Sojourner was sure came not from wish but rather from his sense of duty.

There was one bond between them, not discovered for many years, and that was their mutual love of music, particularly of the Negro folk songs. Sojourner sometimes sang with him in her little voice. Then she learned to drum out accompaniments to his singing on the old piano, and while she knew little music, she had an extraordinary sense of tone and rhythm.

It happened almost by accident that she found the instrument suited to her taste, and that was the violin, hidden in the attic, which the uncle who was killed in France had once owned and discarded. She tried it for several months, and then, gathering together her savings, went down to a second-hand music store in town and the proprietor sold her what was in fact an excellent violin but one which he was glad to get rid of because it had been so long on his hands. It was then that Sojourner found her vocation and her love.

It was difficult, of course, to find anyone at Macon to teach her, especially on the violin. The colored people associated the violin with rather low class assemblies. They wanted their children taught the piano or the organ. So that Sojourner was very largely self-taught. But she followed the few text books that she could find and really did extraordinarily well. Then she discovered that there was in town a very great teacher of the violin. He was mentioned when the Metropolitan Opera came to Atlanta, and he took part.

Herr Max Rosenfels was a German Jew who had left Germany when Hitler's power began to increase, fearing the future which came to the German Jews in the next few years. He came to America with the idea that here he would find musical appreciation, especially among the Negroes, in whose music he had long delighted. Naturally, he was disappointed, particularly when he went to the South and began to inquire into Negro music. It was admitted of course that the Negroes did have some ability, but he was told it was of a low order and no great musician could waste his time on this vulgar stuff. At first, he attended Negro churches and was entranced at their group singing when they sang the "Spirituals" and not the "Gospel" hymns. To his surprise, the churches did not want his presence because they thought he was making fun of them and because he preferred the Spirituals. They thought this was because they were slave songs. The whites strongly objected to his hanging about Negro churches if he expected to teach their children, which he did not but had to, to earn a living.

He found his way to Macon, at last, and was enabled to make a fair living by giving music lessons to more or less gifted white children and youth. Yet, he always had in his mind the idea that he might come in contact with ability among Negroes. On this particular afternoon, when Sojourner went to see him, he was looking, as usual, for some colored girl or woman to help in his bachelor establishment. He had tried several with disappointing results, and he smiled kindly but unenthusiastically upon this queer-looking thin little colored girl when she presented herself. She had a shawl wrapped about her and as she came in he said:

"Oh, you have come to work for me?"

She was a bit taken aback but said in her low, hesitant voice,

"Perhaps I could—" and then the shawl fell away from the violin. He took the violin up and looked at it. It was a good violin and he said to her with some surprise, "Can you play?"

She put the violin beneath her chin and grasped the bow. Then she closed her eyes and played one strain, one of those inimitable bits of pure music which the soul of the slave evolved in his days of martyrdom. It was that song, "I Stood on the River of Jordan." She played it simply, unerringly—a stream of utter music. He was entranced. He was filled with enthusiasm. He said, "Who taught you?"

"I taught myself," she answered, "from books which I bought. I thought perhaps you might tell me where I was wrong and how I could improve."

"To be sure," he said, "but, can you help me in the kitchen?"

So it was arranged that a couple of hours during the afternoon, three days a week, Sojourner should come over and wash up the dishes and sweep the house and then receive a half-hour's instruction. Of course, her family knew nothing of this. She simply disappeared these afternoons. But to Herr Rosenfels, this was a time of perfect joy. He had at last a pupil. He had, at last, knowledge of a music which he had only glimpsed before and yearned for, and the two went to work with a will.

Of course, this idyllic situation could not last long in a city like Macon. Some of Herr Rosenfels' rich white supporters came to his studio one afternoon to arrange for him to furnish music for a soiree. They heard heavenly music and burst in without ceremony.

"Where on earth, Mr. Rosenfels—oh!" This Jew was actually taking Negro pupils. It was outrageous. It was insupportable, and they said as much.

Herr Rosenfels in turn was outraged, and expressed himself in no uncertain terms. Of course, there was on inevitable end. He forfeited the patronage and tolerance of white Macon. Sojourner's lessons had to stop and Herr Rosenfels had to look for support elsewhere. Naturally, he applied to the colored state college. White members of the unions objected to his appointment to the state college. There was no musicians' union, but the members of other unions, knowing that Rosenfels did not belong to a union, saw that pressure was brought upon him and they themselves brought pressure upon the college trustees.

He taught at the school a year and continued Sojourner's tute-lage. However, it was evident to Manuel Mansart that he would simply be courting trouble if he continued to hire this white man to teach music in his school, especially since he had been teaching white children in the city. And so, sorrowfully, Rosenfels moved away, but the results of his teaching Sojourner remained. The family, and especially her father, were astonished at her ability to play and her interpretation of music. With some misgivings, she was even listened to in concerts at the town's colored churches. These churches were not yet used to having "fiddles," as they called them, played in churches, but they had only to hear So-journer a few times to change their attitude. She became repeatedly a welcome guest in the basement auditoriums. It was at one of these church concerts that she again met Roosevelt Wilson.

Of course, she had known him. All the Mansart children had known Roosevelt for he was long one of the family. That was back at the time of the Atlanta Riot, in 1906, the year before Sojourner was born. He was the son of a colored shopkeeper, killed on the last day of rioting, when the mob looted South Atlanta and killed and burned.

It was after this that the mother asked Manuel Mansart to let Roosevelt board with his family and attend school, for she was going out to service. A rich white family in the Peachtree district felt a certain responsibility for the Wilson family. Why, they did not say; but the murdered mulatto who had worksd up from the fields to the city and built him a family and a home had in some dark past a relationship to this white family which could not be broken. So the mother went to their kitchen and the boy to board with the Mansarts, where he could go to school. Manuel did not really have room and his wife already had too much to do; but Roosevelt lived with them as one of the family for ten years until he was graduated from high school.

Roosevelt Wilson was a strong, big, good-looking boy, yel-low in color, with bushy hair. He had a good mind, always follow-ing his own ideas until gradually he got a clear outlook. Unlike the Mansarts, he neither liked nor hated white folk, but viewed them with unprejudiced eyes. They could be beaten with brains and hard work, but this would be no easy task and called for plans and courage. They were enemies, but not always, nor inevitably so. They could be won or cajoled. He proposed to win recognition by thought and effort: meanwhile, they were to be held strictly under suspicion.

Looking about carefully, he determined at an early age that he was going into the ministry. Partially, this came from his mother's insistence and urging. But in great part, it was his own conviction. There was no sentiment about it. He saw in the Negro church the most powerful organization extant among these people. Unless a man was going to start out on some new and uncertain path like that of business or a profession, the clear road to power and influence was the Negro church. It represented the people, served and catered to them, and what was more, it escaped more than any other social institution the influence and domination of the whites. Naturally, it did not entirely escape. It had to have the cooperation of the white ruling classes. It found some support from their gifts, and the recognition that the black pastor got from the white world was almost indispensable for real success. At the same time, no Negro institution so escaped the daily dictation of the whites, and the envy and interference of the poor whites, as the Negro church.

On the other hand, of course, there were clear drawbacks. Wilson naturally believed in religion. It had never occurred to him that there was anyone who did not. But his belief was vague and not particularly important to him. God ruled, of course. He sacrificed his son Jesus for the people. You had to get religion by some kind of miraculous interference, and you had to cater to the "Spirit," especially of the old folks and the more emotional.

All this was routine to his rather casual thinking. But beyond it, he had ideas. There was a lot of social work that could be done in the church that was not well done. There was the matter of getting employment for the members; of distributing charity systematically; of looking after the children who did not go regularly to school; of establishing various kinds of cooperative enterprises; getting the contributions to come more regularly so that preachers could get their salaries and get more than they were now getting; hiring assistants; and of building new churches with more thought to their social work than to preaching exhibitions and religious performances. All this he had in mind, not clearly but more and more definitely because while rather careless, he did really want to do something worthwhile and decent with his life.

His mother, as housekeeper in the white family, did not earn enough to help him much, but on the other hand she did not require his help. He had no brothers or sisters and thus was free to make his own way. After high school, he entered the college department of Atlanta University as a boarder, and so left the Mansart family. They moved to Macon, and he graduated. For a while, he was not sure of his next step when, having made known his determination to go into the church, to his surprise he was offered a scholarship at the Hartford Theological Seminary, up in Connecticut.

He went there, not because he wanted to study theology, which did not strike him as important, but because here was a chance for support during the two or three years when he was finding himself. He went up there and was not particularly happy. He found his fellow students cold and critical. He did not like it and he kept pretty well to himself. He won a reputation of being sullen and uncompaniable, but he learned a lot; there was little that he missed.

He did not like the course of study at Hartford. Seldom did it come to grips with reality. They studied the making of sermons and the essential difference of dogmas. He spent most of his time in reading, and the very breadth of his reading made it impossible for him to fail in any course.

He was pretty clear as to what New England was and meant. It had no attractions for him. He hated the climate, the snow, the cold, the thawing. He loved the sunshine and flowers of the South. He determined to work in the South, but on the other hand he hadn't the slightest idea of becoming a Congregational minister.

Negro Congregationalists, Episcopalians and Presbyterians, were few and far between. Individually, a good many of them were well off. They escaped into these churches to avoid the religious customs of their people and to associate with their own better classes; but that did not deceive Wilson at all; he knew that the colored Baptist Church was the place for him. There he would be free of control, he could practically believe what he pleased, and he could do what he wanted.

He had been at Hartford two years when his mother in Atlanta became desperately ill. She sent for her pastor, the head of the Wheat Street Baptist Church. Then and there, P. James Bryant called young Wilson home and offered him a position in his church. With a song of joy, his mother died.

Bryant was efficient and had built up a tremendous organization in the Wheat Street Church with thousands upon thousands of members. He himself had only a common school education, but he respected educated men. He needed their knowledge, but knew that none of them could cope with him when it came to leading and swaying men. He liked Wilson. He had a symbol of his own possibilities, had he been trained. He even liked his skepticism and hesitations, and the continuing memory of the hurts he had from the world. If he could get Wilson under his wing and use his brains in church life he might make him his successor. What difference did it make what he believed, so long as he said and did the appropriate thing?

So, for a small salary, Roosevelt began working in the church as something between a business manager and lay preacher. His lectures on current events were popular with a certain element in the church, while others shook their heads and said there was not enough religion in them. Meantime, Wilson began to become acquainted in the city.

The people of the church were mainly servants and laborers, with a sprinkling of professional men, a few physicians, one or two dentists, and a lawyer. There were also a half-dozen small businessmen; but the great bulk of them worked in white people's homes or in warehouses, stores, and on the railroads and streets. They were good-hearted people, very religious, but narrow, envious and credulous. At first, the bulk of them resented Wilson. He had not been "called" to preach; he was one of those educated preachers. And then, in addition to this, they were not at all sure as to whether he had really "experienced" religion. He talked about every day matters instead of the Love of God. He related no religious experiences. In fact, it was doubtful if he had had any.

Some began campaigning behind his back and avoiding him. They anticipated by their action the suspicion of a feeling that he thought himself better than they. But on the other hand, his mother had been one of them. Many remembered her spectacular dedication of her son to God. And then, too, Wilson was personally very pleasant. They could not resist his honesty and sympathy. He began to feel that if he could bring them into his home, he could get a closer grip on them.

He was not sure as to just what he wanted to do with them,

but he saw tremendous possibilities. They were normal, good-hearted folk. What they needed was ordinary opportunity. Their real problem was this problem of jobs and decent wages. With regular work and a fair income, they could educate their children. buy homes, and make their organizations work for culture and uplift.

Here was a chance for developing a business from the other end, from the opposition pole from that which he saw in the general business of Atlanta—business for the benefit of people and not people for the benefit of business. It was going to take, of course, shrewd guidance and manipulation to do this thing in a church and in spite of a religion in which he only half believed. He respected their religion, the longer he stayed with it. It was, of course, bizarre, but underneath it all there was a real appeal to character and goodness. And that was basic. If now, he had a home with a sympathetic wife, he might make that the real transforming cell that would leaven this economic aspect of his church work.

Wilson saw that his rise in a Negro Baptist church could be rapid. This type of church was not part of any national organization. It was an autonomous, self-centered body, self-ruled and self-financed. Each local church was its own boss in doctrine, in type of work, in manner of worship. It was Negro and Negro-ruled. Whites could get no foothold within, but exercised their influence only indirectly. Any body of Negroes who liked a preacher, could choose him as their leader in a Baptist church. Henceforth, he was head of their group. He might be almost absolute king; more often, he was the most powerful of a group of leaders called "deacons," backed and financially supported by masterful women.

Their activity centered in the Sunday church service. Here, the Sermon was the magic word which held them together. It must be strong, loud, entertaining and orthodox. This orthodoxy was built on three matters; God the creator, Jesus his son and their friend, and the mystic rite of baptism. Beyond these, the people cared little. The preacher might embrace black magic, unitarianism —anything, so long as he returned to the three fundamentals. Consequently, a colored Baptist church might be anything from a center of mystic, yelling, heathen orgies, to a well-governed social center.

Wilson's first step was to become assistant pastor of Wheat

Street Church. But he wanted his own church, and after two years, Bryant saw that it would be wiser to let him try a church of his own. Later, he could come back to Wheat Street. So he recommended him to Macon as pastor of the First Baptist.

During this time, one of his personal problems was that of women. He was sexually strong. He had begun his sexual experiences in early life and followed them up irregularly with a sort of careful selection, but nevertheless vigorously. He did not want to be tied down to one woman. He did not believe in what was called "Love." At the same time, he knew that in the older type of Negro churches there were sexual opportunities among certain females of the church who were not unaccustomed to having advances made to them by their white employers and by their colored preachers. And while this had to be conducted with a certain care, it was well known.

On the other hand, in the newer type of churches there were girls who wanted marriage and whose parents were desperate for good marriages. But it was hard to find a colored man of position and manners who was willing to take a young colored girl to wife while he was struggling to succeed. After success, he was often too old for a successful union. There was too much attraction outside of marriage. So that Wilson for a long time avoided marriage. He courted the girls but did it carefully, with restraint, without commitment. He let the married women approach him, those who would and could. And there again, by exercising care he avoided scandal and jealousy.

At Macon, he met Sojourner Mansart, not as a woman but as a musician; because buried deep within Roosevelt Wilson's soul was a love of music and of drama. When he heard Sojourner Mansart play sonatas and bits of symphonies, when she interpreted Chopin on her violin, he was pleased. But when she played the Negro spirituals, he was transported. He had hardly noticed her at first— she was quite unworthy of notice. But the music gripped him. And then he had an idea. It seemed to him almost brilliant. Why not marry this girl? She would make few demands upon him. She would protect him from women, in fact. Also, she was the child of the powerful president of the Colored State College. And on the other hand, she was an outlet toward something fine and uplifting in the church. He kept thinking of her.

She wasn't a doll, she was no fool, she had ability, and he

sensed that she was loyal. You do not find much loyalty in the
world and he instinctively distrusted women, especially pretty
women. It occurred to him that a house with Sojourner at the head,
and music in the heart, would have certain attractions and would
help his whole life. She was about the last type of woman he had
in his dreams; but that was just as well, because this dream woman
was a person whom he never would have approached. She would
have been much too beautiful and unpredictable and unreliable.
But here, as he gathered slowly point by point, from time to
time, was a very real, unselfish and beautiful soul.

Sojourner was a curious enigma, silent, never answering, hiding
away, and yet with something that she wanted to hide, something
very precious and fine that was her own. He would not have said
that he loved her because he did not believe in love, but he felt
drawn to her more than to any person that he had ever known;
not even excluding his mother.

She was what men would call black and ugly; that is, dark seal
brown in skin, wtih close curled hair and a face that had no comeliness which accorded with Nordic ideals except perhaps the eyes.
Outside of that, she was rather scrawny, with poor physical development, and inordinately shy. She tried in every way to withdraw
from the world. And everywhere she turned, in some way she was
hurt. She liked to read and read devouringly, but she stopped
reading fiction because always the women, particularly the women
who fell in love, who were chosen, who had any chance, were
beautiful. Without any exception, they were "beautiful": "beautiful" flowing hair, "beautiful" white skin, beautiful bodies, beautiful clothes. She had none of these. She did not long for them, she
was not bitter at their absence, but she was hurt and turned back
in upon herself because there seemed no place for her in the world.
There was nothing in particular that she apparently could do.
No one paid her any attention except perhaps to laugh at her or
to insult her.

Of course, Wilson had known her and her family when a
student, but she had been so timid and retiring that he had almost
forgotten her and had hardly ever spoken to her. But now he
was thrilled by the music she played. It was not often that Wilson
was thrilled. He spoke to her when he could, and tried to call
upon her but to his surprise she would not receive him. She apparently did not want to know him further and seemed to have

forgotten that she ever had known him. But he drew her gradually into the church music. His choir gave concerts with her as soloist. And after one of her brilliant concerts in the basement of the church, William summoned Sojourner to his office. She stood breathless and preoccupied, filled with the memory of the music. He walked over and put his arms around her.

It would be difficult to say just what Sojourner's response was. She was astonished beyond words. This was something that had never occurred to her in her life. She shrank and started back. She was in deadly, almost uncontrollable fear. She was 23 years old, yet to her men, so far as any expression of masculinity was concerned, were cruel beasts. Just what they did to women, she did not know, in fact, she could not imagine. But her mother had warned her; her brothers had ominously threatened her. All the world seemed agreed that men were something to be avoided. She herself had seen the cruelty of boys and the viciousness of some men. She had often rushed away and hidden. All her life she had essayed to escape the half-recognized gleam of casual lust which she detected in men's eyes, especially white men; and the sort of bold contempt which some black men displayed.

Music had veiled the manhood of this man from her eyes. She had forgotten that he was a man. He was just someone for whom she played melody, for whom she worked, in whose church she was happy to find refuge. She had entirely forgotten the beast of prey and sensed only rhythm and tone—the ecstasy of that world joy that comprehended neither dirt nor mist. In this world of sound there was no evil nor terror, only communion of souls in common dreams.

And now, suddenly all this was gone. There stood before her, clasping and gripping her, a strange and unknown man. He was laughing at her, he must be laughing. Nobody had ever before made even pretense of love to her. He wanted to hurt her and gloat over her. She fluttered like a caged bird, tried to scream in her terror, struggled, nad then fainted.

Wilson was astonished and terrified. No such experience with women had ever come to him. He simply could not understand. He sat down helplessly with this girl nestled in his arms, until he looked down and saw her wide eyes fastened upon him, and they were the eyes of the Sistine Madonna. Without further word she arose and ran from him.

Suddenly, he made up his mind. He wanted her. He could trust her. She could piece out and complete his life. It was a week before they met again when talk was possible. He did not hesitate. He said,

"Will you marry me?"

She stared at him. "Oh, no," she said. "Men marry girls that they love. Beautiful girls."

He said, "I love you."

"But," she said, "you can't. Brides should be beautiful, even if brown. Usually they are white wilh blue eyes and golden hair and fair skin. I am ugly and black. I—" She sat staring at him and for several moments was utterly speechless, and then she said, "I am not pretty, I have no great education, I dropped my work in college. I do not love you, I do not know what love is. All that I have read about it has to do with women who are charming and well-dressed, and particularly white. I am none of these. Are you sure, quite sure that you mean what you say? Aren't you somehow deceiving yourself?"

He said, "Sojourner, I want to marry you. I am very, very fond of you and I am afraid that when I first kissed you, you did not realize this and perhaps I didn't either; but now I want to say it calmly and with utter honesty. I want you to be my wife, to come and take charge of my home and to have time for your music and for friendship among people who need music. I think it will be a splendid arrangement for you, and I know it will be for me."

Gently he drew her to him until she was nestling in his arms. "Most human beings," he said, "are not particularly pretty. And the beautiful are not always the good or even the useful. We have a silly habit of painting everything which is good and true as 'beautiful.' What we mean, of course, is that it is wholesome and satisfying and fulfilling. All that you are. See how velvet is your skin and how lovely your eyes?"

"Did you ever read what Countee Cullen wrote:

" 'The night, whose sable breast relieves the stark, white
stars is no less lovely, being dark'

"Or again, 'Who lies with his nut-brown maiden,
    Bruised to the bone by her thin black hair,
    Warmed with the wine that her full lips trade in,
    He lies and his love lies there.'

"Or again, 'And when your body's death gives birth to soil

for Spring to crown
Men will not ask if that rare earth was white
flesh once, or brown.' "

She whispered to him, wanting to believe, and then said, "But—
my hair."

And he replied, "Most hair does not fly in silken streamers.
Many golden curls are as stiff and unyielding as yours, even if less
tightly clenched. Hair is a covering and protection. If it is thick
and clean what more can one ask? Your limbs are long and lithe,
your little breasts are soft cones of chaste beauty, and anyway, I
love you. Can't you love me?" And he knew that he now meant
what once he had but pretended.

"Yes," she cried, "if I dared."

They sat silent. Then he said practically, "Will your family give
you up?"

"Oh, yes, gladly. I'm only in the way. I never fit in anywhere.
People laugh at me, always people laugh."

"No, no, dear. That is not so. You imagine it. Your music
will charm all that away."

"I want to come to you so much, so terribly much. Even if it
don't work out. If I can just try once to be happy, I shall be glad
to die."

She so dreaded a public wedding that he yielded. Her family
was so evidently surprised, almost incredulous that he should want
Sojourner, that he retorted sharply: "Have you been too blind
to see this jewel?"

Manuel was ashamed, and apologized. "You are right," he said.
"Roosevelt, we are blind. This child has a lovely soul. Take it.
Only, dear God, be sure you really want to assume this task. It
will kill her if you fail."

And so they were married. And so, to the astonishment and
constant titter of some of the church members, the Reverend
Roosevelt Wilson, the handsome and learned pastor of the First
Baptist, married an ugly little black girl who played the fiddle.

But it was the young body as well as the soul with which Roosevelt Wilson was enamoured. He went to Sarah Linton, the girl
whom Bruce Mansart had once seemed to love and who had a
beauty parlor. She knew him; in fact, once they had flirted, but
casually. Both, at the time, were too clear-headed to be serious.

Sarah's parlor was well-equipped and modern. A friend's dressing establishment undertook the clothes, and Roosevelt, without saying anything to her or the family, ordered a complete outfit of tasteful, simple robes, with colors set out and contrasted with the dark beauty of Sojourner's skin and of her well-formed but thin body. Her hands and feet were little and long, and he had to send to New York to fit them properly with gloves and shoes.

The trouble about her hair she made herself. She seemed to feel that she was in some way honor bound to keep it just as it was, to do nothing to make it pliable or beautiful. Wilson had to sit down and argue hard. And just as stubbornly she argued back. He was ashamed of her hair. Perhaps he wanted her to powder her face white and to cut back the folds of her nose and lips!

"No, no, darling. Understand, I want you as you are, and yet as comely as you easily can be. We do not leave our nails uncut or our skin unwashed or our bodies unclothed. There is nothing disloyal to nature in making ourselves as lovely as possible. It is falsehood in adorning and not in revelation of loveliness that is wrong."

She yielded, finally, not because she was convinced but because so evidently he wanted her to yield. It was actually a sort of sacrifice to Love. She was startled when her little head stood forth covered with tiny shining coils, clean and oiled and clinging to her dark, well-formed head and above the slight curve sof her breasts. Her long, slender hands and her lithe, well-clothed body made a pleasing whole. The whites stared, the blacks goggled. The dining room of the pullman was very still as they entered on the honeymoon trip to New York.

Sojourner sat in a sort of dream. Her violin spoke low and yearning words of sorrow and laughter, and people paused at the drawing room door and begged leave to listen. At night, Wilson insisted on climbing to the upper berth, and left her lying and staring wide-eyed at the hurrying, passing world.

At last, at the great hotel, with its magnificence and adornment, she came behind closed doors to the duty of sleeping in one bed with a stranger, even though a known and well-loved stranger. She crept to bed in darkness and silence, nestling away in a corner away from the bulk of his body, the sound of his breath, and the consciousness of him beside her. Then, after the excitement and the fear, she fell asleep, and found herself dreaming in his arms, felt his hands creeping along her limbs, and heard her heart pound frantically as the undreamed of thrill of pain and joy inconceivable lifted her beyond all living; until she slept again in utter content and perfect oblivion.

Wilson had known women. Many times he had slept beside comely beauties and looked down at pretty faces. But this bridal night was something utterly new, not so much in physical satisfaction or triumph, but rather in the knowledge of something unutterably sweet and yielding, beyond flesh, that pulsed on the part of a spirit entirely given to him in sacrifice beyond pain, and devotion beyond all knowing. He knew that never again could he have supreme communion with any other soul but this; that here alone lay his greater self. When, at last, he woke in blazing sunlight and complete comfort, the low strains of Handel's "Largo" were creeping gently through his ears. He knew, and she subtly sensed, that if this new life was to be caught and kept, it must be lived now and here in the hard real things of earth and time.

So they lived in New York many days, almost alone for a while. They did not go to church to worship; they went to several churches to see how they were planned and built and what they cost. Not what these churches proposed to do, but what, as a matter of fact, they did. They spent days at social settlements. They selected a few books and read them together. They went to concerts.

Sojourner began to develop her ideas about Negro music. She picked out the pure melody of the older hymns; she found the tragedy of the work-songs; she sensed what Burleigh and Dett were doing to develop new music on this ancient and utterly beautiful foundation. She met Handy and learned of and listened to the "Blues."

They come home to Macon to try to make the First Baptist the best church in town, colored or white, in work, in spirit, in organization. Wilson returned with two ideas: first, to build a church house as center of his social activities, to avoid hiding them in the dark and unsanitary basement; second, later, to build a new and imposing church, second to none in the city. As a step toward this he proposed to have Sojourner play Spirituals in his regular church service. He knew what opposition this would arouse from the older members at hearing a "fiddle" in the sanctuary of God; from the more modern members at having the music of old-fashioned revival orgies replace the more modern "Gospel hymns." Wilson said nothing of his plans. He preached a sermon on "The Music of the Slaves," and then said that his wife would play.

Sojourner glided into the pulpit swathed in white silk, which emphasized her dark features, black shining hair and her long, thin black arms. She raised her violin but kept her head lowered until its music began to creep out, and then quickly she threw her head back and thrust up her chin. She lifted the violin level to her shoulders—and then perhaps the audience did not hear so wonderful a music as they seemed to. They sat entranced, enthralled, almost motionless save for vagrant tears. Into that music went all the woman's soul. She rose above the place and the time and played to the world and its peoples, until, in from the street, stared pale vagrant faces and rose hushed voices. Perhaps none will ever know just what it was they heard in music that day, but that they heard the utmost none doubted. She played until she almost swayed on her feet, and the music died away. And then up from that black throng arose a chorus that shook the city with an obbligato of high human shrieks:

"There was a mighty shouting that day!"

Her husband put his arms around her and wrapped the violin in with her body, and took her silently away. She slept all next day and at night crept again inio his arms and nestled there; all night she nestled in his arms.

Physically, Sojourner was developing. Eating now regularly, good and nourishing food in happy companionship, the flesh began to cover her bones, her limbs rounded, her breasts developed, her little hands and feet stood out in contrast. She sat up and looked straight and walked with less slouch. She wore a look of happiness, and was a charming woman—not pretty, never beautiful, but always lovable. Wilson looked on his wife with growing delight.

The colored First Baptist church of Macon prospered. Wilson attracted a large and young audience. He instituted regular contributions. He raised his own salary and had comfortable furniture at the parsonage. Then he organized a social center, with an auditorium, committee rooms, kitchen and dining room. There were recreation rooms, and he thought of a bathing pool. He organized an employment bureau to get jobs for his parishioners and to furnish good servants for white Macon. He tried less successfully to find employment for skilled artisans, and even consulted with labor union leaders. He rented a home for the aged in the country, which had work at gardening and sewing.

White Macon, after a period of suspicion because of his education and dress, came to support the pastor and his wife. They were
especially enthusiastic about the reliable servants he got and even
consented, in some cases, to talk with him about their traetment
and wage. They loved Sojourner's concerts and attended largely,
sitting in the special seats reserved for them.

Then Wilson got ideas. He bought a corner lot on the main
thoroughfare, running out from the city past the old colored section and then past the school and the new plantation. Wilson
added several lots beyond the corner along the thoroughfare. He
had plans drawn in New York for a fine new church, parsonage and
social hall.

The white city was aroused. The old church was on a side
street, some distance from the main road. The real estate interests
had lately determined to let the Negroes develop their community
down that way, and while the college land bordered the highway,
its growth and main buildings were to face the other way. They
decided to buy back the old Negro slum now being bought by
Negroes under President Mansart's Building and Loan Association.
All these new plans of the whites had followed a new proposal to
pave the highway with federal funds which would turn it into a
main thoroughfare north. Wilson's plans were unthinkable. His
church would be the finest in town. So the banks haggled about a
mortgage, but an Atlanta bank offered to take it.

Then the white city began really to move. It seemed that a new
textile mill was considering coming to Macon if it could secure
a good site for its factory. A lot in the colored district near the
Negro college was eminently suited and the city threatened to
zone this area for industry. The college trustees protested and put
pressure on President Mansart to induce him to advise Wilson to
sell his lot and give up his plans for so elaborate a church. Also,
some of his oldest and best parishioners told Wilson that they
might lose their jobs if the proposed church was built. A less
elaborate church on the present site of the old would be better.
Indeed, the Depression now enveloped the land and area, and plans
for spending large sums of money were futile.

Wilson gave up his plan. He was bitter. He was now 35
years of age and uneasy. He was dissatisfied with his work. As
churches go, his church had been successful. His marriage had

been satisfactory. But he was operating on too small and limited a scale and he saw no future. He was bothered about the church itself. He was bothered about the situation in the South. He was bothered about the nation. There were bigger things that he wanted to do and there was nothing further that he could accomplish, so far as he could see, through the Baptist church or in Macon.

He had served time, attended the Baptist National Conventions with their huge masses of men, some earnest but many of them bent on pleasure and distraction, drinking, gambling, running after women as well as trying to attend to some of the business of the church. Their publishing house was really making spectacular advances so far as facilities and machinery were concerned. But it needed something to publish, something worthwhile. The Sunday School literature was hackneyed and old-fashioned. The general outlook was based on no real knowledge of the world and what was taking place.

When Wilson tried to do something about it, there was no way of getting this separated, unintegrated mass of people working as one real organization. They were separatists; they were chiefly interested in their own little churches. Those churches were supreme, their pastors were little monarchs. The over-all organization was simply a truce between monarchs, with very little that could be done. He was disgusted, particularly when he realized that even this ineffective and unwieldy national body had long been divided into two major factions. His efforts to re-unite the two by running for president in each was a farce. He was too little known to undertake what veterans knew was well-nigh impossible. His vote in both conventions was too small to count.

Returning to Macon, he met the Bishop of the African Methodist Church who presided over this district. The bishop sensed Wilson's disappointment and general unrest, and ventured to broach again a subject which he had before mentioned; and that was the advisability of Wilson's entering the ministry of his church. He pointed out the strength of his overall organization which, through a board of powerful bishops, directed and led the vast number of member churches. He showed how this guidance made for strength and efficiency and avoided local weaknesses and jealousies by sending strong men to places where they were needed and supporting them by central funds. And the bishop concluded by suggesting, without exactly saying, how much his church needed men of Wilson's caliber, not only as ministers but as Presiding Elders, as the next step in the hierarchy was known, and even on the Board of Bishops.

When, the next year, the Board of Deacons of his church refused even to consider renewing Wilson's project for a new church building, he resigned abruptly, leaving his flock in dismay. Thus it was that Roosevelt Wilson joined the A.M.E. connection. He left Macon, to Sojourner's great unhappiness. She had found her little niche in Macon and had built it up around herself. She had made music there and a little beginning in pictorial and plastic art. She had friends, she knew people. She felt that she had amounted to something. For the first time, she became a member of her own family. And now, suddenly, and almost without consultation, she was transplanted to a great city, Birmingham, in Alabama, and she hated it. But, characteristically, she said nothing. She made no complaint. After all, Roosevelt was master.

It was in Birmingham that Sojourner, to her surprise, met again that Herr Max Rosenfels who had first taught her music and then had himself taught at the State College until dismissed, when he went to New York. He gladly accepted their invitation to dinner, although they were hardly settled in their new charge. Rosenfels was traveling on a fellowship to collect Negro music, and just how this happened he was eager to tell.

"Sir and madame, I have had an unusual experience and I am eager to tell you. When I returned to New York, I went to Harlem, and to the Lafayette Theater. I got acquainted with Marion Cook, the composer, and Jesse Shipp, the manager. I learned about the Provincetown Players and saw "Shuffle Along." I heard the lovely voice of Florence Mills; the 'Emperor Jones' was still playing; 'All God's Chillun' was about to be staged. I asked these men and others about possible voices, as I said in my innocence, 'for the Metropolitan Opera!' They all laughed in my face. They said, 'Yes, we have got the voices, but nothing could get us into the Metropolitan.' I disputed them.

"Then I went down to the Metropolitan and introduced myself again to the director, Gatti-Casazza, who remembered me. We talked about music and voices. Of course, I did not mention Negroes. He was in sore straights for help. Meantime, he put me in the orchestra and commissioned me to look about for any unusual voices I might find.

"I started on a systematic search, by letter and some travels, but for Negro, not white voices. At last I got four voices—a tenor and a bass, a soprano and alto. They were all black folk. They were young and, of course, unknown, but they had unusual ability. I knew they had. But by that time, I was sure that there was no use introducing these singers at the Metropolitan and getting them auditions. But since the director was going to have a luncheon for some of his rich donors, with Herz and Toscanini present, and others who were really connoisseurs of music, I had my singers in the dining hall behind the great curtain. And there I asked permission to let them sing, unseen, the old quartet from ''Il Trovatore.'

"Then came the night. The guests, a score or more, were assembled and well-fed, and drinking the best vintages. They were in fine fettle. The richest and most ornate lady had her mind not simply on music and the need of a new opera house. She said, 'What I really need is a good cook. Can any of you help me?'

"And then suddenly the quartet began. There was no doubt of its quality. They sang the 'Miserere,' and it seems to me that it had never been so well sung. Certainly, I know it could not have been sung better. The tenor was simply magnificent, outstanding, vibrant. The soprano might have been matched, but that would have been hard to do. The alto was good, although perhaps not so outstanding as the others. But the bass was one of those voices one hears once in a generation. The roll of that great and unrivalled music was magnificent. Gatti-Casazza leaned forward and gripped my shoulder. 'My God,' he said, 'Where did you get those voices? I have searched the nation and the world!'

"And then the curtain drew aside. All the singers were black. The audience literally gasped. The Director went red with anger. He threw me back in a chair. 'You God-damned fool,' he said, 'what do you mean by doing this thing to me? Don't you know that these black voices are absolutely impossible in the Metropolitan Opera?'

"I said, 'I think I do now. But I did not before this.' And then the wealthy old lady woke up and belched. And she said, looking at the alto, 'She looks as though she could cook'."

From that day, Sojourner knew that Negro music was not simply her pleasure. It was her life.

CHAPTER XV

THE BLACK SHARECROPPERS

It had long been Manuel Mansart's conviction that the final settlement of the race problem in the South would find the Negro settled on the land to furnish raw materials and food for the nation; that white workers would live mainly in the cities and process these raw materials. Of course, Mansart expected some Negroes to live in the cities at work as laborers and servants, in business and the professions; and naturally, many whites would remain as farmers on the land. Still, Mansart believed in this wide general division.

For this reason, he was from the first especially interested in those who came to his school from the country districts. Quite a large number came, but only a minority of them could be admitted because they had had such poor elementary training. Most of them had attended school only a few months in the year for a few years. Some of them had studied by themselves or with the help of individuals. But a very large number simply could not be admitted even to the preparatory school of the State College. The most that could be done was to encourage them to try to get more elementary training in the city schools near their homes. This distressed Mansart very much because evidently here was a great deal of good material going to waste for lack of opportunity.

A few were admitted and these and some city students Mansart was eager to encourage to take up agriculture as a living. He had gotten this idea from the teaching of Booker Washington and others, but especially from his own thought. It seemed to him ideal for Negroes to get small plots of land, to cultivate them scientifically and carefully, and thus build up in that way communities of colored owners and farmers.

He talked of this to the students at chapel exercises and to many individually as a solution of the basic problem of the South. But, somehow, it did not seem to impress them. Most of them wanted to enter the professions—law, medicine, dentistry or pharmacy. A few wanted to enter business and a few to teach, but in that case, teaching often was a last resort rather than a real choice for a vocation. Very few were willing to take up agriculture. He could not see why. He talked to one young student particularly, a city boy from an educated family, searching for a career for their son, as Manuel knew. He outlined his dream of an agricultural community. But the boy's father came in for a talk.

"Did you ever live in the country, President Mansart?"

"Yes," answered Mansart, and he told him about his school at Jerusalem.

The man smiled. "But that wasn't quite the country. That was the town. And I take it you didn't have any too good a time there. You didn't stay there and you don't plan to go back."

Mansart smiled and admitted that it had been pretty difficult in many ways. But that wasn't an example of the idea that he had.

"I know," said the father. "Of course, you think of a nice community of homes, with colored owners, their own churches, schools and stores. But don't you see, President Mansart, that that's impossible?"

"Why impossible?" asked the President.

"Well," said the man, picking them off on his fingers, "First, lawlessness and cheating; second, lack of capital and credit; and last, the subjection of all agriculture to manufacture and trade. You see, sir, that's the Southern pattern. The farmer is ignorant and doesn't know what's going on in the world. He is taxed by the state, cheated by the merchants, given no credit by the banks, and dominated by the big landowners. That's the custom. I tell you, sir, the farmer, whether he is white or black, don't get justice in this economic system."

Mansart knew that there was truth in this, but he insisted that there was a possibility of breaking the system and doing the sort of thing that he had in mind. All it needed was courage.

Soon an opportunity for experiment came. There was his wife's family in Savannah, the mother and the younger sister of the boy who died in the First World War. The younger sister, born in 1904, wanted to come to the big city. When the school opened in Macon, Manuel welcomed his sixteen-year-old niece, Betty Sanders, as a student. There she met Jack Carmichael, who came from Liberty County. He was a light mulatto and good-looking, but cut out for an artist and never for the farmer which his mother wanted him to me. He and Betty fell deeply in love and Mansart encouraged the couple when Jack wanted to marry and take Betty to his mother's farm in Liberty County.

This county was in the lower southeastern part of Georgia and was almost entirely inhabited by Negroes. But instead of it being, on that account, under the control of Negroes all the more, it was after a time under the complete control of local white landlords or of white city merchants. It was, however, near the sea. Mansart dreamed of helping build up a seaside community which should share in fishing and commerce, in addition to the planting. But all that needed thought and capital. And above all, it needed careful organization.

For a time some of the colored teachers up in Atlanta seriously thought of coming down to Liberty County and forming a rural organization. But the fact of the mattetr was, it was too risky. They would have no protection. They had no political power. The countryside through the southern South was at the mercy of the small town and the small town was at the mercy of the mob manipulated by the Big Planter. Any sign of planning and of forward movement of a body of Negro planters would have been sure to run into mob violence sooner or later; so that gradually and in great disappointment, they had to give up their plans.

And as he looked about and travelled about, he saw the same sort of situation. It was possible to build up black peasantry which should be the foundation of a new South. But it was only a possibility where there was careful and organized help from without.

"Under the circumstances, it can't be successful," said Jean Du Bignon. "Suppose, Mr. President, that after all, you're not going to find it feasible to make the Negro a successful peasant in the South? Suppose he moves to the city instead?"

"That would be a calamity," said Mansart.

"Calamities happen," answered Jean.

But Jack and Betty married and went happily in 1923 to live with his mother on a heavily mortgaged 40 acres, none too fertile.

Liberty County was, for 20 years after the Bargain of 1876, represented by two black men in the legislature of Georgia. They were ousted after the overthrow of the Populists and by the time the Carmichaels came, Negroes had no political power, not even a Justice of the Peace or Notary Public.

Carmichael was trying to write and paint as well as raise cotton. Cotton prices had collapsed and the big landholder whose land surrounded the Carmichael plot, and who owned the mortgage, was transforming the Negro landholders into sharecroppers. He came over one morning to drive Jack to field work and found him sketching a cotton field in bloom. He cursed him, struck him and drew his pistol. Jack seized the pistol, knocked the landlord down and tried to shoot him but the pistol only clicked. Carmichael was aghast. He was almost a murderer and certainly now a hunted criminal. There was but one thing to do. He ran away, deserting mother, wife and child. When he attained success somewhere, somehow he planned to redeem his family.

About this time, Mansart came to hear of conditions in the Arkansas Delta. His friend, Will Benson, told him. Mansart liked Benson, of Kowaliga, whose father owned a large plantation not far from Tuskegee, and Benson had an idea of making this the center of an agricultural and industrial development. He proposed to raise the necessary capital by getting Northern philanthropists to become interested in looking over the agricultural and industrial possibilities. It was really a fine scheme and Mansart spent long days talking with Benson over these possibilities. Some of Benson's white friends from the North came down and talked with both of them. The possibility of securing considerable sums of money seemed to be good.

Then there came subtle opposition from Tuskegee. Booker Washington and his friends began to look upon Kowaliga as a possible rival to Tuskegee. Benson disclaimed this and tried to show how the two had no real competition, but Washington refused to encourage the enterprise or to advise philanthropists to invest. Then, of course, in addition to all that came the matter of transportation. Kowaliga was an island in the center of Alabama. The railroads did not touch it. The motor truck had not yet come into use. Just as on a larger scale, far away, Ethiopia was successfully shut in from the sea by the imperialists, so Kowaliga was shut in from the possibility of marketing its goods even if it could make and prepare them for the market.

While Benson was pursuing his plan, he visited Arkansas and on his return told Mansart of a young boy whose father wanted him to attend school but was hindered by local conditions which had for two years delayed settlement of the cotton crop. Mansart gladly offered to let the boy come to his college to study and pay later when his father made settlement for his crops. Thus, Mansart came to know of the Delta.

The Delta of Arkansas was a wide green billowing sea, lighted with flowers. The sunlight was warm and glowing, and the broad dark rivers east and west rolled calmly by to the Gulf. There were birds and little animals, and the soil was black and deep and rich.

Yet, one would hesitate to call this a happy land. Here and there was a home that looked like a mansion, with pillars, trees and flowers; here white folk lived. But the mass of people were Negroes and lived in drab and broken cabins, unpainted and crouched unhappily on the ground. These were one-room homes, often without floors, sometimes without windows. The chimneys invariably were old and broken and seldom dependable.

There was some laughter and joy, especially toward sunset, the time of the evening meal, where dark, ragged, tired workers came trooping in from the fields; and children shouted, ran and played. Yet it was not a land of happiness. People were poor, and some were sick, and they did not know much of the other regions beyond the rivers.

Cotton they knew—how the furry seed was planted, how it was hoed and attended as it grew, how it came up through the furrows and waxed green and lush, and then burst into a great sea of lovely flowers—white and yellow and purple. And then, finally, came the miracle. Out of the swelling pods below the flowers came great fistfuls of silver lint that burst into five glimpses of a new world of clothes. And the people with bent backs hoed it and hoed it again and "chopped" to keep back the weeds.

It was not a happy land but it was a rich land, for the cotton that grew here was needed south and north, across both the seas, over all the earth where long and cruel wars had stripped the people naked. Great sums of gold were offered for this cotton. Yet, somehow, when this gold drained down and through it was not the workers with the bent backs who received much of it, or even saw it.

Just at sunset, back in 1904, there was a little black boy sitting on the step of one of the cabins. This cabin was a shade better than most of its neighbors. It had a passage through the middle which left a room on either side, and a porch in front and behind.

It had floors, two glass windows in front and the chimney stood straight and attracted most of the smoke. There was a vine in front, and flowers.

Supper was just over, and mother was clearing up. But the little boy sat on the step staring west where the setting sun threw the last glow of day. He had come to try to see the big buildings which were in Little Rock. He couldn't see them, but they were there, way back yonder beyond Uncle Joe's. He knew they were there because he had it on the very highest authority, namely, his pappy. Mammy sometimes said she could see the towers just after sunset, but Mammy sometimes made jokes. Still, he was sure that back somewhere far to the west there were towns, with houses crowded right next to each other, and some of them as high as that tree, well, perhaps not that tallest tree but very, very tall, and filled with people. And the people had their pockets full of money.

Now, it was the firm resolve of little Henry Moore, one of these days when he was a bit bigger, to go to that city or some city beyond, perhaps even Memphis or New York, and live there. Because while he loved his home and his parents and brothers and sisters, and while the cotton at times was beautiful, he had gotten pretty tired of it. There was always something to do with it. One had to bend the back and pull and stretch and after all, it didn't make very much difference. They still were poor and of course black people had to be poor. But not quite so poor as these now. Even his pappy acknowledged that.

His pappy told him how he already owned this bit of land, and that when Henry grew up they would buy more and then perhaps they would have a nicer house. Mammy was not enthusiastic. She said that colored people who built nice houses had them burned down sometimes, and even when Uncle Joe painted his house there was trouble.

But nevertheless, since the local school ran only three months, this little boy was going to school in Elaine. He was learning to read and write and could count considerable sums and then, later, he was going off to Tuskegee to learn farming. His pappy was very anxious to have him learn how to farm effectively. Of course, little Henry Moore assured his father that he already knew all about farming that he wanted to know. He had picked cotton when he was seven years old and now he knew how to plow, and to be very frank, it was work that he didn't like.

Years passed on and the boy grew up. By 1914, he was ten. There was war in the world and then, after the war, the demand for clothing increased all over the world and especially the demand for cotton. The price began to rise and new ideas began to sweep over this great sea of delta cotton. Charles Moore planned to send his boy to Tuskegee.

While he was waiting and the uneasiness in the county was increasing, some visitors came by. There was a Negro lawyer, Scipio Jones, from Little Rock, some of his professional friends, and especially a young man from Alabama who lived not far from Tuskegee. His name was William Benson and he was a handsome young mulatto, brilliant brown in color, with beautiful hair and enthusiastic eyes.

Moore was very glad indeed to have a chance to talk with these men. Benson, especially, wanted to know about conditions in this part of Arkansas, and they were explained to him. Benson then revealed some of his own plans, his father's large plantation at Kowaliga, and how he had put a school there and begun to found a cooperative settlement. They talked about young Henry and Benson did not favor sending him to Tuskegee.

"You see, Mr. Moore, Tuskegee is good for those who cannot do better; for those who must work to get through school; those who are backward or retarded. Now Henry is bright, and considering his poor school facilities he's done very well. What he needs is to learn to read, write and count better. Then, he needs a background of general knowledge in a high school and if possible in a good college. Don't try to build science on the ignorance of a ten-year old boy."

Moore was impressed but pleaded lack of funds at present, although high cotten prices might make Henry's schooling possible soon. Benson brushed that aside and offered to take Henry with him to Kowaliga at no cost at all. So Henry finished the elementary school in Kowaliga in two years and then, in 1921, Benson brought him to Mansart at Macon.

President Mansart welcomed young Moore as one who might carry out some of his rural dreams. Moore began the regular college preparatory course with the idea, as Mansart suggested, that later he might go to one of the great agricultural colleges of the North. He turned out to be a sturdy, straightforward young man, and told Mansart an interesting story. His father owned a small farm in the Delta region, which was the lowlands between the Mississippi, Arkansas and Tennessee Rivers, extending down into Louisiana. Here, much cotton was raised on 700,000 square miles of rich land, and three-fourths of the people there, if not more, were Negroes. His father lived a short distance from the town of Elaine, and in his community most of the Negroes could read and write and 500 owned their farms, although 3,500 others were sharecroppers. They did not vote and Negroes were never represented on juries. Their schools were poor.

Henry said the colored people raised between 25,000 and 30,000 bales of cotton a year. And nearly all of them are "supplied" by the landlords and merchants; that is, the local store furnishes them their goods and seed for the year and then at the end of the year when settlement is made they are paid the balance due from the price of the cotton. Even owners like his father were "furnished" by the store because they had to sell their cotton to the only gin there, which was owned by the white landlord, and he paid annually through the store. Of course, the store prices were high. They calculated that they paid 25-50% interest a year, and Charles said it was well-known that the landholders and merchants down there didn't make money on their cotton except in very good years, but made it always on the store charges. The Negroes could seldom get a statement of their account, but simply a report of the goods purchased and the amount of money due them. The landlord took the cotton, ginned it and sold it, and then made settlement.

There was trouble when his father tried to get payment for the last crop in order to send his son to school. There was almost a row at the store, but Charles Moore was well-known and was a quiet, self-controlled man, so that one could see his shoulders stiffen and his eyes flash; nevertheless, he had gone without benefit of the money due now for a year. It was particularly annoying since the price of cotton was going up. Back before the World War it was only 9 cents a pound. Then, during the war, it rose from 11 cents to 20 cents and was 28 cents a pound when the United States entered the war, and now it was 40 cents a pound. This, of course, made it difficult to keep the Negroes in debt and so hold them to their work and not have them straying off to the cities. But nevertheless, the payment was not made, and by July, 1919, they had not yet made settlement for the 1918 crop. Charles Moore, having sent his son away, finally proposed to take measures to force payment.

Meantime, the rise in the price of cototn was galvanizing the South. John Baldwin, of Atlanta, asked his correspondents in Memphas to buy and ship him as much cotton as possible and suggested that with the proceeds they might invest in oil, in rising stocks, in railroads. Memphis bankers ordered consignments of cotton from the Delta at high prices, and were tempted not only to order the cotton but not to pay for it immediately, and to buy on credit oil stocks in the southwest. They also bought some of the foreign stocks that were being offered and which were paying high interest.

The rising price of cotton, the stirring of war, were arousing the Delta, and arousing not only the white merchants in the cities and the colored sharecroppers, but also that group between—the planters, and the poor whites. There was, for instance, in the small city of Elaine, a leading mrechant, John Grey. He owned large amounts of cotton land, did a good trade with Atlanta and local Arkansas merchants, and sold cotton. He had been prosperous and easy-going, and now his wife was trying to get him to branch out. She said: "We have been comfortable but stodgy. There is no reason why you shouldn't be rich. Now that our daughter, Jeanette, has become engaged to a rising young Northerner, we ought to build a new home and give her a striking wedding celebration."

So the Greys began to make plans for a new life. They got an architect and planned a rather elaborate home. In order to do this, it was necessary to get in as much cash as possible and to pay out little. As a result, the small merchants, sharecroppers and the laborers who had raised cotton for Grey in the Delta district did not get their settlement. Grey argued that the Negroes didn't need the money anyway, they would only waste it. They could keep on buying food on credit from his commissary and when he got ready, Grey would settle with them. It was for that reason that he did not settle for the 1918 crop which was still owing in 1919. His wife was delighted with the necklace which he bought for her and the family rode pleasantly out into the country districts in their new Pierce Arrow.

Charles Moore was mad. He sat down in the grove back of the church after the monthly sermon and drew some of the sharecroppers and owners about him. He said:

"We've got to do something about this situation. The whites are spending money like water and getting rich and we are getting further and further in debt. We've had no settlement now of our cotton for two years. Now what I propose is that we get a lawyer and bring suit."

There was a silence, because it was not a popular nor altogether a healthy thing in the Delta region to go to court under any circumstances, and especially against a white man.

"Of course," said Uncle Joe, "there are some good colored lawyers in Little Rock, like Scipio Jones, who could advise us."

"That won't do," said Charles Mooe. "We don't dare hire colored men. What standing would they have in an Elaine court? They might be mobbed. No, we have got to get some good white lawyers right in Elaine, and I think I know the ones to hire."

So during the next week this scheme was carried out and a meeting was arranged in the church on the following Sunday with two white lawyers from Elaine. In addition, Negro cotton pickers organized a union to raise wages. Many of the Negroes in the sawmills organized, and nearly all Negro workers began to refuse to allow their wives and daughters to work for certain white planters. These movements became known, and the white planters determined to break up the whole business and put the Negroes back "in their places." The Negroes, on the other hand, knowing of the race riots in all parts of the country, began to buy firearms. There was indicated a widespread revolt of the black workers against the whole industrial system of the Delta, and the planters determined to attack it head on and wipe out the rebellion.

One Sunday, a drunken white man came to Elaine and proceeded to shoot up the colored district. How far this was a prearranged incident no one knew, but the Negroes refused to be incited to riot. They kept off the street and phoned to the sheriff at Helena. The sheriff did not come. Then white men ambushed one of the secret night meetings of the group arranging the lawsuit. Both sides fired, killing a white "special agent" and a deputy sheriff. Immediately, it was reported that a Negro insurrection had taken place.

An old pattern of Southern life leaped into sudden being— slave insurrection and revenge; murder, poison and rape; the terrible danger to women and children; the fear of the whip, the branding iron, the dungeon; the loss of home and savings; the flame and bullet. The Delta went temporarily mad. The white women and children, loaded on trains, fled to town. The armories of the towns were opened to the white public. Dozens were sworn in quickly as deputy sheriffs. Ammunition was free, and plenty of horses and autos filled the roads. The burning crosses of the Ku Klux filled the nights with terror.

There was something about a manhunt that was superb. Fox-hunting was child's play, even to the few local gentlemen who had been in Kentucky or Maryland. Big game hunting had its attractions—an elephant could shriek like a man; a tiger could scream a blood-tingling defiance. But to get on the trail of a running Negro, mad with fright or hate; to see him twist and turn, to hear him curse and pray—by God that was sport unequalled in modern life! Thus some of these white men thought, as they rode yelling through the blood-stained land. They thought this even if they gave their thought no word. They stared furtively at each other. Some feared blood and hated riot, but how could it be avoided? Here were Negroes; here was Civilization. The result was violence and death.

Train loads and auto loads of white men, armed to the teeth, came from Marianna and Forrest City, Arkansas, Memphis, Tennessee, and Clarksdale, Mississippi. Rifles and ammunition were rushed in. The woods were scoured, Negro homes shot into, Negroes who did not know any trouble was brewing were shot and killed on the highways.

Some young white men looked across a brook where a thin blue wisp of smoke rose from a tiny dun-colored cabin. There were greens and potatoes growing in the rear, and red roses bloomed over the door. A baby was playing on the steps.

"Wait," said one as he unslung his gun. "If that there 'nigger' is home I'm going to run him off. He's got a damn pretty little black filly there. I've had my eye on her some time, but he sticks too close. Here's my chance. I'll flush him, you keep him running like hell, while I have me a little fun."

His companions guffawed. He crept down the bank noiselessly. A little young black woman sat sewing on the narrow porch and singing:

"Way over in Jordan, Lord—"

Then she saw the white man and opened her mouth to scream,

but he was on her before she made a sound. He bore her down to the floor. She twisted and struggled and then lay still. The baby on the steps whimpered, and then for a long time all was silence. The man at last rose, and stretched.

"Aw, shet up, honey—you ain't hurt. Here's a dollar. I'll be back—"

He swung around, looked up and saw Death. He started to yell but the gun roared and his head was a red pulp. The waiting men on the bank above started and yelled, but the little black man with the gun in one hand and his baby in the other plunged across the creek. He shot, and one of the men fell. Two answering shots rang out and the black man fell dead into the muddy water. His wife fell dead across his baby. The baby climbed slowly up the bank and went toddling along the highway.

Lawrence Sells saw all this. Lawrence was a young white man from Illinois, and had just come south to make his fortune. He had stopped in Elaine to kiss his sweetheart, Jeannette Grey, whom he had met through business deals with her father, and to arrange for the spring wedding. She was a lovely and happy young fiancee, and there was a new and beautiful home. He had hurried out into the Delta country to see the cotton land his father had just bought for him. His white fellow owners were genuinely sorry that he had arrived at this critical time; but he might as well learn soon as late. He rode out with a posse and joined the disorder. He saw murder for the first time; and fire, beating and whipping. He was aghast and half-consciously became separated from his companions as he rode along the highway.

A baby—a little black baby of perhaps three years, came toddling toward him, screaming, with tears. He heard shots and then three young white men came full tilt from the side. One swung and raised his gun. He was yelling and cursing:

"Kill that little black brat—his father got John."

He cocked his shotgun, but a great black man arose from across the road and fired first. The man fell dead. The white men turned and galloped away. The baby toddled on. Lawrence Sills rode back. He saw a house burning. There was some commotion within, but he did not pause.

It was undoubtedly the best country house in this part of the land. Sid Gower, a local small planter, struggling up out of share-cropping to land owning, had borrowed money and starved his black laborers to have it finished this spring. Especially was he mad at John Grey, of Elaine, who owed him for cotton and would not pay.

There was his hard-working wife, whose face lit up with a pride that brought tears when the last nail went home. There were his three grown daughters, plain and thin but tough and determined. They had worked for this, even picking cotton in the fields when the dirty "darkies" struck for higher wages and left. His two stalwart sons were hard, ignorant, but desperately striving men. This family was figting and rising from the depths; they'd be "Quality" yet.

The sons, armed, rode off with the mob to steal, beat and kill. The daughters reluctantly rode to Elaine. But the mother would not stir. She wasn't afraid of no "nigger!" She heard the shouting and shooting pass by and spread out across the field. She heard the screams and saw the fires. Then she walked silently through her kitchen, lovingly fingering the new running water tap. How she had longed for this! She turned happily—and then saw him.

He was big, black and sullen. Blood dripped from his shoulders and a red welt crossed his face from ear to ear. She was in deadly fear but did not show it. She stared straight into his eyes and snarled.

"What d'ye want?"

She stood straight and still as he glided to the stove, dragged out the burning wood and coal and scattered it over the floors. The flames rose and curled. She shrieked. "Don't burn it, dear Christ, don't burn my home."

He turned slowly. "That ain't all I'll do, you damned White Cracker."

She sank to her knees and tried to whisper but said nothing. She did not struggle as he crushed her back. She did not cry out, even when after long pain she heard her husabnd's heavy step amid the mad crackling and roaring of the flame, the red hell of all she had lived for.

The Gower boys rode hurriedly on. They stopped only to lash chance Negroes out of their way, or swing hastily aside to avoid a posse of whites. They knew the Negro homes which were furnished with lamps and bedding; with crockery and even bits of silver plate; there might be a little cash and good clothes in homes like the Moores', and small pieces of furniture that were portable. All day they looted from the Negro homes, until dark night fell. Then they drove their horses, hitched to carts gathered here and there, across country toward home. It was past midnight when, approaching home, they saw the red glow in the sky.

" 'Nigger' cabin," they growled at first, and then, "Mighty near home—wonder whose it can be?"

"Don't know no big buildings so near!"

"Sid, Sid, h'its mighty near our home—my God, can it be home?"

"Sam, Sam, Christ a-bighty—h'its home—h'its gone! H'its burned to the ground!"

Meantime, telegrams were sent to the governor of the state. He called for Federal troops and five hundred were rushed from Camp Pike, armed with rifles, cannon, gas masks, hand grenades, bombs and machine-guns. The Colonel took "charge of all strategic points," and "mobilized his men to repel the attack of the black army." The country was scoured for a radius of fifty to one hundred miles, covering all of Phillips and part of adjoining counties, for "Negro insurrectionists."

The soldiers arrested over a thousand Negroes, men and women, and placed them in a "stockade" under heavy guard and kept them there under the most disgusting, unwholesome and unsanitary conditions. They were not allowed to see friends nor attorneys, but all of them had to be separately and personally "investigated" by the army officers and a white "committee of seven." Even if, after the "investigation," a Negro had been proven completely innocent, still no Negro was released until after a white man had appeared and personally "vouched" for him as being a "good nigger."

If the Negroes had been in actual conspiracy or armed rebellion against their serfdom there would have been a small civil war. But the Negroes were mostly unarmed and their intelligent leaders were only appealing to law for wages withheld, or forming unions to secure higher wage. As a result, they willingly surrendered to the law, and among the first was Charles Moore.

Two currents of opinion now struggled for control. Those poor whites who wanted to kill "niggers," steal their property and settle on their land had the guns and horses and wore the badges of the law. Allied with them were the owners and employers who wanted to cow Negroes so thoroughly that they would never dare try to form unions or appeal to the federal courts against white planters and their methods. These latter citizens did not object to a few murders, whippings and torture.

The big landholders now became frightened. This movement of gins and stores got quickly together and consulted. This movement of Negro labor toward courts and labor unions was dangerous to the system; but on the other hand, black labor was their livelihood and path to wealth, and now with rising cotton and soaring business it was crazy to let this labor be driven away or discouraged beyond hope. The poor whites would jump at this chance to kill and steal, and some harsh measures must be applied and let the white riff-raff do it. But it must be curbed and kept in bounds.

So it was that Federal troops had been summoned, not, as was intimated, to repress the Negroes, but to keep the whites from going too far and ruining the labor market. There was, of course, no plot to destroy the whites and burn property, but a strong case for this must be made to impress the nation and to excuse some excesses, and some day—some day—.

Meantime, the planters were getting matters in hand. With help from the federal troops, they rapidly organized a committee of planters and merchants together with the sheriff and local judge. This committee assumed charge of the matter and proceeded to have brought before them a large number of those in jail and examined them. If evidence satisfactory to the committee was not given, their keepers would take them to a room in the jail immediately adjoining the room where the committee was sitting, and torture them by beating and whipping them with leather straps with metal in them, cutting the blood at every lick until the victims would agree to testify to anything their torturers demanded of them. There was also provided an electric chair in which they would be put naked and the current turned on to frighten them into giving damaging statements against themselves and others; also strangling drugs were put up their noses. By these methods, false evidence was extorted from Negroes to be used against the accused.

Every day the white press carried all sorts of inflammatory articles calculated to whip up hysteria; and mobs in Helena, composed of hundreds of men, repeatedly threatened to lynch the prisoners. The United States troops interfered and promised the prompt execution of those found guilty.

On October 27, a grand jury of white men was organized. On

October 29, a joint indictment was returned against a group of these prisoners, accusing them of murder. On the third of November, the prisoners were taken into the court room, and told of the charge. They were denied the right to choose their own lawyers but had a lawyer appointed to defend them. He did not consult with them nor take any steps to summon witnesses nor prepare for their defense. They were immediately placed on trial before a white jury and the trial closed, with only the witnesses for the prosecution. The jury, in two or three minutes, wrote a verdict of "guilty of murder in the first degree as charged," and twelve Negroes were summarily sentenced to death and 67 others sentenced to long terms in prison. All during the trial, the courthouse and the grounds were thronged with a white mob demanding death. Ex-servicemen, the Rotary Club, and the Lions Club, passed resolutions asking the governor not to interfere.

Here, by all precedent, the matter should have ended and the Delta should have settled back to the calm of complete exploitation. But this time this was not the case. The new Northern organization, called the 'NAACP, entered the case. It appealed to the Arkansas Supreme Court for a writ of *habeas corpus*, which the court summarily denied. Then, to the astonishment of white Arkansas, the Supreme Court of the United States allowed it.

The fight lasted four years and cost over $50,000. On January 9, 1923, Moorfield Storey argued the case before the Supreme Court. On February 19, the United States Supreme Court reversed the convictions of six men. Oliver Wendell Holmes delivered the majority opinion of the Court, which was concurred in by Chief Justice Taft and Brandeis. The other six men were allowed the writ of *habeas corpus* by the State Supreme Court and freed from custody. Finally, the last of the 67 were freed from custody in 1924.

It was one of the greatest victories ever won by black folk in America; but for four years Charles Moore lay in jail under sentence of death. It broke his health and spirit and he died. Henry Moore finished his college course in 1924, the year his father died. Then he went back to the farm. Under the circumstances, not much could be done. The whole situation was upset throughout the country. It was going to be a pretty difficult thing for Moore to take care of his mother and educate his little brothers and sisters. He looked for work in town.

It was a bleak prospect there for a young Negro. There was common labor with poor pay and worse treatment. Most laborers alternated with town work and work in the fields, but Moore had his own father's farm for summer work. He had to find town work for the winter. There were the trades if he had skill, which he had not, and if he could have entered the unions of the organized trades, which he could not. There was domestic service of various kinds, and work as a porter or a laborer.

His final choice came through acquaintanceship with a friend of his father's who was head cook in the Grey family, of Elaine. Moore helped him out on several occasions, making needed money and discovering an aptitude for cooking, together with a liking for the work. The pay for house service was good—far better, considering the board, than the skilled trades or the professions like teaching or even the beginnings of medicine and law. Henry sat down and faced frankly the prospect of becoming a servant. The old cook was delighted and the employer was pleased.

Yet, Moore disliked house service. Not altogether because of the kind of work. At home he often helped his mother with the washing and the ironing, and daily with the dishes and the cleaning. But there were certain things about this service for white people, which he greatly disliked—being called by his first name, being regarded as an inferior order of being, having no regular hours, being supposed to be at call any time of the day or night, and so forth. On the other hand, he really liked cooking. He had experimented at home. He had bought cook books. His old friend had a long lore of cooking information which came down from his former residence in New Orleans. Henry even went over to Tuskegee and took a summer course in cookery. He carefully considered the problem of life as an "upper servant." He made certain demands. He wanted to be called by his last name instead of his first; he wanted definite hours of work, and he wanted the proper sort of modern equipment.

When he first made some of these demands, the head of the house, Mr. Grey, immediately told his wife and daughter that he wasn't going to have any "damned uppity-nigger in this kitchen." But Mr. Grey was tired and old-fashioned, and just at this time he suddenly died. It was found that he was a very rich man. The wife and her daughter and son-in-law, Lawrence Sills, determined to move from Elaine to the capital of the state, Little Rock.

Here was a chance for broader life and wider horizons.

The women of the family had had experience, not only with servants in Elaine but with servants in the north, where they went on vacations. They rather liked Moore's attitude. They knew his training. He got up one entertainment, acting as butler in excellent uniform and serving what was really an unusual dinner. The guests spoke of it and wanted to know about her chef. She made a few explanations, and afterward had a conference with Henry.

Henry Moore was frank and she was intelligent. He told her that he didn't like house service and they agreed with him that there were reasons why he shouldn't. He explained that as a Negro he wanted to do something else simply because he was sure he could. But, on the other hand, he had had no opportunity for training or skills; his education could not continue and now he had to stay with his family and try to support his mother and educate the children.

This was the atmosphere about young Lawrence Sills as he visited his bride in Little Rock. The Delta uprising had long been quelled. The black prisoners were all freed. There lingered fear and resentment. It was a dangerous precedent for Negroes to beat white men in a federal lawsuit. It boded ill for the future. It showed a growing unity and knowledge of methods of cooperation which meant trouble in the nation and in the world.

Lawrence Sills was particularly unsettled in mind. His investments were prospering, his cotton land paid for; his bride was beautiful. But he had to talk life over with somebody. They were in the sunken gardens, surrounded with the beauty of land and tinkling water, flower and fruit. He said: "I am not quite happy in Arkansas."

Jeannette was piqued. "But Lawrence, what a thing to say just after your wedding."

"No, no, dear, you know I don't mean what you intimate. I have a beautiful bride, and I'm very, very fond of you; and these surroundings here are simply too lovely to forget in any way. Existence here just as a matter of looking, feeling, eating and drinking, is hardly to be bettered. Especially this food. Where did you get your extraordinary cook?"

"You know, dear, that's a rather strange story. His father owned a little land down in the Delta where you have your cotton acreage, and got in trouble down there during this recent upset.

Henry, instead of becoming the farmer his father wanted him to, came to the city and has become an 'upper servant.' Well, naturally Henry had ideas, and my father at first was not going to have anything to do with him; but Henry is a little different from some folk and particularly from Negroes. He has studied cooking and house service. He has brains. And he demands wages! Well, to cap it all, we've got him here and certainly he does a good job. But that, my dear, has nothing to do with this unhappiness of yours."

"Yes it has," returned Lawrence. "That's just the trouble. Where are we going? That turmoil in Elaine and the Delta—that really was not settled right. You can't beat workers back into their places. You can't have a riot in the South every time a Negro demands higher wages or steals something. There's got to be a better system in general."

"Of course, Lawrence, I know that. But I am, just at this time, very, very happy. And I don't see why our happiness cannot go on. We've got to have servants, naturally, not only because we want them but because they have got to live, and what else is there for the Negroes and a good many of the whites to do, but to work for their betters at such wages as we can afford?"

"Very satisfactory," said Lawrence, "but it doesn't seem to work out, somehow, as it should. Who decides who is better and who is worse? There was a time when the employer told the laborer what his wages would be and invited him to get out if he didn't like them. Now we're right face-to-face with a time when the laborer is telling the employer what he has got to have. And no matter how far it goes, we've got to face the question as to whether the majority of men must accept what a powerful minority is willing to give them, or whether we can look forward to a time when everybody has a reasonable income."

"My dear Lawrence, that is possible, barely possible, with the mass of white people. But really, when it comes to colored people, Negroes, Indians, east and west, Chinese and all that, it's simply unthinkable. You'll always have this mass of incompetence down at the bottom of society, and the best that can be done is to keep a reasonable number of them alive.

"But now, this is going really too far into things. After all, whatever is going to be the outcome we can't settle it now, can we? But there are certain things that we can settle. We can keep a home like this going with well-paid servants; we can travel in

Europe which I'm simply wild to do. We can read, and we can have pirtuses and things of that sort. We can associate with—with —nice people. I don't mean merely rich people, but people of knowledge and taste. That, it looks to me, is the future toward which we can work, and really Lawrence, don't you think that under the circumstances you can be happy?"

It is not at all wonderful that Lawrence decided that he could be very happy under circumstances such as those which surrounded him at the moment. But sometimes, as time went on, he looked out into the Delta, the beautiful and tragic Delta; there was scarce happiness and no contentment there. There, hopeless black serfs still crouched on the soil. Filthy cabins fifty years old leaned crazily; or flimsy makeshift hovels replaced their ruined forerunners. The Negroes still had almost no schools; they received wages too small to live decently; they were jailed if they openly tried to quit their jobs; they were lashed for impudence if they did not work their guts out; they died of easily preventable disease, with no nurses nor physicians to help.

Why did they submit? They did not. They escaped, by night, in swamp and river, by rail where possible. There were left here in slavery, with no vote and little decency, only those who could not get away. Even these kept trying; year after year they tried. Some day they would succeed or die trying. Thus, the self-supporting, independent black peasant of the South was being year by year driven to extinction or to the slums of Memphis, St. Louis or Chicago. At the gates of these cities two veiled figures welcomed them —Crime in crimson and Disease in gray. Some day, on the bones of the black Delta dead, a new white peasantry would be born, unless the big Monopoly Farm choked even that.

CHAPTER XVI

THE WORLD FALLS

At the end of the First World War, the United States reached the apex of political and financial power in all the world. Of all nations, it had more capital to loan than any other, and had already loaned sixteen billion dollars worth of materials to Europe, Asia, Africa, the Americas and sea islands.

At home, our wealth began to pile up from less than a hundred billion at the beginning of the century to nearly 400 billion in the fateful year of 1929. While the number of our manufacturing establishments remained the same, the workers in them had doubled in number and the value of their products had increased six-fold. We had, in 1929, one sixth of the land and people of the world; but we owned 60 per cent of the telegraphs and telephones, 30 per cent of the railroads and of the water power products, and three-fourths of the motorcars. We produced a third of the coal and the lead, half of the copper and steel, and two-thirds of the petroleum.

But the singular thing about our power was its mastery. We were ruled not by responsible individuals, thinking, seeing, hearing and feeling, but by monsters called Corporations; human ability and science straitly bound and strapped into two hundred irresponsible, soulless, eternal groups, stronger than human muscles and armed and equipped with superhuman power. Even these different groups were coalescing into one single group of powerful men who controlled all the group of groups; so that 350 men, in 100 corporations, owned twenty-two thousand million dollars of capital. Among these corporations were 200 giants each with 100 million dollars of assets, and fifteen with over a billion.

Who could touch such massed might? Were we not supreme and invulnerable? Yet, we were an integral part of a world which had been gravely hurt; near forty million men had been killed, wounded or lost; uncounted property had been destroyed. Thousands died by disease and hunger after the war. The peace congress admitted Japan, excluded Russia, and left all the colonies still in chains.

Churchill, of Britain, turned to crush Communism by force, and Foch, of France, wanted two million American soldiers to help in this enterprise. In the covenant of the new League of Nations, Britain and the United States refused to declare races equal, and Japan withdrew. Foch finally said, "This is not peace; it is an armistice for twenty years." He was right. Trotsky, who wanted world revolution to bring Communism, was driven from Russia to Turkey, France and Norway, and finally found sanctuary in Mexico, whence his propaganda turned the liberal United States against Stalin, despite the protest of Bullitt and Robins. Bliss said, "We seem to be drifting into another Dark Ages."

Yet, here in America there were warnings in the air. Little things were happening to little people who counted as nothing in the minds of most men. Girls were going to hell; democratic methods of control were failing; race and religious hate were rife; war and war psychoses were spreading; and revolution against Wrong threatened with force. Business was running wild, and insanity expressing itself in Art.

In Atlanta, for instance, one especially minor matter might have been noted. In 1928, Daisy was about to enter on the world's oldest profession. She was frightened but outwardly calm and self-possessed despite her sixteen years and slight frame. She was a pretty yellow girl, unobtrusively but tastefully dressed, with soft, low voice and excellent grammar. She was standing quietly in downtown Atlanta, near the conflux of Peachtree and Auburn, where in the past she had been most frequently accosted. It was in the cool dusk, when her color was not too conspicuous to the casual eye. Soon she saw the white man approaching whom she had chosen and who many times had appeared to wish to choose her.

It had all begun a year ago when she went to help her old grandmother who, since the city fire, had cooked for the Baldwin family. She was to leave school and be a sort of extra housemaid, paid little at first because of her inexperience, but in time to become a secure fixture in the great, rich family on this lovely estate. The family consisted of the lordly old lady, **Miss Betty Lou**, the young banker, Mr. John, his beautiful and haughty wife, and young Lee Baldwin. Especially young Lee Baldwin—tall, thin and sixteen, perfumed with Turkish tobacco and expensively dressed. She soon found him always lurking about in unexpected places, stroking her cheek and pinching her arm. She was at once scared, flattered and excited.

Young Mrs. John Baldwin, returning unexpectedly from a trip to Charleston, had discovered them together in Daisy's little bedroom up under the roof, overlooking the velvet sheen of the meadow. Daisy had been awakened from her nap and let him have his way. He was emitting cries of ecstasy just as his mother entered the door.

Mrs. Baldwin was relating the frightful incident from which she had scarcely recovered to a coterie of friends, over tea laced with rum.

"There that nasty little bitch lay, holding closely my frightened boy. He did not know what was happening—what it all meant. I struck her across the face and half dragged, half carried him downstairs. He explained amid tears how he had rushed up to her cries of 'Fire,' and she had seized him like a mad thing. I had her out of the house within the hour."

Mrs. Ried, of the Macon Rieds, tapped her cigarette. "As I remember, isn't she a bit young and small to exhibit such—strength?"

"Old enough and quite experienced," snapped Mrs. Baldwin. "Lee might have been infected with some loathsome disease. Dr. Gaines has taken him in hand and promises no harm will come. I tell you, my dears, between these black wenches and the white riff-raff from the hills, our men scarce dare walk the streets these days."

"Or slip into strange beds," retorted Mrs. Ried. "We may have to castrate them in sheer self-defense."

Mrs. Baldwin and all the others ignored the vulgarity of the remark. Mrs. Ried was noted for her advanced thought. Even now she had to add: "And didn't you have some such maid trouble last year?"

They turned to the business at hand which was this proposed Florence Nightingale Home that the white First Methodist church was promoting. They voted an appropriation of $500, without deigning to answer Mrs. Ried's query: "Will colored girls be admitted?" Mrs. Ried bordered on the frivolous at times. "I noticed," she shot at parting, "that Lee is up and able to be about."

But Mrs. Ried was really neither flippant nor shallow. In a prosperous and progressing Southern world she was trying to make her class rise to a vision of a broad human duty among the Negroes and poor whites at their doors. She was a leader of the interracial movement as well as one of the inner social circle. Her efforts to bring the two races together were continuously in vain. Just because she in her social incarnation was also active in inter-racial meetings, did not mean the two movements were in the least beginning to coalesce. Almost the contrary, the one was but escapism for the continued indifference of the other.

John Baldwin had been a little disappointed when, after having served as mayor and gone to war, he had come back and been put into command of Big Business. Of course it was fun. He was making money and was already a millionaire. But, like his mother he wanted a little of the pomp and circumstance. He would like to be governor of the state. He wanted to go to the United States Sennate, and of course this was not only what Betty Lou had always prayed for, but even Mrs. Baldwin was sighing for more worlds to conquer. They had had one son and that, so far as young Mrs. Baldwin was concerned, finished the matter of sex and reproduction. She proposed to have no more children, and she wanted not only money to spend but a wide and ever widening area upon which to exercise her taste in expenditure.

Her son, Lee Baldwin, as he grew became increasingly a problem—partly from a quirk of nature, partly from neglect and indulgence. There were painful incidents in school and on the streets and even in liquor saloons. Time went on and soon Lee Baldwin was running after the Coypel girl who was older than he. Mrs. Baldwin spoke to her husband who had long been intimate with this impossible family. He paid little attention, but the intimacy seemed to stop after that policeman's murder. There was some whispering which connected Zoe Coypel with that incident, but it never reached actual words, and was soon forgotten.

John Pierce, the second, whose protege young John Baldwin was, began to be frightened in 1927. He was nearly 80 and he was frightened at the very prosperity of the United States, of the state of Georgia, and of the city of Atlanta. Things were going too fast, and furiously. Wealth was piling up, and power was concentrating. It was not that he was against this development in principle. It was what he had dreamed about. But it was coming too fast. His New York representative, Haynes, was going insane over investments in French and German cartels. Brakes must be put upon investment and expansion. He called in Baldwin, of Atlanta, and talked to him, but Baldwin at 48 felt young. He had just returned from New York and Washington and was full of enthusiasm.

"I tell you, Mr. Pierce," he said, "this is a new era. We are coming to the place where we are simply going to transform industry. We are going to wipe out poverty. We are going to be masters of the glorious possibilities of this world. Our development is going beyond anything which we have experienced before, and it would be foolish for us to be afraid of the mighty tide on which we are rising."

Pierce looked him over and grunted. This was the kind of thing that he was afraid of. He said, "Well, my boy, you may be right but I doubt it. The world is not in the habit of changing so fast as this. There is something wrong when people are willing and eager to pay for six-percent property, prices that would only be justified by 25 percent. It may come out all right, I would not dare deny it, but it's time for us to watch. For example, Democracy in this land has gone straight to Hell."

"Why shouldn't it?" asked Baldwin. "Can the mob handle the Machine which we are building?"

"No, and can we?" retorted Pierce.

'Our wealth can," answered Baldwin.

"Wealth? Hell! Wealth is a thing, not a person; a result, not the understanding of it. I distrust the people who today are controlling our wealth. What are they doing and why? What training have they for the job? I'm frightened!"

"Nothing ventured, nothing won."

"Everything ventured, everything lost. I'm going abroad to look things over. I know I'm too old, but you are too young."

There came an election in 1928, which John Pierce watched narrowly and President Mansart followed more carefully than ever he had watched a presidential election before. He gave no thought to national politics in 1920, when he had made president. He and all other Negroes heard the rumor of Harding's colored blood, but that did not interest him. Coolidge in 1924 seemed equally unimportant. But in 1928, the situation was different. A Catholic was running against a millionaire and neither evinced any interest in the Negro. Indeed, as the campaign progressed, it was evident that the Negro was being less than ignored—he was being treated worse than in any election since Emancipation. Mansart hesitated but finally joined in signing a nation-wide protest sent out by twenty-five of the principal colored leaders in the nation:

"The persons whose names are signed beneath are alike in the fact that we all have Negro slaves among our ancestors. In other respects, we differ widely; in descent, in dwelling place, in age and occupation, and, to some extent, in our approach to what is known as the Negro problem.

"More especially we differ in political thought and allegiance; some of us are Republicans by inheritance and long custom; others are Democrats, by affiliation and party membership; still others are Socialists.

"But all of us are at this moment united in the solemn conviction that in the presidential campign of 1928, more than in previous campaigns since the Civil War, the American Negro was treated in a manner which is unfair and discouraging.

"We accuse the political leaders of this campaign of permitting without protest, public and repeated assertions on the platform, in the press, and by word of mouth, that color and race constituted in themselves an imputation of guilt and crime.

"It has been said, North and South, East and West, and by partisans of the leading candidates:

1. That Negro voters should not be appealed to, or their support welcomed by the advocates of just causes.

2. That colored persons should not hold public office, no matter what their character may be nor how well they do their work nor how competently they satisfy their constituents.

3. That the contact of white people and black people in government, in business, and in daily life, in common effort and cooperation, calls for explanation and apology.

4. That the honesty and integrity of party organization depend on the complete removal of all Negroes from voice and authority.

5. That the appointment of a public official is an act which concerns only white citizens, and that colored citizens should have neither voice nor consideration in such appointments.

"These assertions, which sound bald and almost unbelievable when stated without embellishment, have appeared as full-page advertisements in the public press, as the subject of leading editorials, and as displayed news stories; they have been repeated on the public platform in open debate and over the radio by both Republican and Democratic speakers, and they have been received by the nation and by the adherents of these and other parties in almost complete silence. A few persons have deprecated this gratuitous lugging in of the race problem, but for the most part, this astonishing campaign of public insult toward one-tenth of the nation has evoked no word of protest from the leading party candidates or from their official spokesmen; and from few religious ministers, Protestant or Catholic, or Jewish, and from almost no leading social reformer.

"Much has been said and rightly of the danger in a republic like ours of making sincere religious belief a matter of political controversy and of diverting public attention from great questions of public policy to petty matters of private life. But, Citizens of America, bad as religious hatred and evil personal gossip are, they have not the seeds of evil and disaster that lie in continued, unlimited and unrestrained appeal to race prejudice. The emphasis of racial contempt and hatred which was made in this campaign is an appeal to the lowest and most primitive of human motives, and as long as this appeal can successfully be made, there is for this land no real peace, no sincere religion, no national unity, no social progress, even in matters far removed from racial controversy.

"Do not misunderstand us: we are not asking equality where there is no equality. We are not demanding or even discussing purely social intermingling. We have not the slightest desire for inter-marriage between the races. We frankly recognize that the aftermath of slavery must involve long years of poverty, crime and contempt; for all of this that the past has brought and the present gives we have paid in good temper, quiet work and unfaltering faith. But we do solemnly affirm that in a civilized land and in a Christian culture and among increasingly intelligent people, somewhere and sometime, limits must be put to race disparagement and separation and to campaigns of racial calumny which seek to set twelve million human beings outside the pale of ordinary humanity.

"We believe that this nation and every part of it must come to admit that the gradual disappearance of inequalities between racial groups and the gradual softening of prejudice and hatred, is a sign of advance and not of retrogression and should be hailed as such by all decent folk and we think it monstrous to wage a political campaign in which the fading and softening of racial animosity and the increase of cooperation can be held up to the nation as a fault and not as a virtue. We do not believe that the majority of the white people whether North or South believe in the necessity or the truth of the assertions current in this campaign; but we are astonished to see the number of persons who are whipped to silence in the presence of such obvious and ancient political trickery.

"It is not so much the virulence of the attack in this case. It is its subtle and complacent character and the assenting silence in which it is received. Gravely and openly these assertions are made and few care, few protest, few answer. Has not the time come when as a nation, North and South, black and white, we can stop this tragic fooling and demand, not to be sure, everything that all Negroes might wish, nor all that some white people might prefer, but a certain balance of decency and logic in the discussion of race?

"We are asking, therefore, in this appeal, for a public repudiation of this campaign of racial hatred. Silence and whispering in this case are worse than in matters of personal character and religion. Will white America make no protest? Will the candidates continue to remain silent? Will the Church say nothing? Is there in truth any issue in this campaign, either religious tolerance, liquor, water-power, tariff or farm relief, that touches in weight the transcendent and fundamental question of the open, loyal and unchallenged recognition of the essential humanity of twelve million Americans who happen to be dark-skinned?"

The *Crisis* had an editorial at Christmas, 1928:
"The Happy Warrior tried to trade the 18th Amendment for the 14th and succeeded in smashing the Solid South and laying its rotten boroughs of wholesale disfranchisement and cheating open to the nation. Silence on fundamental human rights of black folk even when accompanied by promises of free blankets to Indians and 'boloney' for newsboys only availed to give Alfred Smith the most crushing defeat in American history.

"But liberal America has no cause for rejoicing. Smith was beaten by Southern and Western provincialism, religious bigotry, moral puritanism and snobbishness; and Big Business was elected to rule the United States by a mandate which limits Wall Street only by the blue sky. Least of all have black folk a chance even for a weary smile. The Lily Whites and the Ku Klux Klan are the political allies of

Herbert Hoover, and our only hope lies in the smashed and riven 'white primary' of the lower South and the faint but heartening promise of the Socialist Third Party."

Hoover, the newly chosen president, had for twenty years been a promoter of Big Business for Britain in Asia, Africa and Australia. In some years, he drew annual salaries aggregating $100,000. He had made heavy investments in Russian oil and lumber before the Revolution. As food commissioner, he helped the war against Russia. As secretary of commerce, he acted so as to nullify the laws against trusts. With the help of prejudice against Catholics, he gained the presidency.

Pierce watched all this with misgiving, as he saw the world from his Atlanta estate. Far from the city noises, it lay in a great meadow below the highway, like a picture of Versailles with its pale rose color, its towers and gardens. His study faced toward the back, over rolling meadow and low hills, with the Blue Ridge in the distance. Between was the glint of running waters. He held a baby's picture in his hand, a painted sketch of a robust child, cunningly crude and vague. He had never seen his grandchild; indeed he had never seen John, his son, since his desertion and marriage. He had half-promised himself to visit his son, but the invitations were never urgent and so he had simply seen to it that the son's bank account was kept replenished, and read the infrequent and impersonal letters.

His son and family did not, apparently, live extravagantly, but spent enough, mostly on a studio which seemed large and always growing larger. His son was now over 40, and this baby grandson must be all of 17. He would like to see what manner of man he had become. Would John IV ever like to return to the firms? He doubted it, with such parents; but he wondered why he had received no later pictures.

But evidently things were not going well in the financial world. Money was being loaned in New York at 15 percent and 20 percent interest. Pierce saw trouble ahead. He was going to see what could be done to prevent financial disaster in Germany, and see the young grandson. He had warned Baldwin, and Baldwin himself, riding on the crest of the financial wave and without fear, nevertheless was going to consult with the bankers as they met in Atlanta.

Baldwin had not taken his warning lightly. The Old Man was getting old and cautious. This was the new day of youthful daring.

He turned almost gaily to the rapidly growing job of guiding the business of Atlanta, and so of the nation and the world. Yet, that Fall he could not help but notice certain signs of apprehension among those attending the meeting of the American Bankers Association, which took place in Atlanta. There was much whispering together. Baldwin, despite his confidence, began to feel a trickle of fear, and he seemed to see it in person when looking across the meeting room, he saw a black man sitting as delegate. It was John Mitchell, of Virginia. It occurred to Baldwin that always the South had a black shadow at every triumphal feast.

John Mitchell was at the time the guest of Heman Perry, the colored insurance promoter, and he and his enterprises were beginning to feel the widening wave of apprehension. As early as 1925, the state warned Perry that despite his prosperity, his reserve funds were impaired. He realized that he must look for more capital, and this capital was offered him through John Sheldon, working with the Tennessee Insurance Company. This money Sheldon was now demanding. Perry was dangerously in debt, and was fighting for time.

He was talking to his collectors in 1928. They said, "Times are getting bad, boss."

"But," argued Perry, "the country is prosperous, wildly prosperous."

"Sure is—too prosperous. Something's going to break. Colored workers are being laid off, white workers are pushing them to the wall, subscribers to small insurance concerns like Herndon's Atlanta Life are falling off in droves. Some of our best prospects have defaulted. There, for instance, is Jackson, a good man but he's failed on his mortgage payments. Must we foreclose?"

"Yes," snapped Perry, tight-lipped.

And so Jackson, who had gone home a month ago maimed by an accident at the plant, an accident which might have been deliberate, lay slowly dying until there was neither food nor fuel, until the mortgage was foreclosed, and until at last, when Jackson died, his furniture sat on the sidewalk in the snow and sleet. The children cowered in dumb horror, and the woman was gray and silent.

Over beyond the hill, where the white small merchants and better class of workers lived, there was dismay. They had organized and marched downtown and warned the merchants not to hire Negroes. Whites must be given work and must be given better pay. But all this had not relieved the family of Mary Hines.

She was a beautiful white girl, just down from the hills, almost illiterate but determined. She passed through the colored Westend settlement, with its flaunting prosperity and its new school. She spit as she passed. She hated "niggers." Her people never had a home to lose. She had more to lose and she was going down to Peachtree Street to sell all she had. She knew well who would buy. He had asked her frankly yesterday. Now she wept as she held her best and only dress up out of the slush. Two little black boys rushed by, yelling and splashing mud.

Meantime Perry, finding that he was losing his grip on Standard Life, gave up his fine home in Atlanta and went to St. Louis. There, he tried to revive his fortunes in a new insurance company, based on the company formed by the postmistress of Mississippi whom Theodore Roosevelt had appointed, and against whom Vardaman crusaded. The scheme did not work and finally Perry committed suicide in St. Louis. His dreams lived after him. The Booker Washington High School still stands, although while built for a thousand pupils, it has four thousand. His bank was still open and the construction company still took contracts.

So the world staggered on to its doom. So Perry lost control of Standard Life. Tennessee refused to pay Sheldon. John Sheldon dared not face Baldwin, and on a morning in May, 1929, shot himself through the temple.

Pierce went abroad. The situation both in England and Germany was uncertain and needed his attention. He planned to go early in the year and see the Spring under the chestnuts of Paris; then perhaps he'd drop down to Cagnes on his way to the high Alps, at Berne, and so to Berlin. He left for Paris in March; sent a cable to Cagnes in April, receiving a brief reply.

The town he found was not gay or lively as he had always pictured the Riviera. It was a bit drab and old-fashioned, but homely and quiet along the sad blue Mediterranean. The studio which everyone quickly and curiously pointed out loomed dark, vast and forbidding in the background of the town. In a wide, deep doorway enshrined with flower, shrub and vine, stood a hag. No other description fitted her. She was old and her white hair straggled down over her pale, bony face and over her toothless jaws like the locks of a witch. She was thin to emaciation and disheveled. "What a housekeeper!" Pierce thought with extreme distaste.

But the woman disabused him. "Welcome, Father," she said in well-modulated tones, smiling grimly. It was Henrietta Sheldon who had married his son. He stared in consternation as she stood aside slowly, and there hobbled toward him from the black interior, in a paint-stained smock, with palette and brushes, a horribly grotesque figure. He knew it was his son. Yet, his every fibre recoiled at this caricature of the young man who left him in Atlanta, in 1908.

"Welcome, Old Man, thrice welcome! Surprised, eh? Knew you would be. That's why I never let Henrietta send you a picture. Wanted you to realize what your profitable war did to a few million youngsters like me. You see, I was 30 when I went into the airforce. One couldn't just paint while men died, and why wait for America when France was in such dire need? Then, one day, being none too skillful, soaring over the Rhine at Strassbourg wth an angry Boche on my tail, I fell!

" *'From morn to noon he fell, from noon to dewy eve,*
A summer's day;
And with the setting sun, dropped from the Zenith
Like a falling star.'

"But smashed! Oh, so smashed and torn. A twisted and bloody caricature of what was once a comely young man. There was left 'no form nor comeliness' that men nor women should desire me. Yet Henrietta clung; why, I can't see. The money perhaps; perhaps something she still pretends is Love. She stuck. We came here and built this shack because of my great Plan. I forced myself, bent my torn arms and twisted hands back to painting; and we worshipped the baby—the ungrateful brat that he proved—Ah! Here he comes to feed as usual."

Pierce saw a thin, leering youth swaggering up the path with a cigarette hanging down the left edge of his thin, sulky lips. He greeted no one but pushed by to an inner recess.

"He writes," growled the grotesque father. "He was an anarchist; then a Bolshevik, now a Fascist. Writes the damnest drivel and calls it Literature. Forget him! But now, listen to me. My life work grows to its mighty end. You are on time. I was just about to tamp your mug on my climacteric drawing. Here are three great rooms. The first is the story of the Witches' Cauldron, as I saw it at Versailles in 1919. I saw it with my own eyes as I shivered and writhed in my pain and black despair. I didn't then realize what a revelation was being vouchsafed me. Look, see!"

They entered a cavern of a room, twenty-five feet high and forty feet wide, swathed in black curtains and covered, wall and ceiling, with paint of every fantastic color and every twist of curve and line.

"The idea came to me when I saw the lovely gardens where the Roi Soliel once strutted on his high red heels. I pictured it raised and tilted over the heads of the 'Peacemakers,' with the fires of Hell flaming up beneath it. Over it, the Three World Witches hovered while travailing in illegitimate childbirth; and all were three-headed, as such impious crones must be, with white, flying hair, slavering jaws and toothless gums.

"Now, here, see here, high up on the right, the Bastard Bitch called Britain, on whom no sun ever dared set. See her triple heads: Lloyd George, Balfour and South African Smuts. And yonder, high on the left, that Latin abortion, France, Italy and Spain, using Beauty, Poetry and Power to nurse the cancer which seeks to transform with blood the flesh of Jesus into the stones of Rome. Look, leering from its gross body, Clemenceau, the Tiger of France; Sonnino, of Italy, thief of Ethiopia, and Venezelos, the Greek, bringing gifts. And now, down here below, filling the whole space across, here sits World Rule by God's Grace: Willy and Nicky, the Great White Czar and the Emperor by the Grace of God; and good old Franz, the Holy Roman. These are the 'Peacemakers.' They begin their incantations: 'Double, double, toil and trouble!' They wave their wands. They prance. They all know what is hidden down there in that boiling hell. There is the poisonous long black snake which is Africa. There is the red writhing dragon which is Asia. There are the fierce alligators, the newts, the frogs and bugs of the island world, all thrust in there years and decades ago.

"They stir the mass and grin and sing as it steams. And then the incredible happens. The whole boiling mass bursts up into their faces, a green and yellow mass of pus and filth comes coughing up. Into the putrid mess drop bloody tears. A clot is formed. A plot of clots, whence all the vermin world starts to crawl free. But before they start come Three Strangers—Wilson the Unready; Gandhi the new Christ, and Trotsky of the Revolution.

"Of one accord, all the witches fly eastward on broomstick,

tank and plane, bearing all murderers, spies and liars. 'O say, can you see, by the dawn's early light, stinking stars and bloody stripes still waving over the Land of the Rich and the Home of the Slave. The witches cry: 'Wipe out forever the black blasphemers of the God of Gold!'

"And then, would you believe it, over all this steaming, sputtering filthy cauldron of 'Peace,' Americans, led by you and your fellows, dear father, stoop to skim off the gold, the steaming putrid, coward Gold, green and slimy. Our own United States—while Wilson battles with Cabot Lodge—defecates gold mixed with poison and fire. And the whole brew spreads in slimy, stinking mess over the world, as the world falls.

"You see what I mean, Dad, don't you? You see the allegory? You helped calculate it in Wall Street and were paid ten million dollars a day for flesh and blood to make yourselves rich.

"For that, come to the second room. What? You want to leave? You're tired? Who do you think you are? No, no, you have got to see this second room. And then, there is the third and last room, too, which is to be my masterpiece!

"Here in the second and third rooms are painted the grim disaster of Europe as it falls before Asia and Africa. I am going to make the paint partly in blood, blood fortified by a secret formula, which will preserve it and intensify its lovely browns and reds. There will be plenty of blood. You see, that brat of mine is tubercular, and every once in a while up from his lungs whirl quarts of crimson gore. There will be quite enough before he dies. This describes the World War of the Color Line.

"This second room is Asia—Asia in Europe and Asia in Asia—yes, and the start of Asia in Africa, for Asia is the Mother of All. I paint Russia as part of Asia, which of course it is. The muzhik, dumb and ignorant; the coolies, dull, driven cattle; the black heathen, poverty stricken and sick; but all alike plowing up the dirt, reaping the grain, digging the metal, draining the trees, dying in filth and pain that the lords of Europe and America may be rich and highly civilized and called of God. Beautiful, logical, complete and right, until the worms, the vermin, the crawling manure pauses, stops, shrieks, fights, and overwhelms the world.

"Great God, how the white world yells; how it prays, how it fights, how it brings down the lightning from its own private heaven, rallies the thunder from its white god, bursts the heart of nature's inner self! In vain. Still they come, still the yellow vomit spews over the world. The Nordic leaps to beat it and dies. Chiang Kai-shek, puppet, liar, murderer and thief, crashes to Hell. China, China of the Thousand Years, India the Unforgettable, they all step forward, they loom and march, they listen to a Songs of Songs. Where are they going, what do they see?

"Listen, dad, look! They see Africa. They hear that song of Paul Robeson:

'Go down, Moses, way down in Egypt Land.'

"This next, then, is the room Africa, painted in black, dark, shining, lucid black, and here in front Robeson himself, shackled by the stars and stripes—stars in his eyes and stripes on his great broad back.

"And then, beyond that, you must of course see the last room. It is only sketched, but it will be my masterpiece. Here at the entrance, all falls apart, the world drops to Hell; here the false frightful faces of the witches change to the horrid lineaments of Universal Hate. You will view the new aspect of the Bastard Bitch, you will see the Latin Abortion again, and the great American Thief, as they all shriek and fight and kill. As Britain again fights Russia, as Germany again fights France, as Italy again fights Africa, as Spain fights itself, as America fights everybody and everybody fights America, while behind rises Black Eternity on a Christian Hell.

"Is that not a magnificent plan? What a climax! Doesn't it beat the devil to see us all going, dropping, plunging down to that blazing Hell which is—What? So you will go? All right, go! But you ought first to have read a few volumes of your grandson's masterpieces. They are awful. They stink!"

John Pierce staggers toward the door, hearing behind him a thin and mocking voice, "There is John the Fourth, by the grace of Gold; King of all stock markets and master of men. What he writes sometime you must read." Thus, his son was still following John Pierce, calling, limping and shouting.

The weary, tottering old man, seeking to escape the blasphemy of his son's voice, turned into a room at the side. There, the pale, thin grandson with the drooping cigarette was languidly dictating to his mother. She sat huddled over the typewriter, painfully writing as the sweat poured down over her pallid face and dimmed her protruding eyes. His voice lolled on monotonously. He said,

"If we, who are as men may well say, in these accursed days of the dispossessed and disinherited and more, much more than that;

the fetid offal certainly of a universe doomed and rightly cursed since creation to die, and fit only for the cruelest of deaths; have the slightest and most remote notion of escape, expiation or salvation in this world or any next; then Hell greet us and kiss us and our spawn to the tenth generation; come back as we may try to dream of unthought-of and almost unseen yet not entirely unsensed phantoms, standing now back in paralysis or paralyzing effort and drear talk or gesture or poise, trying to emit, discharge and loose such drivel as we may, if in truth we may, crazy with regurgitation and repetition of crime and blood and hurt, I say, I repeat. I thunder and scream, that there is not, nor was nor will be, nearly nothing at least as nothing now seems, and should be even if it be not so called, that can be seen and heard, smelled or touched, assumed or dreamed; but that all creation, blackened as it is or darkened or enshrouded and must be, with ignorance and senseless knowing as everything has been or will be or if not, then—"

He paused, whirled about and sat up straight. His eyes burned. He shrieked as his mother stopped typing. He yelled: "Hey, where are you? What are you doing, you blundering old idiot? Why do you dare stop, you imbecile? How can you pause, woman, and lift your claws between me and prophecy?"

The mother cringed and whined. She whispered, "But he must eat, son. Your grandfather is our guest and must eat. It is late. He will surely be hungry. Come, help me, what is there in the larder? Is there anything? If not we must market—yes!"

The elder Pierce stood distraught. He asked himself if he was really alive. Had he fallen in some insane asylum? He staggered and then ran out of the door and down the path. Dimly he sensed the smell of flowers and heard the sad moaning of the sea. He heard, or thought he heard, the scream of his misshapen son further and further behind. He tore through the streets as men stared, women laughed and dogs barked. He hid in an alley and slept in a warehouse.

Next day, paying a fabulous bribe to a hesitating innkeeper, he cleaned and arranged his clothes, retrieved his bag at the station, shaved, and caught the bus to Nice. He saw the magnificent curve of that bay, but refused to glance at the slums behind. He began to regain his normal self as his plane soared over Turin, the Bernese Oberland, the Rhone and Rhine. Then across Thuringia and Saxony, he came to Berlin, and at last felt that the nightmare of that extraordinary visit was over. He thought of stopping the allowance to his son, but dismissed that idea. But certainly, he would never visit that madhouse again.

After a week of rest, he still felt jittery but was able to look about him. He saw what might be happening in the world—the start of the fall of the capitalistic system, the attempt of the United States to boost the economy of Germany at a cost of $200,-000,000 a year. The fifteen billions of dollars, which the United States was spreading over the world to have a system of making, buying and selling for private profit, seemed coming to an end.

John Pierce realized that Germany had lost an immense sum by war and had destroyed the wealth of others. To restore her own losses and repay the losses, she needed first to recover her power of creating wealth. If this capital were loaned her, the German industrial machine might recover. He saw German intellectual culture, that fine flower of the 19th century, falling in ruins about the ears of a distressed and punished nation. He glimpsed the lithographs of Kathe Kollwitz. He saw the cynical youth, the impoverished intellectuals, the corruption, the whores filling the streets and alleys, and he heard the first hoarse scream of Hitler.

He talked over the business status of Germany in sumptuous offices with keen-eyed men. He realized how, on the back of bankruptcy and distress, German Big Industry had rebuilt its plants and modernized them and was ready to enter the world of commerce with new and better goods. Moreover, that world they proposed to extend and dominate. They no longer were demanding English and French colonies in Africa and Asia. They had vaster ambitions. To explain these, they called in an old and stately man of 78. He was still vigorous and charming. He was medalled and be-ribboned, with monocle and gold-headed cane and faultless clothes. Sir Basil Zarahof, the richest man in the world, explained on a great map: here was the heartland of the world, modern Russia, reaching to China and India, dominating the Middle East. This vast area of industrial development and commerce, of cheap labor and endless consumption, had been lost to the world temporarily by the Russian Revolution. The time had now come to regain it.

"But," objected Pierce, "I thought you had been putting down the Bolsheviks for ten years and had failed."

Zaharof waved his hand. "Bungling with fools and traitors.

There was, first, Wilson's silly project of a meeting at Prinkipo. Then the British messed up things in Archangel and got British, French and Americans quarreling and beginning to mutiny. Then followed blunder after blunder. The Germans marched against the Finns and Hoover furnished food. Yudenitch prepared to march on Petrograd, and ran away with his pockets full of money. Deniken, bearded and mustached, began organizing in the south, backed by the fleets of England and France and helped by the savage Wrangel. They reached Tsaritsyn in June, 1919, but soon were running away in panic and disorder. Kolchak started in from the east to capture Moscow. Instead, he was captured with 2,000 bags of gold, and shot.

"The Poles, with 50 million dollars from the United States, drove into the Ukraine and were hurled back. A Baltic aristocrat, with blonde hair and red mustache stole, whored and murdered in Siberia. He was captured in his silk Mongolian robe. 'I refuse to admit working class authority!' he screamed as he was shot.

"And then," continued Sir Basil, "there were Churchill's spies: Sidney Reilly, Boris Savinkov, and others—all fools. There was the impractical Hoffman plan. But finally, we came to our senses and got together. Deterding joined us and we are glad to welcome Sir Henry here today. The Torgprom was organized. An army of a million men is to be gathered at a cost of 500 million dollars. The French General Staff will furnish leaders, and the French airforce is to be used. Germany is to supply technicians and the British will lend their navy. Russia is to be attacked on all sides and Professor Ramzin will furnish military assistance from within the Soviet Union. The force is to march late this summer or at the latest, the summer of 1930. We subdue Russia and Siberia. Then we take the Balkans into tutelage; we bring order and oil in the Middle East. We overwhelm China, India, Africa. There begins the greatest industrial and commercial era the world ever knew. . . ."

Pierce was obstinate. He had the American dislike of all this "side."

"But," he growled, "this new Russia has already repulsed four-teen nations at a cost of millions. Who did this? If the present Russia has done this once, why not again? And what about this Trotsky? Why are you backing a world communist against a national communist like Stalin? I don't understand—What?"

A servant handed him a cablegram. He fumbled for his glasses and glanced at it. He read it again and stared at the company blindly. They stared back, and rising, huddled about him. He mumbled, "Industry in the United States has crashed! Six million shares have been sold in Wall Street at a loss of fifteen billion dollars. Samuel Haynes, my partner, has shot himself."

In New York, Haynes staggered into the hospital room on the arms of attendants. She was bright and shining but he saw her the moment he entered, sitting in the corner, black and forbidding. Pain gripped him in the breast as he sank on the bed. He lay long days in coma, and then wakened suddenly. She was there, as he knew she would be. Thin, and in rags, dark and dirty and vicious. Poverty—that was her name. She talked swift and low so that not even the nurse could hear.

"Everything smashing, everything going to Hell—good! But I've saved some fine bargains—see this batch of prostitutes? Some pretty, some old and nasty with disease. Here's what they earned last year. I can trade it for a mink coat to fit your wife. Or, here's what a thousand Georgia 'niggers' earned last year from their cotton. It'll pay for a fine Cadillac. Now look sharp, here's something big—a thousand Kansas farms. They'll buy a nice sea-going yacht, with crew and a cellar of fine liquors."

The nurse soothed him and talked to the physician. "He's in delirium," she whispered, "Shall I administer a sedative?"

Haynes tried to say, "That black phantom there—take it away." He went down to the dark waters of oblivion and still saw that sinister figure as he dropped into deeper oblivion and forever.

Pierce caught the *Bremen,* one of the new German luxury liners, built with money borrowed from the United States. He felt sick and discouraged. For himself, he had been conservative; he still had enough for living, untouched by disaster. But many of his friends were ruined and his own zest for life was gone. He drew up a new will. He left his crazy son a small annuity; he wired to see that Baldwin, his Atlanta protege, had enough to weather the storm if it did not last too long. He left a few personal gifts and the residue to charity. He had the will witnessed and sealed. Then, late at night he dropped off the lonely after-deck of the swift steamer.

There came to the United States a day of disillusion such as it had never before seen. Neither at Valley Forge nor at Bull Run nor in the Wilderness, did the nation so lose faith in itself. The foundations of a solid universe tottered. The meaning of Life changed. The greatest thing in American life—Gold—disappeared. Its dwelling places, the noble, dignified and ornate banks, closed their doors. There were no savings; those who had skimped and denied themselves, now wept. There was no work. The nation stared Poverty straight in the eyes and saw Hunger, Disease and Suicide. Millions on increasing millions wandered the streets, idle, begging or too ashamed to beg. Where now was the richest land on earth? Where now were the canniest, sharpest, most successful and resourceful people of the earth?

What was the cause? The cause was not Communism. It was not the system of money or the after-effects of the world war. It was simply something wrong in the system of production. Our two-hundred leading non-financial corporations had assets equal to the combined wealth of the whole United Kingdom. How was our wealth distributed? Eleven million families got less than enough to support them. One half million families got $10,000 and more a year. Twelve million families received 13% of the national income. Thirty-six thousand families reecived the same percentage.

The man in the White House, Herbert Hoover, who had got his wealth in China and Russia kept yelling: "Prosperity is just around the corner!" As President, he drove the veterans out ot Washington and signed the highest tariff law in history against the advice of the economists. And when the crisis broke, he refused the demands of Congress for aid to the unemployed, but hastened to help the banks.

Thus, when capitalism collapsed throughout Europe, our business enterprise was largely under control of trusts, our international trade stopped by tariffs, the whole of our banking system near bankruptcy. The Gold Standard began to totter and ten million American workers were unemployed and facing starvation. Hoover remained stubborn. This was but a temporary upset. Our economy was fundamentally sound. Capital, once owned by individual rich men had been transferred into trusts and was near disaster under Populist attack. Now, under corporations, it was on the road to recovery if not attacked by Socialism. Despite this argument, the losses of sixteen billion dollars quickly grew to fifty billion.

And then, in 1932, came thirteen years of power to a young aristocrat who had entered politics after his fine body was hopelessly crippled. He knew what Courage was and he talked to the nation, saying, "There is nothing to fear but Fear itself!"

CHAPTER XVII

ORGANIZED LABOR

The great Steel Strike came in 1919. Joe Scroggs heard about it when he returned to Atlanta from consultation with labor leaders in Washington. He was in the smoking car, which meant that he and other white men occupied the back half of a coach next to the engine. The front half was the "Jim Crow" car, for all Negro passengers. In the "Jim Crow" end, Joe heard a man talking. He was black, thick-set and strongly muscled. He was happy because he was returning from Pittsburgh for Christmas with money in his pocket.

Even as they all got out of the train at Atlanta, the two groups of white and black had to mingle, more or less, as they walked upstairs and along the corridor to the place where the paths to the white and black waiting rooms separated. The black man, in a loud plaid suit and a new overcoat, talked vociferously and swaggeringly.

"Yes, sah!" he said, "I'se a steel-makin' man. I works in the bigges' damn plant in old Pittsburgh. Did you evah see steel made? Man, it's a wonder! In goes the iron scrap. Huh! Up roahs de fire. Hah! Big spoon swings and opens. Melted iron, red hot, po's into de big pot. Pot blows and blows. Steel busts out lookin' like de sun at noon, only ten times hottah. Hotter'n hell. Ovah goes the kettle. Steel swishes and hisses; stars fall. It's done. We's made it. We falls out, wringing sweat, naked and half dead. We'se finished and steel is done bown!

"Strike? Yep. Dey struck. Me? No, not me. I didn't belong to no union. Yes, ah tried to get in fust—tried hahd, kep on trying 'dough I didn't know why. Jes though ah must. De organizah of dat AFL says 'No "niggers" 'lowed.' I asks 'why?' 'Lazy, cain't work. Don't know nothin'. Won't strike. I say, 'Try me.' He say 'Git out!'

"Me, ah damn't near stahve. Couldn't get nothin' to do. Sent ev'y cent ah had to the ole woman an' kids down heah in Georgia. Money gone. White boss man see me and say, 'Stick around, boy.'

Ah sticks. Had to. No place to go. I'se cold and hongry. Lived in a dump. Yanks, Paddys, Dagoes, Hunkies, all works. No 'niggers.' Whites go on strike—300,000. Pickets tell me 'Don't scab.' And ah says, 'How'll ah eat?' White boss man keep tellin' me—quiet like—'Stick around.' Then bimeby he say, 'Want work?' I say, 'You bet, by God, yes!' Strikers yell, women scream, 'Wanna starve us?' I say, 'Ah done been starved mahself 'an froze, too.' Strike pickets threaten: 'Keep out.'

"Jus' then de goons move in. De goons and police. It was turrible bad. I close my eyes. But I mus' eat. Ah gits work. Boss man ask: 'Know any more black folk wants work?' 'Sure,' ah says, 'dey all do!' I writes my brothah down here, writes my cousins in Alabam. Dey write deirs. 'Niggers' pour in; 30,000 come. Strike is broke. All de whites crawl back.

"Yes, suh! I'se a steel-makin' man. I gits money enough for ole woman an' kids to live on. I buy us clo'se. I gits more than I evah got down south. 'Cou'se I don't git as much as de white man used to git in the north. We'll all git more when we all git together.

"Gwine to join de union? Don't know. I he'ps dem as he'ps me. Ef a man cain't know me when ah'm down, he can go to hell when ah gits on mah feet. Gwine to join? Ah dunno. Dey ain't no hurry!"

This Negro's talk lighted in Scroggs' mind the battle he saw raging in the South. It was not merely along the color line, although it looked like that and was that in part. But it was more than that. It was a fight of employer against laborer, and the poor against the poor, and of the rich against the rich. In the midst of that battle was Joe Scroggs.

Scroggs was related to that Sam Scroggs whom we met in Charleston, and to the Abe Scroggs who was in Jerusalem at the time Manuel Mansart was teaching there. Joe was born in 1880, in Atlanta, where his family worked in the cotton mills. Manuel Mansart as a boy had dropped a brick on his head. But this incident both had forgotten. Joe was thus born in the midst of the poor white workers in the city and came to represent them in many ways.

The Scroggs family all presented the same type—tall, thin bodies, ugly faces, kindly but rather evasive eyes, wiry, drab and untended hair, smooth-shaven, when shaven at all. They gave an impression of lack of cleanliness and of slovenly habits. Yet, within they showed a hard core, a steadfastness and a determination of effort combined with uncertainty as to the objects of those efforts. Usually, they developed an exaggerated inferiority complex and were desperately afraid of losing their heritage as "white folk," of sinking to the level of Negroes. They represented, on the whole, disinherited people, dispossessed of land and property, but frantically clinging to their "rights."

Over Scroggs and his friends the city of Atlanta loomed like the wilful, jealous bird of prey, with mighty shadows of wings. Scroggs loved the city and hated it and feared it. He knew that the full growth and the vast stretch of the wings of Atlanta was coming with these first decades of the 20th century. There was something immeasurable and titanic about this festering, industrial ganglion which they shadowed; and yet, with all its minute, penetrating, devastating intelligence, it was in essence a vast Unknowable, an immense Ignorance which not even God could comprehend. Its slimy pus exuded both faith and syphilis, palaces and brothels, murderers and prostitutes, births and suicides.

There hung a gloomy veil above these sun-drenched hills that, from time to time, could drop down and blind the people. Here, one saw the unleashed anarchy of energy, and yet, of the real inner End of all this, nobody knew anything. It was singular how suspicious this made Atlantans. They believed in signs and incantations, they crossed palms with gold, they saw ghosts, they used love philtres, they told fortunes, they saw witches, they were possessed of devils.

Below all this curious, inexplicable Thing called Atlanta lay in plain sight a simple dichotomy, two worlds of black and white— the white ruler, employer, owner; the black servant, inferior, pauper. But now, in this clear and understandable division the edges, in the new century, were becoming blurred. There were now Negroes who owned homes and automobiles; there were whites who were poor. Of these, Scroggs was one. How did that come and whither would it lead? Of course, few whites became servants and nearly all whites, even in Joe's own family, managed in some way to have a black woman drudge in the kitchen, even if at times she was kept there almost by threat.

But where did Joe's folk really belong? If they were, as they fiercely declared, part of the white half of the world, they must have more money, houses and property. This was their right. When this did not happen, it must be because Negroes were taking what belonged of right to them. As Joe grew older, this belief was shaken. Sometimes, it almost appeared as if instead of two classes of white and black in the world there were three: the white rich, the white poor, and the Negroes. Then it even seemed there might be a fourth class of high Negroes—but this thought he repudiated out of hand. Such a class didn't exist, or if it did, it must be wiped out by force.

This confused thinking came to him first when he was about fifteen in the case of the Black Fireman. A white fireman and his family lived next to Joe. Scroggs did not like the dirty job, but the wife, in defense, explained that the job of fireman was no longer what it used to be when it meant shovelling coal and waiting on the engineer. Now, with mechanical stoking, it had become a white man's job, a stepping stone to the position of engineer. It should, however, be better paid and would be if they didn't keep cheap and subservient "niggers" still in the job.

"Don't you see what the railroads are doing? They hire 'niggers' as firemen. They pay them less than white firemen. The 'niggers' are not mechanics, they are servants of the white engineers. And yet, if they are admitted to the union, they will have the chance of seniority eventually to become engineers, and our wages will be pulled down. We'll have to live beside them, we'll have to have them in our homes, they'll be marrying our sons and daughters."

The Georgia Railroad had began to hire Negroes as firemen in 1905, but there had been a strike against them, with recriminations, negotiations and violence. The black union had fought back. They were willing to join the white union but the white firemen refused. The white leader said:

"I hope and pray that I may never live to see the grand old Brotherhood of Locomotive Firemen so disgraced as to take into its protecting folds this class of God's creation."

The white firemen, despite the fact that they were paid more than Negro firemen, blamed Negroes for their low wages, and in 1909 the Georgia railroad removed white assistants who were getting $1.75 a day and filled their places with Negroes at $1.25 a day; at the same time they gave Negroes equal seniority rights. The result was another strike, and the leader in Atlanta could hark back to the Atlanta riot.

"We should have white supremacy!" he yelled, and the city of Atlanta and the towns through which the firemen ran came to his aid. The Georgia railroad service was crippled. Witnesses were called who declared Negroes too ignorant to make good firemen; but the railroad defended their efficiency and admitted that Negroes were employed because they were cheaper.

"If we can get what we want cheap, is it a crime to take it?"

Finally, the arbitration board decided that Negroes must be paid the same rate of wages as white men, and the conclusion was that Negroes would thus lose their jobs. Still, some Negro firemen remained. An agreement was finally signed with all the Southern railroads that the percentage of Negro firemen would not in the future be larger than it was on January 1, 1910. Thus, the future entrance of colored firemen into employment was blocked. Even then, whites furiously resented the retention of any Negro firemen, and began to attack them from ambush whenever and wherever they could be found.

Scroggs sat down and tried to think it out. He heard the challenge of Joe Hill as it swung from the west over the mountains:

"Work and pray, live on hay,
You'll have pie in the sky when you die."

He heard, too, the shots that killed that martyr despite the President, despite Sweden, despite the Workers of the World. Thousands marched behind his coffin.

"I dreamed I saw Joe Hill last night,
Alive as you and me. ..
Says I, 'But Joe, you're ten years dead.'
'I never died,' says he."

Scroggs was in a poor cottage on the outskirts of Atlanta. He had been asked to come, and scrawny children had said that mother would return soon from market. He saw her coming along the street, slattern, dead tired. She had asked for his help, his protection and advice. Her husband was a locomotive firemen, and her father had been one. She sat down beside him, sighing, and told him what he knew.

"My husband has just killed a 'nigger' and he's been arrested. He had to do it, don't you see, he had to. You know these Negro firemen have got to be driven back and beaten back and killed. We've simply got to drive all of them out of railroad jobs, and we're going to do it. My husband was chosen by lot to do this job and did it, and now he's in danger. You've got to get him out. You've got to."

Joe promised he would. Yes, he had to. The blacks had to be kept back, but how far could this thing go? It might be done in employments where Negroes were comparatively few. But how about his own textile union? One of these days, Negroes were going to get into the factories. He saw it. You couldn't kill them all, there were too many of them; and besides, the blacks were human beings. You just had to admit that. There must be some place for them. There must be some way of regulating this relation between white and black workers so both would help each other and not kill each other.

Joe Scroggs had just come from a meeting of the executive committee of the American Federation of Labor, in Washington. He went over again, in memory, some of the discussions which took place in session and at lunch, in their hotel rooms. He tried to explain to them as well as to himself just what was taking place in the South.

"The mass of Negroes still work for whites. Most employers are whites and employ whites and blacks. The whites get the better paid jobs. The color line stands, in separate churches, separate schools, with poorer schools for Negroes, separate graveyards for the dead. But some blacks are beginning to employ other Negroes, and thus, as employers, they are above the mass of white laborers. Then, there are Negro teachers and professional men. As a result, larger numbers of Negroes, instead of living in the backyards of white people and the side alleys, are beginning to live in places that are not slums. No white man enters such a home except as police agent or grocer, and less and less seldom. So, increasing numbers of Negroes are becoming better in income and homes than large numbers of whites."

A Northern labor leader shook his head. "Yes, yes, of course. Here, then, in America a laboring group of at least 12 percent of the whole labor group is beginning to divide itself into classes. A small group is in alliance with white capital, and a great mass, mostly unskilled, is ready, indeed compelled, to compete with white labor by underbidding union standards, so long as unions exclude them. White labor, by excluding Negroes from their unions, have made the situation worse, especially where the Negro workers have been disfranchised."

A Westerner intervened: "This is leading damn near to foolishness. Either the Negro is here or he ain't. If he is here and aims to stay, you can't starve him out without starving yourselves at the same time. It seems to me that what's needed in the South is teaching of the laborers. They've learned the old 'Rags to Riches' crap. They think as we used to, that all workers are going to become rich, or at least most of them, including us.

"Listen, boys, we're kidding ourselves. The Southern white worker thinks he must in time become rich, with Negroes working for him and also, perhaps, a few highly paid whites. No Southerner sees his children as wage earners, and therefore sees no need of making the whole wage earning situation bearable. He shrinks from this because this must include Negroes. Therefore he thinks he is going to get rid of Negro competition by disfranchising him, or in other words by cutting off his nose to spite his face. It didn't work. That's the reason the Southern workers followed Watson and Hoke Smith like dogs, and cut their vote in two. Did it work? Tell us, Scroggs, did it work?"

Scroggs was thoughtful. "No, it didn't. It sure didn't. We formed a State Federation of Labor in 1899, but excluded Negro unions. We fought Negro skilled workers and Negro capitalists. In 1910, we voted against Negro disfranchisement, but the very next year reversed the vote and favored it. At that time, the leasing of convicts to private capital was legal and profitable; the age of consent for girls was ten years; and graft ruled the state.

"In 1902 came the Georgia Industrial Association of Millowners, a powerful body. Already, milliowners had been working hand in hand. They had defeated the first law against child labor. It was forty years before child labor was even partially abolished, and in 1900, one-fourth of the eighteen thousand white mill workers in Georgia were under seventeen. The new organization brought pressure on the legislature; it spent money on welfare work; it bgan to move the mills out from the cities toward country towns where the mills owned the homes and school houses and churches and bought and paid for the teachers and preachers; and they had the votes in their own hands.

"There were a few Negro unions, but they were not recognized by the white unions. Nor did they receive any encouragement or advice from black leaders, teachers, nor business men. Booker

Washington himself was an outspoken enemy of union labor and a friend of white capital. Labor cnditions in the South, in Georgia and Atlanta, were not good. The very fact that they had an abundance of labor made for trouble. There was white labor and black labor, and they had to be carefully balanced against each other. The Negroes were stirring and the stirring of the Negroes meant jealousy among the poor whites.

"Joe Brown, representing the railroads and elected governor in 1906, pointed out that in trying to organize labor, white union men were also seeking to raise the wages and shorten the hours of Negro servants and farm laborers. Class lines thus were deftly twisted into racial lines. What poor white family was so poor that they did not want a Negro servant? What white farmer could get on without severely exploiting Negro laborers?

"White and colored labor in Atlanta just didn't get on. White teachers organized and joined the Georgia Federation of Labor, but would not admit the colored teachers. White barbers tried to stop colored barbers from serving whites, and especially white women. They forced the Legislature to establish a state board of control and a system of licenses; but the executive wouldn't carry out the law, because the rich whites preferred Negro barbers.

"The prosperity of Negro capital, even with its losses, fanned the flame of race hatred between Negroes and poor whites. The factory workers were aroused. They were having hard hours and low wages. They feared Negro competition. Twice at the great Fulton Mills, textile operatives struck against the attempt to introduce Negro workers, and won. But that did not better the condition of white workers.

"In 1914, the union determined to take a step in advance and strike for their own betterment in wages and conditions of work. I argued that such a state appeal would get the sympathy of the white public. We brought our grievance to the notice of newspapers and churches. The powerful white State Baptist Convention took a stand against the trade union movement. Workers were discharged when they joined unions. They had to leave a week's wages with the mills, which they lost if they left without a week's notice. They had to make good damages to the machinery, and the mill would not pay for lost time.

"There was much child labor, and despite a long fight, no bill against it could be forced through the legislature. The manufacturers said:

" 'The incidents where a child learns to read and write after it obtains the age of fourteen years are exceedingly rare.'

"There was no need then, they argued, to keep such children in school.

"We struck. A great mass meeting was held in Atlanta. The Baptists reversed themselves and began to ask people to give to the sufferers from the strike. In the *Constitution* appeared 137 columns of advertisement with 'appeal to Christ' and saying 'God asks results.' But the strike failed. It petered out and failed. We tried to turn to politics and there we saw our weakened labor vote. Disfranchisement and the 'White Primary' had left but one party in the state. At the convention of this 'democratic' party, held that year in Macon, discussion became a riot. Listen to this clipping:

> " 'All rules of parliamentary law were ignored; and men resorted to methods which would not be countenanced in well-organized mobs. Chairmen were disregarded; age, office and distinction were lost sight of; opponents were howled down; the governor of the state was not allowed to speak.'

"But what difference? There was no other party to turn to. Big Business ruled the state, and labor was beaten, divided and helpless."

Some of Scroggs' colleagues sneered: "So there's nothing left but the Ku Klux Klan. Kill the darkies off or drive them North for us to handle. Do you know what they did to us?" They told the story.

Since the Homestead Strike of 1892, Steel had remained an open shop industry. Attempts were made to unionize it in 1901 and 1909 but had been defeated. The industry was run on the principle proclaimed by one of its executives:

"If a workman sticks up his head, hit it."

The 12-hour day was in force for most steel workers. The homes were hovels, the wages were low since most of the workers consisted of immigrants and Negroes. In 1918, the American Federation of Labor attempted to organize the steel workers into a union which excluded Negroes. One hundred thousand white workers joined and started a strike. But the employers refused to negotiate. The strike spread. Within a month 350,000 men had quit in nine states.

But the Steel Industry was prepared. Thousands of deputy sheriffs had been recruited; the state constabulary of Pennsylvania had been concentrated; authorities had organized bodies of war veterans as special officers. Strikers were clubbed and shot. Homes were invaded. Men, women and children were trampled beneath horses.

Strikers were attacked not only as "Bolsheviks" but as "foreigners." It was said, "You can't reason with these people any more than you can with a cow or a horse. The only way to reason with them is to knock them down." National and racial differences were made to divide the ranks of the strikers. Industrial detective agencies were used.

Negroes of the South poured into the North after the World War, and there had been fighting, hatred and murder in East St. Louis, in Chicago, and elsewhere. Now, they were brought into the Pittsburgh area by the carload. In four months the strike ended in complete defeat. The effective cause was 30,000 Negro strike breakers and untold other thousands ready to come.

It was this story from a Negro strike breaker, which Scroggs heard when he returned to Atlanta. He reviewed his own career as he went to his union's office. The failure of the great strike of 1919 convinced him that labor must go into politics and form a union with the farmers, as Watson had once tried to do. But while Watson had concentrated on the farmer, there was now an organized labor group in the cities, with great power. Where now, in such a combination, would the Negro come in?

When the United States entered the World War, Scroggs saw in this an opportunity to advance his own political fortunes. He was 27 years old and could easily have obtained exemption. But he did not; on the contrary he volunteered and went to France as a private. He was in France about eighteen months, long enough to be wild at the way the French received and treated colored troops.

He returned to Atlanta with the stripes of a sergeant. His hatred of Negroes and opposition to their advancement had been increased rather than diminished by his experience. His animosity had been concentrated on social intermingling in France and withdrawn from the economic picture. He saw the Negro as threatening to marry white girls, and not as earning a living while helping white labor to earn one, too. This contradiction was increased by the fact that in America the race difficulty was increasingly economic, and least of all one of social contact.

Trouble flared again on the railroads, and from railroads Atlanta had been born, and on them now grew. Because of change of jobs and the conditions after the war, two million jobs were reduced to a little over a million and a half. There was increased competition for this work. Negroes still held on as firemen and were edging into other railway jobs. The policy of murder began again. But it did not seem so clear to Scroggs as it had before.

Suppose, right here in the South, Negroes were kept out of the unions—and Scroggs wanted them kept out of his own textile union —would they not as soon as opportunity offered underbid the whites and drive them out of decent, well-paid employment? On the other hand, could they be let to come in?

He heard of the Sacco-Vanzetti case. Seven long years it dragged out before they were executed. Did they die because they were murderers or because they were poor foreign workers?

In accordance with his plans, Scroggs soon went into politics, and was easily elected to the City Council from the mill district. His election was openly sneered at because he himself had nothing that could be called a formal education. He could read and write and he had done a lot of reading in a miscellaneous and unorganized way. He was a rabble-rouser with a bitter tongue, and was feared and hated on the one hand and idolized on the other. He went to the City Council with the distinct purpose of giving the poor white workers better opportunities, and curbing the competition of Negroes.

Leading the white trade unions, he backed every bond issue for schools, and proposed to provide new schools for the white children. But he forgot that while the Negroes were disfranchised in general voting by the White Primary, they could vote in the matter of bond issues. This right was based on property, and the white property holders did not dare disfranchise property. This fact the Negroes had begun to understand, and they defeated the proposed bond issue decisively, until at last the whites had to yield, in 1922, and to promise the Negroes five new schools.

Of course, they needed schools, Scroggs had to acknowledge.

Of every dollar spent on a Negro school child, six dollars were spent on whites. But Scroggs and his supporters insisted that the white schools were still poor and that they first must be made adequate before the needs of the Negroes were met. Despite this, the Negroes forced the city to build its first Negro high school and several new elementary schools.

White labor stuck to its guns. It tried to forestall the employment of Negroes on a building in the municipal airport, by asking the city council to appropriate to the contractor $4,300 which would be the difference in wages paid white and colored labor. This ordinance, the mayor vetoed. Thereupon, the Atlanta Federation of Trades joined with the Phohibition forces to recall the mayor. In this election, again the White Primary could not be used. The colored people registered and kept the mayor in office, because through him they had received their first high school, after they had systematically defeated bond elections.

All this began to give Scroggs food for thought. He grew less dogmatic on questions of labor and race. He had to face the dichotomy between the problems of labor and race. He realized the fight which the rich were making on the poor, the employers on the laborers. The honeymoon between owner and worker which appeared for a while, early in the century, was not real. The object now was to stop labor unions, to make laborers accept without complaint the wages and the conditions offered, and yet the great organizations of industry and concentrations of wealth were growing more and more powerful. The lost Steel Strike of 1919 set a national pattern. Hysteria over Bolshevism prevailed throughout the country. Mitchell Palmer, attorney general, sent hundreds of agents throughout the country to round up reds, radicals and "Bolsheviks."

Few labor leaders, no matter how sincere, could see their way clearly in this day of contradiction. It is true that in modern society the actual worker has a wisdom and point of view which is indispensable for comprehending human progress. He alone knows the modern industrial process from within; from the personal experience of the man whose muscles start the movement and who then must live on that portion of the value which he creates which is given him.

But on the other hand, this knowledge alone is not enough. Beyond this, there must be knowledge and understanding of human beings of all sorts who join in some way and at some time in the final product and service—of their thoughts, ideals and emotions in the world beyond and above food and clothes. This understanding, men like Scroggs did not have. They not only knew little of human history, but less of working conditions in places other than their communities, or of life in groups which they did not know or did not see; or even of neighbors from whom they were rigidly separated by iron bars of prejudice and inherited hate.

Scroggs saw that what he and his fellows knew was not enough. What did white workers want? All to be rich? Impossible. Could a few, including himself, be rich while the rest remained in poverty, ignorance and disease? Who could or would decide which were the undeserving? It might include white as well as black. Or, perhaps all the poor should be comfortable, educated, with good homes, enough food, and with physicians.

Then, always came the question:—must this include "niggers?" No, no! Who would be the servants which even poor whites must have? And then, foreigners like Sacco and Vanzetti—the North perhaps had no right to kill them, but they were only "Dagoes." Take that Jew teaching "niggers" the violin down in Macon—run the "sheeny" out of town! Yet even in this reasoning Scroggs knew something was wrong. Back in his puzzled mind swam that strange song of the blacks:

> *"Ezekiel saw a wheel—way up in the middle of the air!*
> *The big wheel run by Love—the little wheel by the*
> *grace of God—*
> *It's a wheel in a wheel, way up in the middle of the air!"*

That was it—wheels in wheels, rich whites, poor whites, uppity "niggers," hard-working darkies, black criminals and whites. How could whites organize labor without the blacks? But that would mean blacks in textile mills, social equality, intermarriage. Never! Death first. Then no organized labor—it was a hell of a mess!

Here, then, in a world developing toward socialism, was a country with Capitalism girding itself to stop the rise of strong trade unions and these unions hobbling themselves by helping disfranchise black labor; black labor was being advised by its own capitalist leadership to distrust unionism and sumit to exploitation. White northern labor, led by socialists like Debs, grew in power and achieved much social legislation, but its Southern wing, filled with race theories of superiority of whites, refused to cooperate with the North and was only too ready to resort to violence and mob murder to keep the black in their places.

The Ku Klux Klan was reviving and spreading all through the nation. But Scroggs knew this was no labor movement. It was, he laughed, exhibitionism and petty graft. When Watson emerged as United States Senator in 1920, Scroggs hoped that around him the poor farmers and the city trade unions might unite.

Between the Atlanta Riot and 1922, when he died, Tom Watson was successively or simultaneously moody, sick, drunk or crazy. He edited and published four different magazines, two of which the government suppressed. Beginning with a fortune of $250,000 he alternated with profits and gifts between wealth and bankruptcy for sixteen years. He broke with friends and supported enemies; he attacked and supported innumerable causes—war, civil rights, prohibition, and the Russian revolution. He was Populist candidate for president in 1908, on a "white supremacy" platform, and nearly won the Democratic nomination in 1920. Egged on by a strong-minded woman who attached herself to him in 1910, he shamelessly, alternatively and simultaneously attacked Negroes, Catholics and Jews. He was repeatedly in litigation for libel and obscenities in cases brought and dropped by the government and private persons.

As a Democrat, he opposed Wilson and then bolted to Teddy Roosevelt. His tirades were responsible for the lynching of a Jew in Atlanta, in 1914, and the mobbing of the governor who had pardoned him. Watson's newspaper made $1,125 a week profit by this scurrilous campaign. Watson was now almost continuously ill, moody, and with "nervous trouble," insomnia, and asthma and bronchitis. He took to drugs and drink and, in 1915, was nearly crazy and found wandering about muttering his old speeches, after the sad death of his daughter and son.

In 1920, he ran for United States Senator and won the election by a large majority despite getting in jail for assault during the campaign. In the Senate he got few committee assignments, but spoke there hours against the League of Nations and followed contradictory policies on labor, war, religion and race. Repeatedly, he challenged senators and army officers to duels. He died of cerebral hemorrhage in 1922, and 10,000 persons, escorted by the Ku

Klux Klan, attended his funeral in South Georgia. His political opponents sighed with relief at Watson's death, and proceeded to arrange for future political control of Georgia.

But meantime, Scroggs met two leaders of different streams of action in the South. One was Huey Long, of Louisiana. Long, too, was a poor white and had just emerged from a turbulent career as railroad and public service commissioner and as governor of the state, fighting the corporations to a finish. Scroggs met him while he was stopping off in Atlanta, and saw in this loud, violent politician a possible example which he might follow. He agreed with what Long said about railroads and public utilities, but was a bit startled at a last word about the Negroes. As Long was departing, he said to Scroggs:

"Watch the 'niggers'! I tell you, in the long run they are our only balance against the capitalists. You can fight capital with black labor, I tell you. But you've got to get rid of some of your prejudices. Oh, you needn't marry them, you needn't even work beside them. But they have got to have work and pay. One of these days you have got to admit Negroes to unions and the polls. Unlses you do this Big Business has got labor strangled. White labor will be underbid by black labor. In my state, I am going to give Negroes schools and I am going to let them vote just as soon as they want to. You've got to do the same thing here in Georgia."

The other man whom Scroggs met was Eugene Talmadge. He was a rangy, keen-eyed man with little background of education, deliberately bad-mannered and ill-dressed, and a demagogue of the most unscrupulous type. His forte was to be pals with the ignorant and envious; in consort with poor envious white farmers, he out-hated "niggers" in every way—no schools, cheating and driving to work, and deliberate insult for educated "darkies." He slapped his cronies on the back, chewed and spit tobacco with them, shed his coat to display his red suspenders, and boasted his kinship with the lowest and meanest. The ignorant farmers worshipped "Ole Gene." He approached Scroggs as a fellow laborer and friend of labor, but white labor, of course; and he avoided the matter of unions. "Joe, we outcast and oppressed must unite!"

"You mean farmer-labor?"

"Yes, that's it."

"Like Watson's dream?"

"No, Watson was a fool. No niggers. Never niggers. That

Tom found out before he died. We'll make no such mistake."

Talmadge thus became a professional "poor white." In truth, he was a big landowner, and descended from slave-owners. He was a small-town lawyer, owner of a saw-mill, and made money on his farm by driving Negro tenants. He emphasized country ways. His plan was to transfer political power from the cities to the country districts where the Negroes lived, and the whites used Negro disfranchisement to increase their own political power. He said nothing of the fact that this would cut down the political power of white labor unions and increase the power of landholders and employers of farm labor.

John Baldwin was astonished and not too pleased when Eugene Talmadge sauntered into his office one afternoon. Talmadge was deferential but independent, and he used his best English.

"Sir," he said, "I won't trespass too much on your time; but if you don't mind, I'd like to talk with you about the proposed Neill bill."

Baldwin looked puzzled, but Talmadge explained: "That's the bill about unit votes by counties."

Baldwin scowled, but Talmadge seemed not to notice this and proceeded:

"By this bill, the old unit system is changed. Each of Georgia's 159 counties is given a certain number of unit votes, the eight most populous counties six votes each. The next thirty most populous have four votes and the remaining 121 counties have two votes each. The candidates for state office who get most votes in any one county win that county's entire vote—that is, the county vote is cast as a *unit*. Eight counties have a total of 48 votes; thirty counties have 120 votes; and 121 counties have 242 votes.

"Thus, Fulton, Bibb, and Chatham, where Atlanta, Macon, and Savannah are, will have 18 unit votes, while my county, Telfair, and eight other small backwoods counties, will have 18 votes."

Baldwin took down an atlas and figured. Then he glanced at Talmadge. "And so 64,000 voters in the backwoods will have political power equal to 740,000 people in our three largest cities."

"Yes," answered Talmadge imperturbably, "and these big cities have almost all the white union labor vote, while in the Black Belt the 'niggers' don't vote."

He got slowly to his feet. "Just think this over, Mr. Baldwin, and see if you can't throw Big Business back of this bill. I think

I can get white labor support." Baldwin stared as Talmadge slouched out.

Talmadge then sought out Scroggs. He dropped in upon him casually, took a large chew of tobacco and cocked his legs on the table. He looked discouraged. "The banks and corporations," he growled, "are going to kill our bill for county unit representation."

"Well, I don't think much of it," said Scroggs.

"I didn't first, but I got to studying it and now I'm fighting for it," Talmadge replied. "Big Business can't push the poor farmer out of the picture if farmers are sure of a few votes that can't be taken from them. Moreover, these farmers won't let 'niggers' vote. Then the white labor unions in the cities can join these farmers and sweep the state." Scroggs sat up and looked interested. They talked a long time. From these two visits, and similar ones elsewhere, the unit bill became popular.

"You see, Scroggs," argued Talmadge, "with this improved unit system, we can unite farmers and the labor vote and defeat the bankers and manufacturers." The bill went through, and for reward Scroggs went to the legislature. The fact that a labor leader like Scroggs held this seat gave union labor prestige, and led to hopes for greater political power. But in fact, Big Business was now in position to control the state by getting power over labor leadership and over the farmers. They did not have to worry with popular elections. Talmadge talked with Scroggs. He himself was not strong enough to try for high office, but he hit on Scroggs as a trial balloon.

"Scroggs," he said, "you should run for governor on a labor ticket in 1926." Scroggs was too astonished to answer. He blurted:

"Hell, no!"

"But union labor is growing strong in cities, and ready to fight. I'll organize the farmers."

"Another Populist effort?"

"Not exactly; but a farmer-labor combine to stop the corporations."

"And how about the niggers?"

"Absolutely out. Only whites. I'll run for commissioner of agriculture and that will give me the chance to get the farmers behind us."

"But the labor unions are not yet really strong and are growing slowly."

"They've got unusual strength in the city White Primaries. We can play up the railroads and other corporations. I tell you, Scroggs, you've got a chance."

The labor leaders agreed with Talmadge, and Scroggs had his name entered into the White Primary. The signs were encouraging. Rising resentment against the upsurge of Big Business favored Scroggs and it looked as though he might become governor in 1927.

It was at this time that Mansart visited him, with the thought that labor ought to realize that Negro labor could greatly increase the power of the labor movement, and also with the fear that if white labor came to power without help from black labor, the Negro would suffer; he would lose the help of white capital and gain nothing in its place. The interview could hardly be said to have been satisfactory, but it was of value. Scroggs, for the first time in his life, sat down with a Negro of education and had a heart-to-heart talk. He disagreed, but he learned something. He thought of Huey Long and began to doubt Talmadge.

But social forces became too strong for him to resist. Soon it began to appear that his chances for election were really good. By the winter of 1925, he himself was practically certain that he would be the next governor. Talmadge especially brought him glowing reports. In view of all this, he began to think of certain minor but important requirements for the successful candidate, namely, religion and family life.

CHAPTER XVIII

THE CAREER OF ZOE COYPEL

There is little worse in the South than the plight of a young white woman of social position without prospect of a suitable marriage. Education and a career for self-support might do for Northerners, but the concept trickled into the South only with the new century, and then slowly. From childhood, young Zoe Coypel, because of her father's positon and her mother's social recognition, had expected to marry "well."

But now this was doubtful. Her social position was not so assured. Her father was on the brink of giving up a good income, and Zoe had no skills and little education. Also, it began to occur to her from experience with men and from wide observation that marriage just to be married, or for clothes and food, might not be after all the highest goal of life. Even dinners and parties had a certain insipid sameness after a few "seasons."

After desultory affairs with Lee Baldwin and others, and some wild dreams and rough wrestling with her football captain, Zoe began to wonder about companionship with men of a different type, who might be more interesting and absorbing. But in the circles where her mother insisted on moving, such men were not easy to meet. She saw hard-working students, climbing young business men, artisans and workers, but they did not see her, or if they did, put her aside as belonging to a world which they either could not enter or did not want to.

Her frightening encounter with Bruce Mansart and the murder of Policeman Brannigan gave her a momentary glimpse of Hell. She saw possible disgrace, total exclusion from the society of families like the Baldwins, and also no real goal in life.

So, as was her wont, Zoe took matters in her own hands and met Joe Scroggs. He was plain, awkward and ill-dressed, which in earlier days would have put him quite beyond Zoe's notice. But he was tense, earnest and working hard at something he seemed to think of tremendous importance. Zoe inquired into the subject and the man. Thereupon, she began to attend some trade union meetings and to take some notice of politics.

At this time, Scroggs was realizing that to be governor of Georgia a man must be either a Baptist or a Methodist; that was folk pattern. Well, he had once joined the Baptist church and left when the church repudiated union labor. He now renewed his affiliation. In addition to that, it was good policy that a candidate should be married. Scroggs was a bachelor of long standing and the problem of his possible official life in the governor's mansion was beginning to present some difficulties. His sisters were scrawny and more ignorant than he. They must be kept in the background. He knew practically no other women except a few political leaders, who did not seem to him to be entirely female.

He must begin to look about with the idea of marrying a woman who wanted him and of the kind that he wanted. He could never see himself with the sort of wife that his father had—the drudge that his mother had been and that most of his fellow-unionists had chosen. Of course, there were different kinds. There were some of the young laboring white women who had got some education and who worked outside the kitchen. But there, too, Scroggs recoiled. They were not well-dressed. They were not attractive. They did not excite his senses. He wanted something beautiful and striking. He remembered that when he was in high school, he had sat beside a girl who once or twice had let him talk with her. She was unbelievably beautiful, rich and aristocratic. One day, in a burst of courage, he had said to her:

"Will you marry me sometime? When I get rich and have a good job?"

She looked at him with great disdain. "I'd as soon marry a 'nigger' as white trash," she said sharply.

And from that day, Joe Scroggs felt that he belonged to the laboring class and he hated the aristocracy.

Mrs. Coypel became positively frightened when her husband began to complain of his work and to intimate that he was seriously considering giving it up. He said at dinner:

"I would like to return to Lanark and my flowers."

"What? And give up a salary of twelve thousand for twenty-five hundred? Are you crazy?"

"I have been, but I feel some sense of returning sanity. Twenty-five hundred or less, with no debts and no headaches, in addition to flowers, is about twice as much as I'm getting now."

"Have you talked with Mr. Baldwin?"

"Several times, and I'm due for a showdown now. Excuse me."
He left abruptly.

Mrs. Coypel was aghast. Only an eligible marriage on the part
of Zoe would save the family from disaster. It was then that Zoe
mentioned Scroggs. Mrs. Coypel was indignant.

"The very idea! A poor white labor leader!"

But Zoe was thinking hard. What did this separation of men
into races and classes really mean? The incident of Bruce Mansart
had shaken her. She knew perfectly well that Lee Baldwin would
never marry her, and she doubted if she would marry him even
if he asked her. Joe Scroggs was not particularly personable but
he was interesting, sincere and eminently manageable. Moreover,
he had political prospects, and in an entirely new line. The labor
unions were fighting a fierce battle; socialism was growing within,
and the IWW had been formed without and carried out that famous textile strike in Lawrence, Massachusetts. The employers
were fighting the regular unions with "company" unions. In 1924,
the unions went into politics behind La Follette. It was a fright-
fully interesting battle. She would never be able to play any part
in the aristocracy. She might play a part in the growing forces
behind labor.

She made it possible to get in contact with Scroggs and to talk
to him. He was frank and kindly. He told her about his work
as leader of Union Labor. He also told her of his practically certain prospects for election as governor. He told her of the money
he was getting for political activity on the side, and she learned
of other money which, unknown to him, the employers were furnishing to the Talmadge campaign fund. But she found out it
was quite true that he was slated to be governor of Georgia next
term. And when Zoe Coypel heard that, she made up her mind
to marry him.

Zoe soon had Scroggs figuratively upon his knees, with "yes
ma'am" and "no ma'am" and more attention to his clothes and
grammar than he had ever given before. The details of Zoe's wooing were never clear nor apparent to Scroggs, and indeed to anyone
except Zoe herself. She was represented by her mother as being
pursued by this frightful man to whom she had never given a
thought. But in fact, her mother now was slowly changing from

outright opposition to tolerance of the idea of marriage, especially if Scroggs became governor, but was able to induce Zoe not to rush precipitously into the alliance.

Meantime, Mrs. Coypel watched her husband's moves. He had had several long conferences with Baldwin and the whole matter of his future was in the balance. Mrs. Coypel herself took a hand and had a long talk with Baldwin. She learned that her husband could retain his position if he so desired. But her talks with Coypel himself convinced her that he did not want to. His confidence tonight might be definitive, and she was in despair when he left.

Coypel and Baldwin had had several conferences, and this one was the climax.

"Mr. Baldwin," Coypel said, "I am discouraged. I have occupied this position now five years and it is increasingly difficult and disappointing. At first, I conceived that I was to plan a system of higher education for the state of Georgia. I went at this systematically, as you know. I examined the state educational systems of every state in the union, and included foreign nations, and even Russia. I then worked out with you a plan which seemed to me to fit this state. I showed it to you repeatedly. We discussed and amended it."

"It was good, as I said, Coypel; only somewhat idealistic and a bit too theoretical. In ten, twenty years, in a generation it might be adopted. Now we could only begin."

"Just so; well, I tried to begin. Beginning to me meant weeding out and classifying the schools according to function and territory; selecting suitable teachers and dismissing incompetents; grading salaries by competency; erecting university buildings according to convenience and needs; and adopting a unified state budget for higher education."

"And of all this I am quite aware, Coypel; you got exactly nowhere. Local interests were too strong; local jealousies too bitter; ambitions, blood relationships too influential, and greed too widespread. And finally, you found that you had no power to do anything or force anybody. Mansart, dealing with small funds and narrow aims, was at least a center of power and could enforce his decisions. Often you could do nothing. I know this, Coypel; indeed, I warned you how little you must expect and how slowly you must go. You know that what we lack is legislative action to give us necessary power. You know that the political situation has completely stymied us.

"With crazy Tom Watson in the field, and equally radical Hardwick in the governor's chair, we could only mark time. Walker got in by Klan support and thus was handicapped for our purposes. Now, we are beginning to move. We are going to succeed him by one of our own business men, Hardman. He married a Colquit."

"I hear that Scroggs, the Commissioner of Labor, is likely to be elected."

"Nonsense; he hasn't a chance. We are letting him think he has, but the matter is settled. And you know that when we decide, the thing is done. Coypel, I beg you to stick with us through this next administration. We'll do things."

Coypel consented, although conscious that a deeper matter had not been discussed at all and that this he did not dare yet to voice. It was the fact that even in the mind of Baldwin himself the great educational interests of the state should be controlled by industry and organized technology.

Coypel's scheme was not easy to carry out. In the first place, Coypel himself had no idea of its intricacy and deeper meaning. He still thought of education as the training of individuals for the broader life and not for the greatest production of profitable goods. He was in difficulty therefore, from the first, not only because of his ideas, but because the proposed Board of Regents of the State University would control so small a part of the educational interests of the state even if their best plans went through. The new white college in Atlanta, instead of being state controlled, had been subsidized by Coca Cola. This, and the great girls' school in Atlanta, owned by the Methodist church, and a number of other strong institutions of the state, would be still outside the university system.

Beyond that, Industry would control Education, and Education would be for the sake of Industry. He was not yet prepared to have a clear showdown on this fundamental philosophy with Baldwin. He therefore consented reluctantly to keep his job for at least two more years.

When he returned home he mentioned the fact that Hardman would succeed Walker, and that he had consented to hold on. The women were startled, and Coypel continued:

"I know Zoe is thinking of marrying Scroggs. Contrary to your assumptions, I've nothing in particular against Scroggs. He's a rather ignorant, ill-bred fellow, but honest and deserving so far as I know. In the past, Zoe, you've shown no liking for this type of man. If you want to marry him, that is one thing. But if you think you are marrying a governor of Georgia, forget it, my dear, because you're not."

He went out. Mrs. Coypel was sure he was mistaken. But Zoe began to consider what she would do in case Scroggs were defeated. It was an entirely new prospect, and it kept her awake most of the night.

Scroggs, too, had his fears, but his hopes prevailed. He would not admit failure for that meant losing office and a desirable wife. It was difficult for him to understand that election to office in Georgia was the decision of a small group of powerful men meeting secretly, and not the free choice of the mass of citizens. This mass, because of fear or ignorance, or especially because they were afraid of Negroes, might be depended on eventually to assent to the decisions of the powerful.

The power of these men came from wealth or social standing, which again was dependent certainly in part on wealth; or from personal characteristics which sooner or later resulted in wealth. These men might sometimes disagree, as they did in the campaign which resulted in the Atlanta Riot. But usually, differences of opinion among them were soon composed because their interests were never greatly divergent. These interests did not involve Art or Literature, Science, nor for the most part, Religion. They were usually matters of present income, or change of income, of industry or change of industrial techniques. Of course, they were limited by ideas about race, but even here it was race as affecting income.

So that the choice of candidates was not difficult to reach, and the man chosen was the one who, in the carrying out of his duties, would most effectively guard present business methods or change them to the advantage of the powerful men and interests involved. Walker could be trusted to follow advice. Talmadge was suspect until he was tried out. Scroggs was quite unknown and tied up with labor unions. If he would guide these unions to keep their demands low, he might make a valuable official; but if he had any radical labor uplift ideas, he would be dangerous.

Scroggs, therefore, was quietly shelved for future reference, while Hardman, the choice of Big Business and himself at once a business man and physician, became nominee for governor by a large majority. Scroggs ran well for an unknown and a labor leader, but to those inside the result was never in doubt. After the primary, a local "election" was held and the usual seven hundred Atlanta citizens, out of the whole city of 250,000 inhabitants, then went through the motions of an election and made Hardman governor.

Scroggs was crushed. He wondered how a nobody like himself had ever been persuaded to dream that he could be governor of Georgia. But, in a sense, more humiliating was his thought of Zoe Coypel. How she must despise him! Naturally, her only reason for promising to marry him was her wish to be a governor's wife. He never dreamed of anything more than that. He was now in a panic as to how to break the engagement decently.

Zoe Coypel hesitated. She was engaged not to a governor from whose mansion she could thumb her nose at Atlanta society, but to a labor leader at a critical time when the unions were fighting for life, and leading them was neither lucrative nor safe. She dropped into her father's office, which was most unusual. She knew that her father thought a great deal of her, but he was shy and had the idea that his daughter was almost exclusively the mother's property, although in this case he was equally aware that the mother was hardly fitted for the task. So he greeted her now jovially and was unquestionably happy to have her come.

"Well, well," he said. "Lost? Glad to see you. Wanted somebody to talk to. You see, Zoe, you and I haven't been as close friends as we ought to have been. I left you to your mother, and I think we both of us see the mistake. I particularly wanted to talk to you just now because I know you're facing a problem.

"When you began to go around with Scroggs, I was surprised and alarmed. And then I began to find out about him and look him up. He is not at all the kind of man whom I would have thought could attract you, and yet, perhaps for just that reason, he may be the man you need. He is not well-bred, and the boys you've been going about with have been much too well-bred. His education is not good, but neither is yours. You might study together, I think he'd like to.

"But above all, he has got or thinks he's got something that he wants desperately to do, and that you've never had. I think if you try to combine that you may find a better and deeper life than your mother and I have found. At any rate. I'm just passing it on. No orders, mind you. Just a suggestion."

Zoe sat for a long time looking at him. And then finally, she got up and put her arms about him and her cheek to his, and said, "Dad, I'm going to marry Scroggs."

The next morning, Zoe walked into Scroggs' office, and to his speechless amazement announced that they were going to get married. She dragged him out to get the license and then they went house-hunting. They found a three-room apartment in the factory district, and Zoe went home to fetch her clothes and other belongings, while Scroggs went hunting second-hand furniture. Needless to say, Mrs. Coypel was in complete despair. Just as her husband had announced that he was going to stay two years, and added, "Mind you, no more," in his present position. here came Zoe already married to a defeated labor leader, a half-educated poor white.

She let Zoe depart, as of course she had to, and then announced widely to all of her social set whom she could reach that she and her daughter were quite estranged by this amazing mesalliance, and that her husband might soon leave Atlanta for a lucrative offer in the North. The first clear response to these maneuvers was failure to receive her annual invitation to the first Baldwin function of the Fall season. She even ventured to inquire casually by phone to be sure the omission was intentional. It was. The Coypels withdrew from society and settled in Athens to await the legislative action on a new University of Georgia.

Hardman did something on an educational program but not much. A Negro university system was arranged by private Northern philanthropy, centering around Atlanta University, in Atlanta. It did not include the Negro State College at Macon, and no such merger seemed likely in the near future. Baldwin, as well as Coypel, was disappointed, but Baldwin assured Coypel of success in 1930.

Zoe Coypel's life for the first two years of her marriage was not exactly satisfactory. She let her husband go ahead with his plans because she had nothing better to offer and because she really did not understand just what he was doing. He loved her very deeply, that she realized. He also was hurt because he had not lived up to the promises of position, and even wealth, with which he had first lured her.

On the other hand, she looked at him with new eyes. She was not madly in love, but she deeply pitied him, and also she respected him for his struggles. She saw that he was uneducated and inexperienced, that he did not know what life was. On the other hand, she also understood that he was worth teaching, and that she was not equipped for the job. Therefore, gradually, she began to understand that she was the one in this combination who must begin to learn.

At this time, the new CIO was forming, and she went with her husband to some of the initial meetings. They were both impressed by the basic idea of organizing the mass of the laborers and not just the skilled elite. They were sure that this sort of unionism was what the South needed. But of course, this brought up the whole question of organizing Negroes.

It was in Birmingham that Zoe felt that at last she was coming to grips with her problem of life. She and Scroggs had gone to Alabama to talk about the effort there to incorporate Negroes into the union movement. Many of the white miners were bitter. She heard one curse as he passed by:

"By God, I'll never work beside no 'nigger'."

Sitting with local union leaders, they listened to a story. The narrator was a grizzled white union man from the North.

"Mind you," he said, "I ain't no 'nigger-lover.' If I had my way they'd all be shipped back to Africa. But by God, I know a man when I see him, and black Jim Henry was a man. It was two years ago. Jim was a good miner, but we wouldn't admit him to the union and he could only scab when we struck. So what? He had to live.

"Then the CIO came and he joined up. We was damn mad but what could we do? We went on strike soon after for better wages and conditions. It was a pretty hard test for the colored men and we watched them. We ought to have known that they would not stand this test right after the treatment we had been giving them. And they would have scabbed if it had not been for one woman. She was Jim Henry's wife. Thin, scrawny and ugly, but God she had guts! When we were on the point of breaking, she came with one of those Negro songs. I shall never forget it. There, straggled in the city square, we stood hesitating, the whites swearing, the Negroes scowling. And then this woman began the march. She began the song:

'Walk together children, don't you get a-weary.'
There's a great camp meeting in the Promised Land!'

"At last we had all taken it up, and she she sang the interlude and obbligato:

'Strike and never tire, strike and never tire!

"And then again, the swing of the march:

'Walk together, children, don't you get a-weary.'

"That settled it. We beat 'em. It took weeks, but we beat the company to its knees. We got our wages. And then, of course, there came the test. The company turned on us. They had yielded to us and it had cost them money. Now they must open some old mines. They must spread the digging. And we were in a dangerous area.

"Jim Henry was a member of my local. And of course, we let him work. But at the same time, he got the worst places on the job. We saw to that. We worked in bad holes, in mud and water. He stood where we feared gas—you know—.

"One day, we was all called to go down into a re-opened mine. Many whites refused outright, claiming it was dangerous, and fearing gas. Others got suddenly 'sick' and went home. But Jim Henry's wife came right down to the mine and said, 'Be a man, Jim, go down—go down!' And this though the food was scarce at home, her clothes ragged, and she was worn by hard work and want. But there was the old fighting spirit in her eyes. He kissed her and went.

"Down into the darkness we entered the old forgotten diggings slowly and with fear. But Jim Henry walked ahead swinging his pick, until we came to the darkest, lowest level. Then some sniffed and muttered, 'Gas!' Jim sniffed too. 'Taint no gas—just rot,' and he strode on. Most of us stopped and stood still. The boss swore at us, as Jim Henry rounded the far curve and went down into the hole. His voice rolled back singing: *'Dey ain't no hammer, ina dis mountain—'* Then it stopped. We looked into the blackness and saw the air reddening. 'Fire!' we screamed. But the mist and fog killed our voices, and thick darkness settled over him.

"We began to crowd back, but Jim Henry went on down into the cold, muddy water. The fire still glowed ahead, flaring up and on. Then, in the smoke wafting back he smelt it. He knew it was the death gas—soon, soon. There was no escape. We saw him straighten. He swung his pick on high and struck. Hell roared, and then it was still. It was still as death.

"Course, I don't know what happened after that. But when they buried what was found of Jim Henry, some went down to the 'nigger' church for his funeral and they tell a tale. They say they heard a crazy preacher, and then they say Jim Henry's wife stood up and talked, which couldn't a been true for she dropped dead when they lifted him out of the mine. But they say she was there an that she was dim and grey and that she talked low and tight with sobs between, till she came to that song; my God that song:

"I've heard of a city called Heaven!"

"She said, 'He saw it. The heavenly city rose before him. Its towns gleamed white and silver; its wall ran up like singing waters that weep, and over all the golden sun poured down the Glory. Behind, above, rose the White Throne, shimmering with jewels, pulsing with music. Over it swept angels, their long sleek wings beating the air, their voices lifted in heart-hurting harmony.'

"Jim Henry said, so she told, 'I've heard of a City called Heaven—Ah aim to make it my home!'

"'Upon the throne sat the Unknown, gowned in silver and gold. He beckoned and Jim Henry stumbled to his feet. He opened him arms and Jim Henry stepped forward, afraid-like. God sent down the Angel with the Mercy Sword—forward, forward—and Jim Henry cried in joy for it was me, Jane, his wife. I was young again and beautiful. A voice said, " 'Come Jim Henry, enter into the joy of Thy Lord.'" Jim Henry said, "I ain't fitten, Lord, but I tried—'"

Scroggs and Zoe stared at the teller of this tale. Finally, and in silence, they went home.

He and his fellows continually came back to the Negro problem. Talk went like this:

"You got the Negro helpless—what are you afraid of, then—of him or of yourselves? I tell you, the white South is in the saddle, on the black mule, don't you see?"

"From where I'm sitting, I can't tell whether it's the South or the Mule—that same nag you're always riding, the 'nigger.' Why, up North niggers are marrying white women. Seen it with my own eyes."

"Did the women make any fuss? And don't white men here still lie with black women as they have done for two centuries?"

"We're going to have laws against such stuff—state and national. We're going to push 'niggers' down to where they'll never rise."

"Why not kill them?"

"I'd like to."

"Of course, you might run on them again in heaven."

"I'd rather go to Hell!"

"Don't worry!"

"If it wasn't for white folk, where would the world be?"

"I don't know, but another war or so and we'll all know."

"I wonder what would happen if we woke tomorrow morning and found there was not a single Negro in the world? What would we do? What would we talk about? Whom would we blame? Whom would we fear? Whom would we cheat? My God! It would be awful! Life would not be worth living. There wouldn't be no world. History would be abolished. The future would be black— or should I saw white? At any rate, I mean there'd be no future worth living for.

"My theory is that you must have a race problem or no culture. Why have feet unless you can wipe them on something? No Negroes, no gentlemen. That's my notion. The South had lots of Negroes and lots of gentlemen—fine ones, lordly, distinguished. North had few Negroes and few gentlemen. West had no Negroes —who ever heard of a Western gentleman? Who? Don't tell me— God knows his business! When he wants gentlemen, he provides doormats."

"Don't you think there's a lot in that?"

"There certainly is. A lot of hooey."

When the Crash came in 1929, Scroggs was ready to quit. His followers were thrown out of work. His unions dwindled in numbers. The rich seemed to think they were the victims of the Depression; but they could not know how horribly hopeless it was for the mass of the poor, just emerging from the dregs of poverty and first seeing the sky. He cursed at the smug advice of Hoover but listened to that talk of Roosevelt: "There is nothing to fear but Fear itself."

After all, here in the South there was still food and new clothes were unnecessary. Scroggs looked about and talked with the crowds who had new leisure to talk. He began to see that as industry rose from the dead—and it must rise—it would need labor as never before. Moreover, he caught a new note and it grew in intensity. There was to be a New Deal and it was to be carried out by a New Man, who seemed to know men and himself to have suffered. That was the point—he himself had suffered.

In the campaign of 1930, Scroggs opposed Russell, the candidate of Big Business and the close friend of John Baldwin. But Russell won. Under Russell, Baldwin's plan for a university system began to materialize. The old University of Georgia, at Athens, was combined with six senior and six junior colleges, and the three small state Negro institutions were incorporated into the Colored State College, at Macon. Coypel, although not the titular head, was made president of the Board of Regents. It was planned that as soon as further mergers were accomplished, he would become Chancellor of the University of Georgia.

Russell, however, did not stay to finish his job but chose to go to the United States Senate in 1932. There came the opportunity of Eugene Talmadge. After four years as Commissioner of Agriculture, he had an unbeatable machine which, by legislation, enabled the country districts to outvote the cities. Even in the cities he had plans, and they included Scroggs. He visited Scroggs secretly and often.

"Joe," he said, "I'm going to be elected governor in 1932. I'm going to serve one term and then, like Russell, I'm going to the United State Senate. I'm going to rise on the current unrest and confusion—right up to the top. Now, if you'll string along with me, I'll pull you up!

"First and foremost, you'll be elected Commissioner of Labor at this election. That'll be a big job under the reorganization, and will give you a chance to organize labor in the cities. After my term as governor, you'll succeed me. With my South Georgia farmers and your city labor vote, you can't miss. You can have two terms as governor and then—then we'll see."

Scroggs agreed to support Talmadge for governor in 1932. The Depression gave him his text. He lashed out against monopoly and Big Business, especially in gas, water power and electricity. He attacked extravagance in the schools and especially in the Negro schools. All this new understanding of Negro labor and its relation to white labor faded before the anti-Negro attitude of Talmadge and Joe was reduced to uneasy silence. The legislature slashed appropriations, and Mansart found it necessary to curtail a good deal of his work, with the prospect of having to curtail more.

Baldwin, evading the storm and being advised of the need which Big Business had of Russell's services in Washington, helped send him to the United States Senate. Eugene Talmadge became governor, and Scroggs, Commissioner of Labor, was one of his chief lieutenants. Here was the germ of a farmer-labor movement like that of Tom Watson, only the Negro was not thought of, or at least not mentioned.

Talmadge was violently anti-Negro, but Huey Long's advice lingered in Scrogg's mind. This was emphasized by the strike of the textile unions just as Talmadge became governor. Several thousand workers struck against the 8½ percent wage cut and the Bedeaux Speedup System, at Callaway Mills, in La Grange and Manchester. Governor Talmadge declared martial law. Against Scroggs' vehement protest, Talmadge ordered the National Guardsmen to stop the strike. It was smashed by the full force of the authority of the state, and the white strikers driven like dogs to their kennels.

Scroggs was furious, but Talmadge explained elaborately. White union labor must not get out of control in Georgia. If once they raised wages unreasonably, the employers would hire Negroes. That would drag wages down permanently. This repression of the unreasonable demands of white labor was simply guarding them against themselves. Anyway, when Scroggs became governor, he could try any policy he pleased.

Scroggs doubted Talmadge; he knew he was acting for the Negro-hating and labor-exploiting planters of south Georgia, and that also he was financed by Big Business in Atlanta. Until the Negro was brought into the labor movement, Southern white labor could never face the employers as a firm body. Scroggs realized this more and more clearly, but he still hesitated at the price labor must pay for such a triumph.

Talmadge was cautious. He persisted in his stand against labor despite the advice of Scroggs, and as a result his re-election in '34 was certain, if he ran. But he had promised faithfully that he would not run if he was sent to the United States Senate, and that after he was sent to the Senate he would support Scroggs for the governorship.

Scroggs lost all faith in Talmadge, but could not break with him. His administration was soon receiving from the federal government hundreds of thousands of dollars annually for relief. Nearly all went to whites and much of it was for political ends. Harry Hopkins at last got angry and stopped payment of funds. Talmadge thereupon became a bitter enemy of the New Deal.

Moreover, Talmadge did not go to the Senate. Big Business did not trust him and did not propose to put another Tom Watson in Washington. Evading its promises deftly, Big Business asked Talmadge to accept another term as governor, and they made his compliance not too difficult financially. Also, they promised faithfully that Talmadge should go to the Senate in 1936. Talmadge's farmers and the gerrymandering of the state in their favor made the farmer-labor candidate unbeatable.

Thus came the second great disappointment of Scroggs' disappointing life. Talmadge broke the news early one morning at Scroggs' apartment.

"Hello! Had breakfast? You look beat," said Scroggs.

Talmadge wept. "Scroggs, I've been up all night wrestling with those lying, double-crossing sons of bitches. I'm ashamed of myself. They won't send me to the Senate, God damn them! They say I must run again for governor!"

Scroggs sat down heavily. Talmadge explained at length. At last, he revealed that Scroggs would again run for Commissioner of Labor, and that in 1936—

But Scroggs was not listening.

The Georgia election of 1936 came. Talmadge, having served two consecutive terms as governor was prevented by law from running for a third successive term. But, as he had assured Scroggs, he had been promised a United States Senatorship. For a second time this was denied him and he became the bitter enemy of the political group in power which now discarded both Talmadge and Scroggs.

Meantime, through the land the battle between labor and capital raged. First came the struggle in the auto industry, where Negroes were in the unions. They were discriminated against, but they remained loyal. The injustices of the assembly line and the speed-up made old men of boys and kept the average annual wage down to $1,000 a year. The new "sit-down" strike was now tried, where the strikers stopped work but stayed in the mill. Their fellows fed them, serving sometimes 5000 meals a day. The companies hit back with hired detectives and thugs, paid thousands of dollars.

There was one pitched battle with guns and gas in Flint, Michigan. Ford defied the law and his police shot down 175, killed and wounded. The steel workers, having admitted Negroes, now organized again under the new CIO. By February, 1936, they had 150,000 members, and by March won the forty-hour week, 10 percent pay raise, and recognition of their union in most of the industry. Workers in rubber, transport, electricity and textiles were organized, and the CIO entered the South.

Here, Scroggs saw trouble begin. His CIO organizers were kidnapped, clubbed, tarred and feathered and attacked by the Ku Klux Klan. He did not give up, and Zoe stood by his side. For the first time, she saw a meaning to life which was more than enjoyment, more thrilling than clothes, and more inspiring than envy. She read books, she subscribed to newspapers, attended union meetings and at the same time kept a small but neat home.

The depth of the Great Depression now came. Huey Long died in 1935. But on the other hand, the government was pouring out relief money and there was no doubt but what the country was going to climb out of the morass. It might mean Socialism, but Scroggs had no objection to that. The government ought to help the people, he argued. And therefore, he made plans to increase the strength of the labor unions, to go in for social legislation, and then, in time, to face the race problem and the relation of black workers to white.

Meantime, Coypel carried out his decision to resign. He was sitting with Baldwin in the lush reception room of the First National Bank.

"Mr. Baldwin," he said, "I'm resigning. I'm resigning whatever position I have and that which you planned me to have. I never have become Chancellor of the University of Georgia, and never will. Moreover, I don't want to be. My idea of what a university should be can never be reconciled with yours."

He explained that he had determined to return to his little town in North Carolina and had learned through correspondence that they would be glad to have him back in his old place, and that even more than that, his old home could be repurchased.

Baldwin was not surprised and, on the whole, a bit relieved. He had long since realized that Coypel was not the man for the work he wanted done on education in Georgia. Moreover, any change was going to be difficult amid the ambitions, jealousies and interests involved. He dismissed Coypel courteously, with a few words of regret. Coypel was at once uplifted and depressed. No one likes to fail, particularly when the task is great. At the same time, he was at last free of a burden he ought never to have undertaken. He squared his shoulders and went home to tell his wife.

CHAPTER XIX

THE SON OF A HARNESSMAKER

Once upon a time, there lived in Iowa a harnessmaker named Hopkins, who liked to play at bowling. He had a son called Harry, whom one day he took to Iowa State College of Agriculture. There, Harry, at the age of about ten, saw a Negro. The Negro, George Washington Carver, was a singular looking fellow, very dark, tall, thin and slouching, with an unexpectedly high, almost soprano voice.

At first, Harry laughed at him, but later he was fascinated by what Carver was telling the white students about plants—grass, grain and weeds. Harry listened for an hour and wanted to come back to Ames and study under Carver as soon as he finished high school. But he never saw Carver again for Carver soon went south to the Negro school at Tuskegee. Harry Hopkins never forgot him.

As he followed Carver's life, he became more and more intrigued and astonished at this man. He cared nothing for gain. He left his salary checks uncashed for months. He gave freely his precious knowledge to the world without money and without price. He loved knowledge for the sake of knowing, for the good it might do the world. He refused to patent his priceless discoveries; he refused positions of income and trust. Homely, ungainly, shy, and self-forgetful, he lived for Beauty and Truth and never noticed the mocking laughter of his fellow-men, like another Gandhi, cast for a role in a corner, and not in a wide world.

Harry went to Grinnel College and studied under Steiner. Steiner was a Socialist. He was born in Czechoslovakia and educated in Germany. He had lived in England and knew the Webbs and the Fabians. He taught the philosophy of Karl Marx, among other social theories, in his classes. This teaching remained a major influence in Harry Hopkins' life.

After graduation from college, Hopkins came to New York in 1912. He had a keen mind and sympathetic soul and very fortunately soon came to be the spiritual son of John Adams Kingsbury. Kingsbury, at the time, was in charge of the poor of New

York, and Hopkins was an eager neophyte in search of truth and life. Kingsbury wanted to know more about the poor as human beings rather than just as city "problems." He set young Harry Hopkins to study poverty. Harry, fresh from the comfortable West, saw such poverty as he had never dreamed of. He saw it face to face with unblinking eyes and made one of the best studies of it which the city ever had.

His health kept him from war service, because of a severe case of typhoid in his youth, from the effects of which he never wholly recovered. It left him thin and anemic, with frequent and severe illnesses. When Kingsbury went to postwar duties in Europe. Hopkins accepted Red Cross work in New Orleans. Here he stayed three years, and then two years in Atlanta as head of the southeastern Red Cross organization. He did not find in the South that opportunity for which he was looking. On the contrary, he found the problems of class intertwined and distorted by problems of race and color.

He was, for the first time, thrown head-on against the Negro problem of the South. Before that, he had known but few Negroes—Carver whom he knew of as a great scientist; and a few Negro workers in New York, but not many, since the poverty which he studied then was on the East Side, where few Negroes lived. Now, he saw the teeming black population of the southern South, and these from the point of view and under the fierce taboos of the whites who held all the political power, most of the wealth, and set the social customs.

The Red Cross there had been annexed by "society." With ample funds, it took over philanthropy and organized public aid with units where only persons of proper social standing sat in supreme control. No Negro could belong to these units, and if perchance Negroes needed help, it was granted in such a way as not to interfere with wages and status. When, for instance, Negroes were driven out and impoverished by a flood of the Mississippi River, the Red Cross took charge of them and herded them in custody so that they would not escape the clutches of their employers. Eventually, the Red Cross returned them to the plantations of the masters who claimed them.

Hopkins was baffled and affronted. He saw the problem of the South—poverty, dirt, ignorance and disease, overlaid with a curious glaze of pretense, assumption and stubborness. He had no way to cope with this, no method of penetration. He was not by nature a leader or a revolutionist. He was an intelligent follower of leaders, whom he trusted and to whom he was loyal. Here, he was quite cut off from the most oppressed classes—the Negroes and poor whites. He could not approach them apparently, nor gain their confidence. He felt trapped and bound amid hate and want.

When he was transferred to Atlanta to head the Red Cross of the Southeast, instead of more freedom he had even less. Red tape bound him and he seemed able to accomplish nothing. He relapsed into a helplessness natural to a shy man; until one day, quite by accident, he found himself in Macon and on the grounds of the new Negro State College. Without introduction or excuse, he entered the president's office and met Jean Du Bignon. He was again disappointed because he thought she was white. But he asked almost pleadingly:

"Say, can you help me? I want to talk to a Negro heart-to-heart. I don't seem to be able to get a decent conversation out of anybody in this damned country. I'm Harry Hopkins, new head of the Red Cross."

"I know of you, Mr. Hopkins—I'm sure the President will be glad to talk with you."

Hopkins was glad to know that at least the president was a black man. He entered his office.

Mansart was a little prejudiced against Hopkins at first; he represented the Red Cross, and Negroes did not like this snobbish outfit. It helped them sometimes, but always last and with marked condescension. Beyond that, Hopkins' manners startled the rather prim president. Hopkins soon had his feet on the table, had lighted a cigarette. Then he burst out with no preliminaries. He was evidently sympathetic and earnest, with no thought of giving offense:

"How the hell do you stand this South?" he asked. "Damned if I can. I'm quitting."

Manuel stared, changed his mind about asking him not to smoke, and said instead, "But don't you head the Red Cross?"

"I've tried to for two years in Atlanta, and before that for three years in New Orleans. What a mess that was. Huey Long is a good socialist and for the people, but first he's for Long and you can never tell where he'll end. But Louisiana is a God-forsaken nest run by murderers, thieves and whoremongers. I had to leave. And what is the southeast? How can you Negroes take it?"

"What else is there to take?"

"I know, and I'm more juzzled than you. So I'm giving up. But tell me what you really think and what are you going to do."

The ensuing talk was frank and fascinating. Both instinctively began trusting each other and they opened their hearts. One had faith in God and in Man's innate justice. The other doubted any dependable interference from Heaven but believed in the justice of the ordinary mass of folk if they ever got power to apply it. Mansart doubted this, if it was the white mass. Hopkins declared that Mansart's "best people" were mostly "skunks." And so on for two hours, until Jean Du Bignon tactfully intervened. They shook hands warmly at parting and never forgot each other.

When Kingsbury returned from abroad he "rescued" Hopkins from the Red Cross, as he later explained, and for three years they lived in New York in close companionship and study. They worked, read, and talked in their neighboring suburban homes, and roamed the woods. Hopkins studied health conditions and especially the ravages of tuberculosis. Thus, armed with knowledge of poverty, health, and disease, Harry Hopkins in 1928 met Franklin Roosevelt.

Here met two men who were opposites and foils to each other; who complemented each other's personalities by their very contrasts. First of all, both were life members of the great Companionship of Pain. The one was hopelessly paralyzed and carrying about daily seventeen pounds of steel to hold his body upright. The other could not digest his food, and his thin, anemic body was repeatedly under the surgeon's knife and in reach of death. Yet, neither complained. Indeed, both were almost gay for the very opportunity to heal a nation's hurt born of cancerous paralysis of the whole country, if not of the world.

Roosevelt was a gentleman by birth and breeding—by wealth, Groton, and Harvard. He was urbane, well-read, well-groomed and tailored. He belonged to the possessing classes of natural reaction. He had chosen a political career and was thrown close to ill-bred and wily politicians who appealed strongly to his sense of "noblesse oblige." He believed in private wealth, hereditary property and investment. But he was honest; he could look at facts. He could do right even if it clashed with inherited predilections.

While no equalitarian, he had the old American sense of fair play. Franklin Roosevelt was indeed two men in one. The sight of poverty in this rich land incensed him; he believed it entirely unnecessary and mainly the result of wrongdoing, conscious or unconscious. For remedy, he sympathized with the socialism of Harry Hopkins and of most of the greater thinkers of his day. His thought was not socialism but it was socialistic. He listened to it from his friends Franklin Lane and Belle Moskovits, from his co-workers Tugwell and Frances Perkins, from great public teachers like Dewey and Veblen, and from social thinkers like Steffens and Croly. The thought trend of his day was socialistic. The other Roosevelt was the English gentleman, with Dutch patroon reinforcement, who saw in the British empire the salvation of all that civilization meant to him, when the Prime Minister of Great Britain appealed to him for support in saving the British Empire from Hitler.

As successor to Al Smith, Roosevelt inherited the philanthropic socialism of Florence Kelley and her Consumers' League, of Jane Addams and her leaders of Settlements among the poor, and of Frances Perkins and her factory laws. But Hopkins was closer to him and nearer to complete Socialism. Perhaps Roosevelt was drawn to him just because, in contrast to Roosevelt's own training, Hopkins was ill-bred, often ate with his knife and swore. But he was a free inquiring soul, a Socialist who voted for Debs, and a free thinker, did not attend church and knew the mass of men because he was one of them. But he had added to what the class in which he was born knew. He studied poverty and disease face to face. He knew the Negro problem of the southern South by living with it. He was clear-headed and absolutely honest, and the only thing he placed above Truth was Loyalty—personal loyalty to friends. For this, he stopped at no sacrifice.

Harry Hopkins became the co-worker of Roosevelt to meet the ravages of the Great Depression. Roosevelt was at the time governor of New York. In New York, the unemployed filled the streets and grew daily in numbers. Roosevelt determined to meet the disaster by direct relief, thus flying in the face of tradition which had long looked on poverty and unemployment as indications at least of laziness, if not crime. How should he start relief?

He put a Big Business friend in charge and he, in turn, invited the best-known social worker of the day to become executive head of the Temporary Emergency Relief Administration. Mr.

Hodgson, a man of long experience, hesitated and consulted his friends. His advisers said the experiment was too unorthodox and was bound to fail and might ruin his career. He therefore refused, but recommended Harry Hopkins. Hopkins, then in the employ of the Tuberculosis Association, cried: "I'd love it." Roosevelt made him chairman of the TERA, which proceeded to spend millions of dollars to save the workers of New York from starvation.

Then, Franklin Roosevelt became Chief Executive of the United States for twelve years, and at his right hand stood Harry Hopkins. But, too, in obedience to his class upbringing, Roosevent already turned for advice to Science and Big Business. His Brain Trust of Tugwell, Berle, Moley agreed on a "planned economy" and even flirted with Socialism. But at last, Sociology and Finance agreed with Hoover—the banks must first be rescued; the government must immediately restore to power that organized finance which for so long had directed business and influenced governments. Next, the railroads, the children of high finance, must be helped. Here, had Roosevelt been a Socialist or even fairly familiar with the growth of the socialist state in the modern world, would have come at least a beginning of government cotnrol of banking and ownership of railroads. And to this end, there were some moves. But the Brain Trust was contradictory in its advice, and no clear and certain path was followed.

On the other hand, in the realm where Harry Hopkins was expert and was consulted, the administration moved swiftly. For Hopkins saw such disaster as this nation had never before known. In 1930, the United States of America went down into the Valley of the Shadow and looked Hell in the face.

On a corner in Chicago, where the bitter winds from Lake Michigan tore through his thin clothing, Jack Carmichael stood shivering. He was a handsome and young mulatto, but drawn and thin; hungry and weak. He had run away in panic from wife and child in south Georgia, lest his failures ruin them. Even then, he could not find himself; nothing he attempted seemed to work out. Yet, he had dreams. His mind glowed with visions and hopes and fantasies of incredible beauty. Then, as he stood there penniless and hungry, across the street right before him a truck unloading garbage and refuse was beset by 35 persons, digging with hands and sticks for bits of food and vegetables. He turned away and vomited.

Five hundred miles west of Chicago, a farmer stood staring at the prairie with hard eyes. He muttered, "I fed and sold 480 head of cattle last year. Today I haven't a bit of meat in my house and nothing to buy meat with."

A thousand miles eastward, in the metropolis of the nation, a family of ten was moving into a three-room apartment already occupied by a family of five. They slept on chairs and on the floor.

But there are worse things than hunger and cold. This the colored man knew who, at the moment, was restlessly pacing his apartment at midnight in Boston. Monroe Trotter, the colored leader who Woodrow Wilson declared had insulted him in the celebrated interview in 1914, had published the *Boston Guardian* for thirty years. Now, he was about to lose it and he was half insane. This weekly paper was his life. With it, he planned to emancipate the American Negro from his shameful three hundred years' slavery. He would accept no half freedom. He would never consent to making his people merely useful and profitable. He wanted full political and civil rights; no "Jim Crow" institutions; no black hospital wards nor "colored" YMCA's. No! Absolute and complete equality. To hell with Booker Washington and his cowardly surrender to expediency.

To this crusade, Trotter sacrificed his fortune and his devoted wife who had died of exhaustion only last year. They never could afford children. Now came the Depression, and the sneering, greedy creditors. His sister helped with time and money. It was not enough. Where were his friends, his people, his race for whom he had given more than his life? Back and forth he paced in wild distraction as hours flew. Then he went out and climbed to the roof to see the stars. There were no stars. He cursed and raised his shaking hands. He remembered that this morning was the dawn of his sixty-second birthday. Then, with closed and streaming eyes, he walked off the roof and they found him next morning dead, crushed and bloody on the sidewalk below.

Franklin Roosevelt was not a Socialist, but he was tremendously impressed by Socialism, by the social legislation of Germany, Britain, France and Scandinavia in the early 20th century. He was attracted by the idea of a planned economy which the Soviet revolution in Russia put forward. It attracted him as it did all inquiring minds of that day. But the educational system of the United States failed men like Roosevelt. It left him groping for answers. Back in 1912, when finance capital was gaining control of the individual capitalists and fathering the Trusts which Teddy Roosevelt had attacked, Franklin was thinking: "Conditions of civilization that come with individual freedom are inevitably bound to bring up many questions that mere individual liberty cannot solve." He therefore proposed a "struggle for the liberty of the community rather than the liberty of the individual." During his first presidential campaign, he went further and declared if private capital will not operate for a reasonable profit, Government will have to operate itself." And again, more definitely: "We cannot allow our economic life to be controlled by that small group of men whose chief outlook upon the social welfare is tinctured by the fact that they can make huge profits from the lending of money and the marketing of securities." Then, in his first inaugural, he centered on the bankers the blame for the depression: "The money-changers have fled from their high seats in the temples of our civilization. We now must restore that temple and the measure of restoration lies in the extent to which we apply social values more noble than money-profit."

Facing 13 million unemployed, daily growing larger, he saw immediately that this was a matter that could not be left to industry. Under the advice of Harry Hopkins, he instituted an astonishing new performance for America, which many thought was the end of the world. Harry Hopkins spearheaded this movement. He said:

"I think it is an outrage that we should permit hundreds and hundreds of people to be ill-clad, to live in miserable homes, not to have enough to eat, not to be able to send their children to schools, for the only reason that they are poor. I don't believe ever again in America we are going to permit the things to happen which have happened in the past. We are never going back again, in my opinion, to the days of putting the old people in almshouses when a decent, dignified pension at home will keep them there. We are coming to the day when we are going to have decent houses for the poor, when there is genuine and real security for everybody. I have gone all over the moral hurdles that 'people are poor because they are bad.' I don't believe it."

Neither did Roosevelt. Certainly, Socialism could not be blamed for the nation's present plight—Business, and especially Trade and Commerce, could. Roosevelt again indicted Finance

Capital: "The rulers of the exchange of mankind's goods have failed through their own stubborness and their own incompetence. They have admitted their failure and abdicated. Practices of the unscrupulous money-changers stand indicted in the court of public opinion. The primary concern of any government dominated by the humane ideals of Democracy is the simple principle that in a land of vast resources, no one should be permitted to starve."

Hopkins knew that the employment problem was becoming more and more desperate and that the only solution was a huge work program carried on by the federal government instead of states or corporations. In 1934, nearly a billion and a half dollars were spent to sustain 20,000,000 people who were in distress. Work was found for millions of individuals. Unemployed American men and women were paid decent wages and constructed thousands of miles of road, thousands of bridges, parks, schools and hospitals; hundreds of airports, playgrounds, swimming pools. There were a million people a month attending schools for adult education in a hundred thousand classes; recreation was superintended in fifteen thousand community centers.

In this day of distress, the Negro group, because of recent chattel slavery, followed by seventy years of almost unchecked exploitation by their former masters and Northern industry, were now the most miserable of the miserable. But a nation so used to failing to consider black folk as Americans, even when much of its wealth and culture was reared on the black backs of Negroes, was again, in this depression, to forget largely the woes of black folk. Just as slavery excluded the poor white from agriculture, so freedom excluded the poor Negro from rising and expanding manufacture. On the other hand, the world-wide fall of agriculture carried the mass of black farmers more and more down to the level of landless tenants and peons.

The world war, and its wild aftermath, seemed for a moment to open a new door; two million black workers rushed North to work in iron and steel industries, to make automobiles, pack meat, build houses and do the heavy toil in factories. They met the closed trade unions, which pressed them to the wall, into the low-wage ghetto, denied them homes and mobbed them; and then, the Depression met all.

In the Depression, Negro workers, like white workers, lost their jobs; had mortgages foreclosed on their farms and homes and used up their small savings. But in the case of the Negro worker, every-thing was worse in larger or smaller degree; the loss was greater and more permanent; technological displacement began before the depression was accelerated. The unemployment and fall in wages, struck black men sooner, lasted longer, and went to lower levels. The *Crisis* was no longer self-sustaining, because its readers could not buy it. Its voice was stilled. In the rural South, Negro educa-tion almost ceased, while Southern city schools were crowded to suffocation.

Negroes reeled drunkenly under the blows of the Depression. The rate of unemployment among Negroes was twice, three times, and four or more times as high as white unemployment. In Harlem, New York, sixty-four out of every hundred men were out of work, and four out of every five heads of families were jobless. Yet, in October, 1932, 74 percent of all the unemployed in Harlem were not receiving any relief at all. In Newark, N. J., over 90 percent of the Negro workers were unemployed.

In Border cities, the rate of Negro poverty was four to seven times that of whites and the relief given in the South was more difficult to get and less per family than that given whites. In Charleston, South Carolina, half of the population were Negroes, but the Negroes formed seventy percent of the unemployed.

The director of the Community Chest in Birmingham, Ala., reported that while in 1929, twenty percent of those applying for relief were Negroes, by 1932 this proportion had increased to 65 percent.

In the steel and metal center of Youngstown, Ohio, Negroes formed two-thirds of all the unemployed. In Chicago, no areas in the city were harder hit than the Negro section. In the Second Ward, over 85 percent of the persons who had been employed in 1930, were unemployed a year later. Bank failures in the Negro community were more complete and devastating than in other sections of the city and some of the middleclass Negroes, who had saved at great personal sacrifice, became poverty-stricken.

In existing jobs, Negroes were being replaced by white work-ers. Many white workers were used to replace Negroes as janitors and bootblacks, at even lower wages than had been paid to the Negroes. In Atlanta, 150 Negro bellboys were replaced by whites. White girls were used to replace colored male employees of over 40 years standing in the check room of the New York Pennsylvania Railroad Station. In Harrisburg, Pa., one of the largest hotels displaced Negro waiters with white waitresses. Department stores in Ohio replaced Negro porters by whites. In Austin, Texas, whites were employed instead of Negroes to deliver goods for jobbing houses.

Public works operated by the national, state, city and county governments, systematically discriminated against Negroes. At the Hoover Dam, in Nevada, no Negro workers were taken on until persistent protests forced the contractors to hire at least a handful out of a working force of thousands. It was publicly announced by the Highway Commission of Mississippi that no Negroes would be employed in the work of public road building.

Negroes were not allowed to work on the river work in Omaha, a Federal job. They were systematically discriminated against at the El Capitan Dam, in San Diego. They were refused work in the building of the new wing at Harlem Hospital, New York, and were not employed to tear up and re-lay 143rd and 136th streets, in the very heart of Harlem.

Above all, in the Negro's case, local and Federal relief helped him last. It was explicable human nature that the unemployed white man and the starving white child, should be relieved first by white local authorities, who regarded them as fellowmen, and often regarded the Negroes as sub-human. Moreover, it might happen that while the white worker was given more than relief and helped to his feet, the black worker was pauperized by being kept just from starvation; even when, finally, plans were in making for national rehabilitation, and the re-building of the whole industrial system, such plans called for decision as to the Negro's future, and his relations to industry and culture in this country, which the country was not prepared to make, and therefore often refused to consider.

In Washington, D. C., Negro jobless received at all times at least one-third less than the meager relief doled out to unemployed whites. If work or food was given, Negroes got less. The unemployed relief station for Negroes in San Antonio, Texas, was closed down altogether. In many cities of the South, the grafting charity authorities forced the Negro jobless to pay for the Red Cross flour which the white unemployed got free.

The white authorities tried in many places to send back to the South Negro families who had come north; they did this through the Red Cross.

The police were vicious against the Negro jobless. In the South, vagrancy laws were used to put jobless Negroes on the chain-gangs. Police often ruthlessly framed jobless Negroes and threw them into jail.

Hundreds of Negro workers were shot down by police and sheriffs for picking up coal along the railroad tracks or for taking a loaf of bread. The nine Scottsboro boys, who were framed on a fake charge of "rape" in Alabama, were jobless boys looking for work on the Mississippi river boats.

The situation of the Negro farmer, share-cropper and tenant became almost one of starvation. The farms were being seized for debt. The landlords refused to "furnish" food for the croppers and their families. Thousands of farms were abandoned by Negro farmers, who could no longer scratch even the barest liivng from the soil.

Ickes, Roosevelt's Secretary of the Interior, knew something of the Negro problem and of Negro leaders: he had once been president of the Chicago NAACP. He began to look about for advice on the relation of Negroes to the New Deal. He moved cautiously. He wanted an adviser on Negro affairs, but did not think it wise to appoint a colored man. It would be more workable to choose a liberal Southerner. He found such a person in the Howell family, which owned the powerful *Atlanta Constitution*. Clark Foreman was under thirty, but he was well-educated, had worked with the Interracial Movement and was liberal minded. Ickes appointed him to take general charge of a Negro Affairs committee; and Foreman gathered Negro advisers about him. Ickes also put Negroes on his legal staff, and on the National Park service. Mrs. Roosevelt met Mary Bethune and was impressed. Through her advice, other Negroes were consulted. Will Alexander, who had inspired the Southern race relations movement, and served in the Farm Security Administration, brought Negroes into advisory positions so that, in the end, Negroes of education and ability had some voice in the Attorney General's office, the office of the Secretary of War, the Federal Housing Authority, the Office of Emergency Management, the Department of Labor, the Youth Administration, and the Federal Works Agency.

The basic problem of the New Deal was whether to make its objective an effort to "restore" former "prosperity" or some more fundamental change in the essential economic structure of the nation to bring greater stability and economic justice. If it was the first, there was not much hope for the Negro. He simply could look forward to being "restored" to a situation in which his prospects for economic development were growing less and less. If Southern agriculture was to be put on its feet again by government aid, the Negro would remain mainly the tenant farmer and exploited casual laborer. If the great industries were to be similarly "restored," the Negro would still be the reservoir of unskilled labor with uncertain employment and low wages. And the restoration of banking and credit would mean comparatively little to a poverty stricken horde of laborers.

On the other hand, if the relation of industry to labor in general was to be overhauled and readjusted, if the whole relation of the farming industry to the other industry of the land was to be carefully readjusted with regard to prices, methods, machines and markets, if unemployment was to be eradicated by shorter hours, a minimum wage, the forbidding of child labor and the arrangement of old-age security, if these and similar measures were going to change radically the basis of American life, then the American Negro, barring gross discrimination, was going to have a "New Deal," a new chance to improve his condition.

Thus, the New Deal met not only opposition of concentrated wealth based on Negro disfranchisement, but also increased the opposition of white labor by increasing, or failing greatly to decrease the number of poor and unemployed Negroes whose plight threatened the white standard of living. The result was violence and race riots.

Through the meeting of Harry Hopkins with Manuel Mansart, in Macon, Hopkins became acquainted with Judge Mansart, in New York, and now and then met in Mansart's living room, Hopkins, the Judge and his wife, and Sally Haynes. This was something new and stimulating in the life of the Mansarts. In 1934, they were talking of the new National Industrial Recovery Administration, and Sally was enthusiastic. Hopkins was hopeful, but the judge was silent.

"Are you afraid of socialism?" asked Sally.

"No, all my life it has been my hope."

',Of course this is not socialism," said Hopkins. "It is an approach."

"Is it even that?" asked the Judge. "Do you realize that at least a third of the working class are excluded?"

"You mean the Negroes; not in PWA."

"True, less in your work. That I knew would be true; but in Agriculture, in the NIRA and in the proposed Tennessee Valley Authority, as many Negroes are left out as the South and the skilled unions can arrange for. Farm laborers and domestics were not included under the protection of the NIRA codes for industry. Thus, three million Negro workers, more than half of the total number who must work for their livelihood, were not covered. These three million were the backbone of the Negro consumer market. For them, an immediate rise in prices meant additional insecurity and suffering. In certain areas, where uniform minimum wages were established for black and white workers, employers replaced Negroes with whites rather than pay the same wages. Did you read the *New Republic?* Here it is:

> "Taken as a group, Negro industrial workers were helpless to defend themselves against demands made, especially by representatives of Southern industry, for longer hours and lower wages for those occupations, industries and geographical divisions of industries in which te predominant labor supply was Negro. Except for a few exceptional groups, such as the miners of West Virginia or the longshoremen on the South Atlantic seaboard, they were unorganized and without any perceptible power to bargain collectively. In nearly six hundred code hearings, fewer than a dozen Negro representatives of organized labor have appeared."

"I know, I know," replied Hopkins. "Perhaps what the Communists say is true. Either the mass of workers are raised, or some climb on the backs of others and oligarchy continues."

"But," said Sally Haynes, "may not this oligarchy gradually grow larger and larger until the exploited disappear?"

"On that I have thought much," said the Judge, "but I doubt it, especially if the exploited group is visibly marked by color of skin. And remember, the vast majority of the world's workers are so marked today."

Hopkins mused: "Beyond that," he said, "even in the white working class there are marked people; the tendency of the skilled, educated and better paid to join in exploiting the common labor-

er, the ignorant and the poor, is tremendous. It plays a powerful part today here in America. Tomorrow, it will play an even
stronger part. Look about! Does union labor today stand with the
mass of workers or beside the rich?

"Instead of decreasing in wealth and power during the crisis of
1929-33, America's richest families were strengthened, while masses
of citizens were reduced to beggary. And even though many people were lifted from low economic levels by some restoration of
employment, the basic inequalities, issuing from no real differences
in skill or merit, remained as great as ever. Paralleling reemploy-
ment, which reduced joblessness from about twenty million in
1932, to half that in a few years, fantastic dividend and interest
payments were at the same time automatically returned to the top
income group of not more than six thousand adults. I don't know.
I get awful discouraged at times."

Sally asked: "What are Negroes doing about this?"

The judge answered: "The Negro mass is writhing. They formed,
in some cities, Colored Merchants Associations to establish their own
retail stores. They organized in St. Louis, Chicago and New York
boycotts against white merchants with Negro customers who refused
to employ Negro clerks. In Washington, there is a group of young
Negro intellectuals. They are talented and for several years now
have fought with vigor and fine courage, and their barbed arrows
of understanding, their loaded documents, are causing the Roosevelt cabinet many an anxious hour."

"They sure are," answered Hopkins. "If they will just stick to
it and not give up."

The Judge hummed: "Work and pray, live on hay!"

"The real difficulty lies here: there are in this land millions of
laborers who instead of supporting socialism, are coming to fear
and dread it. Some time, when progress needs their support, they'll
be on the wrong side!"

Eventually relief was divided into two parts: a general clearing
house designed to help private business by pump-priming; and
the WPA, under Hopkins, designed to furnish work regardless of
its commercial value or ability to earn private profit. Eventually,
Hopkins' program cost the nation ten billion dollars.

It was Harry Hopkins and his WPA that saved the lives and
happiness of Betty and Jack Carmichael. Betty was that niece of
Manuel Mansart's wife who, with her young husband, Mansart

had encouraged to settle on a farm in south Georgia. Jack had run away to Chicago. They did not even know of each other's whereabouts for years. After Jack's inexplicable desertion, Betty for a time found work as teacher of the local colored school.

The landlord, Cranston, the attack on whom had frightened Jack into leaving, said nothing. He hoped Jack would return and thus give Cranston the chance to bind him legally to work on his land indefinitely. When he was convinced that his family really did not know where Jack was, he simply waited, hoping that Jack would think all was well and return. He therefore helped to get Betty the colored school to teach.

But Cranston, like all farmers, was in sore straits himself. Production had increased during the First World War and in the boom which succeeded it. Farmers had piled up surpluses. When the crash came, the farmers cried out in distress. In the South, they passed on their suffering to the sharecroppers who faced starvation and the chain-gang.

Roosevelt responded here with half-measures. Rejecting the socialist dole or the Big Business method of scarcity, the New Deal combined these methods by destroying food and limiting planting and then paying farmers for their co-operation. When the federal dole payments came to Southern farmers like Cranston, they pocketed the cash and let the sharecroppers starve or run away. Betty Carmichael at last chose to leave. Her mother-in-law offered to attempt to run the little farm with her own efforts and hired labor. She secretly believed her son, Jack, would return.

Betty went north. She planned to find work and as soon as possible save enough to send for her mother-in-law and the boy. She worked in New York as a servant in a well-to-do family, and studied nursing at night. Then, when the family had to give up servants, they secured admission for her in the Cresswell Hospital to study nursing full time and support herself by night work.

This hospital had just tried the experiment of admitting Negro nurses, but of course did not dare mix the races in the dormitories. When Betty arrived there was but one vacant room for two, and she could not be accepted unless the next applicant was also colored. Meantime, however, the attendant let her go to the room to await the next applicant. This applicant proved to be Sally Haynes, who had been assigned unexpectedly to this area by Harry Hopkins for a temporary survey of conditions. She was the daughter of that partner of John Pierce, who committed suicide after the Crash. Sally had rushed home from college after the news to take charge of her totally inadequate mother.

Mrs. Haynes had been summoned to the hospital suddenly. She was pale and swaying as she entered her Rolls-Royce. Her mind was bewilderment. How could her husband be ill? He seemed well that morning although perhaps worried with these accumulating business cares. But it was more than true. When she arrived, he lay white and dead, with a cloth covering his temple where the bullet had entered. The bank manager was less deferential than usual as he accompanied her downtown, to the great banking institution with her husband's name in gold lettering in the window as "President." The manager hurried into the stately office and sat down heavily. He lost no time in amenities but said brusquely,

"Madame, you'd best know now—you are penniless."

"I do not understand?"

"You will; nothing is left—the home, the car, most of your clothes and jewels; everything of his, of yours—and of mine, too."

And he sat there crying unashamedly. He let the tears stream down his face. For he thought of his new-built home in Westchester and the bright lawn on which he used so proudly to toil at sunset; he thought of his happy wife and the two lusty babies; he thought until he dared think no more and rushed and stumbled through the bronze doors of the great and famous bank.

Mrs. Haynes and her daughter faced the ghost called Poverty. It was not so horrible as frightening. It was not real, of course, this awful vision, and yet it was real and it seemed to haunt the whole nation—not only the 600,000 families like hers, who used to have at least a thousand dollars a month, but also the six million families who earned a thousand dollars a year and less.

The Haynes family had never been close-knit. They were three —the absorbed, very busy and often absent husband; the unoccupied, beautifully groomed and usually languid wife; and the daughter, Sally, well-built, tall, strong and always busy. She had been at Bryn Mawr, finishing a four-year college course in three years, and planning post-graduate study in social science in London and Paris.

This plan she had not yet announced at home, when the news of her father's suicide reached her. She was not really surprised, nor too much cast down. It would change her plans, of course.

She could no longer spend five thousand a year, and she shrewdly surmised that this would not be so bad a thing for her own soul.

Her mother was hopeless and apathetic. Sally soon had the lease cancelled, the servants dismissed, the furniture and jewels sold, and all available resources turned into cash. They moved to the lower East Side and they began living the life of the respectable working poor. The mother kept house for her—an entirely new experience. She sweated and thrilled at it, and said one night when the stew turned out unexpectedly good, "I never knew it was such fun to be poor."

The girl, who had been discoursing on the total abolition of poverty, paused in astonishment; paused and stared. Then, she arose and kissed her mother as she hurried out. The mother, with tears in her eyes, touched the kissed cheek gently.

Sally went seeking a job which she knew she must find soon. Lillian Wald, of the Henry Street Settlement, liked her looks, discounted her lack of experience, and gave her a meagerly-paid clerkship at the Settlement, where she met many interesting persons, among them Harry Hopkins.

In this organization, Sally Haynes found work which she loved, and also found a colored girl, Betty Carmichael, from Georgia, who was also facing difficulties and was bitter at her prospects. Sally had been asked to take temporary residence in the Cresswell Hospital to study social conditions.

Sally rushed into the room where Betty was awaiting a roommate. Sally was willing to share a room, but of course had not expected a colored roommate. She burst hurriedly into her new lodging, stopped and stared, and met the stony eyes of Betty. They were both startled, but Sally's training enabled her to snap into normal reaction first.

"Oh," she said brightly to hide her astonishment, "what a heavenly view!" And she stared across the Hudson at the pale Palisades.

Betty was desperately trying to reply accordingly, when the manager of the dormitory burst in, breathless.

"Oh, Miss Haynes," she gasped, "such a terrible mistake. This Miss—er—what is it, was assigned here by mistake—"

"But," interrupted Miss Haynes, "there's room enough, and we both like the room."

The lady from the South sniffed and bridled. "But naturally

colored and white cannot sleep together." She glared and added, "At least, so we Southerners think."

"Indeed, I thought colored and white people had been sleeping together in the South for ages," snapped Miss Haynes.

The official was gone, and Betty was trying to meet the situation in a nonchalant and dignified way, when she simply collapsed and burst into tears. So the two became friends. Harry Hopkins soon had matters straightened out, and Sally became familiar with a social problem new to her experience—that of Negroes. They talked long and often about family problems and the general situation. Sometimes, Harry Hopkins had time to join them, and one night brought a letter.

Remembering Harry Hopkins, Mansart had written him, outlining the misuse of federal relief funds in Georgia. Characteristically, Hopkins never answered his letter, which hurt Mansart. But Hopkins stopped handing out relief funds to Governor Talmadge, which made Talmade furious and drove him completely into the all-too-willing arms of Southern white reaction. Hopkins handed Mansart's letter to Sally. Sally showed it to Betty, her colored friend, and Betty was convinced that her boy and his grandmother must be brought north at the first moment. She would finish the nursing course in another year and paying work was certain. She began to look for an apartment.

Meantime, the grandmother had seemed to be getting on, and her letters which friends wrote for her had few complaints. Then came Mansart's letter to Harry Hopkins, and at last the little boy himself began to write; at first, scrawls almost illegible but increasingly coherent, until at last there crept through a picture of poverty, oppression and striving which frightened the mother. She increased her remittances home, but evidently she could not much longer allow the boy to stay in Georgia. She hesitated over the cost of transportation for both, but at last when she secured an apartment of three rooms in Harlem, she put a money order in the mails and wrote, "Come!"

The letter came and the little boy of eight was hastening across the fields to bring it to grandmother. He was in a terrible hurry. It was a letter from Mommy and had money in it; he could feel it. He left the highroad, cut across a new cotton field, as he knew he shouldn't, and even had the effrontery to dash through the front yard of old man Cranston's home place, which he knew was sacrilege. But he was sure no one was at home, and this bypass brought him almost to his own yard.

But Cranston was at home and so was his wife, who had just planted roses in that bare front yard which once had been so beautiful. There was now little beauty in their lives, and old man Cranston was surly and discouraged. His boys, after army service, had stayed north and seldom even wrote. The one girl had married and gone to Texas. With her raft of babies, they heard nothing from her now. The home place had wilted and gone to dust. The tenants and farm hands had deserted and drifted away, complaining because they received neither pay nor wages. How could they? Cranston was bankrupt. The banks would give him no further credit; the merchants granted his workers less and less support. With the fall of farm prices, his only hope was government subsidy and the amount of that depended on the farm hands and tenants he could claim.

The sight of that little black devil trampling his growing cotton and defiling the sanctity of his own front yard aroused him to fury. That boy should be in the fields, anyway, instead of in school, and his old grandmother must hereafter work in his fields instead of dawdling away her time on that bare bit of ground which she claimed. He was going to foreclose the mortgage right away. It wasn't due yet and the title was good, but he knew the officials in town and they knew how to drive "niggers" off the land. They had no business owning land nohow. He could point out a thousand acres in this very county which landowners had stolen from Negroes who wanted to ape white folks and own land. He'd always said he wouldn't stoop to cheat even a "nigger," but times now were different. It was every man for himself, and he must live.

He had told the black hag only yesterday how it would be, and she had paid him no mind except to demand the back wages which he could not pay, and would not if he could. Didn't the old bitch steal more than enough to support her and that brat? After all, she got money from that girl who had run away north owing him for supplies. He snarled at his silent and shriveled wife, took his horsewhip from the wall and started out the gate and down toward the old woman's house. It angered him every time he saw it and thought of that cocky "nigger" who tried to buy and live on land next to his own home place, and then tried to kill him. He had damn well got rid of him!

The boy was nestled down beside his grandmother and slowly deciphering his mother's letter from the wonderful place called "North."

"Dear Mother and darling Jackie:
"At last I am writing what for these two long years I have so wanted to write. Here is the money order. Come to me at once."

He started to yell, dance and hug his Grandmaw—and then old man Cranston appeared at the front door. The old woman straightened and the boy slid stealthily out the back door and gathered two big jagged pieces of rock.

"God damn your soul to hell, haven't I told you to report to the field for work hereafter and bring that brat? How long do you think you can defy me? By God—"

"Don't you cuss before my boy. Pay me what you owe me. I'm leaving tomorrow."

"Like Hell you're leaving. You're staying right here as long as I say. Do you hear?" And suddenly, he raised the long black whip and brought it down full force across her face and shoulders.

And then the most unbelievable thing happened. A rock—a big, jagged stone struck him beside the head and sent him reeling; before he could recover either his balance or sanity, a second rock knocked him out the door and a little hyena landed on him with flying fists and heels, shrieking:

"Don't you tech my Grandmaw—don't you dast, you dirty old devil—I'll kill you—I'll kill you—"

Old man Cranston struggled to his feet, saw the boy pick up two more rocks, and turned away. He staggered at first, then walked quickly to his house. He'd have both these "niggers" in jail before night. He'd—then he saw the crowd ahead and remembered he was pledged to attend.

It was down in the bottom of the valley, on land too torn and sterile to be plowed, and where for long years the Negro Baptists were wont to meet in a dilapidated church which served also as the Negro school. A committee of white planters had arranged with the black preacher to bring together here, this Saturday afternoon, the tenants and black farm laborers from nearby regions to talk over the new Federal grants to farmers. Some silly Negroes were getting it into their heads that the government was going to help them. That notion must quickly be dispelled before it got fixed. It must be clearly undertsood that the relief payments went to landholders and employers.

Of course, when the landholders received government money they would be able to pay the laborers, after their indebtedness to the farmers had been met. This must be accomplished peaceably and in good spirit so as not to antagonize the government. If the Negroes got obstreperous, or kept drifting away north without settling their just debts, all would lose, both landowners and workers. It was suggested to the preacher that he look up and bring to the meeting some Negro who had gone north and returned. He might be induced to tell how awfully the Negroes were suffering in New York and Chicago, and how anxious they were to get back to the good old South.

Cranston now remembered this meeting. He would go there and tell of this assault on him and scare the darkies present into quick compliance. He wiped his face, mounted his horse and rode down the declivity into the valley through which a little stream gurgled. The preacher was talking:

"Sam, I wants you to tell truly what you'se been suffering in New York these last awful weeks. Don't be afraid—talk up."

Sam glanced a litle uncertainly from one side to the other, took a reassuring touch on the bills in his pants pocket, and began.

"Fore de lawd, brethren and sistern, I hain't never seed such a mess in my borned days—"

"Was that in Atlanta," called a voice, "or Macon?"

A white man spoke up. "That will do; let Sam talk."

Sam talked, loud and long. He let his vivid imagination soar. He told of Negroes dying in the streets, of black folk being kicked and cuffed, of their horrible plight in New York, of how they longed to get back to the "dear old South" and their kind white folk.

A woman shouted: "You wasn't in New York last week! I saw you in Savannah!"

Again interruptions were stopped, but there came a greater interruption. On the brow of the hill appeared a tall old black woman, emerging suddenly from the forest and brush. Her dusty black gown was stained with the blood that dripped slowly from the scar across her forehead. Yet, she walked straight and grim and beside her, closely clasping her hand, was an angry little boy with a rock in his hand. As he came in sight of the crowd, he screamed:

"Old Man Cranston—he done tried to kill my Grandmaw—he tried to kill her!" He pointed straight at Cranston.

The black crowd shuddered and began to murmur. The preacher straightened in his pulpit and raising his hand, cried:

"Brethren, quiet now. Let us sing. *'Shall I be carried to the skies'—*"

But a grim voice in the audience growled: "Don't want no more them God-damned hymns."

The boy kept screaming, and old man Cranston moved back into the white crowd. Then, the leader of the white group who had come out from town to superintend Sam's revelations, moved forward to the pulpit and said:

"Now, boys, let's not have any trouble. We'll see to this old woman. You make that child stop screaming. There isn't going to be any violence today here. We came here for understanding and to help each other, and that's what we're going to do. Now, there's going to be a meeting in town. We'd be glad to have you folks come. Remember, the government is going to help us out of the mess that we're in; it's going to help you and it's going to help me. But only if we all are law-abiding citizens. Suppose now we adjourn this meeting."

Still growling, the crowd began to move and disperse. They went to the old woman and washed and bound her wound. "Come on, we'll take you to the train. You shall go to your daughter tonight. We'll get the money order cashed. We'll see that your things are brought from the house. Come on."

They began to sing as they started away. But the preacher and Sam were still in the pulpit and looked as though they wanted to interfere in some way to regain leadership of the dispersing throng. The preacher glared at the boy.

"Come here, boy," he said, and started toward him.

But the boy raised the hand that had the rock and the rock, flying straight to the pulpit, barely missed the preacher and Sam as they dodged behind it. They were not in evidence again that day.

Old man Cranston was angry. He started toward his home to get his wound attended to, and the leader of the white group rode along with him. Cranston insisted,

"I want to put both those 'niggers' in jail. Do you know they nearly killed me? They're living on my property. They owe me money."

"Yes, yes, I know," said the man. "But can't you see, Cranston, that our methods have got to change? No, I don't mean that we're going to invite 'niggers' to dinner. But this business of kicking them and pushing them around and killing them now and then in order to get our work done, won't do. In the first place, we'll have the whole damned federal government down on us if we continue. Now the government is coming in to help us. Most of that money is going to us, of course, as it ought to. But most of the Negroes, on the other hand, are going to leave us and we can't help ourselves. Do you see that crowd marching over there toward town? Well, that's the way they're marching all over the South. They're leaving the farms and going to the cities. They're leaving the southern cities and going to the northern cities. They won't have any good time. They'll starve and die and live in crowded pigpens. All right. That's the business of the northern cities. But it don't help us.

"Our whole Negro probem is going to be changed. We're going to have some Negroes left and more whites, and they're going to work and they're going to work for the wages we set; but we must not act like damn fools. I'm not going to open the armory and arm the white hoodlums in the city and start a race riot. We ain't going to have no lynchings. That technique's out. It's been overworked. We think we can live on white labor and have white labor live on black labor. Can't be done. We're going to live on labor, and we don't care a damn whether it's black or white. But tonight we're going to have peace, and tomorrow we're going to have money from the government and put it in our pockets. Now, just make up your mind to this, Cranston, because that's just what's going to happen. If that old woman wants to go North, let her go. It means one less pauper to feed and one less little black firebrand to beat our heads in."

Cranston was as angry as he was speechless. But there was nothing he could do. He rode into his yard, almost fell from his horse, and cursed his wife. The white men moved toward town. The black crowd went singing ahead of them. They put the old colored woman in the "Jim Crow" section of the train that rolled from south Georgia toward Atlanta, and landed days afterward in New York. They gave her and the little boy fried chicken and corn pone. But he couldn't put them in his pockets until he had emptied out the jagged stones that he was carrying. But he was a happy little boy. He was going to see his mommy.

CHAPTER XX

THE VISION AND THE CLOUD

Harry Hopkins and his WPA were starting a revolution in the nation. From a day when literature and art had to depend entirely on publisher's profit or chance philanthropy, down to depths where no artist or writer could hope to make a living, even at physical drudgery, there dawned a plan for the federal government to subsidize art, drama and literature. What had at first been a makeshift scheme to keep labor from starvation by made work, which was sometimes raking and re-raking leaves, there succeeded careful plans for socially necessary work of all kinds which was not easily adapted to promotion for private profit. This Ickes encouraged. But Hopkins then came forward with a new and breath-taking vision, which Ickes and many other Liberals viewed with jaundiced eyes. It was a scheme directly to subsidize writers and painters, to furnish music and drama not for private profit but for the value of the result in itself, as artistic accomplishment.

Writers were given a chance to write, and artists to paint, and actors to act, and musicians to compose. They produced music for millions of listeners, and experimented in new forms and horizons in all the arts. The proposal took root and fairly reeled forward. Roosevelt himself believed in the experiment and, more than that, he believed in Harry Hopkins. He gave him large funds, while Ickes growled.

Jack Carmichael, in Chicago, got a chance to write and paint and disclosed real talent. He began to make enough to live on and, what was more important, he began to have confidence in himself. He wrote to his mother but got no answer. He planned a trip south as soon as he could find time.

Many and new plans for artistic work appeared. An excellent series of books on state history were begun. An encyclopedia of the Negro was projected. Shirley Graham interrupted her music course at Oberlin and gave a city opera in Cleveland. The beauty and innovations of this work startled the musical world. She was urged to go to Vienna. Instead, she took charge of the new Negro

Federal Theater, in Chicago, and presented the "Swing Mikado," which swept the city and fascinated Broadway.

Three thousand writers and artists came to be permenently employed. Applause came from the artistic world—and moves for a Federal Theater. A great sculptor, Borglum, wrote Hopkins, "You have the only department that is free to help the creative forces of the nation."

Then came a halt. Big Business had been furious at this "Socialism" of crazy Harry Hopkins from the start. No deed of the New Deal received such bitter criticism. It was said that his schemes cost too much money, when as a matter of fact they cost too little. The superintendent of schools in a great steel trust town declared that a member of Roosevelt's Brain Trust had revealed to him that Roosevelt was trying "to overthrow the government and establish Communism."

The total social situation in the United States called for an overall and interlocking plan of reform. This the New Deal did not have, and this the Brain Trust was not ready to furnish. A part—a small part, covering some fields of Art—Harry Hopkins worked out. Its very success brought frenzied opposition from business adventurers. "Swing Mikado" was driven from Broadway by entrenched theatrical monopoly which foresaw competition and loss of profits. They hired a well-known Negro dancer, "jazzed" the production up for popular taste, and let "Hot Mikado" displace the earlier and far better production.

The magnificent vision of a Federal Theater, state histories and frescoes, was beaten down by 1939. But this simply centered attention on larger projects—production by farming, processing, transport and sale, called urgently for plan and regulation; for here the whole economic system had broken down. A measure of democratic control must be injected into the industrial process, and this meant attention to the labor problem. Finally, if federal subsidy could encourage Art, how about federal taxation to undertake jobs for the welfare of the nation, which private enterprise could not carry on with profit unless it exercized governmental functions?

These matters landed the New Deal face to face with age-old problems of government control of industry, which merged into government-in-industry and the socialistic state. Industry itself first posed the problem when banks came begging handouts from

Washington, followed by railroads, farmers and public power corporations. The government started to plan relief while the corporations were off-base and not alert to where all this was leading.

But still, unified and far-sighted plans sagged. The farmers shrieked for help, and the nation must eat. Their low prices could be pieced out by direct subsidy or by artificial scarcity. The New Deal chose both and met trouble, naturally. It turned to manufacturing and sales, and projected a bold socialistic experiment of nation-wide agreement on wages and prices to be enforced by voluntary consent, backed by aroused public opinion. It was unexpectedly successful. By the end of the first year, the industrial leaders of the country were supporting the NRA. Minimum wages were fixed, and hours of labor. Sweat shops were abolished, so was child labor; and business men were asked to submit to an examination of their books by government inspectors.

Such a measure took imagination and courage, and organized industry accepted it only because it feared something worse. Organized labor was turned by the NRA into a semi-public species of national trade union. Employers were forbidden to discharge men for belonging to a union; the open shop was abolished; nor could employees be forced into company unions. But before this act had been thoroughly tried out, Industry began to fight seriously against the "Red in the White House." The Supreme Court went into action and out of Roosevelt's nine main measures, the court declared seven unconstitutional. The attempt of the President to curb the reaction of these "nine old men" failed, although in the end, Death helped him out.

In 1935, by direct congressional action, labor was given the right to bargain. Court injunctions were curbed so that at last the unions might, if they would, form a real Labor Party.

But this greatest effort of America to adopt socialism, using voluntary cooperation backed by social threat, never came to full trial for the Supreme Court outlawed it. However, there was in the Tennessee Valley Authority a clear case of socialism, of government intrusion into an area of economic endeavor where private enterprise could enter only if it exercised government powers. Such grafting of government powers to private organization had been common in the past.

For years, Senator George Norris had tried to force through this organization of water control in the Tennessee Valley. But

Industry was too strong in the Senate. It was recognized that this was an opening wedge for similar projects covering the river systems of the whole country and breaking the private monopoly of public wealth in agriculture, forestry and power control.

Roosevelt made the experiment. He said that this development was but a small part of the potential public usefulness of the entire Tennessee River. Such use, envisioned in its entirety, "transcends mere power development. It enters the wide fields of flood control, soil erosion, reforestation, elimination of agricultural use of marginal lands, and distribution and diversification of industry. In short, this power development of war days leads logically to national planning for a complete river watershed involving many states and future lives and welfare of millions."

Now the South began to understand. There was a conference called in New Orleans where Huey Long, the stormy petrel whom Industry feared worse than the devil, had just been murdered. The state seemed redeemed from a union of white laboring classes and the farmers, with Negroes in the background, which had for ten years threatened the current organization of the whole South. There was frank talk in this conference:

"Gentlemen, our real enemy today is the New Deal. Even with it, we can in part exclude Negro labor, but not for long if socialism triumphs and Negroes fight their way into the unions. We must plan ahead. Socialism threatens private industry, and industry is moving south and southwest. Agriculture is no longer our main resource. Our cotton crop has moved to Texas and California. But in its place is coming oil, sulphur, and chemicals. We must pioneer in the new chemicals, in plastics and synthetic yarns. We must control a vast and cheap labor force. The old game of splitting the labor force by race is becoming untenable. Union organizers are coming south to unite white and black. We must stop it. We must stand with organized industry the world over to stop the spread of socialism through present democracy and to impose control of the state by organized industry. How? Send your brainiest men to Washington and let's get together and plan!"

So, suddenly, the governor of Georgia gave up his job of reorganizing the state government, refused the traditional second term, and went to the United States Senate. And while the white primary of 1933 was planning, John Baldwin and the political leaders had dinner in private with Eugene Talmadge.

Baldwin gave up his plans of solving problems of race and industry by education. Let education wait! It was, after all, a question whether white or black really benefited from it. He and his colleagues, fearing the alliance of Talmadge and Scroggs, now proposed to split the following of Talmadge from the labor movement in exchange for the governorship. Talmadge was willing but for a price; and that price was the transfer of the balance of power from the cities, where labor was strong, to the rural farming districts where he had control. This would make him political czar of the state and such a contingency was not palatable to Baldwin and his friends. But they whispered together. Money could always keep small farmers in line and no czar lasted forever. Moreover, the prospective Negro vote was also bound to be strong in cities, and the race hate of small white farmers could be depended on to hold such a new crop of voters in check. So, at three o'clock in the morning, the deal was closed and next day Eugene Talmadge was nominated governor of Georgia.

Manuel Mansart was puzzled. The depression had affected his school, but not seriously. Students continued to come but they brought less money. Many turned to school because there was no work for them, but they had nothing with which to pay even the low fees. The school became, thus, in part a relief institution, and Mansart could no longer boast of the considerable part of the school costs that were met by Negroes themselves. On the other hand, this made the problem of education, of teaching these youngsters what was happening to the world, all the more pressing; and here Mansart was puzzled. Here, more than ever, he felt how cut off he was from the real world. He was in a world apart— a worthy world, a world which must and would survive and yet, if it ever was to become a part of the white world, these worlds must understand each other increasingly. And they did not. The part which Mansart represented was moving away from the greater world. The better and more efficient his school grew, the thinner and more brittle were his ties to the white world. Acquaintanceship, friendly gossip, social understanding became less and less. How could he bridge the gap? He felt now, more than ever, the loss of Coypel. They had never been close companions—that their time and place would not allow—but they had been companions. Each was able, now and then, to learn from the other something of each other's worlds, which otherwise would have been veiled.

In one of their last conversations, before Coypel left for his flowers in North Carolina, Mansart had shown him a clipping about the Communist Convention in Chicago, in 1932:

"Fifteen thousand men and women waving red banners, singing, cheering. Brass bands, slogans, color, excitemet, earthquake, sunrise, hope. Foster has just been nominated for President; Ford, for Vice-President of these United States. Negro Ford was a native of Georgia. His father was a tenant farmer and his grandfather had been lynched because of a dispute over the ownership of a pig. The family moved to Alabama, where father and son worked for the Tennessee Coal Company. After working his way through Fisk University, James Ford joined the army in 1917. He was denied admission into the army radio school, but entered the radio school of the French army and served with distinction. After he left the army, he came to Chicago and entered the postal service, and was active in the Postal Workers Union. In 1926, he joined the Communist Party and rose rapidly because of his fight against segregation and his energy as a trade-union organizer."

"What does this mean?" asked Mansart. Coypel smiled and took out a clipping from his pocket. He read:

"We have aligned ourselves with the frankly revolutionary, the party of the workers," signed by Theodore Dreiser, John Dos Passos, Waldo Frank, Edmund Wilson, Sidney Hook, Frederick Schuman, Lincoln Steffens, Matthew Josephson and Ella Winter.

"Some of these I know," said Mansart: "others I never heard of."

"Same here, but we've got to face Communism," said Coypel slowly, "and we will not answer its challenge by silence or lying."

"I read the *Communist Manifesto* last night," said Mansart. "I like it, but will it work? Looking at its advocates, I should say no. But I do not know yet. As a practical and present matter, I've got to ask myself what shall I say to my students about Socialism? How shall I guide them? They are bound to ask searching questions and my teachers must answer honestly and know what is true and right."

Coypel smiled grimly. "Under Eugene Talmadge, you'll have a hell of a time."

The Crisis said in February, 1932: "There is absolutely no hope for the Negro in the United States from public charity and relief. This emergency ought to spell in the minds of American

Negroes the last syllable of philanthropy so far as they are concerned. With 1931, the Negro ceases to be a problem of philanthropy, and becomes to himself and to the world a problem of self-help. Unless the Negro can pull himself out of the present economic struggle by his own bootstraps, he is doomed to a more terrible slavery in the future than he ever suffered in the past."

Colored weeklies commented: The *Journal and Guide,* of Virginia, stated the problem simply:

"Communism is one of the factors in a growing world-wide ideal to improve the conditions of the underprivileged and to give to those who labor a liberal share in the fruits of production."

Dabney's radical sheet, out in Ohio, said:

"Communists come not bringing charity but brotherhood."

The *Tribune* of Pennsylvania, admired the ideals of Russia "because they give hope of that equality of opportunity which America denies Negroes."

The *Afro-American,* of Baltimore, said frankly: "No white group is openly advocating the economic, political and social equality of Negroes, except Communists."

The Crisis summed it up:

"Back of all this ever lies the basic question: Is Communism, as illustrated in Russia and America, a theory good for the world and for the American Negro? The world is ill. It has desperate economic problems intertwined with its problems of racial prejudice. It does not make any difference what Communism says or does, these problems are there. It does not make any difference what Capitalism does or has done in the past. It has left this sinister heritage of poverty, maladjustment, and race prejudice. These problems must be solved, and only thought, study, and experiment can bring intelligent action on the part of Negroes as well as whites."

Mansart remained in deep doubt.

When the WPA ceased to function, Jack Carmichael came east to New York. He had no clear idea as to how he would earn a living. He was still upset by the loss of his family. He had, from shame, avoided asking his uncle by marriage, Manuel Mansart, in Macon, to secure some work. Meantime, he stopped in New York. Here he finally found work in the office of the *New York Age.* The *Age* was one of the oldest of the many weekly Negro newspapers which had defended the colored folk, and distributed news of their actions since the late nineteenth century. The *Age* had been founded by the militant T. Thomas Fortune as the *Globe,* and after his death became one of the periodicals controlled by Booker T. Washington.

Jack found Harlem both inspiring and upsetting. Dirt and crowds and at the same time enthusiasm and song, signs of bursting life. He found himself one day looking particularly at the little boy who was throwing dice with the crowd of hoodlums in the gutter at Lenox Avenue and 135th Street. The little fellow was swearing bravely, but with some difficulty. Jack knew that he was not used to swearing and that the older boys were egging him on. So he went over and put his hand on the boy's shoulder.

"Hey, boy. Don't use that word and stop gambling. Your father will give you a strapping."

The little boy turned and glared at him.

"Ain't got no father. He scared and run away. Who you?"

"No father? Well then, I'll tell your mother. What's your name?"

The little boy stood up straight and said: "I'm John Carmichael II, and my mommy don't whip me."

Jack almost staggered off his feet, and said uncertainly and then sternly, "Take me to your mother."

"I won't."

"Please."

"No!"

"Not for a dollar?"

"Why? Who you, anyhow? Oh, all right. Gimme the dollar!"

The flat was in a crowded section and on a dirty side street, but inside it was a neat place. It was clean and silent. The door flew open. It was his wife, Betty.

"Jackie! Where have you been, anyhow? You are so late!" And then, "Oh, my God—you! How dare you! Oh Jack, come in!"

There were long explanations. John Carmichael said, "Betty, everything I try fails. My work in school was not good, as you know. My farming was a mess. I had to leave you. I was going to murder Cranston. I had his pistol close to his back and pulled the trigger. The thing missed fire. Suddenly, I realized I was about to be a murderer and drag you and my mother and the boy down. I ran. I ran away. I've been running ever since. I wrote you and mother but there was no answer. I tried again and again to get work. I floudered in the depression until the WPA gave me a chance to write and draw, and I sort of found myself."

"Well, Jack, let's try it here in New York for a while. I've got a good job nursing. We'll move out somewhere to find better schools for Jackie. Perhaps you can build up the *Age* to a well-paid job and a public service. If not, we might go east to New England and start a new life in a free land."

In Washington, three men sat watching the world. They were men of substance and power and they were afraid. One was Herbert Hoover, late President of the United States; one was a millionaire banker, once his secretary of the treasury and now near death; the third was a German and represented the Farbenindustrie, as well as other international cartels. He was talking in excellent English: "You know, of course, gentlemen, that the day of the individual capitalist, even when united and guided by finance capital furnished by great banking institutions, is past. It began in the crisis of the seventies, and ended in the crisis of the nineties. This is the day of the Corporation. This culminating invention of the capitalist age—immortal, omniscient, omnipotent, impersonal and amoral—is bringing all industry under its control and Industry is becoming Government. But where will control of this colossus lie? In the hands of the indiscriminate masses of men of all colors and kinds, or in the hands of a chosen and tried elite? The first is unthinkable, with human nature as it is. Very well. Yet, Russia is trying to put its masses in control of Industry. Despite world effort, it has not yet failed. But it must. It pretends to be giving a hold-over dictatorship control until the dream of Communism becomes true. This is crazy and the Russian leaders know it. Yet, they conspire to delude the world until they conquer."

Hoover groaned. "I tried to tell Roosevelt that poor relief and helping bankrupt farmers was not the way to fight depression. It would only make our morons, incompetents, the dupes of all those who dream of raising the dregs of men created to work and not to think, directors of trade and industry instead of its pensioners, to be fed and clothed and not coddled. We whites, and we alone, can direct the world's work and make the goods it needs. For this we need capital in huge amounts for labor and materials. This can come from colonies in Asia and Africa and our Governments can secure and hold colonies and colonial regions. We need Russia and the Balkans, China and India, and the South Seas for land and labor, and they need us for brains. Yet, this young idiot and his worshippers, Hopkins, Ickes, and Perkins, are driving us straight to Hell with Socialism."

"There is hope still," said the ex-secretary. "We must stage a battle on an unprecedented scale to preserve intact the power of the world's elite—the British, French, Germans, and the North Americans. We must arm to the teeth and make our people think as we do by scientific propaganda, fed by news we collect and screen, books we publish and schools we own. We must frighten would-be leaders by taking their jobs, jailing or even killing them. We must infiltrate their trade unions and buy union leaders. We must hire, bribe, and control ability. We will rule by democracy, but will own the voters. We must fight to the finish, even if we put mankind in jeopardy of death."

The group winced at this plain speaking. Almost, they saw the shadow of death hovering above this cadaverous figure. Silence fell on them.

Not far away, late that same night, two men in Washington were also looking East. President Roosevelt had cast the heavy burden of his steel harness aside and sat slouched in his great bed, facing the city fading into nightfall. Beside him sat Harry Hopkins, drooping and downcast. The President spoke in a low voice:

"Harry, I'm tired—dead tired."

"I know; and Chief, I'm sick and in pain."

The president reached out his hand and gripped Hopkins by the shoulder. "I wonder how long we have?"

"Ten years at most; but before then—"

Roosevelt hummed: " 'The City called Heaven'—remember that Negro spiritual?"

"Yes, I've often heard it in Georgia. It starts deep and slow in the 'Low ground of sorrow,' such as we've seen."

There was silence as out beyond the Potomac the rising sun cast a light.

"Yes, I see the 'City called Heaven.' No poverty, homes for all, no fear of age, children in school, free music and theater, good food, and all men daring to say what they think. My God, Chief, that's not asking much!"

"No, and I can see it; the towers and the minarets—the streets and flowers—I planned 'to make it my home'—but I won't!"

"No, Chief, we won't. The Valley of the Shadow lies before us and it'll be tough going!"

Hopkins added: "Do you think—do you dare dream that British socialism and the American New Deal can break this world alliance, especially with Churchill representing the very socialism he tried so desperately to kill in Russia?"

"Perhaps not. But we must try."

"The price asked by the Rockefellers, Morgans, and Mellons for helping save their industrial rival Britain is surrender of your New Deal, bound hand and foot. If you pay that price, what is left?"

"I'll bargain hard. I'll save something, unless I die. I must do this. Harry, I'm British bred. England is in my blood. I believe in Britain as I believe in God. Besides, there is no other way!"

"There may be another."

"Where, what, who?"

"Russia!"

"Nonsense. Russia is dying, or at least doomed to sickness for many centuries. It is our fault, ours and Britain's; that I know. Nevertheless, it is true. We nations of the West have set the Russian revolution so thoroughly, completely back that whatever it might have done, it now probably will not even attempt."

"Chief, I don't believe it. I prophesy, I stand and swear, that Britain and Europe and our America will yet be saved from Nazis and Fascists by the Communists, fighting under Stalin. Russia and Russia alone, representing the white race, will yet prevent an awful World War between the white and colored worlds. The possession of modern industry by Russia, and Russia's stand against colonialism will make the exploitation and decimation of Asia and Africa by Britain, France and the United States impossible."

"I wish I could believe that too, Harry. But it is crazy; it is impossible. But I'm weary. Good night, my friend, I must sleep."

The President of the United States, shed of his iron armor, lay lax and stared at the stars. He sensed clearly that Great White Flame which blazed out of the North in the days of his fathers and lighted the Earth; he saw it flare and spread over all the world and, too, he saw it fade to the dull white ash of today. He wept as it faded.

Below, Harry Hopkins, prime minister to a king, plodded along in a lonely world. The city slept and lights went dim; sinister shadows flitted by. Only above, the stars blazed; beyond the stars, he saw suddenly the rise of that Red Flame, flooding the East and pouring over the Earth. He knew that flame of revolution would sweep west until it faced the Atlantic; East, till it fired the Pacific; and South till it lit the ocean of India. It frightened him, but he could not stop it. He did not want to stop it. He groaned in vain distress.

Six hundred miles south by west, Manuel Mansart, President of the Georgia Colored State College, wandered sleepless about his college grounds, as so often he had been wont to do in the early days of its beginning when evil lurked. He saw the same stars that shone on Washington, and the mist which started toward them. He believed that beyond the mist burned the Black Flame. How could it be black if it flamed? How could it burn without heat and wild destruction? Yet all this it did, and the dark blaze of its urge as it rolled and roared out of the South bound his heart and world, into one whole of Power and Peace, of Freedom and Law, of Force and Love. But not yet, not for a long, long time yet; and his tears blurred the mist that hid the stars.